PENGUIN B

A Storm in a Teacup

Lucy Cavendish has spent most of her working life in journalism. She writes for the the *Sunday Telegraph*, the *Observer*, *The Times*, the *Daily Mail* and a variety of glossy magazines. She also writes a column about her family life in *Stella* magazine, part of the *Sunday Telegraph*, and she writes a blog on mumsnet as Samantha Smythe. She lives in Oxfordshire with Michael, a graphic artist, and their four children.

This is the final novel in a trilogy, following *Samantha Smythe's Modern Family Journal* and *Lost and Found*. She has also contributed two short stories in the collection *The Leap Year* (available from www.queenbee.co.uk).

A Storm in a Teacup

LUCY CAVENDISH

PENGUIN BOOKS

PENGUIN BOOKS

Published by the Penguin Group
Penguin Books Ltd, 80 Strand, London WC2R ORL, England
Penguin Group (USA) Inc., 375 Hudson Street, New York, New York 10014, USA
Penguin Group (Canada), 90 Eglinton Avenue East, Suite 700, Toronto, Ontario, Canada M4P 2Y3
(a division of Pearson Penguin Canada Inc.)
Penguin Ireland, 25 St Stephen's Green, Dublin 2, Ireland (a division of Penguin Books Ltd)
Penguin Group (Australia), 250 Camberwell Road, Camberwell, Victoria 3124, Australia
(a division of Pearson Australia Group Pty Ltd)
Penguin Books India Pvt Ltd, 11 Community Centre, Panchsheel Park, New Delhi – 110 017, India
Penguin Group (NZ), 67 Apollo Drive, Rosedale, North Shore 0632, New Zealand
(a division of Pearson New Zealand Ltd)
Penguin Books (South Africa) (Pty) Ltd, 24 Sturdee Avenue, Rosebank, Johannesburg 2196, South Africa

Penguin Books Ltd, Registered Offices: 80 Strand, London WC2R ORL, England

www.penguin.com

First published 2010
003

Copyright © Lucy Cavendish, 2010
All rights reserved

The moral right of the author has been asserted

Set in Garamond MT Std 10.5/13pt
Typeset by Palimpsest Book Production Limited, Grangemouth, Stirlingshire
Printed in England by Clays Ltd, Elcograf S.p.A.

ISBN: 978-0-141-03536-9

www.greenpenguin.co.uk

For Jeremiah

Prologue

It happened one Wednesday morning. I was doing the laundry, drinking a coffee, listening to the radio. It doesn't really matter which. Maybe I was sitting down trying to do the crossword, for on most Wednesday mornings my two eldest sons, Edward and Bennie, are at school. Their younger brother, Jamie, was at nursery. But on that Wednesday morning, as I was maybe sitting down with a cup of something hot, the telephone rang. Perhaps I tried to leave it. I do sometimes when I have a few minutes to myself for then the telephone seems like a squat toad bleeping and burping at me. But this time I didn't. I picked up the receiver.

'Hello,' said a nervous voice. It was the nice lady from the nursery. I knew she was nice because she always sneaked Jamie an extra Rich Tea biscuit at the end when everyone was leaving.

'Mrs Smythe?' she said, even more tentatively.

'Yes,' I said.

'I need you to come to the nursery.'

'Come to the nursery?' I asked, feeling rather confused. 'Why?'

The nice lady from the nursery sighed.

'I don't want to explain on the telephone.'

'What? Is Jamie OK? Has something awful happened to him?' I suddenly had visions of Jamie walking out into the road and being hit by a car, or somehow toppling into a pond, which they don't actually have. I've read about these things. Children go to nurseries and never come back.

'No, Jamie's fine,' said the nice lady quickly, too quickly. 'I just need you to come right now.'

The nursery is five minutes away. As I drove there my heart was beating so fast I could barely hear myself breathe.

When I got to the gates, a member of nursery staff motioned for me to park my car alongside the playground. Jamie was waiting there. He seemed totally fine, if a little forlorn.

'Jamie,' I said. I bent down to hold him. He wouldn't look at me.

'Jamie?' I said again.

The nice lady came into the yard.

'Come with me into the office,' she said. She gave Jamie a pitying look. 'One of our staff members will take care of everything out here.'

We went into her office and sat down, her on one side of the desk, me on the other.

'It's very hard for me to tell you this, Mrs Smythe,' she said gravely, 'but I'm afraid that you will have to take Jamie home.'

'Take Jamie home?'

'Yes.'

'What, right now?'

'Yes. He's going to have to stay at home for the time being, I'm afraid.'

'Why?'

She sighed again.

'Jamie committed a misdemeanour today that was so awful there may be an investigation into it by the nursery.'

'What on earth did he do?'

'He hurt another child.'

'What do you mean "hurt"? What did he do?'

'He lunged for a child with the sharp end of a paint-brush and tried to stick it in the child's eye. If one of my staff members hadn't been nearby he could have blinded someone.'

'He must have slipped!'

'No,' said the nice lady, kindly but firmly. 'He didn't slip. I was there and I saw it. He meant to hurt that child. It was alarmingly deliberate.'

'No, not Jamie!' I said defensively, shocked. 'Which child was it?'

'It was Isla. I don't know why he did it. Isla wasn't even that near him. She'd just toddled over there. She's barely more than a baby girl . . .'

The words 'baby girl' hung in the air.

'Mrs Smythe,' she continued, looking embarrassed, 'I'm not sure how to help. Jamie's behaviour has been . . . well, it's changed, if I can be frank. He's quite aggressive with the smaller children and I've found recently that he's become very disruptive . . .'

'I'll take him home,' I said, maybe a bit too abruptly.

'And you also need to know that Isla's parents have the right to make an official complaint.'

'I'm going now. I'll take him home.'

'Isla was very badly bruised and quite hysterical. Jamie didn't try to harm her just once. We pulled him away, but he was going for her again. I've had to tell her parents this. They may ask for an investigation. We are a state nursery. There are procedures we have to follow . . .'

I got up.

'I'm going,' I said. 'Don't worry. I won't bring Jamie back.'

The nice lady started wringing her hands in a concerned fashion.

'This gives me no pleasure, Mrs Smythe,' she said. 'I have, in the past, found Jamie to be a most charming child . . .' but it was too late, for now I was out of the door.

I took Jamie by the hand and marched him out of the playground. I gave the young girl who had been overseeing everything a falsely jaunty wave.

'Everything's fine,' she said. 'Not even a murmur.'

'Thanks,' I said.

I didn't speak to Jamie as I put him in the car, but he soon spied what it was he wanted. I watched him carefully through the rear-view mirror. I could see him leaning over towards the baby seat. Then suddenly he reared up, opened his mouth as wide as he could and yelled, 'Wake up, Baby Sparkle!'

My newborn baby daughter's grey-blue eyes snapped open and filled with tears.

'Waaaa!' she cried.

'Jamie!' I said.

Jamie sat back into his car seat, popped his thumb in his mouth and smiled to himself.

This is how it all started.

1. Distinguishing Features

Jamie is sitting in an over-large chair wearing a tight pink gingham dress. I'm sitting next to him trying to ignore this fact. I'm wearing a skirt – I never wear skirts – and a shirt that I've ironed – I never iron – and I'm hoping that, with my ironed shirt and smart skirt, the child psychologist sitting opposite me might take me a bit more seriously than before. I'm here not simply because of what happened just under a year ago but also because, since the paintbrush calamity, Jamie's behaviour has got worse.

This change in Jamie – insisting on using baby talk even though he's four years old (such as saying 'my' instead of 'I' and 'sike' for 'like'), trying to drink his milk from a baby beaker and sometimes becoming aggressive towards his brothers when he gets cross – has caused undeniable ripples in our family. Where once we were all united, now we are pulling in different directions. We are a large family. There are six of us in the Smythe household and we all have different needs and desires. My husband, John, who is my second one as I was married to a different John before him, wants me. I want him, but I also want my children. Edward, the eldest and son of John the First, wants me, as do Bennie and Jamie and, of course, Baby Sparkle. I have, over the years, cut myself into ever-decreasing portions to satisfy their need for my love and attention. I have, I think, done well. Sometimes I even catch sight of myself in a random mirror and, although

I'm shocked by what I see – a wild-haired woman shedding children as rabbits do kittens, all re-attaching themselves to me as I shoo them away – I realize I look like a mum. I act like a mum. I sound like a mum. I shout like a mum. And I have, after all these years, given myself a teeny bit of space and told myself I'm good at this. I eased Edward and myself through the parting of his father. I then eased John the Second into our lives with barely a ripple (hmm, I think), and I've gone on to pop out three more babies. Yet here I am with my Jamie, and life is not as it is supposed to be.

I was so shocked after he almost blinded Isla that I telephoned John when we got home, feeling nearly hysterical, imagining that, somehow, he would feel nearly hysterical too.

'Isla's parents will call the social services,' I said to John in a panic down the telephone. 'Then they'll come to our house and take the children away at midnight . . .'

'No, they won't,' he said, surprisingly assured considering I'd just told him his youngest son had been excluded from nursery. 'Jamie's just suffering from a bit of sibling rivalry. He didn't actually hurt Isla.'

'The nice lady at the nursery says she's bruised. He lunged at her, twice!'

'Maybe he was a bit fed up.'

'Fed up?' I said. 'Have you got any idea how bad this is?'

'No,' he said calmly, 'because I'm here in London working so I wasn't at the nursery and I didn't see the bruises on Isla. Did you?'

'Well, no, not exactly,' I said, wrong-footed, 'but the nice lady there said there'll have to be an investigation. She said they have to write all these things down in a book and if the child is badly hurt then procedures happen.'

'There won't be any investigation,' said John. 'It's all fine.'

But it wasn't really. Isla's parents were not at all happy about what Jamie had done. They asked the nursery to look into what had happened and I spent an awkward morning with the nice lady on one side of me and Isla's parents on the other. John couldn't come to the meeting as he was working so I went on my own and squirmed in embarrassment as I apologized to them profusely, explaining that Jamie had recently had to cope with the birth of a baby sister, but they remained hurt and unmoved.

'Isla's our only child,' they said.

'I'm so sorry,' I said.

The upshot was I decided to keep Jamie out of nursery and to monitor his behaviour. John, it has to be said, did not agree with my decision.

'What's he going to do now?'

'He'll be with me and Baby Sparkle. In that way I can help him to adjust.'

'He doesn't need to adjust,' said John. 'He'll get over it.'

'I can't trust him with other children,' I said. 'You should have seen Isla's parents. They were not at all happy.'

'Jamie's always been the easy one in the household,' said John. 'Do you not think you are overreacting somewhat?'

It's true that before Baby Sparkle was born Jamie was a happy-go-lucky soul who could occasionally be quirky. Our eldest son, Edward, who's now nearly thirteen, was immensely difficult as a small boy. He was cross and angry and couldn't speak properly. Bennie's also had his problems.

Two years ago he nearly drowned in a freak accident on holiday and has since developed a stutter. However, despite the semi-traumatic state the Smythe family seemed to live in, Jamie waddled through life merrily eating butternut squash and, oddly, not liking sandpits.

Since the paintbrush incident, however, he has started shouting and becoming rude. He calls people 'stupid idiots' all the time, he refuses to eat and he swears. When the telephone rings, he picks it up and shouts 'Bugger off!' into the receiver.

At first, everyone thought it was funny – angelic Jamie with his blond hair, green eyes and cute face shouting 'Bugger off' was amusing – but now we're all sick of it.

'Why does Jamie tell my friends to bugger off when they ring?' asked Edward, who was lolling on the sofa watching the television. 'Why doesn't he bugger off?'

My mother told me I should grin and bear it. 'All children feel cross when another baby comes into the family,' she said. 'Your sister refused to stop using a potty for years after you were born.'

But then everything got much worse. For a start, Jamie kept stealing all Baby Sparkle's clothes. It started with her knickers, which means he's spent most of the last year waving baby knickers above his head, once he found out they were too small to fit on his bottom. Then, when he realized that if he were smaller he too could wear gathered-up silky little pouffy underpants with roses on, he virtually stopped eating. I'd find all sorts of things to try and tempt him – bagels with melted cheese on them, delicious, creamy fish pies, meaty shepherd's pie topped with piles of mash. I tried yoghurts and croissants and chopped-up bits of fruit and fromage frais. I cut up paw-paws, pineapple, melon, bananas. I made puddings and tarts and soufflés and stews. I flash-fried steaks and baked lamb chops and peeled prawns. I scoured the shelves of the supermarket and even put things such as cheese strings, Cheez Dippers and pizzas into my shopping basket. All to no avail. And now the weight has fallen off him and he looks so skinny and tiny I'm amazed I haven't had a visit from the social services on the charge of starving my child.

When we went out for a walk once, Jamie and I met the nice lady from the nursery and I could tell she was shocked by how he looked.

'Jamie!' she said, her hands flying to her mouth.

'I'm so thin!' he announced to her and ran his hands over his tiny, skinny body.

As Baby Sparkle emerged from her Babygros and began to be put in dresses, Jamie started wanting to wear dresses. When I drew a line at this behaviour, he stopped eating again, even pushing bowls of Rice Krispies away, until one day I bought him a dress. We went to the shop and I pretended we were looking for a dress for Baby Sparkle. 'Look at this lovely dress,' I said, pulling out a purple one with a discreet bow at the back. 'This would look nice on Baby Sparkle, wouldn't it, Jamie?'

'I think that might be a bit big for your baby,' said the helpful shop assistant, hovering behind us and peering into Baby Sparkle's pram.

'She's a big baby,' I said.

'She doesn't look that big,' said the shop assistant.

'It's for me!' yelled Jamie crossly.

After that, Jamie and I got into a sort of code. He made up an imaginary friend called Sophie and we'd often go and shop for her. For a while this worked very well. Jamie seemed to be able to express himself in the form of Sophie, and this imaginary Sophie seemed a far more reasonable person than her alter-ego. 'Sophie likes a bit of butter on her bread,' Jamie would say pertly when I'd ask him what he'd like to eat for dinner, and he'd say that he wouldn't like anything but he was sure Sophie would love some toast. He'd then eat rounds and rounds of toast to keep up with Sophie.

'God, I love Sophie,' I said to my mother one day after Jamie had devoured some baked beans, scrambled eggs and a cup of milk followed by two yoghurts because, Jamie told me, 'Sophie is very partial to yoghurts.'

But soon things started to go awry with Sophie. For a start, she gradually became more and more demanding.

'Sophie would like a Flower Fairy cup,' Jamie would say when we were in the toy shop. 'Sophie would like a tea set. Sophie would like a pink bath robe.'

In the end I told Jamie that Sophie couldn't have *everything* she wanted and the next morning Jamie woke up and clamped his mouth shut again.

'I've made toast with butter on for Sophie,' I said in my most persuasive voice one lunch time. 'Sophie's about to eat it all up.'

'No, she isn't,' said Jamie. 'Sophie's got too fat. She's on a diet now.'

And that was that.

The nice lady at the nursery, who I contacted for help as I thought she might know about these matters, suggested

I go and see my doctor. After much thought, and some persuasion on my part, Jamie was referred by the doctor to a child psychologist.

I don't hold out much hope though. When I first went to see the child psychologist a week ago – 'Hello, Candace,' I said, noticing that her name, CANDACE HARRIS, was typed neatly on the questionnaire I was asked to fill in all about Jamie's behaviour – I felt we got off on the wrong foot. She said, 'Please call me Miss Harris in front of your child,' and I felt scolded like a little girl. Later on, Candace, who I from then on called Miss Harris, explained to me that she always felt it worked better for the children if the parents called her by her surname, as it meant she maintained a position of authority.

'Is that important?' I said to her.

'Yes,' she said. 'If I want Jamie, for example, to sit down and try to vocalize what is going on in his life, in his head, then he has to respect me, and in order for him to respect me, I have to be perceived as being in a position of authority over him.'

'But he doesn't do anything I say,' I said. 'If I asked him to call me Mrs Smythe, do you think he'd behave himself a bit more?'

Candace-Miss-Harris looked at me as if I were mocking her.

'Of course not,' she said coldly. 'You can hardly expect your own son to call you by your surname.'

'Oh, I just thought it might help,' I said.

Candace-Miss-Harris didn't say anything. She just watched Jamie who, at that first meeting, insisted on having a dummy in his mouth even though he'd never used one before.

'Is this your baby daughter's dummy?' Candace-Miss-Harris asked me.

'No,' I said, 'she doesn't use a dummy.'

'So where did Jamie get it from?'

'My mother bought it ages ago for the baby, but I never used it. Jamie found it in a cupboard. He's just playing with it. He likes to play with it. He keeps it under his pillow. Is that not good?' I said, seeing how cross Candace-Miss-Harris looked.

'It's an inappropriate object for a boy of four years old to play with,' she said. 'He should be playing with toys that ask questions of him, not baby things.' Then she turned to Jamie. 'Give me the dummy, Jamie.'

Jamie just looked at her. He shook his head.

'Dummy please, Jamie,' she said again, giving him a stern look.

Jamie stared out of the window.

'Give Miss Harris your dummy, Jamie, will you?' I asked him in the most conciliatory tone possible.

'Could you let me do the talking please, Mrs Smythe?' said Candace-Miss-Harris.

'Jamie,' she said, 'I want that dummy now. I have asked you nicely three times and if you don't give it to me I will come over and take it off you myself.'

Jamie just looked at her and kept on sucking in a determined fashion.

'One, Jamie, two, three . . .'

Suddenly Jamie spat his dummy out and, at the same time, flew like a demon over to Candace-Miss-Harris, and he moved so rapidly that no one could have predicted what he was about to do. He sank his teeth into Candace-Miss-Harris's outstretched arm.

'Arrgghh!' she screamed, clenching her fist in pain.

'Oh God, I'm really sorry, Candace,' I said.

'Miss Harris,' she said through gritted teeth.

'Jamie,' I said to him, now holding him firmly by his arm. 'That's very naughty of you to bite Miss Harris. What on earth has got into you?'

'Bugger off!' he screamed. Then he ran out of the door.

I turned to Candace-Miss-Harris. 'I'm so sorry,' I said. 'He doesn't usually bite. I mean, he did try to stab a girl's eye out with a paintbrush, but the doctor's told you all that so . . .'

'Clearly, there is a lot of work to do here,' said Candace-Miss-Harris through her grimaces. 'Come back again next week.'

I nodded meekly and then followed after Jamie.

So this time, in our second session, I'm trying to show Candace-Miss-Harris that I'm in control. I'm trying to say to her, through my smart new clothes, that instead of being a frazzled mother of four I am, in fact, totally organized and cool and sanguine. I'm hoping that my skirt and ironed shirt are showing Candace-Miss-Harris that I'm the type of mother who can make a nutritious breakfast that all my children eat at the table with nothing spilled anywhere, certainly not on me, get them all out of the door for school and then put on my superbly neat and ironed clothes for a trip to the psychologist. In fact, I'm hoping to give off the impression of a mother who is so supremely together that I actually put on my neat, clean, ironed clothes *before* breakfast. That's how bloody controlled and together I am and, as I think this, I smile confidently at Candace-Miss-Harris.

But at this moment Candace-Miss-Harris seems to be

staring intently at Jamie, who's smiling back at her in a helpful fashion.

'How are we today, Jamie?' asks Candace-Miss-Harris.

'Happy,' says Jamie, fluffing his dress up around his legs.

'Jamie, why are you wearing a dress?'

'I like my dress,' he says. Then he cocks his head to one side and opens his big green eyes. 'Is your name Sophie?' he asks, smiling at the psychologist.

'Sophie?' she asks, looking at him and then looking down to write some notes. 'What does the name "Sophie" mean to you, Jamie?'

'Sophie's his imaginary friend,' I explain.

'No, she's not!' says Jamie angrily, his eyes glinting. 'She's my real friend. She's Sophie and I'm Dorothy from Oz and Mummy is Truly Sumptious.'

'Ah,' says the therapist meaningfully, writing yet more notes. 'You like watching these films, do you?'

'Oh, yes,' says Jamie.

'He doesn't watch them that much, Candace,' I say. 'I just let him when he's tired because . . .'

'My name is Miss Harris,' says Candace-Miss-Harris.

'Sorry,' I say.

'I want Mummy to wear a white dress like Truly Sumptious.'

'You want Mummy to look like the character in *Chitty Chitty Bang Bang*?'

''Es,' says Jamie.

'Why is that, Jamie?'

'I want her to look like a dolly. I like dollies.'

'He likes to line them up in his cot,' I say.

As soon as I say the word 'cot', I realize I've said the wrong thing.

'Cot?' says Candace-Miss-Harris, her eyes flashing. 'At the age of four?'

'Well, he loves his cot,' I say apologetically. 'He just adores it and I didn't think there was a problem with that really because it's such a big one and . . .'

'Will you please let Jamie answer, Mrs Smythe?' she says. 'Jamie, why do you still sleep in a cot?'

'Girls like sleeping in cots.'

'So do you think you're a girl?'

Jamie shoots me a look and then starts struggling to get off the chair.

'Which little person is really supposed to wear a dress in this family, Jamie?'

Jamie struggles some more.

'Come on, Jamie,' says Candace-Miss-Harris. 'I can help you.'

'No,' he says. 'I wanna go! I wanna go!'

'All right, Jamie,' says Candace-Miss-Harris, suddenly rather weary. 'Why don't you go? There are some toys in the waiting room and Nicole, the lady at the reception desk, will play with you.'

'I want Mama to come,' says Jamie truculently.

'Well, I need to talk to your mother.'

Jamie comes towards me and starts tugging at my hand.

'You come with me, Mama,' he says.

'No,' I say. 'I have to stay and talk.'

Jamie starts to cry. He tries to get on my lap. I stroke his hair and pull him towards me.

'I need some help, Jamie,' I say. 'We both do. I just need to do this, OK?'

Jamie looks at me. Then suddenly we hear a gurgling from outside the room. I remember the baby is there. She's been sitting quietly on the floor in the reception area this past half-hour, playing with a plastic toy Nicole gave her.

Jamie follows my glance until he sees his little sister. His face contorts into an angry, scrunched-up ball.

'Twinkle, twinkle, little willy. Baby Sparkle is so silly. Baby Sparkle's a bum-bum!' yells Jamie. Then he runs out of the door, slamming it behind him, making Baby Sparkle jump in surprise.

'I'd better go,' I say to the psychologist.

She nods. She's taking notes. 'I've observed everything that's come up today. I'm writing up what I think.'

'Same time next week then?' I say to her desperately.

She nods again.

I go back into the waiting room. Nicole, the receptionist, gives me a sympathetic smile.

'Your baby's been marvellous,' she says, retrieving the plastic ball from Baby Sparkle, who raises her arms for me to lift her up. 'Your little boy . . . he's waiting for you in the hall.'

I thank her and go towards the hall to get Jamie.

'Shall I book you in for next week?' she calls after me.

'Yes,' I say, but I'm lying. I know we won't be back next week. We won't be back at all.

We are all too far gone for that.

When I get home to our old brick and flint cottage in our quiet valley tucked away inside a crease in the Chiltern Hills, John is up in the attic. 'How did it go?' he yells down at me from the very top of the house. 'Did she find out what's wrong with Jamie?'

'No,' I yell back as I watch Jamie put on the *Chitty Chitty Bang Bang* DVD. 'He wants me to dress like Truly Scrumptious and he called Baby Sparkle something rude in front of the psychologist.'

'What?' John shouts. 'I can't hear you.'

'Come downstairs then,' I retort.

There's no answer from John so I go into the kitchen to watch Baby Sparkle from the window. She's asleep in the back of our car that's parked in the driveway. We often leave her to sleep in the driveway where we can see her. It always seems such a shame to move her when she's so happy in her car seat. Her baby head lolls over to one side, her pert little mouth is open and she's breathing heavily, in and out. I love watching her sleep. I love the way she twitches and jerks until she finally goes off into this deep, utterly uninter-ruptable torpor. I feel John beside me. He has come downstairs. He puts his arm around me.

'You know, I don't think there's anything wrong with Jamie,' he says quietly, kissing the top of my head. 'It's just taking a bit of time for him to get used to the baby being around, that's all.'

'Why do I feel so miserable then?' I say as I sit down at the table. 'You have no idea how it all sounds, how guilty I feel.'

'Why do you feel guilty?'

'Who lets him wear dresses? Who lets him sleep in a cot? I do. When I told her Jamie still slept in a cot she gave me such a look.'

'Maybe she has a point,' says John.

'Well, thanks,' I say, sinking my head down. 'Thanks for the support.'

John sighs. 'Samantha,' he says. He tries to stroke my hair. I push his hand away.

'I'm tired of this, John,' I say. 'You know, Baby Sparkle

isn't really a baby any more. She's over a year old, yet Jamie still likes wearing dresses and he has an imaginary friend who's spending all our money and neither of them will eat.'

John laughs. 'What's wrong with that?' he says.

'Oh, come on,' I say wearily.

'He'll adjust. I'm sure he will.'

'What if he doesn't? What if he has become seriously psychologically disturbed by Sparkle's arrival? I've heard of siblings who are so scarred by the rivalry in their childhood that they've never spoken to their sibling again. My sister Julia told me that her friend's brother took a knife to her throat when they were little and said he'd kill her unless she sang every verse of "All Things Bright and Beautiful" for him.'

'Oh God,' says John. 'Who on earth knows all the words to "All Things Bright and Beautiful"? It's about a million verses long.'

'Actually, it's only four.'

'Is it?' says John, sounding astounded.

'That's not the point. According to Julia, those siblings never spoke to each other again.'

'Well, at least Jamie's not that bad,' says John.

'I think he is,' I say. 'I think he's really disturbed.'

'Yes,' says John, 'I know that's what you think. In your mind, he's disturbed.'

'What do you mean by that?'

John doesn't answer.

'I don't believe this,' I say, turning towards him. 'My God, you think it's just me. You think I'm over-worrying.'

'Yes, I do, to a certain extent,' he says simply.

'How can you be so relaxed about this?' I ask, almost shouting. 'I mean, has the thought never occurred to you that maybe we're seeing a psychologist because he's disturbed? Or do you think we're going there because Jamie and I have nothing better to do?'

'No,' says John slowly. 'It's just that I . . .'

'You haven't even been to a session with us. How come this is all my responsibility? I need some help and if you won't help me, and bloody Candace-Miss-Harris won't either, then I'm going to have to find someone who can.'

'Oh, Samantha,' says John, kissing the top of my head. I let him this time. 'I am trying, you know.'

'We've got one summer,' I say to him. 'He starts school in September and he cannot be swearing and sleeping in a cot by the end of it. Something has to happen, John, and you have to help me. They're *our* children, not just mine.'

John and I then turn to watch Baby Sparkle, who's still asleep.

'Look at that peaceful baby,' says John. 'See? She's fine.'

Suddenly, Jamie appears from the sitting room. He has taken off his dress and is clad in nothing but a pair of light-blue knickers.

'Hello, Jamie,' says John.

Jamie looks at John. He looks adorable, as he can do sometimes. He gives his most winning smile.

'I'm watching Chiccy Chiccy Bang Bang,' he says to John, batting his eyelashes at him.

'I can see that,' says John.

'I'm not wearing any clothes.'

'I can see that as well. Aren't you cold?'

'No.' Then he says he wants to whisper something to John. 'I wanna tell you a secret.'

'What?' whispers John loudly, bending down and cupping his ear.

Jamie leans forward and says, rather loudly, 'I want Mummy to wear a Truly Sumptious dress.' He sits back, looking very pleased with himself.

John looks at me and raises an eyebrow.

'God, John,' I say, 'I just don't know how we got here. I really don't.'

2. Flight Season

It was Edward who came up with the idea of a change. He suggested it after a letter flopped down on our mat a couple of Saturdays ago. It was addressed to Edward. In fact, now Edward is getting older, many things appear from the postie's bag addressed to him. For example, he gets flyers for football courses he has done before. They say things like, 'Bored over the summer? Come and have a kickabout with representatives from your local LEAGUE team. Bring packed lunch and a drink. No nuts please.' Edward stares at these things with complete bafflement.

'Look,' he'll say to me, 'I'm being invited to play football with our local LEAGUE –' he shouts the LEAGUE bit because it's in capitals and he thinks that's what you do when something is written like that – 'team. Why do you think that is?'

I'll explain to Edward that it's not just him who's being invited, but many other children as well.

'But how do they know we're good at football?' he asks, moving his eyebrows up and down in a quizzical fashion.

'They don't,' I reply. 'They send these out to everyone who has done a course with them before.'

'Have I?' he'll say. 'Then what's the point of doing a course I've already done over again?'

At this stage I usually give up.

Edward took his letter on this particular morning and told me he wanted to read it in his room. 'It's my letter,' he said defiantly, 'and I'm going to read it in secret in my room,' and off he went. I looked at John, but he just shrugged his shoulders in a 'boys-will-be-boys' type fashion and carried on opening the letters that had come for us while I peeled the potatoes to make a cottage pie for lunch.

'Here's one for you,' he said to me. 'Shall I open it?'

I nodded. We regularly open each other's post. In fact, I always think I should open John's post in case there's a bill in it that needs paying. It would never get paid if it were left to John for I know what he'd do. He'd write 'To Be Paid' on it and then leave it lying around the house on top of his motley collection of other Letters To Be Dealt With, such as council tax bills, self-assessment income tax forms and notification of appointments at the dentist until, eventually, the bill would work its way to the bottom of the pile and then it would shuffle itself, somehow, into the newspaper recycling pile and get chucked out on a Friday morning and, a week later, I'd get a call from the gas/water/electricity people, who would threaten to cut us off because of the blasted unpaid bill.

'Oh,' said John, having opened the letter. 'It's from Wheelers in Barnstaple. They say that the couple who are renting the house in Devon have given notice. From the first of May the house will be made empty and, basically, what do we want to do about it.'

I groaned. 'Oh, great,' I said. 'Here we are trying to sort Jamie out over the summer and now we're going to have to do something about the house. What a pain.'

The truth is, though, the house in Devon hasn't really been a pain at all. It's a truly beautiful house tucked into a cove, but not quite on the sea, and it belonged to Janet, Edward's father's mother. It's a place the three of us used to go to years ago to visit her, before John the First and I separated and then divorced. Janet left it to Edward in her will four years ago, stipulating that he must share the house with his brothers.

For a while we weren't sure what to do with the house, so we've just rented it out on an annual basis. There was always some idea we'd go and see it, but life had taken over somewhat.

'Don't worry about the house,' said John. 'I'll just ring them and tell them to re-let it. Problem solved.'

But, ten minutes later, Edward appeared with a strange look on his face.

'I'm not sure I understood the letter that came for me,' he said, 'but I think the people who are living in my cottage in Devon are moving out and it is my house still, isn't it?'

'Yes,' I said carefully, realizing this was leading somewhere, but not quite sure where it was going. 'Your Granny Janet left it to you, but she did say you must share it with your brothers,' I reminded him.

'And the house will be empty?' asked Edward.

'Yes,' I said even more slowly. 'Until it's rented out again. Why?'

'Where are Bennie and Jamie?' he asked.

'Outside,' I said.

Edward then wandered outside, leaving John and me puzzled.

'What's he up to?' I asked John.

'Don't know,' said John.

When he came back in five minutes later, he was followed by his brothers.

'We've got a plan,' said Bennie, beaming at me.

'Shut up, Bennie,' said Edward.

'Edward!' I said.

'No, it's just that it's my plan,' said Edward. 'I want to tell you.'

'OK then,' said John, 'what is it?'

'I think we should all go and have our long holiday in Devon!' said Edward, his eyes shining. 'I've talked to Bennie and Jamie and they all agree and I can't talk to Baby Sparkle because she's asleep and, anyway, she doesn't count because Granny Janet said I had to share her house with my brothers and she never said "and your sister", so we've ruled Baby Sparkle out anyway.'

'Why do you want to go and spend the summer in Devon, Edward?' asked John patiently.

'I miss that house,' said Edward rather dramatically. 'I loved Granny Janet and she loved me and I haven't even been to see the house since she died and I want to go to live in it for a bit and so do the others because I've told them all about it.'

'It's near the sea,' piped up Bennie.

'Is hot there,' said Jamie. 'There daisies in the garden. My sike daisies.'

'We want to go,' said Bennie.

'See?' said Edward. 'You and Mum are always saying you want to live near the sea and now you can!'

We sent them outside and sat in the kitchen and discussed at length what should happen. Could we go to Devon for the summer?

'It's not a bad idea,' I said to John. 'We've got no holiday plans and Wheelers could rent it from September and . . .'

John sat silently for a bit.

24

'It would be fun, wouldn't it?' I said. 'Sea and sand and that lovely house.'

'I haven't seen the house,' said John shortly.

I realized, then, that it might be hard for him to go to a place that was so resonant of Edward's father and grand-mother. I would holiday with my first John there sometimes as much as three times a year.

'Maybe you're right,' I said quickly. 'We could find some-where in France perhaps.'

John looked at me and he looked very serious.

'No, let's go,' he said. 'I can probably take the summer off and a change of scene would help Jamie. Maybe it would take his mind off whatever's troubling him. What do you say?'

I thought for a bit and then I said, 'Do you think a change would really help Jamie?'

'Yes, actually, I do. Sometimes it's hard to see what's going on if everything stays the same. We're busy, you're worrying, the telephone doesn't stop, I've been working . . . it's hard to really concentrate on Jamie with all that going on.'

'A holiday would be good,' I said, feeling happy in a way I hadn't felt for such a time, 'and the sun and sea would be lovely and it would be great to be together as a family. Oh, John, you could really spend time with Jamie. It's been so hard to do that with the baby.'

'I know,' said John, ruffling my hair. 'Yes, we should go for the summer. In fact, I'm sure of it. Why not? Let's commit to it once and for all.'

'It would make the boys very happy,' I said.

'It would make me happy,' John said, smiling. 'It's time we had a proper summer together and I really do think it will help Jamie — so it's settled then.'

We called the boys in and Edward cheered when John told him we'd be in Devon for weeks on end over the summer.

'Imagine it, Edward,' said John, whirling his coffee mug around. 'We can go surfing and rock-pooling and we can eat chips on the beach and . . .'

'Chips on the beach! Yummy!' said Bennie.

'Hate chips,' said Jamie.

'. . . and we can sunbathe and sleep and eat cream teas and fresh fish . . .'

'I think Baby Sparkle might need her first bathing suit,' I said.

Jamie's ears pricked up.

'New bathing suit?' he said. 'Me want one.'

'Of course,' I said smoothly.

'When do we go?' asked Edward.

'As soon as the summer holidays start,' said John.

'Will you be there, Dad?'

'Absolutely. Me and Mummy and all of us.'

'It'll be an adventure,' I said happily. 'A real family adventure.'

3. Migration

It is a beautiful day when we leave the valley. Edward stares out of the window of the car as John waves us goodbye.

'Is Dad not coming with us?' he asks.

'Not today,' I say, as breezily as I can. 'He's working this week. He's coming down at the weekend.'

Edward shoots me an odd look.

'Working?' he says, staring at me. 'I thought we were going away on holiday all together.'

'Yes,' I say, 'well, we were, but Daddy has to work.'

'What's he working on now?' says Edward, looking mildly interested, which is odd as Edward is rarely interested in anyone's work. In fact, it always comes as a shock to him that I work at all. Even when my first book, *Our Fridges, Ourselves*, became a best-seller a couple of years ago, he nearly fell over when a friend came up to him and told him his mother loved my book. 'What's your book about then?' he asked me. I told him it was a coffee-table book about what famous people keep in their fridges.

Since then I've done *Good Fridge, Bad Fridge*, which analysed the contents of people's fridges in terms of their nutritional value, and now I'm researching a book on glamour fridges. Somehow the fridge formula has worked. *Our Fridges, Ourselves* has been turned into a television show which involves a well-known presenter nosing around people's fridges while other people guess who each fridge belongs to. The show became a daytime television hit and has, since then, been formatted across the world. Every time another country buys the rights to the television show, I get a cut of the money, so it has proved to be a nice little earner for me.

I told Edward that John was spending his summer designing sets for a puppet show.

'That wasn't what was supposed to happen though, was it?' says Edward, now looking at the road in front of him.

'No,' I say shortly. 'It wasn't.'

'And you're not fine with that, are you, Mum?' says Edward.

'No, I'm totally fine with it,' I say. 'Everything is really, really fine.'

I am, of course, sort of lying and Edward knows this. He has caught me out. This is partially because, now he's 'almost a teenager' as he puts it, he stays up later and also because, as John often works until way into the evening, we spend time together alone, just the two of us, after the younger children have gone to bed. We're very companionable, Edward and me. We watch television and play Scrabble and do crosswords together.

But one night, after John came home, I forgot Edward was still up. He was in the study playing on the computer when John bounded into the kitchen looking very pleased with himself.

'I've got a great gig over the summer,' he said, as he looked for a corkscrew to open the bottle of wine he was brandishing.

'What?' I said, all thoughts of wide-awake Edward now out of my mind.

'It's an incredible job,' he said, coming round the breakfast counter and grasping me about the waist. 'I'm designing sets for a show called *Pulcinella.*'

'What?' I said again.

'Why are you saying "what"?' said John. 'I'm doing sets for *Pulcinella*. It translates into *Mr Punch* and I'm going to be doing a whole set of props for this fantastic French outfit that travels round Europe putting on shows about Mr Punch in the court of the Ancien Régime.'

'Hang on a minute,' I said, refusing the glass of wine John was offering me. 'There's something I don't understand here. Are you seriously telling me that you're not coming on holiday with us?'

John stopped his search of the fridge, looking for something to eat. He stood staring at me, as if he was hurt.

'Of course not,' he said, looking almost puppyish, a look he always uses when he knows he has done something wrong. 'I'll be there. I just won't be there all the time.'

I could feel it coming then, the anger, the waves of exhausted anger I'd been keeping in. I closed my eyes.

'You won't be there all the time,' I hissed, like a bicycle tyre pricked by a thorn.

'I think it will be good for my career, Samantha,' he said pleadingly. 'Imagine my designs being shown in Prague, Paris. I can't turn that down, can I?' He looked at me appealingly. 'I'll come every weekend,' he said.

'Not good enough,' I said. 'Jamie is more important than your career. Jamie is more important than anything.'

'Jamie is fine . . .'

'NO, HE IS NOT!' I yelled, suddenly losing control. 'He is not bloody fine and I can't do any more and you promised, you bloody promised me you would help. I can't balance everybody. I've got a new baby, in case you hadn't noticed, and you, as per usual, you are walking away from a problem.'

'I am not walking away!' said John indignantly. 'I am trying to provide for my family.'

'It's one summer. One bloody summer that you agreed to. I need you there. We all need you there because I can't do it alone and I won't do it. I just won't. I'm tired and sad and exhausted and I'm the only one who cares. I'm sick of being the only one who worries about this family. It's only bloody me . . .'

And then suddenly I heard a small subdued voice coming from the direction of the kitchen door.

'I'll go to bed, shall I?' said Edward.

I took a deep breath in.

'Yes,' I said, still not opening my eyes.

Later on, after we had sat in silence for half an hour, John told me he'd turn the job down.

'It's not worth it,' he said, not looking at me. 'If you want me to, I'll turn it down. Yes, I'll turn it down. There, that settles it.'

Half an hour after that, I told him to take the job. I told him we'd all be fine.

'Do you really think so?' he said.

I didn't say anything because I felt on the verge of tears.

'I'm sorry,' he said.

Then I went to bed and, some time later, John followed me. I pretended to be asleep.

'Samantha,' he whispered to my back. 'I really am sorry. I'm a thoughtless pain in the neck, aren't I?'

I turned towards him then and saw his face in the half light.

'No,' I said, reaching out to stroke his cheek. 'You're not. I'm just a bit cross, that's all. I just worry so. You know I do.'

'You mustn't worry,' he said gently. 'I really do believe Jamie will be fine. If I didn't think that, I would move a mountain to be with him all summer. You know that, don't you?'

'Yes,' I whispered back. 'I do know that but, you know, John, it's my job to worry.'

So, as we set off I tell Edward about the glove puppet set John is making. Edward is boggle-eyed.

'He's making a Punch and Judy tent?' he asks.

'Not a tent really,' I say. 'He's actually making a stage, but he'll come and stay with us at weekends.'

'Oh,' says Edward. 'So he'll be down at weekends?'

'Absolutely.'

Then I can see Edward's brain working very hard.

'I'll try to help with Jamie,' he says.

'Oh, Edward,' I say. 'It's not your job.'

'But I heard you tell Dad you were tired. It's not good to be so tired.'

'You shouldn't have heard that. You mustn't worry about it, really you mustn't.'

'Did you use to argue with my other dad? The one whose mother owned the house we're going to?'

I stop the car momentarily and turn to look at him.

'I'm not doing this, Edward,' I say to him, looking at him straight in the face. 'I'm not having this discussion with you. This is not about anything major. I wanted Daddy to come and I was angry that he took the job and now I'm over it. We will have a lovely time all together and Daddy will come at weekends, OK?'

Edward pulls a face.

'I was only asking,' he says as I start up the car again. 'Nothing wrong with that, is there?'

But five minutes later, he's off again.

'Did Daddy actually help with anything for the holiday?' he asks.

'Yes,' I say, 'he helped with the packing.'

Edward snorts.

'Hey,' I say, 'packing is an art. Very few people know how to do it.'

HOW TO PACK FOR GOING ON HOLIDAY

You have two choices here. You can either do 'The Samantha', which is to think methodically and thoughtfully about what might actually be needed on holiday and then pack accordingly, or you can do 'The John'. This version involves shoving everything you see into any bag, in any order, and stuffing the bags on to the aeroplane/boat/car and then discovering, to your dismay, that although you have toothpaste you have no toothbrush, you may have a large beach towel but no swimming trunks, etc. A true aficionado of 'The John' will then turn round and shout 'Why didn't you pack my toothbrush?' at their poor, hapless partner standing not so far away who is, herself, trying to work out why she has seven pairs of black knickers and no white ones even though she had specifically said to her husband that it was very important to pack white ones or else she would have nothing to wear under her white long linen dress.

But those who opt for 'The Samantha' also face a difficult and trying time. For they shall be responsible for everything from packing playing cards to matches, T-shirts to shoe laces.

Before we go on holiday I spend, ooh, around six weeks

thinking about what we all need. I start off with the practical things like candles, matches, citronella, mosquito repellent, fly spray, Anthisan, Wasp-Eze, mosquito coils, mosquito coil burners, Elastoplast, Piriton, calamine lotion, Calpol for the over-6s, Calpol for the under-6s, Benylin, Tixylix, Lemsip for adults and Night Nurse.

Then, five weeks before, I shall think about what to take in my first-aid kit; all the medicines known to humankind including the ones listed above, plus gauze and syringes and splints and a thermometer and scissors, plenty of scissors. You always need scissors on holiday. And one of those funny little pen things that's supposed to neutralize the itching sensation you get with mosquito bites. And Friar's Balsam in case of nasal congestion. I also take Rennie tablets for indigestion, Rinstead pastels in case someone gets an ulcer and Arnica pills and lotion.

Four weeks in advance and I'm now on to electrical equipment. This is a pretty short list as we're hopeless with electrical things. We tend to take only a camera and memory cards and the video camera and Digi8 cassettes and then tape players for the children and a hairdryer and hair straighteners for me and chargers for all of them and plug adaptors.

Three weeks before we go, I start looking for the luggage. 'Where are our suitcases?' I'll ask John. 'I don't know,' he'll say. This is his most irritating characteristic. He has this amazing ability to say 'I don't know' about everything. For example, let's say that John has, the day before, been out digging the garden. Everyone has witnessed him. But the next day, when I need to clear up the dog mess because all the children are running around in bare feet and one of them has already stepped perilously close to a dog turd, I'll go to the garden shed to look for the spade. The spade shall not be there so I shall say to John, 'Darling, where's the spade?' and he'll say 'I don't know.' Why does he say this? I'll point out to him that it was he who last had the spade and that, therefore, 'I don't know' is the incorrect answer. 'I didn't have it last,' he'll say with some conviction. I'll then state that we all saw him digging the garden the day before and so he definitely had the spade last and all I want to know is where he has left it. 'In the garden shed,' he'll say. I'll tell him that the spade is not in the garden shed as I looked for it there and couldn't see it. John will look at me in an amused fashion as if I'm a blind idiot and go and look in the shed himself. He'll then come back and say, 'You're right. The spade's not in the shed. Someone must have taken it.' 'Who could possibly have taken it?' I'll say. 'I don't know,' he'll reply.

In the same way, John never knows where the suitcases are even though it was he who was supposed to have put them back in the attic after we came back from holiday all of a year ago. This means I have to go on a suitcase hunt. I usually inveigle Edward and his friend Stanley to help me. Last year they found one under Jamie's cot and then they realized that Bennie had stolen a small one and turned it into a case for all his trucks. They found my large one squashed behind the Welsh dresser in my bathroom and another squished into the back of Edward's cupboard. This year I sent them off on the same task. I heard them thundering up and down the stairs, closely followed by Bennie. They ended up finding one under Jamie's cot again and another in the attic. 'I'm not sure the attic is safe,' I told them when they reappeared with a third suitcase. They were covered in cobwebs.

Over the next two weeks I start sorting out clothes. I make little piles of clothes for the beach, clothes for wet days, clothes for dry days, clothes for hot days, clothes for days which are not hot but not wet, and then an underwear pile. I put a suitcase in each child's room and then fiddle-faddle about trying to fit everything in. Should I take a towelling robe each? I love the boys in towelling robes. They look so sweet in their matching stripy blue ones and they're handy for after swimming or on the beach, but those robes take up so much room.

'Should I take their towelling robes?' I ask John when he's home from work.

'Yes,' he says. 'Why not?'

'But they take up so much room.'

'OK, don't take them then.'

'But that's not the point, John. Should I take them? I don't mean in a moral sense or a fashion sense, but do they justify their usefulness proportional to the space they take up?'

'How on earth am I supposed to know?' he says, laughing. 'It's only a holiday, Samantha. Take what you want.'

But that's not the point of packing for there's nothing as frustrating as unpacking once you're on holiday and then watching at least half of your clothes sit unworn for the entire time. So I'll pack and unpack and repack and have little private conversations with T-shirts and shorts and knickers and socks, and I'll edit the three pairs of pretty pyjamas I'm packing for Jamie down to one and I shall only pack five pairs of pants for Bennie because I can hand wash the rest. Oh God, the handwash! And then I'll empty out all the summer clothes from my wardrobe and pack every single item into the large adult-sized suitcases, along with six pairs of shoes.

Then, with about four days to go, I have a panic about the pets. This happens every time we go away. It's as if John and

I are in some unspoken world of denial when it comes to the pets. I keep thinking he will organize dog and cat care (oh, why do I think this?) and he obviously assumes I'll do it. Eventually, once we establish that neither of us have actually done anything, we make frantic calls to our next-door neighbours hoping that maybe one of them will agree to come in on a daily basis and feed the cat and then, once we establish that someone will do that, we call my mother. 'Mum,' I say in my fake oh-please-help-me tone of voice.

'What do you want, Samantha?' asks my mother, knowing already that I'm about to ask her something.

'Oh, nothing,' I'll say.

'Good,' my mother will say.

'It's just that, well, you know we're going away . . .'

'Yes.'

I hesitate for a bit. This is not an easy one. My mother hates being obligated to anyone and she's not going to like what I'm about to ask her. 'Beady,' I say. 'I have no one to take care of Beady.'

'You have no one to take care of your dog.' She says it as a statement.

'Erm, no.'

'You are going away in four days' time and you have not arranged for anyone to look after your dog.'

'Erm, yes. I mean, no, we haven't.'

'Have you tried the kennels?'

'Yes,' I lie. Kennels? Kennels for my Beady? I don't think so. At the mention of kennels, Beady hangs her head down and looks at me with her soft brown eyes. She has Catholic guilt, this dog. My mother sighs.

'I suppose you want me to take her then?'

'Erm, yes.'

'God, Samantha,' she'll say. 'How can a daughter of mine be so disorganized?'

All this just to go on holiday. Is it worth it? I wonder sometimes, I really do.

But now, today, I've packed and re-packed and packed again and I haven't had to worry about the dog as we're taking her with us and my mother has promised to come and feed the cat when John eventually gets down to visit us and, somehow, we're going to lurch off down the motor-way, all of us stuffed into this small space. Somehow John and Edward have fitted the bags in and now we're on our way. John stood in the road, seeing us off. I've kissed him goodbye. I've given him a meaningful kiss, a long one, a sorry-you-are-not-coming-with-us type of a one. I watched him in the mirror as his waving hands got smaller and smaller and he got further and further away. It suddenly occurs to me that this is how things end. One day you're waving goodbye to the man you love and the next second he's gone. It jolts me suddenly. I remember so clearly waving Edward's father away as he went off with his guitar to find himself and he never came back, and then, years ago now, when Edward and I went to say our farewells to his pater-nal grandmother. She was dying of cancer and she wanted to see us to say goodbye and I remember Edward happily chatting on about 'Granny Janet', as he called her, and how much he wanted to see her, but we never saw her again either. This is what happens to people: they disappear. Sometimes, like Janet, they know they're dying. They make preparations for it. They say goodbye to people and hello to others, ones they haven't seen for years, ones they have fallen out with and feuded with, and then, pretty soon, they have to say goodbye to them as well. But sometimes people leave unexpectedly. They are, say, driving to Devon with four noisy children in their car and as they lean over to feed the baby with a bottle that has fallen on the floor or turn to argue vehemently with their youngest son, they lose their concentration for a second and the next thing they know, they have ploughed through the central reservation into the path of an oncoming juggernaut and they're all . . .

'Mum!' yells Edward suddenly in my ear. 'You're weaving all over the road. What's the matter with you?'

'Oh, Edward,' I say. 'I'm so sorry. I wasn't concentrating. I was just thinking, what if we all died in a car crash on the motorway? Wouldn't that be awful?'

'Yeah, well why don't you look at the road,' he says truculently, 'and then we'll all live?'

4. Distribution

We get to the hill above Lower Strand at three o'clock in the afternoon. We've been in the car for five hours, more or less. We did have a stop at Leigh Delamere service station – the only one worth stopping at – on the way down because Baby Sparkle, who spent virtually the entire journey asleep, woke up and needed her nappy changing.

It was Bennie who noticed it.

'Poor Baby Sparkle,' he said anxiously. 'She really smells.'

So we all got out and trooped off to the loos and then went to Marks & Spencer to get some sandwiches. 'I DON'T WANT SANDWICHES, I WANT CAKE!' said Jamie loudly as soon as we'd got into the shop. So we bought cake for Sophie – you have to give in on long journeys I find – and sandwiches and wiggly-worm sweets, and then we went back to the car and set off once more, at which point Baby Sparkle, now clean and happy having munched down some crackers and cheese, fell asleep again. In fact, by the time I reach the long hill that snakes down the side of the sea cliff that takes us to the valley of Lower Strand and the road that goes on further to the beach and the sea, everyone is asleep apart from Beady the dog, who is sitting up on the back seat, squashed between Bennie and Baby Sparkle, with her tongue hanging out.

'Can you smell that sea air?' I say to Beady and she wags her tail, and then I drive very slowly down the hill towards the wooded valley with the fuchsias hanging down from the sides, towards a little village and a little house that I used to know so well.

'I used to come here all the time,' I say to Beady as we pass the rock face with water dripping down it and then the big fern bush. 'There's a small school here on the right just after the hanging ferns and the village hall is over there.' The village hall looks exactly the same as it always has. It's made of dark wood with an ancient tiled roof. It has a clock face above the door. I notice that the hands are still stuck on a quarter to three. 'It's been that time for years,' I say. And then I drive down a bit more and to the left and there is the house. It looks almost exactly the same as it did when Janet was alive, although it's a bit more run-down. It's hard to see a portion of it as the garden hedge has grown somewhat. I notice that some of the slates on the roof are tilting at crazy angles and that the paint on the window frames is obviously peeling.

What of the garden? Janet loved her garden. I crane my neck to look over the hedge until I can see the gently sloping garden and the buddleia bushes and the roses which always seemed to be in full bloom. It all looks rather overgrown. The wisteria has all but obliterated the view from the French doors that open up from the drawing room into the garden and the trellis that John the First bought and put up for his mother, so that she could grow honeysuckle and jasmine up it, has been swamped in a mass of greenery beyond all recognition. Oh, what would Janet think of all this? That was the thing about Janet. She was mad on gardening. I remember her so clearly being out in that garden, kneeling down on her pad, her little trug beside her. One year she told me she was entering the garden for the National Garden Day that happened annually in the area. 'I've never felt confident enough to enter the garden into the National Garden Day before,' she told me as we watched Edward, who was tiny then, toddle round the flower beds. 'Not all gardens are accepted,' she said. 'They have to have something special about them.' A week later, once we had left Devon, she telephoned and told me her garden had been accepted. She said she was delighted.

But now . . . her poor garden, all unloved and rambling. I promise then and there that I will try to restore the garden over the summer. I'm not a great gardener, but I can try. The children can help and maybe we can all learn about gardening together.

The house is more of a large cottage really, with six bedrooms and three bathrooms and a rather wonderful wrought-iron balcony that runs all the way round the first floor. Janet never really bothered about the interior of the house. She only ever cooked on a small electric stove, rather than use the magnificent Aga, and she refused to light the fire in the huge but beautiful fireplace unless it was terribly cold. In the summer she'd take her indoor furniture outside and we'd sit on a comfortable squishy sofa of a Sunday morning, reading the newspapers and listening to the bees and the sea, and it was all very relaxing.

I park the car and turn the engine off. Baby Sparkle immediately opens her eyes. She always does this. She can be fast asleep, but as soon as you stop the engine she snaps open those eyes of hers and smiles.

'Hello, darling Baby Sparkle,' I say to her. 'We're in Devon now. We're near the sea.'

'Near the sea?' says Edward sleepily, his head still lolling against the window.

'Yes, Edward,' I say. 'We're at the house, at Granny Janet's house.'

Then suddenly, just as I'm saying this, the smell of roses floods the car and I feel rather tearful. God, how Janet loved those roses, that smell. I think of Janet when she was here and she was alive and vibrant and then I think of her lying there dying in Prestwood General.

'Do you know something, Edward?' I whisper to him. 'We must make this place lovely again in the memory of Janet, for every sod of earth you tread on has been trodden on by her before you. This is Janet's legacy to you and you must honour it.'

Edward, now fully awake, looks at me in a peculiar fashion.

'You've gone quite mad, haven't you?' he says.

'No,' I say. 'I'm just saying that we'll restore this garden to its former glory. Maybe we can even get it back into the Garden Open Day. That's what Janet would have wanted.'

'OK,' he sighs. 'I have no idea what the open day is, but you said the house and garden belongs to Bennie and Jamie so they must help too.'

Edward then looks out of the window. 'I don't really remember being here,' he says as he reaches for the front-door key to the house and gets out of the car. Beady jumps after him and sniffs the air. 'Does it smell of the sea?' Edward asks her.

'Are we near the sea?' asks Bennie, waking up.

'It's just down the road,' I say. 'You can't see it from here, but if you go down the road towards the village, you'll see it.'

'The sea! The sea!' trills Jamie, who is now also climbing out over the seats of the car. 'Baby Sparkle will go in the sea.'

'No,' I say, gazing at Baby Sparkle who is gazing fixedly back at me. 'She's too little to go in the sea.'

'No,' says Jamie, jutting out his chin determinedly. 'I shall put her in the sea. She can sink.'

'In a beautiful pea-green boat?' asks Bennie.

'With some honey and plenty of money, wrapped up in a five-pound note?' I ask, ignoring Jamie.

'Yes,' says Bennie, giggling. 'Actually, I'd like some honey right now, Mummy, if there is some. On toast, please.'

Then he gets out of the car and follows Edward through the garden gate.

'Come on, Mum!' he yells. 'Come on, Jamie.'

Jamie holds my hand as we walk through the gate.

'How messy,' he says, looking at the garden. 'Sophie doesn't like mess.'

'Sophie doesn't like mess?' I say. 'But we're going to clear it up. Now why don't you let go of my hand and go into the house and choose a bedroom.'

'No,' says Jamie, keeping my hand firmly in his. 'I not go in without you. Sophie is afraid of this new house.'

'Well, I need to get Baby Sparkle out of the car so maybe you and Sophie can wait here for me.'

'No,' says Jamie again. 'We can't.'

'But Baby Sparkle will cry,' I say as I hear some whimpering emanating from the car. 'She'll get sad because she doesn't know where we are.'

'I SAID WE CAN'T!' yells Jamie. 'SOPHIE IS SCARED.'

Suddenly Beady races out of the house and starts barking.

'Mum,' says Edward, running into the garden. 'There's a man coming up the road. I saw him out of my bedroom window.'

'You got a bedroom?' says Jamie crossly. 'Sophie wants that room!'

'You don't even know which room I'm having,' says Edward. 'You haven't even been into the house.'

'Not me,' says Jamie. 'SOPHIE!'

'Jamie,' says Edward, 'there is no such person as Sophie.'

'There is!'

'I don't care,' says Edward. 'You're not having my room.'

'Yes!' yells Jamie, beginning to cry loudly.

'No!' says Edward.

I suggest we go into the house and sort things out.

'Bennie,' I say to Bennie, who has just appeared from the kitchen and has somehow found a biscuit that he's munching on. 'Can you please unstrap Baby Sparkle and bring her into the house?' Bennie nods and disappears off into the drive. 'And Jamie and Edward and I will sort out the rooms.'

'I want the blue one,' Bennie calls out from behind the hedge, 'and Baby Sparkle can sleep with me if she wants.'

'Bennie loves that baby,' says Edward.

We go into the house and we're about to go up the stairs when I hear a coughing noise coming from the kitchen.

'That man is in our house,' whispers Edward loudly. Beady starts barking again.

'Who is he?' I say.

'Probably a nosey neighbour,' says Edward. 'He came through a hole in the hedge and . . .' Then Edward stops as we hear a voice say, 'Hello, dog! Guarding your family, are you? I like a dog that does that.'

I turn and go back into the kitchen. There at the back door, blocking out the light, is the figure of a man.

'Hello,' says the man to me. 'Are you Ms Smythe?'

'I am Mrs Smythe,' I say, trying to make his face out from beneath the hat he's wearing.

'You are not a Mrs Smith, but a Mrs Smythe, spelled S-M-Y-T-H-E?'

'Yes,' I say cautiously. 'I am most definitely a Mrs Smythe. And you are?'

'Good,' says the man. 'And you are Edward Smythe?' he says to Edward. Edward nods. 'Thought you were,' says the man. 'I'm Noel Rideout. It's spelled Rideout, but it's pronounced Ridout. Thought I'd let you know as everyone gets muddled when they see me write cheques.'

'Right,' says Edward.

'Well, can I come in?' asks the man.

'Oh God, I'm so sorry,' I say. 'Yes, please do.'

The man enters the kitchen and I see then that he's probably in his late sixties and must have been, as a younger man, startlingly attractive, for even now he's a good-looking man. He's tall and has that brown skin that people get when they have lived near the sea for a long time. He has a long, thin face, crinkled with lines, an aquiline nose, blue eyes and silky grey hair that pokes out from under his hat and curls down the nape of his neck. He also looks terribly smart. He has on a tweed suit and shiny brown brogues.

'So, the famous Edward then?' he says, raising an eyebrow at him. Edward shifts about a bit from foot to foot.

'How do you know my name?' asks Edward.

'Oh, I know all about you, Edward,' says Noel. He turns back to me, leaving Edward looking rather uncomfortable. 'I was a very good friend of Janet's, you see. Not only was I her neighbour and her friend, but I helped her buy this house.'

'Is it part yours then?' Edward asks a bit nervously.

'Oh no,' says Noel, now looking at Edward again. 'You have no worries on that account. The inheritance on this house goes solely to you.'

'How do you know that?' asks Edward.

'Because I was Janet's solicitor and I was very close to your grandmother. I remember the evenings we sat together on the veranda drinking a glass of something cool and refreshing.' Noel pauses. 'So tragic she has gone. I do miss her company. Oh, well. I drafted her will for her so, you see, I really do know all about you, Edward, because she talked of you often.' Noel looks very sad.

He then turns back towards me. 'Don't mind me,' he says. 'I'm only being maudlin. I have come to relieve you of some things I have in this garden that I must now remove.'

'Like what?' says Edward, looking intrigued.

'Like a wine rope,' he says, striding off into the garden.

'A wine rope?' I ask, following him. 'What's a wine rope?'

Noel Rideout doesn't answer me. He's staring into the garden.

'What an extraordinary little boy,' he says. 'That is a boy, isn't it?'

I follow his gaze. He's staring at Jamie who has wandered outside and, unbeknownst to me, taken off all his clothes and put on a pair of knickers, the ones covered in rosebuds that we bought from a catalogue for him.

'Hello,' says Jamie, waving at him and wandering towards us. 'I know the f-word. It begins with a b.'

'Does it?' says Noel Rideout. 'How interesting. Now, I must say, what wonderful underwear you have on.' Jamie gives him one of his most heart-melting smiles. 'My grand-daughter would love those.'

'Is she called Sophie?' asks Jamie. 'I have a friend called Sophie.'

'Do you?' says Noel Rideout, smiling down at Jamie. 'And where is your friend called Sophie?'

'She's right here,' says Jamie, opening his green eyes wide and motioning towards the space next to him, which is occupied by nothing more than thin air.

Noel Rideout bends down towards Jamie and puts his hand out. 'Hello, Sophie,' he says, pretending to shake someone's hand. 'How charming you are. Your friend Sophie has wonderful manners,' he says to Jamie.

Jamie primps and preens a bit. 'Yes, she does, doesn't she?' he says.

Then Bennie appears, manfully trying to hold Baby Sparkle.

'Ah, another boy, I see,' says Noel Rideout.

'And a baby girl,' says Edward, as I go and take Baby Sparkle from his brother.

'Have you seen my wine rope?' he asks Jamie. 'I've put it in some flowers to attract moths.'

'What are moths?' asks Jamie. 'Do they begin with a b?'

'No, they don't, but they are like butterflies and butterflies begin with a b,' says Noel.

'Sophie likes flutterbyes,' says Jamie, holding out a hand to Noel.

Noel takes Jamie's hand and then pretends to hold another hand on the other side.

'Sophie likes holding hands,' says Jamie, noticing what Noel Rideout is doing, and then the two of them – or three of them if you count imaginary Sophie, who now seems to be almost real – wander towards the bottom of the garden. The rest of us follow.

47

'Can that man really see Sophie?' asks Bennie dubiously as we watch Noel Rideout talk to Jamie and then to Sophie in turn.

'No,' I say. 'He's just being nice.'

'He's being really nice,' says Edward. 'I decided to stop talking to Sophie when she nicked my remote-control dragonfly and flew it into Jamie's bedroom wall.'

Just then Noel stops by a rather straggly bush situated next to a squat tree that has branches sticking out at all angles.

'Now, let me see,' he says, finding some glasses in his jacket pocket and putting them on. He starts rummaging through the leaves of the bush. 'Ah, here it is.' He extracts a rope from the foliage and stares at it. The rope is thin and stained a deep pinkish colour. 'Best way to see moths,' Noel says to no one in particular. 'You soak a rope in red wine and sugar and you leave it out at dusk and then the moths come and you can look at them. I saw a Red-belted Clearwing the other day. Quite rare, you know, but then again, this tree here is a crab apple and they love crab apples. I reported the sighting to the *Entomologist's Gazette* in Truro and it made the front page – "*Synanthedon myopaeformis* seen in North Devon garden". Oh, sorry, am I boring you?'

'No,' I say as I watch Jamie alternately staring at Noel and then at the rope and back again. 'Jamie is obviously fascinated. And Sophie,' I add hurriedly as I see Jamie giving me a beady look.

'The Red-belted Clearwing has a lovely red band on its body,' Noel says to Jamie and Jamie smiles. 'Hence the name. It likes to feed underneath the bark of a tree, especially a wounded tree.'

'A wounded tree?' says Jamie. 'How it be wounded?'

'Does that mean someone has attacked it?' asks Edward.

'No,' says Noel. 'It's normally when the main trunk has divided, when there's been a storm for example and a tree's been struck by lightning.'

'Sophie's scared of lightning,' says Jamie, shivering.

'Lots of people are scared of lightning,' says Noel, 'but the Red-belted Clearwing loves it because it means it can lay its eggs in the bark of the tree and when the larvae hatch they feed immediately. You need to look for exit holes in the bark, you see.'

Jamie positions himself closer to Noel, using him to balance by holding on to his bent-down knee, and leans forward to peer at the bark.

'You can't see any?' Noel says to him. Jamie shakes his head. 'Can Sophie see any?' Jamie shakes his head again.

Noel straightens up. 'Never mind,' he says. 'Now, that's enough of all that. I'll find somewhere else to put the wine string.'

'No, please, leave it there,' I say. 'Please do. Jamie would probably love that. He's had a difficult year and . . .' I stop talking. I'm not sure why on earth I'm telling this slightly odd man about Jamie's problems.

Noel smiles and nods.

'I can see he is wearing female knickers and that he has a lovely invisible friend with him, but no more. Do not concern yourself, Mrs Smythe. Do you need some help with your children? I only say this because I happen to have noticed a sign in the village hall stating that a local girl called Shelley, who is apparently very nice, is offering herself up as a summer babysitter. I just thought I'd let you know.'

'Well, that's very kind of you.'

'Don't mention it. Now, if your youngest boy and his

friend are into moths then would it help for me to re-soak the rope and bring it back?'

'I'm not sure he's into moths, but . . .' I say.

'You bring it back?' says Jamie, smiling away. 'You bring pretty flutterbyes to our garden?'

'Moths, dear boy,' Noel says. 'Wonderful moths.' He puts the rope in his pocket. 'Not now, but later. I shall go and leave you in peace,' he says.

'But maybe you'd like some tea?' I say. 'Sorry. I've been terribly rude. Aren't neighbours supposed to offer each other cups of tea? Isn't that what neighbours do?'

'Are we neighbours?' says Noel.

'I don't know,' I say falteringly. 'Don't you live near here?'

'Oh, yes,' he says, 'but I don't tend to drink tea.' Then he sets off towards the gap in the hedge. As he's about to disappear through it, he turns to me with a thoughtful look on his face and says, 'Don't you find that houses reflect the character of the person who owns them?'

'I don't know,' I say.

'This house was very suited to Janet, you see. It's rambling and welcoming with a beautiful, flowering, abundant garden. It's the type of property that attracts things: people, insects, butterflies, moths. People like being here. I'm sure you will too.'

'I do hope so,' I say. 'But where do you live?'

'In a former pub,' he says, raising an eyebrow. 'It suits me very well.'

Then, just as he is about leave again, he stops once more. 'There's a meeting tomorrow night at seven thirty in the village hall. It may be of interest to you to come. This Shelley could babysit for you and then you'd realize that this is a working village, Mrs Smythe, not just somewhere for tourists to use as they wish.'

I'm about to tell him that I have no intention of 'using' the village, as he has put it, but before I can say anything he strides off, leaving me gaping after him.

'Has he gone?' says Edward, coming to join me.

'Yes,' I say, still looking down the road at Noel Rideout's retreating figure.

'He reminds me of something,' says Edward, screwing his face up. 'Now what is it?'

'He looks like a fox!' says Bennie, who is halfway up the crab apple tree. 'He has a long nose just like a fox.'

'I don't know if he's a fox,' I say thoughtfully, watching Jamie who has voluntarily gone back to the car and emerged into the garden eating one of his packed lunch sandwiches, 'but Jamie seems to like him.'

I call John when I get back into the house.

'You're there?' he says. 'How was the journey?'

'Well, you know, four kids, one a baby, loo stop, food stop, too many children and one dog and not enough hands,' I say.

'Ah, that type of thing,' says John.

'Yes, that type of thing,' I say.

'But you've got there OK?'

'Yes, we're here now.'

I then go on to describe how ramshackle the house and garden have become.

'The house is cold and damp.'

'That's because no one's been living in it since May, isn't it?'

'I suppose so,' I say, 'but it feels odd to be here somehow. As if the house knows we're strangers.'

'What? You think the house knows you're strangers? Samantha, my darling, it's a house.'

'Yes, but maybe it knows that Janet died and . . .'

'Where on earth are you getting all this from? Houses don't have feelings. They are nothing more than bricks and mortar.'

'That's not what Noel Rideout said.'

'Noel Rideout?'

'Yes, his name is spelled Rideout, but you pronounce it Ridout.'

'But who on earth is he?'

'He's an old friend of Janet's. He seems really nice. He showed Jamie some moths in the garden and he pretended Sophie was really there and I've never known a stranger do that.'

'What did Jamie think of it?'

'He loved it!' I say.

'That's great,' says John enthusiastically. 'You see? The change has already been good.'

'Not that you're here to see it.' As soon as I say it I feel sorry. 'I mean, I wish you were here to see it all. It's really rather lovely and I have hopes here, real hopes, that this might help Jamie. Mind you, the garden's terribly run down and Janet loved her garden, so I thought I'd try to clear it up and restore it back to its former glory. You know how I like a project.'

'I think that's a great idea,' says John, sounding relieved. 'The kids will help you. I'll help you when I come down as well. Call me tomorrow when you get up. I've got to get to London now and pick up a pile of wood to turn into a French chateau.'

'A French chateau for puppets?'

'Oh, don't start,' he says. 'Anyway, how are the kids? Are you coping with all four of them?'

'Just about,' I say, 'but Noel told me about a local girl called Shelley. Apparently she's available for babysitting over the summer.'

'That's a good idea,' says John. 'God, we might even get to go out one night together without the kids. That would be amazing.'

'Don't get your hopes up,' I say. 'She might not be available. It may not work out.'

'Why wouldn't it?'

'The children might not like her.'

'Really, Samantha. You're not employing her as a nanny. You're only asking her to babysit.'

'I just want to check her out first,' I say defensively.

'This is about Baby Sparkle, isn't it?' says John. 'I don't know what's happened to you since you had that baby.'

In truth, neither do I.

WHAT HAS HAPPENED TO ME SINCE
I HAD BABY SPARKLE

Something has happened to me since I had Baby Sparkle. This is obvious to everyone I know and even to me. Actually, maybe it was happening to me before I had her, but it has become increasingly pronounced over the past year since I had my sapphire-eyed gurgling girl. I seem to worry all the time and recently I've started getting worried about my worrying. I used to be a pretty laid-back person. Most problems slid away from me. For example, I never worried about having change to pay the parking meter in the local supermarket car park in the way my mother does. She nearly had an apoplectic fit at me once when we took Edward, then aged about four, to see an am-dram version of *Puss in Boots*. We drove into the car park and I parked and then set off with Edward to the church hall.

'You haven't paid for a ticket!' my mother said, looking amazed.

'No,' I said breezily. 'I don't have any change.'

'You don't have any change? How can you not have change?'

'Because there isn't any in my purse.'

'But why not?' she spluttered. 'I always have change in my purse and you knew you were coming to the play. You know the car park charges forty pence and yet you've come out without even two twenty-pence pieces!'

'I know,' I said patiently.

'Well, you'll get a ticket,' she said. 'I never get a ticket because I always have change.'

'Good for you,' I said.

So I never worried about the small things, but I did worry about the big things. I was very nervous that there would be nuclear warfare. Where I grew up, in an old Victorian rectory, there was an air-raid shelter in the back garden and one day, after a particularly worrying news report, my father decided that it would make a perfect nuclear bunker, so he went out and bought about a hundred tins of baked beans and alpha-betti-spaghetti and he lined the walls of the air-raid shelter with them. Unfortunately, he also forgot to take the right change with him for the car park and came back from the shops wielding a parking ticket, which made my mother purse her lips. Anyway, we spent months practising our nuclear warfare drill, which meant my sister, Julia, and I had to grab the pets and stand in a line clutching the two cats and two dogs and then march into the air-raid shelter. But after a while the shelter began to smell of mould and we puzzled over the problem as cans of food, my father assured us, could not go off. It turned out that in the dark of the concrete bunker, my father hadn't seen the piles of apples the gardener had put there at the end of autumn to last us the winter.

'Oh dear,' my father said as he rummaged around and came up holding a brown, deflated apple specked with spots of mould. 'I think there are loads of them.'

After that we moved out of the air-raid shelter and the threat of warfare passed and, pretty soon, we all forgot about the bunker, apart from my mother who made us eat a tin of baked beans and spaghetti a night for ages afterwards.

Also, I worry about the fact that I have a decreasing desire to work. I get *offered* work. My *Fridges* book has, oddly enough, brought in lots of job offers. I get asked to write about people's fantastic interiors, but I find I don't want to. All I really want to do is hang out with my baby and do some vague research into my glamour-fridges book. I don't think I've ever felt quite so strongly about this before. John keeps saying things like, 'Aren't we going to have to get childcare for you to continue to work?' and I look at my beautiful Baby Sparkle and then I think of someone, anyone else, holding her and I immediately want to kill them. This is a very odd sensation for me. I've spent years of my life having au pairs. In fact, when Edward was born I would happily have given him to anyone who wanted him; the problem was that no one did for he cried so much. Eventually I found an au pair and, since then, there's been a run of them. There's been Santa and Wendy, and I have quite happily watched them hold and kiss and cuddle my children, but now we have no childcare and I find I like it that way. Whenever someone rings up to see if I want to write an article on someone's beautiful home, I find myself saying things like, 'I'm afraid I can't as I don't have any childcare,' and then I can almost hear the person on the end of the line snort derisively. 'What kind of woman doesn't have childcare?' they're probably thinking.

Conversely, until recently, I had no desire to be proud of my house. I hate cleaning. It's the most boring job known to humankind and no one should have to do it unless they are paid or they choose to do it. In the past I would go round to people's houses and note the women in their spotless homes, beaming away as if I were supposed to pat them on the back and say, 'Jolly clean house!' Why can't they see that no one cares, I'd think. Then again, my sister, Julia, was constantly cleaning her house. Every time anyone threatened to come round she'd get out the duster.

'Why are you dusting?' I'd say to her.

'Because Robert's friend's mother is coming round for tea and the house is a state!'

I would say that a) the house wasn't in a state at all and b) that her son's friend's mother probably wouldn't notice anyway.

'But she'll think less of me!' Julia would wail.

I would then say that I was sure people didn't think less of me because my house was dirty and Julia remained silent.

So I got a cleaner, but we don't have one any more because everyone I find resigns after a few weeks. I asked the last one – Carlotta, an Austrian lady who was recommended by my friend Adele who lives near me and is always telling me how to run my life – why she didn't want to clean for us any longer. She had only been with us for a month and I'd only just had the baby, and I was so desperate I couldn't believe she was abandoning me. I wept on her shoulder when she told me she wouldn't be coming any more. 'I am zo zorry, Zamantha,' she said. 'It's too far for me to travel.'

'But you only live a few miles away!' I said, clinging to her. 'I'll pay you petrol money! I'll up your wages. Please stay. I need you!'

'I cannot ztay,' she said. 'I cannot clean round zose toyz and zat mess in zose boyz bedroomz.' Then she walked out, taking her duster with her, and I collapsed in a heap which made the baby cry even more than me.

The upshot is that, for the past few months, we have had no childcare and no cleaner and no anything really, so it has all been down to me and something miraculous has happened. I've got so used to doing it all that I cannot imagine anyone else doing it. I have to admit that I've become rather obsessive. Since the birth of Baby Sparkle, I now take some sort of strange pride in having a clean house and a well-stocked fridge and a stockpot on the go, while also looking after three children and a baby. Before friends come to the house, I clean and tidy and plump cushions and dress the baby in her finest and persuade the boys to clean their teeth and then maybe bake a cake, and when my friends arrive and say, 'Gosh, how on earth do you manage it all?' I smile serenely as if it's nothing, a mere trifle, to run a family of six and the house and laundry and food and everything else.

Adele thinks I'm crazy. She has one daughter and a rich husband and spends most of her days having botox and micro-dermabrasions. She'd never clean her own house.

'Why don't you get an au pair again?' she says as she watches me tearing around picking up errant boys' knickers and reuniting socks. 'Do you really want to spend your life doing this?' The truth is, I seem to think that I do. I met Adele's friend Susie the other day at Adele's house where I had gone for a coffee. Susie told me she had two children and no job, but somehow she also had staff. 'I have a cleaner and a housekeeper who cooks and an au pair called Jolka.'

'But isn't it rather annoying to have all these people in your life?' I asked her. 'You have to manage them and look after them and listen to them.' I was going to say 'and pay them', but it was obvious that this wasn't a problem for Susie.

'No!' she said, looking astounded. 'It's amazing. I get to do anything I want. What woman doesn't want that?'

I told her I didn't think I wanted that really. 'I want to look after my children,' I said.

'Of course you do,' she said. 'But why on earth do you want to do everything else as well?' She then went on to tell me how she and her husband take Jolka on holiday with them. 'It gives us such freedom and it's much easier to manage on the beach if you have an extra pair of hands,' she said. 'I actually get to read a book.'

For some reason, this remark made me rather cross. 'But isn't the point of going on holiday that you actually spend time with your children?' I asked tetchily.

Susie raised a perfectly manicured eyebrow. 'Yes,' she said, 'but it's also about us relaxing together as a family and them playing safely, and me not being fed up with them, and my husband and I having time out in the evenings to enjoy each other's company. Do you have a problem with that?'

After Susie had left and I had become increasingly silent, Adele asked me what the matter was. 'You're being chippy,' she said.

'No, I'm not,' I replied.

'Yes, you are. You're trying to turn everybody into you, but you can't. Just because you've got some idea of how a woman should be doesn't mean that everyone falls into that category.'

'What do you mean?'

'Oh, you think everyone should be with their children all the time and then clean their houses and cook piles of home-made food.' Adele yawned.

Now, as I struggle to do everything, I think that Adele has a point. I decide I will look for a cleaner when we get back from Devon but, in the meantime, maybe there is someone local who wants to help out while we're on holiday. Then John and I could have some time together away from the children and the baby . . .

5. Species Identification

The next day, I wake up to the sound of Baby Sparkle crying. I've managed to find a small room in the house in which to fit her travel cot. It was obviously once a dressing room for it's tiny and a bit airless, but it's next to the master bedroom and I thought it would suit her perfectly. That's the thing about Baby Sparkle – she doesn't seem to mind where she sleeps. Last night I squeezed in through the dressing-room door and gently put her in her cot and managed, somehow, to wind her musical teddy up and she just lay herself down, popped her thumb in her mouth and went to sleep. I then squeezed myself back out of the room and went downstairs.

Yesterday, Edward had bagged the best room and virtually barricaded himself in due to the advances of Jamie who, at the first sign of Edward actually finding somewhere to sleep, tried to bed down in that room as well.

'Mmm,' he had said, casually putting his Buppie on the bed. 'Me and Sophie sike this room. We sleep here.'

'Jamie,' I said, 'it's me and Sophie *like* this room.'

I heard Edward thundering up the stairs.

'No, Jamie,' he said, 'this is my room. You're not sleeping here and I get to say that because this is also my house, so GET OUT!' He tried to push Jamie out of the door.

'Get off me!' yelled Jamie. He bared his teeth at Edward, who then lunged at him, and all I heard was a lot of caterwauling and angry screaming until I announced to both of them that the room they were in, the room with the balcony, was in fact mine.

'I need a big room,' I said, grabbing Jamie and holding him to stop him from leaping on Edward. 'I need to be near Baby Sparkle's room and Daddy is coming at the weekend and he needs some space.' Edward rolled his eyes, so I told him that I also deserved to have a balcony with wisteria growing up the side and a view of the valley sloping away in front of the house. I craved the sound of buzzing bees in the morning, I said, and I wanted to wake up and see the sun rise and smell the flowers and look out over Janet's exquisite garden.

'Why don't you have the attic room with the skylight?' I suggested to Edward. 'Then you can watch the stars at night.'

'I need some space, Mum,' said Edward.

'I know,' I said patiently. 'That attic room has lots of space.'

Eventually Edward agreed and picked his bag up to mooch along the corridor, closely followed by Jamie who seemed determined to share a room with Edward. 'My love you, Edward,' he said dolefully when Edward tried to eject him from the skylight room as well. 'Sophie love you too.'

Bennie, however, had happily chosen a room at the side of the house with two single beds in it. I found him in there eating a yoghurt and unpacking his bag in a surprisingly organized fashion.

'Where on earth did you find that yoghurt?' I asked him in amazement as I hadn't unpacked the food bags yet.

'I looked in the bags downstairs,' said Bennie, scooping the yoghurt out with a finger. 'I've got a chocolate croissant as well.' He produced a rather squashed croissant from underneath him. 'Do you want some?'

I sighed and shook my head. 'Are you all right in this room then?' I asked.

'Yes,' said Bennie. 'I can see the sea from here. I like it.'

By the time we went to bed, we had sorted everything out. Edward gave in to Jamie and said that if he would sleep on a camp bed then he, Edward, didn't mind sharing a room with him. 'You are my baby brother after all,' he said to Jamie, and then, looking pointedly at me, 'I'm here to help you.'

'Where's my cot then?' said Jamie.

'No cot,' said Edward, 'just a lovely camp bed.'

Then Edward began to put his blue pyjamas on and Jamie got into his pink ones. They both lay and looked at the sky and, eventually, they must have dropped off, for when I went to give them the cups of hot chocolate they'd asked for, they were asleep. Bennie was waiting for his chocolate though and a plain biscuit.

'I love it here,' he said, his eyelids drooping.

I went to sleep not long after the boys. I opened up the balcony doors and smelled the jasmine from the garden waft over me and felt extraordinarily happy.

This morning though, Baby Sparkle is crying and fractious. She doesn't want the milk I offer her. She spits out the banana Bennie says he will share with her. She tips her porridge up all over the table.

'Baby Sparkle,' I say to her, 'what are we going to do with you? It's only eight in the morning and you're so cross.' Baby Sparkle just wails at me.

'Shall we go to the beach?' Bennie asks when he sees how red-faced his sister is turning. 'Then she can play in the sand. She might like playing in the sand.'

I tell Bennie that going to the beach is a very good idea.

'You play with Sparkle,' I say, 'while I go and get everything we need.'

It takes an age for us to get to the beach. We have to pack everything – towels and buckets and spades and lotion – and then I nearly miss the turning over the dunes to drop down to Beachcomber Bay. Luckily Edward sees a sign for it.

'Go left, go left!' he shouts as I'm about to sail off further down the road. We turn left and drive for about half a mile, the road gradually sloping downwards until we turn the corner and there it is.

'The sea!' yell the children as Edward reads the sign at the car park.

'Yes, this is Beachcomber Bay,' he says.

We unpack the car and load up Baby Sparkle's pushchair with buckets and spades, nets and towels. I put Baby Sparkle on my hip and hang the three huge beach bags over the other shoulder.

We all march down to the beach, past the café which isn't open yet, and set up camp next to the rocks.

'This is a perfect spot,' I say to Edward as I look around. 'It's small and sheltered and there's a café which, if I remember rightly, opens for lunch or something.'

'There're rocks as well,' says Edward. 'We can look for crabs.'

'We can catch them in our nets,' says Bennie.

'Don't sike crabs,' says Jamie.

So now I'm on this wonderful beach. I like the fact that it's small and rather protected by the cliffs, which gives it some shade. The sun is beginning to get hot. I've put a hat on

Baby Sparkle and she's sitting at my feet, sinking her toes into the wet sand. I'm watching the children run around with Edward, who's kindly building his brothers a sandcastle. He told me that, later on, he will let Bennie and Jamie bury him.

'I'm in a good mood,' he said to me, 'so they can throw sand on me. It will be funny.'

Jamie is wearing a pair of girl's bikini bottoms that he insisted I buy for Sophie from the same catalogue that stocks his pink knickers. I was reluctant to get them. 'I think Sophie has a bikini already, doesn't she?' I said to him.

'NO!' he yelled. Actually, here on the beach, Jamie looks sweet. He has a little boy's body – thin and lithe and tanned. He's the only member of our family who doesn't have a huge round belly and that's because, unlike the rest of us, he doesn't stuff himself stupid every day. I eat so much breakfast sometimes I can barely do my jeans up. Often I make eggs and bacon for everyone, then I stand back and watch. Usually Bennie is the first one at the table. In fact, Bennie is often hovering round the table before there's any food on it, so desperate is he to get as much food inside himself as quickly as possible. If I'm not fast enough in making and doling out the food, Bennie will sometimes open the fridge door and abseil up its shelves to find something he wants. Once the egg and bacon is ready, Bennie will hoick himself on to a chair and start banging the table with his knife and fork.

Edward will then mooch in, sitting reluctantly and silently at the table.

'I'll have it,' Bennie will say, leaning over precariously on his chair to fish the egg off Edward's plate.

At this point, Jamie will still not be with us. He'll generally be watching something on the television, but as soon as he hears me coming, he'll dive under the cushions and hide.

'Don't sike breakfast,' he'll say.

'Yes, you do,' I'll say. 'It's eggs. You like eggs. Sophie likes eggs.'

'Sophie sike eggs?' Jamie will say, now looking curiously out from under the cushions. Then he'll follow me into the kitchen and I'll lift him up on to a chair.

'Is this an egg?' he'll say, looking directly at the fried egg on his plate.

'Yes, Jamie,' I'll say. 'That is an egg, the type of egg that Sophie just adores. Now why don't you eat it with her?'

But Jamie will put his head on one side, stick his thumb in his mouth and push the plate away from him.

'Sophie no sike this type of egg. Neither do I,' he'll say.

This game of what Jamie does and doesn't like can potentially go on all morning. For example, he'll say he wants Rice Krispies, so I'll pour him a bowl and put it down in front of him. He'll then look at the bowl in a way that suggests it has somehow offended him.

'These Rice Krispies?' he'll say.

'Yes, Jamie,' I'll say.

Then he'll push the bowl away again. 'Sophie no sike them.'

I'll offer him – and, of course, Sophie – about a million different types of things. I'll run through the cereal cupboard – Cornflakes, Branflakes, Puffed Wheat, Honeynut Loops, Weetabix, Weetos, Crunchy Nut Cornflakes – and Jamie will look soulfully at each and every packet before saying mournfully, 'Me and Sophie don't sike them.'

Eventually I'll give up and put on some toast for myself, whereupon his little eyes will light up.

'My toast,' he'll say, and I'll stand back and watch him nibble on the small square of dried toast that he has deigned to eat. Meanwhile, Bennie will have polished off his own breakfast and turned his attention to Jamie's.

'This food is great!' he'll say. 'I'll eat yours as well, Jamie!' He'll reach for Jamie's toast.

Jamie will turn and look in a horrified fashion at Bennie.

'That's Sophie's food!' he'll say, dropping his minuscule morsel on to the floor. 'I don't sike you, Bennie!' and then he'll burst into tears and refuse to eat anything at all.

I can always spot Bennie on the beach. He's tall for his age, but has a long, round body and short legs. He also has mad, sticking-up blond hair and very pale skin. Unlike Jamie, who still hides behind my legs when he meets people, Bennie is very sociable. Within about a minute of being on the beach he has hooked up with another boy who is the same height as him but much thinner and, once I really look and study this boy, seems maybe a year older. I've already noticed who the boy's mother is because I've done one of my beach-scans, which involves, the minute I get to the beach, checking out all the women lying in the vicinity of me. John noticed me doing this once when we were on holiday last year. I was fiddling around with towels and searching for sun cream, but really I was looking around me, while pretending not to, taking a quick peek at everyone.

'What are you doing?' asked John, noticing that I was being rather absent-minded with the towel unfurling.

'Oh, nothing,' I said breezily.

'Yes, you are. You're looking at everyone, aren't you? You're looking at all the men's bodies!'

I then explained that actually I wasn't looking at the men at all because a) the point of the beach-scan is that it gives women a chance to size up what the other women around them look like with their clothes off – the 'clothes off' bit being the most terrifying part for every woman over the age of thirty – and b) there was no point looking for men to oggle because there weren't any.

'No men here,' I said. 'They're all either surfing or down the pub. The beach, dear John, is purely the domain of women if you hadn't noticed.'

So I've already done my beach-scan here. I did it when I first arrived on the beach. As I fussed around laying out the towels and putting the baby down and finding all the millions of things I needed – water and hats and suntan lotion – I also surreptitiously glanced around to see who else was near me. It was then that I singled out the mother of the boy who's playing with Bennie. She's sitting down by some other rocks nearer the sea than I am and I noticed, rather happily, that her body was no better or worse than mine. This is always a very good thing. No one wants to hang out with the slim, lithe, athletic mother who makes them feel like a heffalump. There's always one of them on the beach, one perfect specimen who lies, legs akimbo – Brazilian waxed, of course – reading a book, hat tipped over her eyes, sunglasses on as if she has no care in the world. This type of woman spends her life getting up and stretching and looking around in a pretty, disinterested fashion and then lying back down again like a cat in the sun and, somehow, you know that she knows you are watching her.

But this woman, this mother, isn't like that at all. What I really notice about her is that she looks Celtic – very pale skin and freckles and copper-coloured hair tucked up under a hat. For some reason, I already feel comfortable with this woman, almost as if we've talked, as if we're friends bonded together by our two sons. At some point, as Bennie and his new friend go off with their buckets to collect water to put round the sandcastle they've built with Edward, she puts her book down and looks up again to check where her son is. She sees Bennie and does her own beach-scan until her gaze settles on me. Something unspoken passes between us as she realizes I'm Bennie's mother. She then notices Baby Sparkle, now eating sand at my feet, and she smiles at me and I smile back.

I'm about to give her a small wave or even possibly pick up Baby Sparkle and go to talk to her, when my view becomes blocked. For there, standing in front of me, and totally unaware of me, is a perfect beach mother. This woman is tall and very slim with long bronzed legs, clad in tiny pink towelling shorts. She has equally tiny pert breasts nestling upturned in her raspberry-coloured obviously designer bikini top. She has long straight blonde hair and she's wearing a floppy hat and huge bug-eyed sunglasses. In short, she looks amazing. I watch her as she holds a hand up to her eyes, shielding them from the sun, looking for somewhere to sit down. I'm so busy staring at this woman that until she says, 'Antigone, Allegra, where do you want to sit?' I don't realize she has two young girls with her who look about the same age as Edward. They're obviously her daughters. They have the same long blonde hair as their mother, only much blonder, almost white like albinos, and they're rather disconcertingly dressed in exactly the same way. They're both wearing short white sundresses and purple flower flip-flops and they have on yellow toy sunglasses in the shape of stars.

'Look,' I say to Baby Sparkle, who's still trying to eat sand, 'identical twins.' I then notice that bringing up the rear of this perfect party is an older, dark-haired, slightly plump girl who looks to be in her early to mid-twenties. She's heaving two huge bags along behind her. The bags are stuffed full of beach toys and towels, and she's dragging them along the sand. She's a few paces behind the Three Graces, as I decide to call the mother and twin combo. The mother turns round to this girl. 'I think we'll sit here,' she says imperiously. The dark-haired girl slips slightly in the sand as she struggles to catch up. 'Here!' the woman says again, motioning to a patch of sand not too far in front of me and Baby Sparkle. The dark-haired girl nods her head fervently and then starts unpacking the towels. The mother and daughters just stand there watching her.

I look around and notice that the mother of the boy Bennie is playing with is also staring at the Three Graces. I try to catch her eye. I think I see her grimace slightly. Once the towels are laid out on the sand, the woman lies down. She stretches on her towel, her endless legs out in front of her, and she sinks her head down on to the sand. Her hat tips forward across her face, almost covering it. The girls sit next to her. One of them takes off her dress to reveal a small flowery bikini. She leans towards her twin, cups her hand and whispers something in her ear. They both giggle. The other one also takes off her dress to reveal an identical bikini, then they get up and, holding hands, wander off towards the sea.

Their au pair – for I've now decided this must be their

au pair – looks distinctly hot and bothered. She has, so far, only just finished smoothing the towels on to the sand. As the girls walk off, she shouts after them. 'Li li! Li li!' she yells. I don't know what she means and I assume the girls don't either as they keep on walking without looking back. 'Li li!' the au pair calls out even more loudly, but the girls either don't hear her or they're pretending that they haven't. The au pair is still fully clothed, but now starts rapidly disrobing to reveal a lumpy body clad in an all-in-one black swimsuit. 'Anti!' she cries after the girls. 'Alli, wait!'

Suddenly the mother raises herself up on to the backs of her arms and sees the girls now getting increasingly more distant.

'For God's sake,' I hear her mutter. Then she says, 'Go after them, will you, Jolka?'

I cannot believe it. Jolka? How funny. Adele's friend Susie had an au pair called Jolka. I stare at the mother. Is she Susie? The Susie I met at Adele's house? She must be and yet I can't tell because her back is towards me and she's still wearing her hat. And everyone looks so different on the beach. I decide this woman must be Susie. Did she tell me she had twins and that their names were Antigone and Allegra? I don't think so, but she definitely had an au pair called Jolka and there can't be many of them around. It was winter when I met Susie so she was wearing more clothes, but she was definitely blonde and beautiful. I'm not sure what to do. Should I call out her name and see what she does? Should I go over to her and say hello? I'm doubtful if she will even remember me, so maybe I should pretend I don't know her. But, then again, what if she turns round and sees me and does recognize me and then thinks I'm inordinately rude not to have introduced myself?

Just as I'm thinking all these things, Baby Sparkle starts crying.

'Ma-ma-ma-ma,' she says, trying to speak through the mound of sand she has wedged in her mouth.

'Oh God,' I say as I grab her and try to hoik the sand out.

'Waaa!' she says once I've done it.

Susie turns and looks right at me. I have no choice.

'Susie,' I call out to her. 'Is that you?' She sits up now and takes her sunglasses off and stares at me. It's definitely her.

'It's me. Samantha, remember? I met you at Adele's house.'

'Ah,' she says, a look of recognition passing across her face. 'Yes, I remember you. You're the one with lots of children and no help.'

'Yes,' I say, a bit taken aback. 'That's the one.'

'Are you here on holiday?' she asks.

'Yes. My son Jamie is just over there.' I point to Jamie, who's pottering around at the foot of the rocks and jabbing his net into pools. 'Bennie is that big one over there with another boy, and Edward . . .' Actually, where is Edward? 'I'm not sure where Edward is.'

Susie raises an eyebrow. 'My children are nearly in the sea,' she says. 'I have Jolka with me.'

'I know. I saw her.'

'And you don't know where your eldest son is?'

'He's nearly thirteen. He's a good swimmer.'

'Well, you have nothing to worry about then.'

I'm about to tell her that I'm not actually worried when a shadow falls over me. It's the boy who was playing with Bennie.

'Are you Bennie's mother?' he asks. He has an Irish accent and red hair.

'Yes,' I say.

'Well, you'd better come quick then,' he says. 'Cos your boy's hurt his leg.'

I get up quickly. 'Is he OK? What's he done?'

'He just gave it a wee bang on a rock and now he's moaning and he's asked fer yer.'

Susie, now lying back down, doesn't move a muscle, but I can just tell she's smiling from behind her hat. As I walk past her, carrying Baby Sparkle, she raises herself back on to her arms. 'I'll look after your baby if you like,' she says, taking me by surprise. I tell her I'm fine actually and she lies back and closes her eyes. 'Shout if you need me,' she says.

On my way to Bennie, who's just a bit further away than Jamie, I see Edward. He's sitting on some rocks, throwing stones into a pool. I shout for him, but he doesn't hear me. I want to tell him about Susie's twins. Maybe he'd like to swim with them, but I'm not sure how it would work. Those girls seem so other-worldly in many ways, like goddesses, and Edward, well, he'd probably get tongue-tied.

Bennie lets out an ear-splitting scream as I get close to him.

'Owwwww!' he yells. 'Myyy leeggg.'

The boy he was playing with makes a tutting noise.

'You only slipped,' he says. 'C'mon now and let's swim.'

'I want my mummy!' wails Bennie.

'I'm here,' I say. Bennie opens his eyes. 'My leg hurts,' he says. 'I can't move. I want Daddy.'

'Daddy isn't here. You know that. Now you have to move,' I say. 'I need to get you back to the towels so I can put the baby down and look at your leg.' I go to raise him up.

'Aarrggh,' he yells. 'I need my daddy.'

'Well, you've got me,' I say.

Just then I hear another Irish voice behind me.

'I bet there's delicious ice cream at that there café,' says the female voice. I turn to find the boy's mother standing behind me.

'Such a shame for the wee lad,' she says. 'I was watching them. They were on the rocks, not too far out now, and your lad just slipped a bit. It's probably just a bang. I looked to see if you'd noticed, but you were talking to your friend.'

'She's not really my friend,' I say.

'Well, I'm Roisin,' says the woman. She's smiling at me. 'My boy's Lorcan.'

'I'm Samantha,' I say, shaking her hand, 'and my son is called Bennie.'

'Now, Bennie,' she says, bending towards him. 'What do you say if me and Lorcan give you a carry? We can hold you between us and take you back to where your mum's stuff is.'

'Nooo,' cries Bennie.

'Oh well,' she says, 'now that's a real shame because I've just given Lorcan here some money to get ice cream and chips, haven't I, Lorcan?' She winks at her son.

'Yes,' says Lorcan.

'And he so wants to share it with you, so if we get back to where your clothes are and you pop some on then we can all go to the café. What do you say?'

Bennie looks at me questioningly. I give him a nod. 'OK then,' says Bennie in a small voice. Roisin and Lorcan make a seat for him by interlocking their hands.

'On you get,' Roisin says to Bennie. 'You are King Bennie wandering through your people back to your throne. Isn't that who you are?'

'Yes,' says Bennie happily, dragging himself up and managing to sit on their hands.

'Or you're Saint Patrick telling all the snakes to get out of Ireland!'

'Yes!' says Bennie. 'Out snakes!' he says, pointing towards the ground.

We all move slowly back to where my mound of clothes lies. We must look a strange sight. Bennie keeps waving a leafy frond of seaweed around him in order to be like Saint Patrick – 'This is my snaker-getta-outta stick,' he yells. Jamie has now joined us and is trotting alongside, still clad in his bikini bottoms, and Edward has come down from the rocks and is capering behind pretending to be a jester.

'Now, this is fun, is it not?' says Roisin to no one in particular.

'It's very kind of you,' I say to her over the top of Baby Sparkle's head.

'It's not a problem,' she says. 'I've only got the one and Lorcan's quite sensible, aren't you?'

Lorcan nods. 'Can I put Bennie down now?' he asks. 'He's really heavy.'

We all stop for a breather. I look over to where we are going, back up the beach, to find there's another woman with Susie. I can't tell if she's short or tall as she's crouched over Susie, and her mouth is moving up and down, up and down. Behind her on the sand sits a bored-looking boy.

'Looks like your friend's got another friend,' says Roisin, following my gaze.

Edward kindly offers to help get Bennie back to the

towels so Lorcan takes over the jester role and, pretty soon, we're back where we need to be. Susie smiles as we go past her. 'Gosh,' she says, 'is your son all right?'

'Yes, I am,' Bennie says to her.

'He hurt his leg,' I say. The dark-haired lady with Susie just looks at us. She is, much to my relief, shorter and dumpier than Susie.

'This is Karin ,' says Susie, motioning her head towards the woman. 'Our children go to the same school.' The lady nods her head at me.

I motion towards Roisin.

'This is Roisin,' I say. 'I've only just met her.' Roisin laughs.

Ten minutes later and we are all at the beach café. It's really rather lovely. It's set up above the beach and resembles a large log cabin. It has a wooden veranda that juts out over the rocks where you can sit and drink coffee or eat anything from its seemingly endless menu. A young girl with long black hair and a nose ring seems to run it, although she seems far too youthful to have set up something that manages to be the epitome of shabby chic. Sometimes it's possible to see the flash of a much darker and slightly older man working away in the kitchen. Occasionally he appears out the front of the café with plates of hot toasted sandwiches. The couple – I assume they're a couple – seem to have got it all right though. They have coffees and café lattes and a selection of herbal teas and sandwiches and salads and salmon fishcakes and steak and chips and also every ice cream on the planet. Once Bennie sees the truly amazing range on offer, he forgets about his leg altogether. In fact, he dances around and asks me to buy him pretty much everything, but settles for a mint choc Cornetto in the end. Roisin says she's hungry and just as we're looking at the menu — toasted ciabatta with smoked salmon and rocket with lemon dressing, that type of thing for a rather over-inflated price of £6.99 — Susie and Karin appear, followed by the bored-looking boy.

'Hi,' says Susie, pushing her sunglasses back on her head. 'Anything good here to eat?'

'There's ice creams,' says Roisin.

'Ooh, great,' says Karin, walking over to look at the menu. The bored-looking boy says nothing.

'Crayfish salad,' says Susie, running down the menu. 'Chicken and polenta. Lulu and Lalith's home-made Sri Lankan curry. How very sophisticated. Shall we all sit and eat lunch together?' Roisin and I both nod and Susie says that if we tell her what we want she will order and then bring it all over to the table as she has to go to the 'little girl's room', as she calls it. Roisin wanders off back up the hill to the car park, her mobile phone in her hand.

I'm left sitting at the table with Karin. She's shorter than Susie and much bigger. She's the type of person I imagine lying on sofas, eating chocolates and watching daytime television. She must have been very pretty once because she has a heart-shaped face and a sweet, small stubby nose, but now she looks overweight and tired. Karin's face has the type of chubbiness about her that makes her look unhealthy. I try to study her without her noticing and I decide that she looks a bit fed up. She's talking in a low voice to her son. They're obviously having an argument about something, so I turn my head to look at the children, who are sitting below me on a bench. They're all eating their ice creams. Edward is sitting a bit apart and staring

76

out to sea. I can hear Karin saying, 'No, Aaron, you cannot play your PSP here on the beach. Why not? Because I said so. Why don't you do anything I tell you? I might as well sit here and talk to the chairs.'

'Yeah, you might as well,' mutters the boy.

'Sorry? Did you say something?' Karin says in an exaggerated fashion. 'God, you're just like your dad. You don't listen to anything I say and then you're just plain rude to me.'

The boy gets up and, without a backward glance, walks away back to the beach. Karin looks after him. She seems a bit upset.

'How old is he?' I say, watching him going down the steps and on to the beach.

'He's thirteen,' she says. 'His name is Aaron.'

'Well, maybe he'd like to play with my son Edward. Look, there he is. He's bored out of his brains.'

Karin's face lights up. 'Oh, that would be great,' she says. Then she stands up and yells, 'Aaaron!' Aaron looks up at her. 'Meet Edward!' she shouts and she gesticulates to where Edward is sitting. I stand up too. On hearing his name, Edward looks up towards the café. He sees me. I point towards Aaron. Edward then sees Aaron or, more exactly, he sees the PSP in Aaron's hands. He turns to me and puts his thumbs up and, the next thing we know, the two of them are huddled in a shady bit under the rocks playing on the portable PlayStation.

'Oh,' says Karin when she sees what they're doing.

'Well,' I say, 'at least they're happy.'

'What I wouldn't give for a Jolka,' says Karin as she sees Susie wending her way through the tables like a streak of honey towards us. 'I mean, look at Susie. She seems so relaxed. She doesn't have the faintest idea where the girls are, but she doesn't need to. God, I envy her.' She looks at me and then at Baby Sparkle, who's playing under the table. 'Your baby is chewing a cigarette packet,' she says.

'Oh,' I say as I scoop up Baby Sparkle and extract the packet from her curled-up and recalcitrant fist and wipe her mouth down. 'Now, where did you find that?' I ask her.

'Do you have help at home?' Karin asks me.

'No,' I say.

'God, why not?'

'I like to do it myself really,' I say, wondering if I sound a bit pathetic.

'Really?' says Karin, looking shocked. 'I'm struggling just doing one. How on earth do you manage four?'

'Well, I'm not sure I do manage,' I say.

'I'd love help,' she says, 'but my husband won't pay for anything. He's a bit on the traditional side. He wants me to stay at home and cook and clean and bring up Aaron, so that's what I do.' Karin then looks away. The cooking and cleaning is obviously not making her very happy.

Susie comes back to the table, bringing with her three toasted ciabatta sandwiches, a rocket and parmesan salad and some bottles of water.

'Tuck in,' she says, motioning towards the sandwiches, 'but leave one for Roisin. I've just seen her halfway up the hill, talking on her mobile phone. I'm not having one. I'm smoking instead.' She looks at Baby Sparkle. 'Do you mind if I smoke near your baby?' she says as she lights up.

Roisin appears, looking a bit flustered.

'Work call, I'm afraid,' she says.

'What do you do?' I ask her.

'I'm a legal secretary,' she says. 'I mean, I'd finished all my work before I came on holiday but . . . oh well, they don't seem to be able to survive without me.'

'But how do you survive?' asks Susie. 'I find working mothers so stressful to be around. They're always dashing here and there and it must be such a dreadful life. Who looks after your son when you're at work?'

'He goes to school and then an after-school club until I can pick him up.'

'Oh,' says Susie. 'Does he do a lot of sport then? My girls go to a private school and that's all they seem to do – endless sport and endless holidays.'

'Well, Lorcan just goes to the local school and he doesn't seem to do much sport or have many holidays. That's why we're here, to have a nice break next to the sea.'

'What, he doesn't do any sport at all?' says Susie incredulously. 'I thought all boys did sport. Karin's husband, Henry, is always off playing rugby and he left school an aeon ago.'

'Well, sometimes he does Gaelic football, but that's about it.'

'I don't know that sport,' says Karin. 'Is it very different from normal football?'

'Yes,' says Roisin.

'Does his father play it?' asks Susie. 'Henry's always trying to get Aaron to play rugby, isn't he, Karin?'

'No, he doesn't,' says Roisin a bit shortly.

'My husband can't believe we haven't had any sons,' says Susie. 'He was desperate for someone to take up cricket, but after we had the twins I told him there was no way I'd ever get pregnant again. Imagine having to go through it more than once!'

'Actually, I don't have a husband,' says Roisin. 'I'm a single mother.'

'Well, good on you,' says Susie. 'Why not be a single mum? Though I don't know how you cope. The only single mother I know has been driven to distraction by her son.'

'Oh, you mean Margaret,' says Karin. 'Oh my God. You must tell Samantha and Roisin about her.'

'She's a nutter,' says Susie. 'One time she left her son on the side of a road because he wasn't behaving and she was late for work.'

'What?' says Roisin.

'Yes,' continues Karin, 'she told us all about it. She went back to get him and got stuck in traffic. Can you believe that?'

'No,' I say. 'Was he all right?'

'Yes, it was a miracle.'

Susie and Karin then went on to tell us a whole plethora of stories about this woman. 'She locked him in the chicken shed.' 'She made him eat his dinner off the floor because he dropped his plate.' 'When he was little, he fell out of his pushchair and she ran him over with it.' After the fifth story, Roisin catches my eye.

'Well, I don't do any of those things,' she says to Karin and Susie. Then she says, 'I think we should go and check on the children,' looking at me in what I take to be a meaningful fashion.

'Absolutely,' I say.

'We've bored you,' says Susie, lighting another cigarette. She looks at Baby Sparkle. I had put her in her pushchair after the cigarette packet-chewing incident. 'Even your baby's asleep, she's so bored.' Then she looks to the beach. 'Oh,' she says, 'what a sweet scene. Look, there's Anti and Alli playing on that thing with your sons.'

We all turn to look. Edward, Aaron, Antigone and Allegra are all sitting on a rock, huddled round each other.

'Where's Jolka?' asks Karin.

'Oh, probably slacking somewhere,' says Susie. 'She can be phenomenally lazy sometimes, God bless her. I suppose I better go and make sure she hasn't drowned. I don't think she can swim. She's a Pole, you see.'

'Shall we do this another day?' says Karin eagerly, looking at all of us. 'It's good to meet other mothers really, isn't it?'

Roisin and I both nod our heads and then go back towards the beach.

'Lorcan doesn't see his father, you know,' Roisin says to me as we walk side by side.

'I don't need to know that, Roisin,' I say, 'but if it helps you feel any better, Edward doesn't see his either.'

Roisin turns and looks at me. 'I thought they were all brothers,' she says.

'They are,' I say, 'in their hearts, but not by blood.'

'That means you've been through it all, haven't you?'

'Yes, I have,' I say.

'It's difficult, isn't it?' she says.

I nod my head.

'Where's your husband then? Is he here?'

'No,' I say. 'He's working.'

Roisin lets out a whistle.

'That's tough, eh? Here on your own with four kids. Why's he working?'

'Search me,' I say. 'He wasn't supposed to be. He was supposed to be on holiday with me helping sort Jamie out, but . . .'

'He's done a runner then?'

'Not a runner as such.'

'No? Yet here you are alone. But, y'know, I came here to meet people and now I've met you. I'm happy to help out, if you want me to. Lorcan and your son seem to have hit it off and . . . we should all have a good summer, shouldn't we?'

'I hope so,' I say and I give her a grateful smile.

6. Baiting Techniques

Tonight, I find myself standing outside the village hall in Lower Strand wondering if I've made a major mistake in coming to the village meeting. I had assumed, for some reason, that there would be virtually no one here, but it looks as if the whole village is present. I peeked my head through the door about five minutes ago and I couldn't believe it. The whole place was humming and absolutely packed out. I looked around for anyone I might recognize but, bar the lady who runs the village shop, I didn't see anyone. I didn't even see Noel and yet I was sure he was going to be here. So now I'm standing round the side of the hall trying to get the courage to go in. I decide that, if I count to five, I might be able to steel myself to walk through the door. But was there a chair for me? I can't remember. What if there isn't? What if I have to walk down the middle aisle of the room, parading myself in front of the entire population of Lower Strand, just to find a space?

I remember how, when I was heavily pregnant with Baby Sparkle, I went to the funeral of the editorial director of the magazine that publishes my fridge articles. She had died very suddenly of a cancer she had told no one about, which seemed terribly sad. Everyone was so shocked.

'Did you know that Helena had cancer?' the editor of the magazine had asked me, her eyes round like saucers.

'No,' I said.

'No one knew,' said the editor, and then we had a conversation about how tragic it must have been for poor Helena to come to work every day and not breathe a word.

'Why didn't she tell me?' said the editor, and I was about to say that it was probably because the editor refused to believe anyone when they said they were ill, seeing it as a personal slight to herself or as an act of sheer laziness when they didn't turn up for work. Of course, Helena decided to keep her weakness under her hat.

The editor and I walked into the church and it was absolutely packed. A lady in front of us got up and gave her space *to the editor* even though I was obviously pregnant and then, in the end, the vicar appeared and gently led me down to a chair next to the lectern, which faced the entire congregation. 'I usually sit here,' he said kindly, 'but you take the seat and I will stand.' It was utterly mortifying. I had to spend the entire funeral staring at the congregation and they all stared back.

So I don't want to have to parade myself to the villagers tonight. I am an 'outsider', after all. I know this because Shelley – the Shelley of the advert on the notice board outside this godforsaken village hall, who turned up to babysit – told me so.

I had telephoned Shelley the night before.

'Shelley?' I said. 'A Mr Rideout suggested I call you.'

'About the advert?' she said.

'Yes. I have four children and I . . .'

'You need help,' she said. 'Well, I'm the girl for you.'

She then told me that she had loads of experience with children because her mother had been a childminder and she had helped her sometimes.

'She even took in babies,' she said. 'She had Mr Rideout's

granddaughter when she'd visit as a baby. I know how to bath them.'

'Actually, I tend to do the baby,' I said quickly.

'OK, well, I cook and clean and iron and . . .'

'You sound amazing,' I said. 'A godsend.'

But when Shelley turned up earlier tonight, just after I'd finished feeding the children their dinner, and had immediately put Baby Sparkle to bed, I got quite a shock. For a start, her overpowering perfume came into the house about two minutes before she did. Edward and I were sitting at the kitchen table when he said, 'Ooh-my-God-what's-that-smell?' and I sniffed the air. It smelled heavily of gardenias mixed with some over-sweet scent like orange blossom. I was about to say that it was obviously the flowers in the garden when we heard a knock at the door and in walked a small, tubby, youthful-looking girl who was very obviously swathed in this perfume which hung like a fug around her.

Edward took one last desperate gulp of air and walked out of the room.

'Edward!' I said.

'I'm not coming back in,' he yelled, now up the stairs. 'I'm only trying to survive.'

'Hello, Mrs Smythe, I'm Shelley,' said Shelley, sticking out her hand. 'Now, don't you worry about your son. I'm very used to naughty children.'

'Right,' I said. 'Edward is nearly thirteen, so he's not really a child. Actually, Shelley, how old are you, out of interest? You look very young.'

'I'm nineteen,' she said. 'But don't worry. I'm always being asked if I'm old enough to get a drink. I tell them, look, I've finished school! I'm a college kid, but no one believes me.'

'Oh, are you at college round here?'

'No, not here. There's no colleges here. No, I go to Cardiff.'

'And what are you studying?'

'Leisure and Recreation. At the moment I'm studying how the presence of vans selling fish and chips on the beach affect tourist traffic. It's fascinating really. You see, the beach near Lower Strand doesn't allow vans, but it does have a café –'

'Oh yes, I know the one,' I said. 'I went there today. It sells great food.'

'– and it's very over-priced,' Shelley continued blithely, as if I'd never uttered a word, 'so although it attracts a certain type of tourist, it doesn't actually increase the overall usage of the beach, whereas the beach at Woolacombe does allow fish and chip vans down on to the sand and it's a far busier beach because surfers all like eating fish and chips.'

'So what do you do with that information now you've gathered it?'

'I put it into a graph,' she said.

'And then what?'

'Well, that's it.'

'Right,' I said, 'but then that information's not very useful, is it?'

Shelley looked hurt.

'Sorry,' I said. 'I just don't know about these things.'

'That's because you're an outsider,' she said. 'If you want to live round here, you have to know about surfing and stuff. Tourism is how this community makes its money.'

'Of course,' I said, feeling chastened. 'Sorry.'

'That's all right,' she said.

Then, suddenly, she spied my laptop.

'Oh, a computer!' she said. 'I don't have one here and I haven't been able to check my emails for ages.'

'Well, why not check them after you've put the kids to bed?' I said.

'Really? I'd be so grateful. I'm waiting to hear from some friends.'

'Check away!' I said and then I gave her the list I'd made of 'How To Put The Children To Bed' and left.

'Have fun at the village meeting!' she called after me.

Now I wonder if she was being ironic. Can a nineteen-year-old who is studying Leisure and Recreation actually be ironic? Then I get the giggles imagining Shelley doing a thesis on the pros and cons of croquet or how a recreational task such as reading a book can be utilized to help tourism in Devon's villages. I'm just wondering who on earth thought up this course when I hear a voice that is obviously Edward's saying, 'You do know you're talking to yourself, don't you?'

'Edward,' I say. 'What are you doing here?'

'I couldn't bear the babysitter's perfume any more so I told her I was going to find you.'

'I see. And did she say that was OK?'

'I'm not a child, Mum,' he says. 'I heard you tell her that. So I said to her, "I am not a child and I have decided to go and find my mum," and she said that was OK.'

'Oh, right,' I say. 'Well, that's not great babysitting, is it? What if you had got lost?'

'How could I get lost?' says Edward. 'This village is tiny.'

'What if you were lying?'

'Lying in order to do what?'

'Oh, I don't know,' I say. I realize that although I'm cross with Edward for just walking out of the house and although

I'm slightly concerned that Shelley let him, having no idea where he was actually intending to go or what he was intending to do, I'm glad of his company.

'Are you going to join me at this village meeting?' I ask him.

'Yes,' he says, not looking at me.

'Is something the matter?'

'No. Why do you think there is?'

'Because I know you. You're pulling one of your "something's the matter" faces.'

'Oh, it's nothing really.' Edward scuffs his shoes on the tarmac.

'No, come on, tell me. Are you upset that Dad isn't here?'

'A bit.'

'He'll be here soon and then you can show him around. Is anything else the problem? You've been quiet ever since we left the beach. Has someone said something to you? I saw you with the twins when you were playing that PlayStation with Aaron. Did they upset you?'

'No, it wasn't those twins.'

'Was it Aaron?'

'Mm.'

'What did he do?'

Suddenly Edward turns on me. 'Aaron has everything and I have nothing.'

'What do you mean, Aaron has everything?'

'*He has stuff!*' Edward says and then he walks off rapidly about a million steps in front of me.

THE PROBLEM WITH 'STUFF'

This is the problem with stuff: some families like having stuff all over the place and others do not, and when I'm talking

88

about stuff I'm not referring to junk or general household detritus, but real stuff the kids like to play with. Now, some parents spend a lot of time investing in this stuff. They buy endless games and toys and gadgets and widgets, and it's not just for Christmas and birthdays but for ever and ever and ever and Easter and Whitsun and St Swithin's Day, and on and on it goes until, when you visit the house of your child's friend and they appear dressed as Doctor Who and then show you the whole range of *Doctor Who* accoutrements their parents bought them, complete with a talking model of a Dalek that's as high as your knees, then you know you're in a house of people who are in thrall to STUFF!

I have, over the past few years, tried to work out why so many parents buy their children so many things. For a while I thought this was mainly what working parents did – reward their children with nice new things to assuage their guilt at not being at home – but then I kept meeting mothers who didn't work and fathers who rushed home all the time to see their children and they had even more stuff than my working friend's children and she works very hard. In fact, my working friend barely buys her children anything so that they don't get hooked on the guilt thing. She told me that after her parents split up and her father left home, she wrote him a letter which said, 'Dear Dad, I hate you for leaving us. I'm so unhappy. How could you do it? PS Can I have a pony now?' Her father duly bought her the pony and then she needed some tack and a grooming kit and a brand new saddle, and then, once she'd grown out of her pony-loving phase, she asked for money for clothes and tickets to gigs and holidays abroad and, eventually, a sports car. Unfortunately her father bought all these things for her and she ended up having no respect for him whatsoever, so he would have been better off not buying her any of this in the first place. Consequently she refuses to feel guilty over the fact that she works and she avoids the stuff trap like the plague.

So I've had to rethink my stuff theory and, in order to replace it, I asked people why they bought the things that they did. My results are rather interesting, I think. One father told me the reason why his children had just about every electronic gadget going was because he liked playing with it all himself. 'I'm a techno-bore,' he told me. He said it helped him bond with his children, although when I went round to his house once and he was playing endless rounds of Donkey Kong, I noticed his son sitting next to him looking decidedly bored. He told Edward later that, actually, he'd much rather play with his friends than his over-competitive slightly trying-too-hard dad.

The other group of people who seem to buy their children loads of things are those that never had anything very much as a child. Their arguments went along the lines of 'Do-you-know-how-awful-it-was-to-sit-and-watch-other-children-get-all-these-presents-and-not-have-anything-like-that-yourself?' These parents go so far as to say that they were bullied for not having a Rubik's Cube or not having enough money to buy popping sweetie crystals that fizzed in their mouths.

The other problem is that the toys' and games' market has become so sophisticated. There are endless things to buy. It starts when children are babies and it never lets up. When I was in hospital having had Edward all those years ago, I kept getting visits from 'helpful' people who were, in reality, trying to peddle me an entire range of stuff I did not want: this type of baby milk, that type of baby food, coupons to get money off expensive prams, a booklet advising me on baby safety in the house, cot mattresses that could tell me the temperature of the baby/the room/the air in the room. I got offered romper suits and fibre-free pillows and sleeping nests and pushchairs with cuddletoes and bears that sang numbers in French and . . . it was so overwhelming that I ended up buying absolutely nothing. But the die was cast and all this stuff has followed Edward ever since. We have argued over him wanting the entire set of engines from the Thomas the Tank franchise even though there are about a hundred and they are, of course, increasing by the day, and they cost at least ten pounds each. Then he went through a mad crazy Pokémon phase and wanted every Pokémon and every Pokémon trainer, and then he wanted diggers and army trucks and telescopes and microscopes and games that involve finding fake dinosaur bones in the garden, and on and on this has gone for almost thirteen years. And the real problem is that the more stuff he wants, the less I want to buy it.

But tonight Edward does seem genuinely upset. He tells me the list of what Aaron has: a portable PlayStation, a real PlayStation, two Nintendo DSs, a Gameboy, a portable DVD player, an iPod, a mobile phone, a Nintendo Wii, a GameCube, an AppleMac computer, an Xbox, a quad bike and even a television and DVD player in his bedroom! 'He has everything,' wails Edward. 'And I have nothing.'

'But what would you do with all that stuff?' I say. 'Your brain would fry. How can you seriously want all that when there are starving people in the world who don't have electricity, let alone something to run off it?'

'That's not the point,' Edward says. 'You always say that,

but you don't understand. I'm the only boy in the class that has nothing.'

'You don't have nothing,' I say. 'You have a brain and you have feelings and you understand the world and the way it works in a way that many other children don't. You have a good heart, Edward.'

'I don't want a good heart,' he says. 'I want a Wii.'

'Like everyone else? You want to be just like everyone else?'

'Yes,' he says.

A few heads swivel round when we walk into the village hall, but at least there are two free chairs at the back so Edward and I hurriedly take these as the meeting is obviously about to start. I look around for Noel, but I still can't see him. Then again, the hall is so crowded and everyone looks to be roughly the same age as him, more or less, so it's hard to tell one face from another. I get a shock, however, when I look past Edward along the row of seats we are sitting on as, about four seats down from him, is a girl who is roughly Edward's age. She's wearing heavy black eye-liner and has very obviously back-combed hair.

'Look, Edward,' I hiss at him. 'There's a girl here who's about the same age as you.' I try to point at her in a surreptitious fashion. Edward looks down the line.

'Yes,' he says. 'A girl, Mum.'

'Yes, I know a girl, but she's about the same age, isn't she? Maybe you could chat to her afterwards. You've been looking for someone to hang out with.'

'But she's a girl. And she looks odd.'

'No, she doesn't.'

'She has black eyes.'

'It's only make-up.'

'And black clothes.'

'Well, maybe she's a Goth.'

'What's a Goth?'

I'm about to reply when a tall, haughty-looking man wearing glasses stands up on a stage at the front of the hall and clears his throat loudly.

'Can I have some quiet?' he says. 'My name, for those of you who don't know me, is Mr Henderson and I'm the Chairman of the Lower Strand residents' association and head of the Parish Council for the Overstrand District and . . .'

'Is he a very important man?' Edward whispers loudly as Mr Henderson carries on listing his various chairmanships.

'Seems so,' I whisper back.

'. . . and elected the local representative for the North Devon ward of Overstrand, Upper Strand and Lower Strand and their environs.' Mr Henderson stops and looks around at the people seated beneath him. 'Now, taking the minutes at this AGM is Mrs Dilys Ashford . . .' A lady in a blue summer dress at the front of the hall raises her hand and waves. 'Thank you, Dilys,' says Mr Henderson. 'And we are joined by council members from various other local villages and towns and any other person who thinks they wish to have a say about what we will discuss today. On the agenda, which those of you who have picked up a white sheet from the door will know, is whether or not we should have a zebra crossing in front of the post office as proposed by Mr Daniel Smullen. Are you here, Mr Smullen?' A man five rows in front raises his hand. 'Good, good. Now, Mr Smullen can argue his case and the person arguing against him is . . . me, actually, as I see no reason to sully the country look of our beautiful village with an ugly zebra crossing, but we will come to that in due course. Then we will look at Map No. 1, for those who picked one up at the door, which shows Bridleway No. 20c which runs from Upper Strand to Lower Strand. According to Mrs Pat Pucklechurch of the Upper Strand Centre of Equitation, this path has become so overgrown that her horses can no longer pass through, so she is proposing the council pay to have it cleared and I, for one, am in agreement with her. Then there's a suggestion from Mr Smith, the groundsman who looks after the local recreation ground, to have someone come and get rid of the graffiti sprayed on the cricket pavilion walls. I just want to take this chance, with my parish councillor hat on, to express grave concern and dismay that some local youths are obviously wilfully damaging the public property of this village and I urge – let this be noted, Dilys – that if anyone knows the identity of any of these youths, they should come and see me after this meeting or even let me know anonymously. Then I think we will turn to the matter of the Cutlass Estate and lighting at night. I can see Mr Cutlass is here –' I follow Mr Henderson's gaze as he nods his head at a rather unremarkable-looking middle-aged man in the front row – 'and, if we have time, we will also discuss the annual village fête . . .'

On Mr Henderson talked and on the meeting went, and as people stood up to either support Daniel Smullen – one lady of eighty-something, who was wearing a mad hat – or not to support him, which seemed to be just about everyone else, all of whom wittered on at length about the beauty of Lower Strand, I found myself staring randomly at people. I realize eventually that not everyone in the room is quite as old as I thought and yet there's no one of my age here. Everyone seems to be fifty at least, apart from the Goth-girl. Why are there no younger couples here?

'Do you know, I'm one of the youngest people here?' I whisper to Edward, who's staring up at the ceiling with his mouth open. 'Why do you think that is?'

'No idea,' says Edward. 'I'm counting the cracks in the ceiling.'

'Oh God, is it that boring?'

'Yes,' says Edward as Mr Henderson's voice booms out above the now-increasing restlessness of everyone seated in the hall. 'Passed! The council will pay for Bridleway 20c to be cleared. Now . . .'

'I think it's because they can't get babysitters. Or maybe they're at home having dinner and drinking wine . . .'

'Passed! The cricket pavilion will be cleaned,' booms Mr Henderson again as noise from the floor increases. 'On to the lighting of the Cutlass Estate . . .'

'Or maybe no young people live here apart from that girl in black,' says Edward. 'Do you think she's the vandal?'

'No,' I say. 'Girls aren't into graffiti.'

'But she looks like a vandal.'

'. . . the issue is whether or not the estate should be lit at night. In respect of this, I think Mr Cutlass has prepared something to say on the matter and, before he does so, I think we should all keep in mind the good works Mr Cutlass has done for Lower Strand.'

There is a general low rumbling amongst the villagers as Mr Henderson drones on about how Mr Cutlass has paid for the church bell to be restored and given money to the local morris dancing troupe and various other good works.

Finally, Mr Henderson looks down at the sheaf of papers he's holding in his hand. 'He also paid for the entire two-week run of last year's sell-out production of *Oh! Calcutta!* I'm sure we can all remember Mrs Pat Pucklechurch's *tour de force* performance.' At this, various people start tittering.

Mr Henderson then sits down and the man who is obviously Mr Cutlass stands up. He looks average in every way – average height, average build, average-coloured mouse-brown hair.

'I shall make this brief,' he says in a small, reedy voice. 'I know that some of you in the village have a problem with the fact that I have put street lamps on the Cutlass Estate. I've heard that villagers are disappointed by this; that some of you feel that the light shines down from the estate and into your homes at night. I'm happy to meet privately with anyone who has a complaint to make, but I also thought it was important for you all to understand why I must light the estate at night. Many holidaymakers come every year to the Cutlass Estate. They feel welcomed here and, most importantly, they feel safe. These holidaymakers, and their warm feelings towards the village of Lower Strand, are very important to our local economy. They use the village shop. They spend money at the pub. They invest in our local area and, in order for them to do so, we have to provide what they want – and what they want is to be able to see their way home after a night out. I'm a resident of Lower Strand and this village is of the utmost importance to me so, in order for everyone to feel happy, I will as of tomorrow replace the light bulbs in the estate street lamps with low-watt energy-saving bulbs, and I hope this will be the end of the matter.'

Mr Cutlass sits down. The murmuring in the room starts up again.

'Well, if that's all,' says Mr Henderson, standing up again and talking in a very loud voice, 'then I think we should finish with the small matter of the village fête, the proceeds of which should go to the maintenance of this village hall, with which I'm sure we are all in agreement . . .'

Just as I'm about to tell Edward that, now I've thought about it, not all graffiti is necessarily bad and that some artists have made a fortune from their graffiti, I hear a voice I recognize say, 'Actually, I'm not in agreement.'

The whole hall falls silent. I notice Goth-girl, who was previously slumped in her seat, sits up rather quickly.

'Who is not in agreement?' says Mr Henderson rather tetchily, his eyes scanning the room.

'I'm not,' says the voice and then, right in the middle of the hall, a man stands up. It is Noel Rideout.

'Oh, Mr Rideout,' says Mr Henderson in a tone of voice that implies a sense of here-we-go-again. 'What objection can you possibly have to the proceeds from the village fête going to maintain this important and worthy hall, which is absolutely central to the well-being, both social and physical, of our village of Lower Strand?'

'My objection is not to deny the village hall funds,' says Noel simply. 'I'm not implying that this hall does not play an integral part of our village life. I'm just saying that this year there is a more worthy cause we should support. As you all probably know, Mrs de Salis is in desperate need of funds. Her house is the most important house in this district. It's the only Grade One listed house for miles around and it has played a very important role in the history of this area. The first Lords of Lower Strand built the original building in medieval times and those foundations still exist. The Manor House reflects the entire history and heritage of Lower Strand itself. Unfortunately, the house is in need of care and attention and I find it terribly hard to sit here and have Mr Cutlass lecture us all about the need to encourage visitors to this area by having twenty-four hour, seven-days-a-week lighting on his holiday home park without any of us talking about the need to maintain a genuine attraction such as the Manor House of Mrs de Salis.'

'Quiet, please,' says Mr Henderson to the increasingly noisy hall.

Noel continues. 'This house is of major architectural importance. It has, or had, one of the finest sunken Italian gardens in this country. These things are rare commodities and I'm sure, if we could help finance the building work that is needed on the house and the restoration of the garden, that people from far and wide will come and visit our area. They will bring in money and possibly more jobs, and all without having to change the essence of what makes the Manor House so special. Not only that, but every year Mrs de Salis very kindly lets us have our fête in her garden, so maybe this year we could help her out. The entire roof needs work done on it, important work to preserve the heritage of this building and . . .'

People are talking more loudly now. Some have even stood up and are making their way to the back of the hall. '. . . and if we don't help her then some unsavoury person will buy that house and that land, and build yet more holiday homes on it –' at this, Noel looks at Mr Cutlass, who is studiously not looking back at Noel – 'and a place of great historic interest will turn into a theme park that has as much to do with the heritage of this area as the Cutlass Estate.'

By now no one seems to be listening at all. They're all talking amongst themselves. About a quarter of those present are filing out through the double doors at the back.

Suddenly Mr Henderson stands up. 'QUIET, PLEASE!' he roars. 'Mr Rideout,' he says to Noel, 'while I'm sure your friend Mrs de Salis would appreciate what you have done for her . . .'

'It's not because she is my friend,' says Noel.

Mr Henderson continues. 'While I'm sure Mrs de Salis will appreciate what you have done for her, I cannot put to the council that we donate the money of the fête to her for, as we all know, the money can never go to an individual.'

'It's not for her,' says Noel. 'It's for the Manor House, and this house should be saved for all of us. It's an historically important house and . . .'

By now even more people are drifting out of their seats and heading for the door.

'It seems, Mr Rideout, that we have gone over the allotted time for our meeting,' says Mr Henderson smoothly. 'Maybe we can discuss this at the next council meeting.'

'It will be too late by then and you know it will,' Noel says angrily. Then he turns round and, seeing that everyone is leaving, pushes past the people in front of him and leaves the hall. The Goth-girl sitting next to us runs after him.

'Oh dear,' I say to Edward. 'What do you think that was all about?'

Edward shrugs. 'All is know is that there are six hundred and forty-five cracks on this ceiling, so I'd say it needs a bit of maintenance really.'

We follow everyone outside. Some people are talking about Noel.

'He's away with the fairies, that man,' says the woman who was sitting next to us to another woman. 'Give the money to save a house? What's he on about?'

'I haven't seen Mrs de Salis in years,' says the other woman. 'Not properly. I only see her at the fête. Why can't she pay for her own house to be fixed? That's the problem with posh people. They always expect the little people to pay for them. That house hasn't been open to the public for years!'

Edward and I turn left out of the hall to go back to our house.

'I wonder why that girl ran after Noel,' I say.

'Why don't you ask her?' says Edward. 'She's just over there, standing in front of the pub.'

'Oh,' I say as the girl looks towards us. 'Do you want to meet her?'

'Not really,' says Edward.

'We have to walk by her anyway. It's the way back home.'

We walk towards the pub and, just as we're about to get to where the girl is standing, the pub door opens and out comes Noel Rideout. He sees us immediately.

'Mrs Smythe!' he calls out, beckoning us over. 'Please do come here.'

Edward and I walk over.

'This is my granddaughter Isabel,' he says, pointing towards the Goth-girl. She doesn't smile. 'Isabel, this is Edward and his mother, Mrs Smythe.'

'Samantha,' I say to Noel Rideout's granddaughter. 'We saw you in the meeting.'

'Yes,' she says. She has a Scottish accent.

'Oh, were you at the meeting?' says Noel. 'I looked for you, but I didn't see you.'

'We were at the back.'

'Well, now you'll know how useless they all are in this village,' Noel says, sighing. 'That dreadful Mr Henderson and that poodle faker Mr Cutlass. Do you know, he went to some appalling minor public school?'

'What's that got to do with it?' I ask.

'Everything, my dear,' says Noel. 'Honestly, you wouldn't believe it. Every time some property developer like Mr Cutlass comes in and buys up some land that *they*, those villagers, sell off, they complain about the fact that holiday homes are built on it. I mean, none of them pipe up in that meeting even though they've all been whinging about the lights on his holiday estate for years. But up gets Mr Henderson to remind us what a philanthropist Mr Cutlass is, and everyone lies doggo. This is what we are now. We've stopped being a village. We are here only to service the holiday-makers who pay ten pounds for a home-made cottage pie from the local shop. Have you seen them? Ten pounds for a cottage pie made by Dilys! I mean, what kind of person does that? Dilys can't even cook! She probably uses cat meat.'

Isabel starts giggling.

'Oh, she does, my dear,' says Noel. 'But then, after the summer, when they've all made a mint, they complain endlessly about the "outsiders"' as they call them and how they're eroding village life in their hallowed Lower Strand. And then they'll complain again about people like you!' Noel Rideout looks at me.

'People like me?' I say, rather taken aback.

'Oh, not you personally, Samantha. You belong here in Janet's house. I knew that the moment I met you. No, I'm talking about the second-home owners who come and cherry pick what they want from this little Devon village life of ours and then return home without a second glance. They take with one hand and –'

'I'm not going to do that,' I say. 'I'm not here to take. I'm here to help.'

'Help?' says Noel archly. 'Good. Well, you can help. You can buy me a drink.'

'A drink?'

'Yes, a drink. I trust mothers are allowed to drink, aren't they?'

'Of course,' I say.

'Then what are we waiting for? You can buy me a drink and I can think of a way you can help. A good deal, I'd say.'

'What about your granddaughter? What will she and Edward do?'

Noel looks surprised, as if he's forgotten Isabel is present.

'Oh,' he says.

'Don't worry, Granddad,' says Isabel. 'I'll show Edward the rec.'

Edward looks a bit alarmed.

'You are the vandal then, aren't you? I said it was you, but my mum said . . .'

Isabel starts laughing and suddenly her face stops looking so sullen and seems younger and prettier.

'No, it's not me,' she says, still smiling. 'Ach, come on, Edward. I'll show you around and all that.'

Edward blushes a bit.

'Why not, Edward?' I say. 'It's great there's someone here of your own age. Just make sure you're back home by nine p.m., OK?'

Edward looks a bit uncertain, but then agrees to go. As they walk off, I hear Isabel say, in her lilting accent, 'Edward, have you ever drunk a Bacardi Breezer before?'

I turn to ask Noel about this, but he has already disappeared into the Poltimore Arms.

7. Pheromone Lures

Somehow it's 11 p.m. before I get in. I have no idea how it has got so late. One minute I was phoning Shelley to make sure Edward had arrived home, which he had, then Noel and I were sitting at a table sharing a bottle of white wine and the next minute I looked at my watch and yelped.

'Christ, Noel!' I said. 'I must go!'

He murmured a bit about not wanting to go home yet and Isabel having a key to let herself in, so I told him that I had to leave even if he didn't and that we'd talk about our solution to the problem of Mrs de Salis's house another time. We had, of course, spent half the night trying to sort out how to save the Manor House. I'd suggested sponsored events such as a walk or a cake-baking contest, or a sponsored surf or something, but Noel had snorted with laughter.

'Oh, it's so lovely of you to try and help,' he said, 'but, my dear Samantha, it costs a fortune to fix the roof of a Grade One listed house. We need at least ten thousand pounds and that's just for starters. I don't want to be negative, my dear, but how much do you think a sponsored cake-baking contest will bring in?'

I told him he had a point.

'But how much does the fête make?' I asked him.

'Actually, last year we raised five thousand.'

'God, that's pretty good,' I said.

'Mr Cutlass probably accounted for about two thousand

pounds of it because he bought nearly all the raffle tickets and then gave the prizes away.'

'Why did he do that?' I asked, surprised.

'Guilt,' said Noel. 'He buys his friends. He's one of those people who wants to be liked. He can't bear it if everyone doesn't think he's marvellous. I mean, it would be fine if he genuinely cared about the village, if he was kind and generous and genuinely likeable. You're very likeable and helpful and we've only just met, you see.'

'Oh, thanks,' I said, feeling flattered.

'I mean, your family have inherited Janet's beautiful house and are you pulling it down and turning it into your version of the countryside?'

'No,' I said.

'No, you're not. You're committed to looking after that house and restoring the garden to its former glory. You *are* doing that, aren't you?'

'Yes.'

'See? I'm right about you! You're just what we need in this village. We need people with spirit, like you and your children.'

'Oh, my children,' I groaned.

'Your children are wonderful,' said Noel. 'Look at your smallest son. He's such a charmer with those green eyes of his and his habit of wearing girls' knickers.'

'Actually, I really did want to thank you for being so nice to him the other day. Very few people seem to understand about Sophie, let alone pretend she's really there.'

'But Sophie's such a charmer too!' said Noel. 'And don't worry about Jamie wearing those wonderful bits of under-wear. In my day, boys who went to public school dreamed of wearing frilly knickers, but no one actually dared to.'

'Oh, you're teasing me.'

'Not at all! No, people like you and your brood of children breathe life back into places like this. We need young people, not old fusty-dusties like me. Young people, families, beautiful women, we love them all!'

'Well, five thousand pounds is not to be sniffed at,' I said, trying to steer the conversation back towards the fête.

'Yes, but in case you hadn't noticed, I didn't get any assurance from Mr Henderson that the funds would go towards it.'

'Could we change his mind?'

Noel thought for a bit. 'Possibly,' he said. 'But it's going to be difficult. Mr Cutlass won't want the money to go towards the Manor House and he'll put pressure on Mr Henderson to do up the village hall. However, I've got a plan. I think I can make Mr Henderson see things our way.'

'How?'

'I can be very persuasive when I want to be,' he said.

Noel then told me that he thought Mr Henderson was having an affair with Mrs Pat Pucklechurch of Upper Strand Equitation fame.

'Actually, she's only got a couple of hunters and a Shetland pony. Anyway, her husband died last year and now that nosey little Henderson man is up there all the time, sniffing about.'

'But is Mr Henderson married?'

'No,' said Noel.

'Then it's not really an affair, is it?'

'Not really. But everyone's gossiping about it anyway because it's a small village.'

'Aren't we gossiping though?'

'Yes!' said Noel delightedly. 'We're having a great gossip

and then everyone will go home and gossip about us because we've been seen together.'

'Will they?'

'Yes, but don't worry, my dear. I'm sure me being seen with you reflects wonderfully on me.'

I laughed.

'Anyway, back to Mrs Pat Pucklechurch,' he said. 'I could go and ask for riding lessons.'

'Noel,' I said, 'be serious.'

'I could tell her she's the most beautiful person I have ever seen, with her long hair and horsey face, and then I could whisper to her, over a pile of pony nuts, that she should persuade Mr Henderson to give us the money and, in return, I'll give her a private tour of the sunken Italian garden. Do you think that will work?'

'No,' I said, smiling.

'Hmm. Thought not. I could try out a few other stories though, couldn't I?'

'Such as . . . ?'

'Daniel Smullen could have an Internet gambling addiction,' he said, 'and the t'ai chi lady could take in lodgers which, actually, she does.'

'What's wrong with taking in lodgers?'

'Nothing, but she doesn't want anyone to know because she thinks they'll look down on her for being short of cash and no one likes her as it is even though they're all nice to her face.'

'Why don't they like her?'

'Because she's a newcomer.'

'What counts as a newcomer round here?' I asked.

'Well, look at that lady over there,' he said, pointing to a woman in a blue woollen suit who seemed to be having a good time, laughing away with three other women. 'She's lived here for probably over ten years yet everyone still calls her a newcomer.'

'What do you have to do to fit in then?' I asked him.

'Stick with me and you'll find out. If you help me and we succeed, you'll feel very much part of this community. I'm sure everyone will love you when they realize how marvellous you are. You're my co-conspirator now, aren't you, Samantha?'

I nodded my head and he patted my hand.

'Good,' he said and then he went off to get some more wine.

A while later I looked down at the table and saw three empty wine bottles. Had we really drunk this much? We had spent the last hour or so talking about my children. I hadn't meant to, but Noel seemed so interested in Jamie that I found myself blurting it all out to him. I told him about how Jamie had attacked Isla at the nursery.

'With the sharp end of the paintbrush?' asked Noel, looking as if he was considering something of great importance.

'Yes, and he meant to harm her. He tried twice. That's serious, isn't it? I mean, my husband John thinks he'll just grow out of it, but I . . . well, I'm very worried about him.'

'I can see that,' said Noel. 'Of course you're worried about him. He's your son! What mother wouldn't worry? I think you're coping admirably, considering. It can't be easy looking after all those children, especially when one is a baby. I was wondering, and without meaning to pry, about the whereabouts of your husband. Why is he not on holiday with you?'

I told Noel the whereabouts of my husband as I drank another glass of wine.

'He's working on some puppet show,' I said, as Noel looked surprised. 'That's what he does, he's a set designer. He's hardly being paid any money to do it, but . . . anyway, I don't know what it is about Jamie. He's changed since Sparkle was born. He was so lovely before she came along.'

I then told Noel about the non-eating and the swearing and the baby talk and the wearing of girl's clothes and how Sophie had come about and how demanding she had become.

'I'll talk to Sophie,' said Noel.

'No, seriously,' I said.

'Seriously, Samantha? Seriously, I do not know what the matter is. Does your son do a hobby? Maybe his father takes him out to do things together, does he?'

I shook my head miserably.

'Well,' continued Noel, 'your little boy did seem very interested in looking for moths. Boys like hobbies, you know. It brings them out of themselves. It occurs to me that, maybe, as his father's not around, I should take him out moth hunting.'

'Would you?' I said hopefully. 'I do think he'd enjoy it.'

'Well, *I'd* enjoy it. Absolutely I would,' he said. 'It's been a long time since anyone in my life has been remotely interested in moths. Most people can't see past their dusk-iness and their feathery wings. People are scared of them and yet they're not scared of butterflies and I've never understood that. But you, Samantha, you're not scared of moths, are you?'

'No.'

'Of course you're not! That's because you're too bright

and too thoughtful to be taken in by that showing off the butterflies tend to do. Don't you find that they show off? Constantly opening and shutting their wings when they're sitting on leaves and that type of thing? A discerning woman such as yourself wouldn't be taken in by a butterfly. No, I imagine you prefer the shadiness of moths, the way they come out to find nocturnal glow. Isn't that what attracts you to them, Samantha? They're always the intellectual entomologist's choice.'

I asked him what he thought Jamie would gain from watching moths.

'It's not just watching them,' said Noel. 'Maybe if I taught your little James about how moths emerge from a chrysalis and how their bodies change and how they feed and all that circle of life stuff, and so on and so forth, it might help. This is what I've been thinking about.'

'Yes, it might help,' I said. Then I thanked him most profusely and he looked embarrassed.

As I left, I told him that I was sorry. 'You must have been very bored,' I said. 'I feel as if I've talked about Jamie all night.'

'Not at all,' he said. 'You're being a good and concerned mother and I like that about you. Anyway, nothing you could do would ever bore me.'

I left him, blushing somewhat, and as soon as I got outside, the fresh air hit me like a breeze block and I nearly fell down right there on the road in front of the pub. I was relieved that Noel wasn't with me. What would he have thought? He seemed so charming, so urbane somehow, and me so drunk. Then I breathed in deeply, which seemed to help. Once my head stopped spinning, I started walking – or weaving, really – back to the house. It was only when

I was halfway home that I realized something important: I was happy. I had a mission to do. I was going to save this house and Noel was going to save Jamie and everything was going to be right in the world.

All the same, I'm giggling a bit as I look for Shelley in the kitchen. 'Shelley?' I say merrily as I can see no sign of anybody. 'Shelley? Where are you?'

'In here,' says Shelley from the sitting room.

I walk in to find Shelley on the computer.

'I've just Googled you,' she says.

'Sorry?' I say, wondering whether or not I should open another bottle of wine and have a glass. Then I remember about Edward.

'Was Edward OK when he got home?' I ask Shelley.

'Oh, yeah,' she says. 'He said he'd had a great time. Oh, and he told me not to tell you, but he's got paint on his T-shirt so I've put it in a basin to soak.'

'Paint on his T-shirt?' I ask, feeling confused.

'Maybe he leaned against a fence or something. He was looking pretty pleased with himself, in a good way,' Shelley says hurriedly. 'Anyways, I looked you up on Google and I found out you write books. Would I have read any of them? I do like reading, you know.'

'Well, they're not exactly books,' I say, feeling a bit deflated. 'They're more like large-format glossy coffee-table books. You don't really read them. You just look at them. And there's a television programme that goes with them.'

'Really? What's it about?'

'Fridges,' I say. 'You have to guess who the fridge belongs to.'

'Oh,' she says. 'Well, I've put a link to you on my web page.'

'Your what?'

'My web page. Don't you have one? You make a web site dedicated to you and everything that you've done and then people access it and become your friends.'

'What kind of friends?'

'All sorts,' she says.

'How many friends have you got?'

'Oh, about three hundred and sixty.'

'Three hundred and sixty friends!' I say. 'How can anyone have that many friends? You must be very popular. Where did you meet them all?'

'Online,' she says.

'So you've never actually met any of them?'

'Some of them. But most contact you through the Internet and ask to be your friend. You can be friends with organizations too. Annie Lennox is friends with the Dalai Lama and Nelson Mandela. I can make you a page if you like.'

'Erm, I think I'm OK,' I say.

'I love it. I spend hours online, you know, because I'm not really going to go into leisure and stuff, even though I'm studying it.'

'Aren't you?'

'No. I'm going to be a rock star.'

'Are you?' I say, somewhat hesitantly.

'Yes. I play the guitar, you see, and I've written some poetry and I've put the words to music and put a video of me singing it up on my web page.'

'And can anyone view it?'

'Oh, yes. I've already been contacted by a couple of managers.'

'A couple of managers? That's amazing! What kinds of bands do they manage?'

'I don't think they manage any. They're just looking for people to manage.'

'And where do they find their acts?'

'On Facebook, MySpace, that type of thing.'

'Right,' I say, feeling confused. 'So they're not really managers at all, are they, if they haven't managed anyone?'

'Don't tell my mum,' says Shelley, ignoring what I've just said. 'She thinks it's all nonsense.'

'But, Shelley, I couldn't possibly tell your mum as I don't actually know who she is.'

'Oh, didn't you know? She's Dilys. She takes the minutes in the AGM.'

'Dilys is your mum?' I say. 'I've just seen her at the meeting. Anyway, thanks so much for babysitting.' I give her a twenty-pound note. She raises her eyebrows.

'Thanks a lot,' she says. 'I'll do this again!'

I'm about to go to bed when I decide to sit for a while on the downstairs veranda. The smell of night jasmine is strong and I breathe it in heavily and deeply. I love sitting here, listening to the night. Some people think the night is quiet, but it isn't. It's really rather noisy. I try to listen very carefully now. I can hear an owl, I think. Yes, there's some low hooting further down towards the valley. What else? Ah, the swishing of a bat as it skims through the air catching night-time bugs. I imagine a fox rustling around somewhere and maybe even some badgers. I wonder if there are moths here now, looking for their night-time nectar? Where are they? I can't possibly see any in this dark. The light is on behind me in the living room. I turn to see some small creatures fluttering around it. Are they moths? I move inside to get a better look. Yes, there are two small brown moths singeing their wings on the light bulbs. I'm just getting up closer to them to get a real look when the telephone rings. My heart lurches. Who could be ringing at this time of night? It must be Noel. He's got back from the pub and he's ringing because he's found a solution to our problem.

'Hello?' I say, picking up the receiver and slurring somewhat. 'Have you got a solution? You have, haven't you?'

'A solution to what?' says a man's voice. It's John.

'Oh, John,' I say a bit weakly.

'Who were you expecting? Who has a solution?'

'Oh, it's so complicated,' I say, suddenly not wanting to share my new-found friendship with Noel. 'I'm too tired to explain.'

'No, Samantha,' he says lightly, 'try harder. I've barely talked to you since you got to Devon. I want to know what's been going on with you and the children. How are they? How are you?'

'Actually,' I say, 'they're all fine. They've all made friends.'

'With who?'

'Edward's met a girl called Isabel.'

'A girl!' says John. 'Well, good on him.' He gives a low whistle. 'Chip off the old block, eh?'

'It's not like that,' I say a bit tersely. 'But it's stopping him from being bored. And Bennie's met an Irish boy called Lorcan . . .'

'Good, I like the Irish.'

'. . . and Jamie's made friends with Noel, of course.'

'As in Noel who talked to invisible Sophie?'

'Yes, him.'

'Isn't that a bit odd?'

'Because he's old? I don't think so. Jamie seems to like

looking at moths with him and he's offered to take Jamie out to look for more moths and I think it may well help Jamie. Noel said it was good for a boy to have a hobby.'

'Yes, I'm sure it is,' says John.

'I mean, at least someone's trying to help Jamie,' I say, sounding slightly aggressive.

'Oh, Samantha,' says John, sounding a bit fed up. 'Please don't start giving me a hard time.'

'I'm not! I'm just saying that I think it's good for Jamie that he's met Noel. I've been talking in the pub with Noel tonight and he agrees that Jamie needs some help and when I told him I thought I was probably over-worrying, he said he didn't think I was.'

'Right. OK,' says John, sounding ever more weary. 'Well, I'm glad you had a good time in the pub.'

There's a pause.

'Are you drunk?' asks John after a while.

I giggle. 'A little bit,' I say.

'How much wine did you have?'

'Three bottles.'

'Between two of you? My God, that's like being an alcoholic.'

'Is it?' I say, shocked.

'No, not in your case,' says John. 'Alcoholics drink that every day, if not more.'

'Then I'm a one-day alkie,' I say, giggling again. 'I'm a modern-day binge drinker. It's only because we had a lot to discuss.'

'Like what?'

I spend the next ten minutes explaining to John precisely where I've been and all about Noel's campaign to save his friend's house.

'Hang on a minute,' John says. 'Are you telling me that you've managed to get involved in some campaign that you know nothing about when you've only been in the village for about forty-eight hours?'

'Yes,' I say, 'but . . .'

John groans. 'Oh, why am I not surprised?' he says.

'John,' I say impatiently, 'I had to get involved. This isn't some village, this is the village where Janet spent half her life. I want to help. I don't want us to just come here and use this house without caring. Anyway, you know what I'm like. I love doing a project and I don't really feel I've achieved anything in ages.'

'You've had four children. You write books that are turned into television programmes the world over.'

'Yes, but they're about fridges and the success of the television programmes has nothing to do with me. I want to be part of something.'

John is silent for a bit. Then he says, 'Look, Samantha, you don't really belong anywhere until you have friends who live there. You can't make friends that quickly. Not even you can.'

I don't say anything.

John sighs. 'OK, are you serious about trying to help this woman save her house?'

'Yes,' I say, speaking up again fervently.

'I'll try to help then,' he says.

I remember that I haven't asked him about his puppet theatre.

'Did you build the chateau?' I ask him.

'Yes,' he says. 'It's very dramatic. I think tickets for the show are selling well. Once it's finished in London, the whole show moves to Paris. I don't have to go with them though, so I can spend all the rest of the holiday with you and the children. I've just got to sort out the preview and then we're fine.'

'When do you need to preview the show?'

'In at few weeks' time.'

Then a thought occurs to me.

'Hey,' I say, 'why don't you bring the puppet show here and preview it at the fête? The kids would love to see it – and you, of course.'

John laughs. 'Now I know you really are drunk. It's an experimental show and it's in French. I can't see that being a sell-out draw.'

'But at least it's something different,' I say. 'And it would be fun, wouldn't it? There are loads of yummy mummies here and I bet they'd love their children to go and see a puppet show in French. I met them on the beach yesterday.'

'And why would these yummy mummies want to come to a French puppet show?'

'Oh, because they're always trying to get their children to learn foreign languages. Honestly, they'll flock to it. And I can't think of anything else to help the fête, so . . .'

John is silent for a moment and then he says, 'Do you know, Samantha, that's not such a bad idea. Test the show on children. Why not? And I'll get to spend some more time with you.'

Then he tells me that he's driving down at the weekend.

'I'm bringing Dougie with me,' he says. 'Is that all right?'

'Of course it's all right,' I say. 'It's more than all right. I love Dougie!'

'Can we go and see where the fête will be?'

'I'll ask,' I say. 'I'm sure we can. I have a good feeling about all this.'

'Great,' says John. 'I'll see you then. I love you, Samantha.'

I go upstairs to bed. I peek into Baby Sparkle's room. I watch her chest as it goes up and down in tiny movements. Then I look into Bennie's room. He's splayed out as if he's being crucified – arms out wide to the side, mouth open. There's a little bundle at his feet, wrapped up in a pink duvet. It's Jamie, curled up into a ball. Poor Jamie. He obviously didn't want to sleep on his own in the skylight room when Edward wasn't there and has crept down to sleep with Bennie. I pick him up. He's as light as a feather, as light as a Rice Krispie. I put him on the spare bed and kiss his forehead. He barely stirs.

'Everything is going to change for you, little man,' I whisper to him as I carefully tuck him in. 'Everything.'

8. Diagnostic Features

It is eight o'clock in the morning and I am, as usual, trying to make the children's breakfast. When I woke up an hour ago, I found out that my head hurt. At first I didn't know what was going on. When I heard Baby Sparkle, I raised my head up and realized it felt as heavy as lead. When I moved it one way, the lead seemed to clunk over that side. It moved back again when I returned to centre. It was really most odd. 'I have a headache,' I thought to myself. 'Why have I got a headache?' Then I remembered the three bottles I had drunk with Noel. I groaned inwardly. What on earth must he think of me? I decided to wake myself up by having a shower and now all the children are goggling at me because I've washed my hair and wrapped it up in a towel and put it on top of my head like a turban. The fact that I've actually managed to have a full-on, more-than-five-minute shower has alerted them that something is up.

'You've showered,' said Bennie, his mouth gaping open.

'Yes,' I said. 'It's a miracle, isn't it?' which it actually is because I never usually get a minute to do anything other than shove something resembling food into Jamie and cook dippy eggs for Bennie while also trying to help Baby Sparkle spoon some gloop into her mouth. Baby Sparkle seems to love gloop. She likes porridge, stewed apples, mushy peas. Anything she can dip her pudgy hands into makes her very happy. If you put her in her high chair and give her a plastic bowl full of anything that has the consistency of blancmange, she almost claps her hands with delight. This morning I've made her porridge with bananas mashed into it. I've strapped her into this high chair that magically attaches itself to the sides of tables. It always appears very precarious and yet they're very popular. They pop up wherever you go.

That's how it is with accoutrements — all parents have the same things. We all have the same baby walker and the same gym. Why it's called a gym I have no idea. It's just a mat that lies under an arching structure which you hang toys off. The idea is that the baby lies on its back and reaches for the toys with its arms and legs.

'What a stupid name for a toy,' I said to my mother one day. 'Babies can't do gym.'

'All babies need exercise,' my mother said. 'In China they sit their babies in a line and strap their arms on to long wooden poles and then they move the poles around so the babies work their arm muscles correctly.'

'That sounds barbaric,' I said.

'It's very good for them,' said my mother.

It's interesting, though, what people call barbaric. I, for example, think it's barbaric to strap Chinese babies' arms to long poles in order to make them move. My mother thinks it's barbaric to have a dog and leave it at home. Sometimes I have to leave our dog, Beady, at home for maybe a couple of hours and my mother always gets very cross with me.

'You cannot leave a dog alone in the house,' she says when I tell her I'm going out to the shops with Baby Sparkle.

'I have to,' I'll say. 'I need to get Baby Sparkle some new vests.'

'Well, you wouldn't leave her alone in the house, would you?'

'No.'

'Then why leave the dog?'

'Baby Sparkle is a human being, Mum,' I'll say.

'There's no difference,' my mother will say. Then she'll threaten to call the RSPCA if I ever do it again, a threat I routinely ignore.

Interestingly, Edward thinks it's barbaric to catch butterflies and moths.

'Isabel told me last night that her grandfather catches moths and then kills them and pins them on to cardboard to keep a record of them. Does he?' he asks me while I'm getting breakfast.

'I don't know. I don't think so.'

'She said she thought it was barbaric. She said that he was barbaric and I agree with her.'

'But, Edward, you don't even know it's true.'

'I'm worrying about it.'

I go to kiss him on the head. He smells of something sweet and strange. I can't quite identify what it is.

'You've had a shower,' he says to me before I can ask him what the smell is.

'Yes,' I say.

'Your hair looks funny all wrapped up in that towel. You look like you're wearing a turban. Where do they wear turbans again? Is it in Arabia?'

'No,' I say. 'There's not really any such place as Arabia and, anyway, they don't wear turbans there. It tends to be more in India and Pakistan.'

'There's a boy at our school who wears a turban,' he says. 'His name is Arjunbir. Apparently he has loads of hair under that because he's not allowed to cut it.'

'Right.'

'I think I'll go and write a story about that. Is that a good idea?'

'In a minute,' I say. 'Edward, I want to ask you something.'

'What?' says Edward, turning towards me.

'How did you get paint on your clothes last night? Shelley told me she put your T-shirt in to soak, but where did it come from?'

'How should I know?' says Edward. 'One minute it wasn't there, the next it was. It was probably from a gate post or something. Is that all you wanted to ask me?'

'No. That's not all. How did it go last night?'

'What do you mean?'

'I mean, what did you do? Did you have fun?'

'S'pose so,' he says, a bit defensively. 'Isabel showed me the rec and then we kinda wandered around looking for something to do.'

'Well, that doesn't sound like much fun.'

'It was all right.'

'What did you find to do after that then?'

'Nothing. Why?' he asks, sounding suspicious.

'It's just that I can smell something on you.'

'Oh,' he says, 'what type of thing?'

'Alcohol.'

'Alcohol?' Edward says in a stunned tone. 'Why would I smell of alcohol?'

'I don't know,' I say patiently. 'Why would you?'

'You know I've never ever liked alcohol! You're just cross cos Dad isn't here and now you're looking for people to blame.'

'Hang on a minute, Edward,' I say. 'This has got nothing to do with Dad and whether he's here or not. It's just that when you left me and Noel last night, Isabel was talking about Bacardi Breezers and now I can smell something on you. You didn't drink one last night, did you?'

'I would never drink a Bacardi Breezer with anyone!' he says, incensed. 'And you know I never lie!' Then he storms out of the door, which worries me for I also know that whenever Edward says he isn't lying is precisely the time when he might be.

'Is Edward lying?' I ask Baby Sparkle as I sit down at the table to butter Bennie's toast. Baby Sparkle stops playing with her porridge and starts laughing. I love the way she does this. Even though she can't speak yet, she's so communicative. If you laugh, she laughs. If you talk, she tries to talk back. She seems to think that talking involves waggling your head and then sticking your tongue in and out rapidly.

'Ra-la-ra-la-ra,' she goes now, moving her tongue in and out of her mouth.

WHY CHILDREN LIE

I always think it unbelievable when parents find the fact that their children lie a source of either great pain or bafflement or both. I meet them all the time. They say things like, 'My little Alfred never eats a chocolate biscuit. He's such a good little boy because we don't like him eating biscuits and we've told him that, so now he never does it,' and I look at little Alfred and I think 'Hmmm' to myself. Then I'll say to the parents, 'How do you know little Alfred doesn't eat chocolate biscuits?' and they'll look very smug and say, 'Because we've taught Alfred not to lie.'

Alfred will look up at me with his big round brown eyes, a bit like a Labrador puppy, and I'll look down at him, and what my eyes are saying to Alfred's are 'And should I tell your parents about the chocolate I saw you stuffing yourself with at a party last week?' For when the parents find out, as they always do, they are furious. They are shocked and then sad and then poor little Alfred is in no end of trouble and I always wonder if it would have been a whole lot better coming from me rather than them having to face the truth after turning up to another child's party a few minutes early, only to catch Alfred in the act of downing a cupcake with half an inch of icing on top. Ah, well, there went poor Alfred, banned from his friends' parties for about a year, two years, for life, and following him out of the party were his parents, heads bowed in shame, eyes red, desperately trying to understand what went wrong, and do you know what I want to say to Alfred's parents? I want to say this: IT'S JUST A BIT OF CHOCOLATE! What on earth is wrong with eating chocolate? In fact, what is wrong with crisps and ice cream and yummy sweets and those gooey, chewy things that stick your mouth together and sherbet lemons and cream puffs and chocolate éclairs and Eccles cakes and lardy cake and iced buns? Why do we spend all our lives telling our children they can't eat these things when they're impossible to avoid? Every time you go to the shops, there these things are, doing enticing little dances of the seven veils in such a way that only children can see them. 'Come and eat me up,' say the Pick and Mix. 'I'm delicious,' squeaks popcorn. All these children are dribble-mouthed and entranced, and what happens? Their boring parents say, 'You can't have any!' So what does their little nipper do? In his mind he hatches a plan, a fiendish plan, whereby when his parents' backs are turned he will in some way, somehow, get the popcorn and eat the whole lot up! But he knows he's not allowed it, so what can he do? The little nipper's brain works feverishly . . . what can he do, what can he do? Oh my God, maybe he will have to lie! And then another part of his brain says to him, 'You cannot lie. Only naughty boys lie. Remember what Mum and Dad have told you.' But the popcorn-eating obsessed part of the brain says, 'Phooey to all that. I know. I'll get the popcorn and eat it fast and then, if anyone asks me about it, I'll lie and say I haven't had it and they'll never find out.'

This is why children lie.

It's the thought of being in trouble that makes them lie. Most children are people pleasers. They just tell you what you want to hear even if that bears no relevance to the truth. All very logical.

So why are parents so appalled by children who lie? I lied with impunity as a child. I didn't intend to be naughty and yet I was. I dropped all my mother's jade animals that she'd brought back from Hong Kong out of her bedroom window to see if they bounced. I probably knew I shouldn't have done it, but I couldn't seem to stop myself. And they didn't bounce. They chipped. As soon as I saw them chip I knew I was in trouble so I ran down and picked up all the animals and put them back on my mother's mantelpiece and hoped she wouldn't notice. But she did notice. She called me and my sister in and said, 'Someone has ruined my jade animals and I want to know who.' My sister and I looked at the floor. 'I won't be angry,' she said. 'I just want to know who it was and if you don't tell me I'll send you both to bed with no supper.' So I looked at Julia and she knew it wasn't her, and she knew it was me, and so I piped up.

'It was me, Mum,' I said. 'I'm sorry. I didn't mean to.' And my mother said, 'I-KNEW-IT-WAS-YOU!' and then she got very angry and smacked my bottom and sent me to bed with no supper.

The other day I took Benny to his friend's house. His mother came out and, looking very apologetic, told me the rules: no running, no shouting, no screaming, no taking outdoor toys in, no taking indoor toys out, no playing in the sand pit, take shoes off before you come in the house, no using the art pencils without supervision, no going outside without coats on, no coats on indoors . . . and on and on it went until, when she'd finished, I said, 'Are they allowed to breathe?' and she shot me a funny look.

I think children should make up rules for their parents: pick me up from school every day, don't make me eat food I hate, be reasonable about my chocolate consumption, read me stories every night, launder my school uniform for me, listen to me, be kind and nice and help me wash my hair even though I hate you doing it, let me see my friends, please stop shouting at me and can I have a puppy/kitten/ goldfish? We spend all our lives telling children what not to do, yet how many of us think about what *we* should do? I see armies of parents not listening to their children, women who have never dropped their children off at school or picked them up because they're too busy, and parents who are so involved in their own individual lives that they only notice what their child is doing when they've eaten the cupcake at the party.

'Edward's gone to write a story,' I tell Baby Sparkle. 'It's going to be about a boy with lots of hair. Mind you, Baby Sparkle, it may not be about that at all. Do you remember the time he was supposed to do an essay entitled "What I Would Do If I Were Prime Minister For a Day"?'

'Ra-la-ra-la-ra,' says Baby Sparkle, waggling her head about.

'He wrote, "If I were Prime Minister for a day I'd get on my presidential plane and fly to Italy and over the sea the plane would crash and then I'd get attacked by a great white shark and die." That's a weird story, isn't it, Baby Sparkle?'

Baby Sparkle waggles her head again.

'Then,' I continue, 'there's the time he insisted that rhyme went "Remember, remember, the sixth of November", and when I told him it was supposed to be the fifth of November he just wouldn't believe me, would he?'

'Is the fifth of November firework night?' says a voice from the door. It's Bennie. He is half naked, having taken his pyjama bottoms off. This is not surprising. Bennie hardly ever wears clothes.

'Hello, Bennie,' I say. 'Yes, November fifth is firework night. Now what are you and Jamie up to?'

'I'm watching television and Jamie is colouring in a story-book called *Rose-Red and Snow-White* or something. Is my breakfast ready?'

'Yes. I'm going to bring it to you right now.'

Bennie disappears again as I crack his eggs open in their cups. I go into the sitting room with a tray full of eggs, toast and Jamie's Rice Krispies.

"Ello, Mum,' says Jamie. 'I'm colouring Rose-Red.'

'Good for you,' I say.

'She has black hair. Do I have black hair like Rose-Red?'

'No, you have blond hair like Snow-White.'

Jamie frowns. 'I don't like her. She ate an apple and died.'

I'm about to tell him that he's got his Snow-Whites muddled up when there's a knock at the door.

'Ra-la-ra-la-ra,' I hear Baby Sparkle say.

I go back into the kitchen to find Noel hovering just inside the doorway.

'Sorry,' he says apologetically when he sees me. 'The door was open so I –'

'No, it's fine,' I say. Just then I remember I'm wearing a turban on my head. 'I've washed my hair.'

'Hence the towel,' he says. 'I can see that. Do you want me to go?'

'No,' I say. 'I'll go and brush my hair out. Have some coffee. I've had about ten cups since last night's extravaganza.'

Noel looks at me. 'Extravaganza, my dear? That's all in day's work for me, I'm afraid.'

'Well, I must apologize,' I say. 'I don't usually drink that amount and turn into a giggling lunatic.'

'Not at all,' he says. 'You were the most charming company.' Then he looks down at Baby Sparkle. 'Hmm. Stodge. Fascinating what babies like to eat. It's the same with old people, you know. Our teeth go so we just eat soft fruits.' He sits down in front of her. 'Now, small person. Are we going to eat your breakfast, the two of us?'

'You don't really have to feed her,' I say, going up the stairs.

I walk past Edward's room. He's busily writing away.

'Edward,' I say, 'I'm sorry if I upset you.'

'I'm not upset,' he says, refusing to look at me. 'I just want you to believe me.'

'I do,' I say.

'Because I'm not lying,' he says.

'OK,' I say. 'Case closed. You're not lying. What are you doing then?'

'I'm doing a great bit of writing,' he says. 'It's about this boy with long hair who gets on a plane and flies to Italy and . . .' He looks at my face. 'It's only a joke, Mum!' he says gleefully. 'I haven't really written that story again. I've done something entirely different. It starts like this. "Every child needs to meet someone on holiday, even if they like them or not . . ."'

'That sounds good.'

'Yes, it's about a boy who goes back to a house he used to go to with his father, but his father has disappeared and the boy goes to try and find him because he misses him so . . .'

'Edward,' I say warningly.

'What?' he says innocently.

Then I hear a banging noise from downstairs.

'Noel Rideout's here,' I say.

'Oh,' he says, looking gloomy.

'Don't be like that,' I say. 'He's eating Baby Sparkle's breakfast with her, so I thought maybe when I've done my hair, we could go downstairs together and ask him about the moths. What do you think?'

'Oh, OK,' says Edward, re-reading his story. 'Do you think if a boy has long hair people think he's a girl?'

'Possibly,' I say.

'Great,' says Edward, picking up his pen again.

Ten minutes later, Edward and I go back downstairs to the kitchen. Baby Sparkle and Noel are nowhere to be seen.

'Oh God,' I say, 'where are they?'

Then we hear some giggling in the garden so we go outside to find Baby Sparkle sitting up on a rug on the lawn. Noel and Jamie are sitting near her at the garden table, looking at a book.

'Now, this one is called a Clouded Drab. That's a funny name, isn't it?' Noel is saying.

'Sophie want to know what drab is,' says Jamie, staring at the book.

'Ah, well you can tell Sophie that drab means dull and lacking in colour. Not at all like you, James, because I can see you're wearing some lovely pink knickers and I do think pink suits you so well.'

Jamie blushes.

'Ah, Samantha,' says Noel, catching sight of me as I come into the garden. 'I have brought your children, well, your two youngest children, outside for some fresh air. It's a lovely day, is it not?'

'It is,' I say, noticing how the sun is now rather warm. I can feel the beginnings of the heat of the day on my arms. The grass is dewy. The bees have already started up their hum. 'Yes, it's going to be a lovely day,' I say. 'Maybe a good day for the beach.'

'The beach?' says Jamie. 'My am wearing my pink knickers to go on the beach.'

'It's "I am wearing my pink knickers", James,' says Noel. 'Do you think you can tell me that?'

Jamie nods earnestly and then he screws his eyes up as if he's thinking very hard. '*I* am wearing my pink knickers,' he says.

'Yes. Well done,' says Noel. 'You certainly are wearing pink knickers, but you're not wearing them to the beach because, this morning, we're not going to the beach.'

'Why not?' I ask.

'Because we're going to visit Sarah de Salis.'

'Are we?'

'Yes, we are. I've decided that it's very important you see the house. You cannot save a house without looking at it first.'

'Yes, that's true, but . . . have you asked Mrs de Salis if it's OK?'

'Yes, and it's fine.'

'What? With the children as well?'

'Yes, Sarah de Salis loves children.'

Jamie gets up from the garden table and wanders over to me.

'Come and sit down, Mummy,' he says. 'Come and look at this book with me.'

We walk back to the table and I sit down on the chair next to him.

'It's a book about moths, Jamie,' I say.

'I hope you don't mind, Samantha,' says Noel, 'but he seemed very interested in the wine string so I thought I'd bring him one of my moth identification books.'

'That's fine,' I say.

Noel turns over the page. 'What's this moth, James?' he asks him, pointing to an illustration at the bottom of the page.

'My . . . I don't know,' says Jamie.

'Clever you, James!' says Noel.

Jamie looks very pleased with himself.

'Does Sophie know the name of this moth?' Noel continues. 'Look at the wings. There's a clue in the pattern on the wings, isn't there?'

'Is it . . . is it . . . a shell?' asks Jamie.

'Yes!' says Noel. 'You are a clever boy. This moth is called a Scallop Shell and its wings always bear these distinctive dark brown wavy crosslines on them. They're very common round here, so you and Sophie must look out for one.'

'Sophie didn't know the name of that moth,' Jamie says to Noel, as if he's telling him a secret. 'Only my . . . only I knew it.'

'Yes,' says Noel. 'You did.'

'We were just looking at this moth,' he says to me, pointing at the page. 'It's the *Apocheima hispidaria*, the Small Brindled Beauty. It feeds on oak leaves and it's been in the news recently because it's been rediscovered in Sherwood Forest, which is very unexpected as it hasn't been seen there since the early eighteen hundreds.'

I study the picture. 'It looks like the moth version of a tabby kitten,' I say.

'I like moth-kittens,' says Jamie.

'James also says he likes this moth.' Noel turns the pages. 'Do you see it? It's the small brown one with the faintly green wings.' I lean over Noel and Jamie to look at the book.

'Is it this one? The July Highflyer?'

'I like the green wings,' says Jamie.

'I thought you only liked pink?' I ask him.

'And green,' he says.

Noel interrupts us. 'Now, I told Mrs de Salis we'd be with her for elevenses, so we'd all best get a move on. In terms of your children, we'll take the young ones and . . .' Noel gets up and walks to the fence. 'Ah, here she is,' he says. I go and stand with him and look up the street to see Isabel walking towards us.

'I thought maybe Edward and Isabel could go and have

some fun,' says Noel. 'It's no fun at all for them to come and see an old lady in an old house.'

Isabel now gets to the gap in the hedge. She bends down. Her jeans inadvertently slip below her waistline. She's wearing a G-string.

'My granddaughter,' says Noel, registering the hint of shock on my face, 'is a very modern young lady,' and we leave it at that.

9. Conservation

It takes an hour and a half to get out of the house. First of all Baby Sparkle fell asleep on the rug, so I put her back in her cot. Then Jamie decided he wanted Noel to explain about virtually every moth in his book and Bennie had a fit because when he found out that we were going to see Mrs de Salis's house and Edward wasn't coming, he decided it was unfair.

'Why should I go and see a house?' he said. 'I want to stay with Edward.'

'You can't be with us!' shouted Edward from upstairs where he was ensconced with Isabel. He'd looked pretty pleased when he'd found out she was in the garden. He'd appeared down the stairs and insisted she follow him back up to his room to read his story.

'I like stories,' Isabel had said.

'Oh good,' said Edward. 'Then we can write one each and read them out if you want to.'

'Sure,' said Isabel.

'I've written one about a boy trying to find his real dad who has disappeared on a holiday in Devon.'

Isabel gave him a queer look.

'Is that true, Edward?' she asked.

'Sort of,' he said as they went up the stairs.

But pretty soon, Bennie had disturbed their peace.

'I'm staying with Edward,' he'd yelled.

'No!' Edward had yelled back again. 'We're going to the

beach to tell each other more stories and you can't come with us.'

'I want to go too!' yelled Bennie.

'We're climbing on slippery rocks, hen,' Isabel said, appearing at the top of the stairs.

'*Slippery rocks*?' said Bennie. 'I love slippery rocks.'

'They're too dangerous,' Isabel said, coming down with Edward following her.

'See?' said Edward to Bennie. 'They're dangerous so you can't come.' He hissed the last bit. Bennie burst into tears.

'It's unfair,' he sobbed. 'I'm good on dangerous rocks.'

I sat down and took Bennie on my lap, which was no mean feat as he's huge for his age. 'Bennie,' I said. 'We will go to the beach afterwards. I promise you. But this lady is waiting for us at her house.'

'Are you going to Mrs de Salis's house?' asked Isabel, looking thoughtful. 'Well, Bennie, you'll like that because she has a gong.'

'A gong?' said Bennie doubtfully.

'Yes, a big gold one and she lets you bang it if you want to.'

'I want to bang the gong!' said Edward. Isabel gave him a withering look.

'Don't be an idiot, Edward,' she said. 'You and I have got other things to do.'

'Like what?' said Edward grumpily. Edward has always liked nothing more than being able to make a lot of noise, usually involving saucepan lids. The idea of banging a gong is about as close to heaven as you could get for him.

'We've got a packed lunch to make,' Isabel said. 'We need food and drink. I've got some back at Granddad's house we can take.'

'Is that OK with your grandfather?' I asked her a bit suspiciously.

'Ask him yourself,' she said, nodding her head towards the back garden.

I went out and asked Noel and he said it was fine for Edward and Isabel to help themselves to whatever they wanted to, then he looked at his watch and said we really had to go right away. He told Jamie they would look at the book later and that he'd hold his hand walking down the lane, so I said I'd get the baby up and then, finally, we left.

We're now wandering down the lane, the five of us. Jamie is holding Noel's hand and listening to him attentively as Noel explains just about everything to him.

'Do you see that house?' Noel says, pointing at an old cottage.

'Yes,' says Jamie.

'That house is made from the local stone. It's called Morte slate and it means the house is very old, built in medieval times, around 1656. It's the oldest dwelling in Lower Strand. And do you see the field next to it?'

'Yes.'

'The yellow flowers in it are called ragwort and do you know what likes ragwort?'

'Eeyores?'

'No, it's poisonous to donkeys, but the Golden-rod larvae love to feed on it. They are very difficult to find, but we can look for some one day if you like.'

'Yes, please,' says Jamie.

Then Noel points out another cottage. 'Now, this one is made from bricks. It's still very old, but not as old as the other house. Do you see the holes in the front of the house?'

'In the bricks?' asks Jamie.

'No. The holes are actually in the mortar because it's made of lime and lime mortar is porous and soft, unlike cement. It means that the damp which is in all houses can move in and out. Only old houses use it. The holes come from mortar bees. This house probably had some wisteria climbing up it at some point and that has attracted the bees.'

'Bees?' says Jamie. 'I don't like bees. I like flutterbyes.'

'These ones don't sting. Do you want to go and look at the holes, James?'

Jamie nods his head.

'Do you want to go and look at the holes?' I say to Bennie, who's obviously still sulking. He has been walking behind me ever since we left the house and he keeps complaining that he's got a stone/twig/bit of gravel in his sandal.

'No, I don't want to look at the holes,' he says. 'I want to go to the beach.'

'We're going to the beach later,' I say. 'Why do I have to keep telling you that?'

We carry on walking and, as we get round the corner, I see a woman and a boy walking towards us on the other side of the road. The sun is behind them so I can't make out who it is. I squint my eyes up. As the woman gets closer I think I recognize her. Bennie suddenly notices them coming towards us. He obviously has better eyesight than me because the next thing I know he has broken into a slow jog.

'Lorcan!' he yells, getting faster.

'Bennie!' I call. 'Watch the road.'

The boy, who is now only about a hundred feet away, also breaks into a run and rushes towards us. As he gets closer I see that Bennie is right. It *is* Lorcan and just behind him is Roisin.

'Hi,' she says when she reaches us.

'Good to see you. I was hoping we'd meet up again.'

Roisin laughs. 'So was I and here we both are. Serendipity, I think.' She looks inside the pushchair. 'Ah, Baby Sparkle looks very sweet today. Such a lovely name for a baby.'

'Edward named her that,' I say. 'Her real name is Kate.'

Roisin smiles. 'Both names suit her,' she says.

We then stand and look at Lorcan and Bennie, who are chatting away to each other as if they've known each other for years.

'Would you look at them?' says Roisin. 'Long lost twins they are. Lorcan talked about Bennie all yesterday evening. It's good Lorcan's met a friend, you know, being an only child and all that. There's a limit to how many sandcastles one woman can build but –' she looks down at the large bucket and spade she's carrying – 'I'm back on duty today.'

'You're going to the beach then?'

'Yes.'

'We'll be down later. We're just off to visit someone.'

The boys come over towards us.

'Mum,' says Bennie. 'Lorcan's going to the beach right now and he says I can go with him. Lorcan's mummy, can I come with you?'

Roisin gives me an inquisitive look and raises her eyebrows.

'Bennie,' I say, 'I'm afraid you can't do that. You can't just barge into someone else's family like that.'

'Erm, well, it's fine by me,' says Roisin apologetically, 'but it may be that you'd rather Bennie stayed with you.'

'It's not that,' I say. 'I just thought it would be too much and . . .'

Roisin laughs. 'You hardly know me. I understand. You're probably thinking "Who's this mad Irish woman trying to steal my child?" but I promise I'll look after him. I won't let them in the sea without me and I'll only buy him ice creams without nuts in or no ice creams at all and . . . it would be great for me really. Lorcan would love it and it would get me off sandcastle duty, but maybe I'm being selfish . . .'

'No, not at all,' I say. Bennie looks at me desperately.

'Please, Mum,' he says. 'I really want to play with Lorcan.'

'Well, if it's so important . . . then yes, OK, you can go.'

Bennie whoops with excitement and puts his hand in Roisin's.

'See, Mummy?' he says. 'I'm already being a sensible boy.'

I tell Roisin that, all in all, I probably won't be at the beach until just after lunch and she says that's fine and that she'll either be in the café or where she was yesterday.

'I'll give you my mobile number. Just call me later and let me know what you're up to.' She writes her number down on a piece of paper she has in her bag and gives it to me.

I tell her I'll see her later and then I watch as she walks off down the road with the two boys hanging off her.

Fifteen minutes later we have climbed up the steep road leading out from Lower Strand and then headed horizontally as if shadowing the coast path. On the way out of the village, maybe a mile or so out, we come across an obviously brand new development of about twenty new houses, most of which are bungalows. They are all pretty much the same – painted white, blue doors, blue window frames, PVC windows in the frames and little bits of garden marked out by blue picket fences. Some of them have the door positioned over to the right on the house, some to the left. Most of them also have washing fluttering out on washing lines. There is a smattering of brightly coloured children's toys in some of the gardens and a few on the road. Most of the bungalows face the sea, but some are set much further back from the others as there's not enough room for all of them to have a view.

'Look at these,' says Noel disdainfully. 'They are monstrosities, aren't they? Why do they have their own road, these ridiculous gates? There used to be a proper gatehouse here with proper gates until it all got pulled down and turned into this.'

I look at the development and I can see what Noel means. As the main road goes snaking onward up the hill, this brand new tarmac road forks off to the left. There are gates, rather hideous ones, flanking the beginning of the road, and large lamps like boulders running alongside the obviously new road that leads through the estate. There is a signpost on the road that says 'Cutlass Estate'.

'Ah, this is the holiday park then?' I ask Noel.

'Yes, the vision of Mr Cutlass made real. Cheap, cheerful and utterly not in keeping with our glorious countryside. It's a total con, this estate, and those street lights shine all night. Cutlass says it's for security. Security! This is the most secure place in Britain, for God's sake.'

Noel strides off, frowning, and I follow him, finding it hard to keep up.

'How has he made his money?'

'Candles, my dear,' says Noel.

'Candles?'

'Yes. There was a firm here in Devon that made candles locally. Mr Cutlass came in and bought them out and promptly moved the manufacturing of the candles out to the Far East. He said it was cheaper. Interestingly enough, the candles are still marketed as "Devon's finest" and they have a dreadful picture on them showing the sea and the cliffs, but they have nothing to do with Devon at all. Mr Cutlass's candles are as much of a con as he is.'

Noel strides off once more and soon we veer away from the road on to a footpath that, thankfully, takes us away from the Cutlass Estate.

It's getting pretty warm now. Beady is bombing along in the distance. Occasionally she stops and turns to look at us, one paw held bent and off the ground, rather like a question mark. As she sees us continuing to walk in her direction, she puts her nose down and sets off again, but I can tell she's hot because her tongue is lolling out. I, too, am feeling the effects of the heat. I'm out of breath and the pushchair, which I've doggedly got up the hill, feels like a dead weight. I stopped halfway up the hill and stripped Baby Sparkle down to nothing but a vest. She said 'la-la-la' in appreciation. I, however, am sweating and I keep having to mop my brow and push my hair back and out from my eyes. I'm sure I look a complete state. I'm also rather thirsty. Noel, however, looks as cool as a cucumber even though he's wearing a heavy shirt and tweed jacket. Sometimes he stops and takes a small canister from his jacket and sprays it in his mouth.

'What is that?' I ask Noel eventually as he stops and bends down to show Jamie some cowslips.

'It's called Gold Spot,' he says. 'It's a cooling mouth freshener.'

'A cooling mouth freshener?'

'That's what it says on the side of it,' he says, 'and I have no reason to disbelieve it.'

'Aren't you hot then?'

'No,' he says, straightening up. 'I'm not. Are you hot? You look hot.'

'Pretty flowers,' says Jamie, stroking the yellowy-orange bell-like petals. 'Small and tiny.'

'Yes and they used to be very rare,' Noel tells him, 'but now they're making a comeback.'

'Is it much further?' I ask. 'I can't believe Jamie's made it this far. I'm not sure how much more he can walk, let alone me.'

'James is fine, aren't you, James?'

'Yes,' says Jamie, standing up. He looks back down at the flowers. 'A flutterbye!' he shouts. Noel stops immediately and crouches down to look at the ground.

'Oh, James, my dear. It's a Common Heath. Oh, well done you! You really are very talented at this. Samantha, can you see it?'

I bend down to see what Noel is pointing at. I see something small and light brown.

'Is that a moth?' I say. 'It looks like one, but I thought they only came out at night?'

'Oh, no. Common Heaths are very active by day, especially when it's warm.'

'I saw a flutterbye, Mummy,' says Jamie, jumping up and down.

'Yes, you're very good at that,' says Noel, smiling warmly at him, 'even though they are actually called moths.'

Jamie puts his hand back in Noel's and we carry on walking.

Eventually we come to an old wall on our right-hand side.

'This is the beginning of the Manor House grounds,' says Noel in a hushed voice.

It's so dark and dank that I look up. Above us soars a canopy of large pine trees that block out the light. On the left-hand side there's a stream, slate in colour.

But now we have got to the end of the curve of the wall and in front of us is a gravel drive. It's not as long as I expected, a few hundred yards maybe. One side of the drive is laid to lawn, the other is lined with rhododendron trees. The drive leads up to the house and ends in a horseshoe shape. I gaze along the drive and follow it until it reaches the house and there it is, the Manor House, the house I am here to save. I stop in my tracks. I'd expected something very traditional, grand, imposing – a magnificent stately home – and yet the Manor House is not like this at all. It is, in fact, more like a bow-fronted, rather beautiful Italian villa. It has what seems to be a copper roof. There is a wrought-iron veranda in the centre of the front of the house, which is recessed back from two curved bows. The outside walls have been painted a pale pink. The windows are long and large and have shutters on the inside. Small mint and white striped canopies on the outside have been let down to shade the windows. At the front of the house is a raised patio area shaded by a trellised rose walk with stone steps that lead down to the garden. There is something terribly graceful about it all. The house, the paved patio with the roses hanging down from the ornamental trellis and the pretty shaded windows all seem redolent of a past life where Edwardian ladies and gentlemen, say, spent long hazy afternoons, lazing around drinking mint juleps and playing croquet. Yet there is something odd about the house.

'I expected a proper manor house,' I say to Noel, thinking of the medieval cottage in the village. 'This house is beautiful, but it's almost like . . . I don't know what really – a villa maybe? It's so fancy, isn't it?'

'Yes it is, isn't it?' says Noel.

'Why is that?'

'There's a simple explanation,' says Noel, 'but you'll have to ask Sarah about it.'

Noel then walks up to the door and raps hard on it with a huge knocker in the shape of a lion's head.

'Sarah!' he shouts, staring up at the blank windows. 'It's me, Noel! I have Samantha with me.'

For a while we hear nothing and then, eventually, there's the drag of a bolt as the person inside pulls back the lock. The door opens and there, standing in front of us, is a tall, thin lady with a quiet but tired-looking face. She has surprisingly dark hair, almost steel grey, not white even though she must be at least eighty, if not closer to ninety. Everything else about her is old, from the frailty of her arms to her stick-like legs, which are clad in thick navy-blue stockings that wrinkle round her ankles. Her face is so thin and sunken it could be a death mask. But when she smiles, she looks kind and strong and somehow really rather appealing.

'Who is she?' whispers Jamie loudly. 'Sophie thinks she's a witch.'

The lady smiles. 'Do I look like a witch?' she says to Jamie, who has now retreated behind Noel's legs. 'I'm very sorry if I do. I'd bend down to say hello to you and then you could see I'm not a witch, but I can't because I'm too old to bend, you see. Do you see?'

Jamie still says nothing.

'Oh, well,' says the lady. 'I'm sure you'll come round.' Then she looks at me and extends her hand. 'Hello,' she says as I shake it. 'You must be Samantha.'

I nod my head. 'I am,' I say, 'and you're Mrs de Salis.'

'I'm so sorry for my appearance,' says Mrs de Salis, 'but I was cleaning the dining room so we could all eat lunch.' She looks reproachfully at Noel. 'Noel had said you'd be here for morning coffee, but then you didn't come so I decided a spot of lunch might be in order.'

'Sorry, Sarah,' says Noel. 'I did try to get Samantha out of the house, but she seemed almost impossible to move.'

'I'm very sorry. I've got four children, five if you count the imaginary Sophie,' I say to Mrs de Salis apologetically. 'Sometimes we don't even get out of the house at all.'

'Well, I'm very flattered that you managed to get here then,' says Mrs de Salis. 'Anyway, it gave me a chance to clean up.'

It's then I notice that she's wearing an ancient-looking pinafore.

'This used to have birds on it,' says Mrs de Salis, noticing what I'm looking at. She addresses Jamie directly as he has now, finally, re-emerged from behind Noel. 'Can you imagine! It had beautiful blue peacocks on it. Do you like peacocks?' she asks him.

'Yes,' says Jamie.

'I thought you might. You look like a boy who likes a peacock. We used to have them here on the estate, but after my husband died ... well now, oh, what am I thinking!' she says. 'You've walked all the way from Lower

Strand, haven't you? On a day like this? You must be panting with thirst. Come in immediately and I'll find something for you to drink.'

She turns round and I park Baby Sparkle, who is now asleep in her pushchair, into the shade next to the front door and we all follow Mrs de Salis into the hallway of the house. The hallway is exactly how I expected it to be. It's quite magnificent. The entire hall is clad in oak and there's a staircase right in front of us. On the walls hang antique paintings of people with gold plaques under their names. The writing on the plaques is so small that I can't read what they say, but some of the men in the portraits are wearing military gear and some have swords. Up the side of one of the hall walls is what looks to be a family tree etched on an impressive canvas. It takes up a whole wall.

'There are so many of you!' I say.

'Not my family,' says Mrs de Salis. 'That's Gerrard's side.'

'It's very impressive, isn't it, Samantha?' says Noel. 'If you ever have time, you should come and study it.'

Right at that moment I hear Jamie yell, 'The gong!' He has wandered off down the end of the hall and found a big gold gong sitting next to what seems to be a Roman statue of a head carved in marble.

'I want to bang the gong,' says Jamie.

'Yes, do bang the gong,' says Mrs de Salis, 'because I think it's lunch time.'

Jamie bangs the gong very loudly five times, which wakes up Baby Sparkle. She starts to cry from outside the front door so I go and undo her straps. 'It wasn't me who banged the gong, Mummy,' says Jamie. 'It was Sophie.'

'Well, that Sophie is very naughty,' I say, picking Baby Sparkle up. 'Hello, darling,' I say to her. She coos back at me. I take her inside and Noel and I follow Mrs de Salis into the dining room. What I see takes my breath away. The dining room turns out to be a huge, grand room with a high decorative ceiling and long walls covered in astonishing murals depicting pastoral scenes. It also has a large fireplace at one end.

'I call this the Long Room,' she says. 'It's fifty feet long, you know, and these murals have been here for years. Gerrard had an eminent architectural restorer, George Oak, re-do them about fifty years ago. I think they've been done in what's called the Strawberry Hill Gothic Revival Style.'

'They're beautiful,' I say. 'And the fireplace . . .'

'It's the original. It's made of veined grey marble and there's a matching one in the smoking room, only no one smokes there any more. Now, I'll go and get the lunch. Do your children eat chicken?' she asks. I tell her that they do. 'Good,' she says. 'I'll bring the food in and maybe, Noel, you can go up to the attic and find a high chair. I know there's one somewhere.'

Noel nods his head and gets up to move. 'I'll take James with me,' he says to me. 'That way he can explore.'

Ten minutes later, Noel appears carrying an ancient, creaking high chair. 'Will your baby be OK in this?' he says, looking at it dubiously.

'I'm sure she'll be fine,' I say, popping Baby Sparkle into the seat. Baby Sparkle looks a bit surprised as I force her in. The chair is much smaller than her capacious plastic one at home, but then she notices that there's a wooden bar on the front. It has wooden hollow rings on it, like an abacus, that she can spin round and push up and down.

'Ra-la-ra-la-ra,' she says happily as she starts pushing a ring from one end to the other.

'What a great chair,' I say.

Jamie is now sitting on a window seat stroking what appears to be a cushion.

'What's that, Jamie?' I ask him.

'That's the Hugger Mugger,' says Mrs de Salis as she appears through the door holding a large tureen. Noel gets up to take it from her.

'That's too heavy for you,' he says.

'It's fine,' she says, putting the tureen down on the table. 'The Hugger Mugger is a very old cat,' she says to Jamie, 'and quite deaf.'

'Oh,' says Jamie sadly. Then he puts his mouth up to the cat's ear. 'HELLO, CATTY!' he yells.

'Jamie!' I say.

'Don't worry,' says Mrs de Salis, 'the cat hasn't even moved.'

Jamie then comes and sits at the table as Mrs de Salis ladles out some soup on to our plates.

'This is beef consommé,' she says.

Jamie looks at it. He wrinkles his nose up. 'Is it from the dishwasher?' he asks.

'Jamie!' I hiss at him.

'Maybe little boys don't like consommé,' says Mrs de Salis a bit mournfully, looking at Jamie's bowl. 'Never mind, I can always get him some bread.'

'Bread?' says Jamie. 'I don't like bread.'

'James,' says Noel lightly, 'shall we tell Mrs de Salis about the moth you found? Do you remember it?'

'Yes,' says Jamie, now rather excited. 'I found a moth. I like moths and I know them all.'

'He found a Common Heath,' Noel says to Mrs de Salis, winking at her. 'Now, James, why don't you tell us all about the moths you've seen since you came to Devon while Sarah gets you some bread, because if a boy is to go moth hunting, he must keep his strength up.'

'Yes,' says Jamie again. 'I do like bread. I will have some.'

'Please,' I say.

'Please,' he says.

As Mrs de Salis goes to find some bread, I try the soup. It is lukewarm and tastes like boiled cabbages. I look at Noel. He seems totally oblivious to how horrible it is and is happily slurping away while Jamie burbles on about moths with red underbellies and ones with green wings.

'Noel,' I say to him. 'I can't eat this.'

'Don't then,' he says.

'But it's rude not to.'

'Yes, maybe, but there's not much you can do about it.' He sighs. 'Sarah's never been able to cook. The aristocracy are hopeless at it.' He looks around the room. 'You could pour it into the plant pot, Samantha,' he says. 'That one over there looks desperately in need of sustenance.'

'I can't do that!' I say, as Jamie starts giggling. Then Jamie gets up and marches over to the plant.

'Jamie!' I say warningly. He looks at me defiantly and slowly tips all his soup into the pot.

'Good on you, James,' says Noel as Jamie comes back to sit down at the table. 'Now, was it you who poured the soup out or Sophie?'

'I did it,' says Jamie proudly.

'Good boy,' says Noel and I'm astonished to find that Jamie has admitted to something rather than blaming Sophie.

Just then the dining room door opens and Mrs de Salis comes back in.

'Oh, good boy,' said Mrs de Salis when she sees Jamie's empty bowl. 'You've finished your soup. I couldn't find any bread anyway. My Gerrard always thought children should eat up all their food and he didn't approve of mopping things up with bread. He'd say, "Children should eat what they're given," but I think that's a generational thing.'

'That's true,' I say, now rather desperately trying to spoon my soup into Baby Sparkle's mouth as she actually seems to be enjoying it.

After we finish our consommé, which doesn't take that long as Baby Sparkle helpfully dribbles most of mine down her front, Mrs de Salis disappears to get the main course.

'It's chicken, isn't it?' I ask Noel.

'Yes,' says Noel, getting up in a laconic fashion, going over to a cupboard in the corner and extricating a bottle. 'I think I'll have some wine. Would you like some with your lunch?'

'Not really,' I say, remembering that we still haven't had anything to drink since we arrived here. I go to pour out some water that's sitting in a jug on the table.

'There are no glasses,' I say to Noel.

He points at a set of deep-red Moroccan tea glasses on top of the dresser.

'Use them,' he says. I pour some out for Jamie, who's now sitting back on the window seat and cooing over the Hugger Mugger, and then I share mine with Baby Sparkle, tipping the glass up to her lips carefully.

'Now,' says Noel as Mrs de Salis comes back in, wheeling a hostess trolley. 'You have to tell Samantha about the house, Sarah. She cannot help us if she doesn't know what she's dealing with.'

'Yes, of course,' says Mrs de Salis, opening up the ancient-looking trolley and putting some rather droopy broccoli on to my plate.

'It's broccoli,' she says. 'You do like broccoli, don't you? I cooked it this morning and it should still be warm as I kept it in this trolley and it's heated.'

'I love broccoli,' I say.

'It's not hot,' says Mrs de Salis, 'so your baby can probably eat it with her fingers.'

Jamie wanders over and takes a look at the broccoli.

'I don't like that,' he says. 'I like biscuits.'

'Biscuits?' says Mrs de Salis. 'I may have some for pudding. First you should have chicken. Your mother told me you like chicken and here I have some in a white sauce.' She opens up the lid to a pot and puts two ladles full on Jamie's plate. Jamie looks at it dolefully.

'James,' says Noel, 'after lunch I'm sure Sarah will take you to see many wonderful things in this house, but in order to see these wonderful things you must eat. Eat, my dear boy. It's so good for you.'

Mrs de Salis then places her hand on top of a big silver dish, a bit like a chef. 'This is the pièce de résistance. Inside here is my favourite thing in the whole world – potato! My specially made, child-friendly mound of mashed potatoes.'

'Mashy potatoes!' says Jamie happily and then he sits down and starts eating a bowlful. 'I like these!'

'Wonderful!' says Noel as I stare at Jamie in amazement.

I give Noel a grateful smile as I serve Baby Sparkle and myself some food.

'I'll pass on the main course, Sarah,' says Noel. 'I'm

happy with my wine and, anyway, I've got to go after lunch. So maybe we could . . .'

'Yes, right,' says Mrs de Salis as she sits down. 'Well, Samantha. I'll tell you all about the house because obviously we're trying to save it and also, for various reasons, I've been going through old records and now I know lots of history about it and it really is a fascinating place. My husband, Gerrard, always referred to it as the "New House". This part we are sitting in was built in about 1806 on the site of the original house.'

'The original house?' I ask.

'Yes. There's documentation to show that there was a dwelling here in medieval times and, at some point, the farmhouse grew bigger and bigger and eventually became the home of the Lords of the Manor of Lincombe and Warcombe, hence its change of name to the Manor House.'

'What happened to it then?'

'Well, it was bought by my husband's family in the early to middle seventeen hundreds and then the original house mysteriously burned down. There are only some foundations and a bit of wall left of it. This New House was rebuilt in the late eighteenth and early nineteenth centuries. The main house is of historical importance because it's a fine example of the Georgian architecture of the day. It was built by a well-known domestic architect, so it's worth preserving, but it's the roof that is so problematic.'

'The problem with it,' says Noel, helping himself to another glass of wine, 'is that it needs a lot of restoration and it will cost a lot of money because only craftsmen who are skilled in traditional building of copper roofs with a leaf edge can renovate it.'

'Not only does the roof need doing,' says Mrs de Salis,

'but the walls are damp and the floorboards need treating as they're being eaten away by worms. This house is becoming virtually uninhabitable.'

We're all quiet for a bit and then Jamie puts his fork down.

'Finished!' he says triumphantly. He shows Noel his empty bowl. 'Can I have some biccies now?'

'Yes,' says Sarah. She disappears and comes back with a decidedly crumbly packet of Garibaldis.

'They seem to be out of date,' she says, passing me the packet.

'Oh, don't worry,' I say, spooning the last bit of mash down Baby Sparkle, 'biscuits never go out of date.'

But when I look at the sell-by sticker it says 'Dec. 1999'.

10. Field Characters

After Noel finishes his wine, he says he really has to leave. He kisses Sarah de Salis goodbye and then turns to me.

'I'll go and find Edward and Isabel,' he says. 'Do you want me to call Roisin for you and let her know how long you'll be here?'

'Oh, that would be very kind, Noel, but I should go now really, shouldn't I?'

Noel looks at Jamie, who is sitting back on the window seat, stroking the Hugger Mugger and singing away to himself.

'Stay here, Samantha. I'll sort everything out with Edward and Bennie for you. I'm sure they're fine and that little boy of yours,' he looks over to Jamie, 'seems very happy here.'

'It's you,' I say. 'I can't tell you . . .'

'You don't need to,' he says. 'I'm enjoying every minute of being with yourself and your family. It's the most enjoyable time I've had in an age, but you really must remain here because you need to see the garden. It's very important as that's where the fête is. You have to find something to make that Mr Henderson let us take the profits from the fête to spend on the roof and the garden. You have to hatch a plan with Sarah.'

He rummages around in his pocket. 'Ah, here's a piece of paper,' he says. 'Write Roisin's number down for me and then we're all sorted.'

After Noel leaves, Mrs de Salis suggests we sit in the

garden. She shows me, Jamie and Baby Sparkle out through the back of the house.

'This area was the old service quarters,' she tells me. We walk down a small dark passageway which houses a large horizontal freezer and many cardboard boxes.

'I keep meaning to unpack these,' she says, waving her hand towards the boxes, 'but I never get round to it.' Then she looks at the freezer as if it's something she has never seen before. 'Goodness me,' she says. 'I forgot about this freezer. No one's used it for years. I'll never forget Cook getting such a shock once. She opened it up and found a deer head in it.'

We pass by a large cloakroom full of coats and hats and shoes, some of which are small and obviously for children. There are some boy's lace-up shoes with clunky heels and some girl's pretty dancing shoes. They are made of black leather and they have bows on them.

We then pass what must have been a dairy, a larder and the kitchen. I can see some ancient scales which have weights on one side of them and a measuring pan on the other. There is a Kenwood Chefette lying on the table, a fondue set on top of the fridge and an old wooden spice rack with ceramic plaques on it saying 'thyme' and 'rosemary'. There is an electric kettle, a wood-burning stove and, set into the wall, a wooden box with a glass cover. In this box there are what seem to be small coloured light bulbs.

'What's that?' I ask Mrs de Salis, pointing towards the box.

'That's for the servants,' she says. 'Every room in this house has a bell, you see, so when someone wants something, they press the bell and the appropriate light goes off in here. If you need matches in the smoking room, for example, you press the bell and a servant sees which room you are in and they come in and find out what you want and then trot off to get the matches.'

'Did you have lots of servants?' I ask.

'Not really. When Gerrard was little, they did. They had a butler and a housekeeper and some maids and Cook, of course, and Nanny, and they had a groundsman and a gamekeeper and a ghillie to manage the pond and the stream, and a groom for the horses and a kennel man and a gardener, if not two or three, and there was a lady from the village who came with her daughter to do the laundry.'

'Good grief,' I say. 'That's so many people.'

'Everyone had staff then,' she says.

Jamie starts tugging at my trousers.

'What is it?' I ask him.

'I want to go and push the bell,' he says.

'Off you go then,' says Mrs de Salis. 'You find a bell and ring it and then we'll find you.'

Jamie trots off back down the passageway. Soon we hear him climbing up the stairs. Thump, thump, thump.

'I wonder where he's going,' says Mrs de Salis. 'There's not much up there, only a day- and two night-nurseries and four maids' bedrooms.'

Suddenly a bell rings from above us and a little light pings into life in the box on the wall.

'He's in nursery number one,' says Mrs de Salis. 'Follow me and I'll show the way.' We all go back down the passageway and up the narrow stairs. 'These are the servants' stairs,' Mrs de Salis tells me. 'Do you see? There's the grand staircase for the guests and this one for the backstairs staff. They both lead to the same place really.'

We pop out at the back of the first floor in another passageway. In front of me is the top hall, again in oak and covered in paintings, and to the back of me is one of the nurseries. We find Jamie in there, dancing around. It's a large room, painted yellow with a bare stripped wooden floor. In the corner of the room there's a basket of toys.

'Look!' says Jamie, showing me the Victorian china doll he's dancing with. 'A dolly! I like this dolly!'

I put Baby Sparkle on the ground and she sits on her bottom and shuffles over to the basket.

'All my dollies!' Jamie yells at her as she tries to pull a toy from the basket.

'Now, now, Jamie,' says Mrs de Salis. 'There are lots of toys for everyone. They used to belong to Philomena,' she says to me.

'Philomena?' I ask.

'Gerrard's sister,' she says. She then tells Jamie to pick a couple of toys as we are going back downstairs and out to the garden. 'If you do as I ask, and you stop swearing, you can bang the gong before you go home.'

Jamie claps his hands in delight. He takes two dollies from the basket then looks at Baby Sparkle. 'Here,' he says, thrusting one towards her.

'Ra-la-ra-la-ra-la,' she says, reaching out for it.

'Jamie!' I say. 'You're sharing with Sparkle. I've never seen you do that.'

'I'm a good boy,' he says, smiling.

Outside, Mrs de Salis takes my hand and leads me off to the left towards an expanse of flat lawn. There's a wrought-iron table and some chairs placed on a section of patio next to the house. Wisteria trails up this side of the house and the leaves offer some shade.

'I'd thought we'd sit here,' she says, 'because your baby can be out of the sun and we can discuss the fête. I always have it on this side lawn, the croquet lawn, because it's so flat.'

I tell her that I think this is probably the best place to hold the fête as it's very pretty. 'You have so many lovely flowers,' I say to her as I look at the beds that border the lawn.

'Yes, I do try to keep them going,' she says. 'I have violets in that shady corner.' She points over to a place where the rhododendrons have overgrown. 'I have primroses and bluebells too. There's also the Italian sunken garden. People used to come from miles around to see it, but now it's not in a very good condition. It really does have some exquisite plants though and I think you'd like to see them maybe.'

I nod my head and think for a while and then I say, 'I don't suppose you could open the gardens to visitors, could you?'

'We used to, but I'm afraid it's become very run down. I used to have a host of gardeners here, but they've all gone now.'

'Surely there's something here that people would pay to see? It's such a magnificent place.'

'That's very kind of you to say so,' says Mrs de Salis, 'but I'm afraid the Italian garden would no longer have the pull it used to have. I understand it was much in demand in its day. It was planted by Gerrard's great-grandfather's wife, Dorothy, as a way of attracting more butterflies into the garden. They were crazy on butterflies then, but now I think a lot of the plants are dead and gone.'

'Do you think we could rescue it? I don't know much about gardening, but . . .'

'Well, maybe in the future, but it needs serious excavation because I fear it has sunk rather more than it was supposed to have done originally.'

'Do you have anything else?' I ask.

'I have a tennis court, but that's overgrown now, and I have the Home Pond. Maybe you saw it on your way in? It's diverted from the stream. We always meant to have a ha-ha there, but the stream at the bottom of the garden gets in the way. Someone diverted it a long time ago and since then it has formed a pond on our land. I get wonderful things in my pond. I used to watch my husband's younger brothers swim in it. They used to catch newts and hold them up and squeeze them until they squeaked. Maybe I could charge people to swim in my pond?'

'No, I don't think that's going to do it either,' I say. 'No one lets their children swim in ponds any more. There's some health and safety rule about it probably.'

We decide to search for inspiration in one of the many outside sheds.

'I've got loads of interesting things in those sheds,' says Mrs de Salis, looking enthusiastic, so I gather up Jamie and Baby Sparkle, who's now looking sleepy again, and we wander back round to the rear end of the house where the old cobbled courtyard is. The back of the house is in a desperate state. The paint is flaking off the walls. The window frames are rotten and some of them have come away from the windows entirely. There are big gaps in the roof where the tiles have fallen off.

'Poor house,' says Mrs de Salis, looking at its arching wall. 'The problem, Samantha, is that I have a duty to maintain it, you see, and I can't afford to . . .' She opens the door of the first outbuilding and three wood pigeons fly out, cooing as they go.

'This is the old coach house,' she says, peering into the gloom. 'We used it as a garage. Now, what have we got here?'

I walk inside the coach house. I can see something large and shadowy.

Jamie peers in too.

'What's that in there?' he asks.

'I'm not sure,' I say. 'There's something pretty big in here,' I call out to Mrs de Salis. 'Do you have any idea what it is?'

I don't think she can hear me as she doesn't respond.

'Come on, Jamie,' I say. 'Let's go and explore.'

Jamie takes my hand and we make our way further into the outbuilding. The thing seems to be enveloped by a huge sheet. I look a bit more closely. 'I can't make it out,' I say to Jamie. 'We're going to have to try and get this cover off.'

I go to one end and grab the sheet and I pull very hard. Suddenly it falls off in a cloud of dust to reveal sheets of dark metal and large tyres with silver spokes and a red leather interior and shiny running boards.

'Oh my God,' I say in amazement. 'It's a car. It's an ancient car.'

'It's Chitty Chitty Bang Bang!' yells Jamie, bouncing up and down with excitement.

'Oh, I'd forgotten that was there,' says Mrs de Salis, now standing next to me and clapping her hands in excitement. 'It's the Wonderful Car. That's what Gerrard used to call it, the Wonderful Car.'

She starts brushing dust off the bonnet of the magnificent antique-looking motor.

'It's an old Model-T Ford. Isn't that amazing? I remember how everyone used to stare at us when we went out in this.'

'Can I get in it and play?' asks Jamie.

'Of course you must,' says Mrs de Salis. She leans in to open the front side door. It gives an enormous creak and then, miraculously for such an old car, opens up. Jamie jumps into the seat.

'Peep peep!' he yells, pretending to drive and moving the steering wheel this way and that. He's covered in dust.

'What a beautiful car,' I say, brushing some of the dust away. 'Look at that wood interior and those wonderful old dials. This must be a collector's item. Surely you could sell this and make loads of money, it's in such good condition?'

'Oh, no!' says Mrs de Salis. 'I couldn't sell it. Gerrard loved it so. I couldn't sell anything Gerrard loved, I'm afraid. I don't have much left of him and this car brings back so many happy memories.'

'Get out of the way!' yells Jamie, pretending to drive. 'Road hog at the wheel.'

'Well, maybe think about it,' I say. 'In the meantime, Jamie seems very happy to play in it.'

Mrs de Salis laughs.

Jamie carries on playing happily in the car as I push my way through some cobwebs towards the back of the garage. There I find an ancient but roomy Silver Cross pram and a very dirty but obviously once exquisite hand-made doll's house.

'There's a pram and a doll's house here,' I say. 'They're a bit dirty, but they do look lovely really. I don't suppose you'd want to sell them?'

'Oh, that's Gerrard's old pram!' says Mrs de Salis excitedly. 'And Philomena's doll's house. I can't believe they're still here.'

Jamie, who has got out of the car, is delighted to see the doll's house.

'I want to play with it, please,' he says.

Between us, Sarah de Salis and I manage to drag the doll's

house out from the garage. In the daylight you can see how beautiful it is. There are two floors to it and an attic and little hand-carved shutters and doors with tiny handles on them, and on the front door is a crest.

'That's the family crest,' says Mrs de Salis. 'It's a griffin on one side and a lion on the other, you see. How clever for someone to have carved such a miniature version of it. I think I'll just go and get a cloth and wipe it down so Jamie can play with it.'

Mrs de Salis then disappears back into the garage and pulls the pram out. 'I'll give this a clean too and then your baby can have a sleep. She looks so tired and I'm not sure if babies should really sleep sitting up in a pushchair like that. My mother always told me that babies should sleep lying down or else it would damage their kidneys.'

After we finish looking through the outbuildings, and once Baby Sparkle is happily sleeping in the Silver Cross and Jamie is playing with the doll's house, we sit down in the garden. There are no figures in the doll's house so Mrs de Salis ties two twigs together using thread from her sewing basket so that the twigs look like people with arms and legs.

'This one is Anne-Mary,' she says, wrapping a bit of cloth over a twig so it looks like a skirt, 'and this is Sebastian and here is Absalom their dog.' She finds a small fir cone that she uses for the dog.

Jamie's so happy with his new twig family that he sits down on the cobblestones and makes Anne-Mary and Sebastian walk up and down the stairs for the next half an hour. He's still happily playing with it as Mrs de Salis emerges on to the lawn pushing her rickety hostess trolley.

'Now,' she says, 'I've made tea.'

I tell Mrs de Salis I really should go, but she reminds me that Noel had promised to check on Edward and Bennie.

'I shall ring him if you like and make sure he has it all sorted out,' she says. 'I'd love you to stay for some tea if you will.' She goes off and I sit in the garden and close my eyes. I can hear the chirping of a bird, the rustling of the grass, a buzzing to the left of me and Mrs de Salis talking on the telephone far off on the right. I take a deep breath and then hone in on Jamie. 'You naughty Absalom,' he's saying in a high-pitched voice. 'How dare you steal the sausages.' Then I hear him say in a low voice, 'Hey, don't worry about that Anne-Mary. Chitty Chitty Bang Bang will come and rescue your baby.'

'He's an enchanting child really, isn't he?' says Mrs de Salis, coming back into the garden. 'I've called Noel and he says that he's talked to your friend and everything is fine and that your middle son can stay with her as long as he likes. Your eldest son and Isabel are also fine and they were at the beach, but now they're back at Noel's house.'

'Great,' I say as I feel myself relax.

'Your little boy likes it here, doesn't he?' she says.

'Yes,' I say. 'I've had a few problems with him, but he seems to be enjoying himself here in your house and garden. Maybe it's the freedom. And it's so relaxing here.'

She smiles wanly. 'Yes, it is, or was. It's too much for me now. I know Noel wants me to continue living here. He loves this house. He loves this whole area. He grew up here and the village is at the heart of his life. I think he feels that if we lose this house, we lose the spirit of what this village is. He has spent his life here working for his family firm, living the life that was expected of him. The only time he deviated from the path was when he married Letitia. She wasn't what Gerrard would call a good egg.'

'Why?' I ask, intrigued. 'What did she do?'

'She was a London girl. She came down here on holiday. It must have been about 1958 or 59. I can't quite remember. It was rare to find a fancy girl like Letitia all the way down here.'

'And Noel met her then?'

'Oh, yes. I remember him coming over to tell Gerrard and myself some terrific news. He said he'd met this girl and that he was totally smitten and he wanted to ask her to marry him. He was very excited and I suppose Gerrard and I were too because we'd had to wait for the war to end before we could marry. I'll never forget Gerrard coming up that drive with his head bandaged. He was never the same after that. He had ringing in his ears and he drank a bottle of wine with lunch every day and then another at night. I got used to it. It became normal for me because it was the only way Gerrard could forget what he had seen.' She shakes herself a bit. 'Gerrard died fifteen years ago, but he hadn't been right for the past half century really. I think that's what happened to many men of his generation. They survived but, in many ways, their lives were cut short in terms of the quality of them. Such a shame, really.'

Mrs de Salis sighs. 'Anyway, Gerrard and I had met Letitia only once on a walk. I didn't like the look of her particularly. She wore a lot of make-up, which I think is odd in a woman when you're going for a country walk. Noel and Letitia were married within the year and virtually nine months to the day later, they had Clarissa.'

'When did they split up then?'

'Not for about five years. Not until Noel found out that Letitia was seeing another man behind his back. Then she took their daughter Clarissa and the next thing we knew Clarissa was sent to boarding school.'

'Why?'

'I must choose my words carefully here. I think Letitia humiliated him in his eyes.'

'How so?'

'Noel was a talented man, very intelligent and ambitious, but he had no choice than to work in the family law firm. I think it hurt his pride when Letitia left him and I think he punished his wife through the daughter.'

'But if that's the case, why does Clarissa send Isabel down here to stay with a man who rejected her?'

'Ah, that's human nature, isn't it?' says Sarah. 'It's like a bee to honey. Clarissa wants her father's love and approval, but she's remote from him both emotionally and physically. She lives in Scotland and doesn't that happen when you're distant from someone? Don't you decide they're the most wonderful person ever? That's what your memory does to you.'

11. Pre-dusk Light

An hour later, Jamie and me and Baby Sparkle have walked back to Lower Strand and are now in the car on the way to the beach. Jamie looks exhausted. He's in the back of the car on his booster seat with the strap going across his front. He's fast asleep and his head is lolling from one side to the other. He has taken off all his clothes apart from a pair of orange and white striped towelling knickers. My mother made them for me when I was small and somehow Jamie found them at the back of my wardrobe. I don't know why I kept them really. Maybe because I used to love wearing them. My mother made me and my sister Julia an identical pair each with matching towelling hoodie robes to wear on top and we spent our childhood holidays clad in these outfits, looking for crabs on the beaches of Cornwall. I've always meant to make my own children similar things to wear on the beach but, unlike my mother, I cannot sew. My mother finds this unbelievable.

'Why don't you make your children clothes?' she asked me when she saw a package from a children's clothing mail order company arriving at our door. 'I made nearly all your clothes. I don't know what's wrong with your generation. You have no concept of what the word frugal means.'

I told her that a) that wasn't true and b) it depended on what meaning you put on the word frugal.

'I understand the concept of frugality,' I said to her. 'I

shall explain it to you. Here I am, me, Samantha Smythe, mother of four, trying to look after my children and look after my marriage and the house and the animals and the shopping and the cooking and do a bit of work. So, do you know what, my spare time is in short supply at the moment and, when I actually have any, I like to spend it having fun with my children rather than making towelling robes which I can buy very easily over the Internet. I could be frugal about spending money on clothes and make them myself, but then I would have to be frugal with my time. Do you see? I choose not to be frugal with my love and so I buy clothes instead.'

'Now you're just being ridiculous,' said my mother rather huffily.

'It's called being Time Poor,' I told her.

THE PROBLEM WITH BEING TIME POOR

Before I had children I thought I was busy. I really and truly thought I was. The fact that I would sometimes lie in until mid-morning at the weekend seemed to be my right. It never occurred to me to truly enjoy it as I hadn't fully understood how it would be snatched away from me in later years. When my sister, who had children much earlier than me, would ring up at 9.30 a.m. for a chat and say things like, 'Oh, I've been waiting for an age to talk to you,' I thought she was mad because 9.30 a.m. was pretty early in the morning in those days. I'd say to her, 'Couldn't you have rung me later?' and she'd say, 'But this is later,' and then I'd yawn and she'd get cross and put the phone down on me. What was I thinking in those days? Not only that, what actually did I do? I didn't really go shopping, not for food anyway, which takes up virtually all my life at the moment. We get through enough food in this household to feed the entire Horn of Africa.

No, I don't even remember what I used to eat then. I never cooked unless I had people round for dinner and back then I didn't have people round for dinner because none of us had children so we all went out for dinner. We never went anywhere expensive, as we may do now on the rare occasion such as my birthday when we venture to our local posh restaurant. We just went to local Italian restaurants and ate pasta. My cooking obsession didn't start until I had children. Neither did my love of drinking wine. I barely touched it before I had Edward. I certainly couldn't have told you if I liked a St Emilion or a Châteauneuf du Pape.

No parents have any time. There is just too much to do in one day, even when that day starts three hours earlier than it used to do. We all know what needs to be done and yet it takes so long to do it. Why does it? This is why: there are forces out there working against the parent. They are invisible forces, but still, there they are making our lives a misery. For example, every day I go upstairs and downstairs and up the stairs again, sorting out laundry. I get the laundry from the dryer and I take it to my bedroom and I sort it into piles on the bed. I've found this is the most time-effective way of doing it. I can then whirl my arms around, just like an octopus, and somehow get all John's clothes and all my clothes put away in a nano second. I will then do the children's clothes. This is more difficult as both Edward and Bennie wear grey socks for school and, even though Edward is twice the size of Bennie, their socks manage to somehow look the same size. This means that I have to hold every grey sock up to every other grey sock to see which ones match in style and shade. I can then pair the socks off and make a stab at separating the underpants, which also look the same, bar Jamie's as most of his are pink, and put their clothes in their rooms.

Then there's the hour it takes to do the shopping order and another hour gone for clearing up the house and then take another two for all the rest of the times I clear up the house during a 24-hour period. Then there's the cooking, which takes an age, and, occasionally, I might even get to answer the telephone. Therefore, because I'm Time Poor, I don't get to go out shopping for clothes. In fact, I barely go out at all. Sometimes I find I haven't ventured out of the valley in which I live for a week. I only know this because I find myself having gibbering conversations with the flowers in the garden. That's when I know I've finally lost it.

Another problem with being Time Poor is that nothing gets done properly. Children's homework is completed in a random fashion while I stir the cheese sauce, feed the baby and persuade Bennie to stick pictures from nursery rhymes into his book. We'll look at the pictures together: there'll be one of an old lady wearing a bonnet looking in a cupboard and one with a dog looking sadly at a bowl and then one of the bonneted woman and the dog tripping off somewhere.

'Right, Bennie,' I'll say in an encouraging tone. 'Now you must stick these pictures in your homework book in the right order.' Just then the cheese sauce is most likely to overflow or the baby will try and do a back flip out of her high chair and my attention will be distracted while Bennie does his cutting and gluing. The consequence of my lack of attention will be that Old Mother Hubbard somehow goes to the shops and then finds the cupboard empty . . .

There's only one answer to being Time Poor and it's this:

throw money at it. Get someone to help with the garden/the cleaning/the cooking/the kids/learn nursery rhymes. If you can't do that, which most of us can't, then find shortcuts. My shortcut is never to own up to being able to do anything much. I pretend I can't mow the lawn (of course I can) or rod the drains or change a tyre on the cars. And never, ever knit or even start to knit unless you enjoy it. Cheat on the cooking. No one needs a home-made pudding every day. Don't make your own mayonnaise. We have to adjust to survive. And never, ever make your own clothes or anyone else's for that matter.

But Jamie has somehow found my ancient towelling knickers and now he's wearing them and looking very cute in them as well. Maybe my mother has a point. Maybe I love these knickers so much because they were made by her. What an act of love, to be sitting there at night cutting and sewing by hand, with nothing more than a taper candle to light the room . . . but now I know I've gone truly mad. I'm stuck in the world of Mrs de Salis. My mother had electric lights, for goodness' sake! But, then again, maybe if I made Jamie's clothes he might wear them and not try to copy Baby Sparkle's.

I look at Baby Sparkle. She's in a pink, floaty smock top with nothing else on apart from a nappy. She has such a sweet face, rather exquisite I think. Even when she was little she was exquisite. After she was born I kept meeting other women with their babies. I remember one lady in the supermarket who showed me her baby and I nearly had to cover my face to hide the shock I felt.

'This is Roseanna,' she said to me as she turned the baby she was carrying towards me. It was the ugliest baby I had ever seen – red face, ginger hair, cradle cap and a head that looked shaved away like a Smartie.

'How lovely,' I said and walked off smartly with Sparkle, who was in her sling. 'Thank God you don't look like that,' I said to her and she furled her little hand round itself and yawned.

But I do truly believe that Baby Sparkle is rather pretty and that's not just because I'm her mother. I'm more than capable of owning up to the fact that both Edward – huge forehead like Frankenstein – and Bennie – looked like an old man who'd been in the war – were not attractive babies. Jamie was beautiful, of course. 'What a lovely shaped head,' my mother said when she saw him and, fortunately for Baby Sparkle, she seems to be heading in the cute-Jamie direction rather than the stuffed-sausage way of Bennie. Poor Bennie. He's now so big that he has to wear clothes for children three years older than him so he can do his trousers up.

I have a slight pang about Bennie. Oh God, I didn't explain to Roisin that Bennie has to eat all the time. I now imagine that I'll turn up to the beach to find Bennie dying of hunger in the middle of the sand, lying there gasping like a beached white whale. When we get to the car park, however, I see Bennie immediately because he's on his way up the steps from the café. Lorcan is walking behind him and behind the two of them is Roisin, talking on her phone with one hand while dragging two sets of buckets and spades behind her with the other. I get out of the car and wave at her and she tries to wave back but is too laden down. Bennie, however, sprints towards me as soon as he sees me.

'Muummmyyy!' he yells, careering into my legs and virtu-ally knocking me over.

'Bennie!' I say, bending down and giving him a hug. 'How are you? Have you had a nice time?'

'I've had a great time!' he says. 'You won't believe what I did!'

'What did you do, darling?'

'Me and Lorcan and Lorcan's mum made a huge sandcastle and then we got lots of buckets of water to put in the moat and then we got really hot so we had a swim and then, guess what?'

'What?' I say, pretending to be very excited.

'Then we went to the café and Lorcan's mum bought us juice and sandwiches and some fruit and a thing called a smoothie and then, because Lorcan's mum said we'd been so good, she bought us an ice cream!'

'Wow,' I say, looking at Roisin, who has finally got up the steps and put down the buckets.

'I had a Glup!' says Bennie.

'They're called Gulps,' says Roisin apologetically. 'I hope you don't mind him having one, it was just so hot and . . .'

'No, that's so kind of you. They've obviously had a great time. You must let me pay for all that food.'

'No,' says Roisin. 'Absolutely not. Now, how was your day?'

'Great,' I say.

'Are you going to tell me about it over a coffee?' she says. 'You were being a mite mysterious earlier on with your older man friend.'

'Oh, Noel,' I say. 'Are you sure you've got time? I thought you might be keen to get home.' I indicate her phone.

'No, I just had to make another bloody work call. Honest to God, you'd think I was a director of this company the work they put on me. If they carry on, I'm going to tell them where they can stick their job. The boys had to come with me as I couldn't leave them on the beach alone. C'mon now. Let's leave the buckets by your car and go and get a coffee.'

I'm about to tell her that, actually, I can't as the younger two children are asleep when I hear Jamie from the inside of the car.

'Benniiee,' he wails plaintively.

Bennie opens the door,

'Hello, Jamie,' he says. 'I had an ice cream.'

'I want an ice cream,' says Jamie, rubbing his eyes and beginning to wail again, which wakes up Baby Sparkle. 'I WANT ICE CREAM!'

'Jamie,' I say. 'You have to ask nicely.'

Jamie looks at me in a cross fashion. 'Please, then,' he says.

'Yes, you can,' I say.

'Looks like ice creams all round then,' says Roisin as I unstrap Jamie and start on Sparkle.

'I can have another ice cream then?' says Bennie. 'Yippee!' Then he and Lorcan and Jamie, who is now out of the car, run back to the steps and start pounding their way down to the café.

'Hungry boys, eh?' says Roisin, raising an eyebrow.

Five minutes later we are in the café. The three boys have got their ice creams and have run down to eat them on the beach. Baby Sparkle is grasping a fruit ice lolly.

'Ra-la-ra-la-ra,' she says, exploring it with her tongue as the lolly melts over her hands. While Roisin gets the coffees, I look out towards the beach. I decide that tea time is a beautiful time to be on the beach. The sun is going down and people's shadows are long on the sand. The air is wonderfully warm, but less hot than at lunch time. I can see people playing bat and ball games. I can hear them laughing. There's a dog careering in and out of the water, chasing a ball.

'It's perfect, isn't it?' says Roisin, sitting down.

'Mmm,' I say. I look at Roisin. 'Your freckles have come out,' I say to her.

'Oh, they always do that,' she says, pushing a strand of hair behind her ear. It strikes me then that Roisin is actually very attractive. I hadn't really spotted it before, but now I can see she has a lovely wide face and red lips and wonderful hair.

'This beach life suits you,' I say.

She laughs again. 'Well, it's very relaxing,' she says. 'At home I'm always rushing about trying to do Lorcan and work and . . .'

'Does he see his father at all?'

'No,' she says. 'He's not interested. He . . . well, we met years ago at school and for a while I thought he was the dog's bollocks, but then he started drinking and spending all the money I earned so . . . I chucked him out. Best thing I ever did. It's not bad being on your own, y'know.'

'I was on my own for a bit,' I tell her, although I'm not quite sure why. 'I was married before to the man who's Edward's father.'

'Aah,' says Roisin, looking interested. 'You mentioned that before. So your husband's not Edward's dad?'

'No.'

'How does that work out then?'

'Fine,' I say. 'Edward calls him dad and he loves his siblings. He gets on very well with John, but . . .'

'But what?' she asks, looking sympathetically at me.

'Since we've been down here, Edward's been acting a bit strangely.'

'In what way?' she asks, so I tell her about how the house down here used to belong to his real father's mother and the fact that he overheard the row between John and me. 'I think he's questioning things right now,' I say.

'I'm sure he is,' says Roisin. 'Well, you best tell your husband what's going on and ask him to get a bit more involved.'

'He is involved!' I say, feeling a little defensive. 'It's just that he's had so much work on and I've been so busy with Jamie and the baby . . .'

'Exactly,' she says. 'You can't hold up the entire sky all by yourself, y'know.'

We sit in silence for a while and drink our coffee, me wondering why I've suddenly told Roisin my life story and she probably wondering if she has, somehow, overstepped the mark. Then she asks me to tell her about my day and what I was up to so, rather relieved to change the subject, I explain everything to her. It seems to take forever, but Roisin listens carefully, head on one side. Occasionally she bends forward to wipe Baby Sparkle's hands for me or she turns her head to see what the boys are up to. When I finish she says, 'Yes, right, I see your problem. You need to save the house and you need to find ways of making money.'

I tell her that's precisely it. Then I tell her about the possibility of John bringing the puppet show down to the fête.

'Now that sounds like a good idea,' she says. 'It would be grand if he was here and you're right about those yummy mummies. They're constantly sending their children off to learn languages. Sometimes I think I should set myself up as a Gaelic teacher in Galway. I could charge a fortune.'

She thinks for a bit and then says, 'Look, the way I see it is this. If you get enough stuff of your own going on at the fête and you publicize it enough, then that man on the village council will have no choice but to let the profits go towards saving the house. You could sort of shame him into it.'

'How?' I ask her.

'Well, you could make flyers, y'know. If your husband is bringing that puppet show then you could make flyers advertising his show and put that it's at the fête and then you'd sort of take the fête over, wouldn't you?'

'Yes,' I say. 'That's a great idea. I'll call John later. And I have a computer here! Edward could do some flyers, and he and Isabel could deliver them round the village.'

'I'm sure me and Lorcan could help too,' says Roisin.

'You should meet John. He's coming down tomorrow night with my best friend, Dougie. In fact, Dougie's single like you. We could be like a committee! We'll show that Mr Henderson. Actually,' I say a bit recklessly, 'why don't you come to dinner? You and me and John and Dougie?'

'Well, maybe,' says Roisin, now sounding a bit doubtful.

'Does it sound like I'm setting you up? I'm not setting you up, honestly I'm not, and anyway, I ought to invite Noel as he's at the epicentre of all this.'

Roisin's face clears. 'Well, yes then,' she says. 'I'd love to.' She looks down to the beach. 'Ah,' she says. 'I wondered when she'd appear.'

I follow her gaze to see Susie coming towards us. She's wearing rolled-up skinny jeans held round her waist by a large leather belt with a huge buckle, Spanish riding boots and a bikini top. She has a pendant, which flashes silver and gold, nestling between her breasts. Karin is right behind her. She's wearing a voluminous pink kaftan that clashes with her face, which has gone the colour of a squashed raspberry.

'Where are the kids?' I ask Roisin, noticing neither Susie's nor Karin's children are with them.

'Probably with Jolka,' she says. 'Can you hear anyone saying "Li li"?'

'No,' I say, giggling. 'So you've heard it too?'

'Apparently Susie makes Jolka talk to those girls in Mandarin.'

'But she's Polish!'

'Yes,' says Roisin, laughing, 'that's why she only knows one word.'

I'm about to ask Roisin how she knows any of this when Susie and Karin get to the table.

'Hi,' says Susie laconically. 'May we join you?'

'Yes,' both Roisin and I say.

'Get us a coffee will you, Karin?' says Susie, not even looking towards Karin but waving a five-pound note at her. 'I'm not supposed to drink coffee really. My Chinese doctor told me I'm hot and wet, or cold and dry, or something like that, and apparently coffee makes everything much worse. Then again, what's worse? Me being hot and wet because I've had coffee or being bad-tempered because I haven't. That's why I bought this.' She points at the pendant. It's very beautiful. It's in the style of a Coptic cross, but one side of it is dark silver and the other seems to be burnished gold.

'What is it?' asks Roisin.

'It's a mood changer,' says Susie. 'It works on my body's electro-magnetic aura and it's supposed to keep me calm.'

'Does it?' I ask.

'Yes, I think it does,' she says. 'It helps me cope with those girls of mine.'

'Actually, where are your daughters?' I ask.

'Anti and Alli?' she says. 'They were in the sea with Jolka about an hour ago, but now I have no idea. Where are all your brood?'

I point towards Baby Sparkle. Her face is covered in melted orange lolly.

'Oh, so attractive,' says Susie. 'What about your boys?'

I nod my head towards the beach.

'Oh, yes. I saw your middle son playing with Lorcan earlier on, but I didn't see you. Where have you been?'

'Samantha's been organizing the local fête,' says Roisin quickly.

'Local fête?' asks Karin, who has just reappeared with some coffee. 'I got us all some chocolate tiffin,' she says in a guilty fashion. 'You know, we're on holiday and all that . . .'

'Not for me,' says Susie, lighting a cigarette.

'I'll have some,' says Roisin firmly, picking up a piece of the chocolate cake.

Susie raises an eyebrow. 'Do you feel guilty when you eat chocolate?' she asks Roisin. 'My Chinese doctor says –'

'No, I don't feel guilty,' says Roisin.

'Neither do I,' says Susie. 'Not that I ever eat chocolate, but guilt is such a wasted emotion.'

'I feel really dreadful when I eat chocolate,' says Karin, putting an entire tiffin in her mouth.

'Why do you eat it then?' Susie asks.

'Why does anyone eat chocolate?' says Roisin. 'We eat it because it's delicious.'

'It's called comfort food though, isn't it?' says Susie, looking at Karin. 'You know, it's the type of thing people eat when they're unhappy.'

'Actually, I don't agree,' says Roisin. 'I eat it because I love it.'

'But maybe you're unhappy,' says Susie.

Roisin laughs. 'Jeeesus,' she says. 'You don't let up now, do you, girl?'

Susie laughs as well and so does Karin as she surreptitiously reaches out for another tiffin.

Susie then turns back to me.

'About this fête, Samantha,' she says. 'Who would have put you down as the organized type?'

I'm about to tell Susie that I am, in fact, highly organized as I have so many children, when Roisin butts in.

'Her husband's bringing down a French puppet theatre. They're doing an amazing show over the summer which is touring all round Europe and it's sold out all over the place.'

I stare at Roisin. She pointedly ignores me.

'Sold out?' says Karin, slightly spitting tiffin from her mouth without realizing.

'Oh, yes,' says Roisin. 'Haven't you read about it? All the tickets have gone in London. They're selling on eBay for up to a thousand pounds.'

'I think I might have read about them,' says Karin excitedly, having finally swallowed her cake.

'Well, you'd remember,' says Roisin, 'because the show is all done in French.'

'French?' says Susie, looking interested.

'Yes,' says Roisin. 'Apparently everyone who's anyone is taking their children to see it because it's supposed to be creative and educational at the same time.'

'And your husband is a French puppeteer, is he, Samantha?' asks Susie drily.

'No,' I say. 'He's designing the set and they need somewhere to preview it and I suggested here, at the local village fête.'

'You are joking,' says Susie. 'An avant-garde French puppet show is actually coming to Lower Strand?'

'Actually, it's a sold-out, much-in-demand French puppet show that's coming to Lower Strand,' says Roisin.

'How much are the tickets?' asks Karin. 'I've been on and on at Aaron to learn French. He went away to Auch last summer to stay with a family, but when he came back he barely spoke any more French than when he went away.'

'Why not?' I ask.

'Oh,' says Karin miserably, 'I think he just played on their PlayStation all the time.'

'I keep telling you,' says Susie. 'You have to stop letting him do that.'

'He was in France!' says Karin. 'What else could I do?'

'Karin,' says Susie sharply. 'Take some responsibility, would you?'

'The tickets are ten pounds,' says Roisin, talking over Susie. I stare at her again. She ignores me again.

'Ten pounds!' exclaims Karin.

'Yes, that's a bit steep, isn't it?' says Susie.

'They're thirty pounds for the London show and you won't get one for those shows anyway, not for love nor money, so ten pounds is a bargain.'

OK,' says Karin. 'You've convinced me. I'll have two then, one for me and one for Aaron.'

'I suppose I'll have three,' says Susie. 'One for Jolka and two for the girls.'

'Aren't you going to come?' I ask her. 'My husband says it's going to be really good.'

'Oh, yes, your husband,' says Susie. 'I keep forgetting he does this strange job. Yes, I will come. Maybe it's worth ten pounds just to meet your other half, Samantha.'

'Where's your husband then, Susie?' Roisin asks her. 'Doesn't he go on holidays? Or is he one of those high-earning banker types who works all the time?'

'Yes, he is one of those high-earning banker types, thank you for asking,' says Susie, stirring her half-fat latte. 'Actually, he's on holiday right now. He's on a beach in Thailand with his girlfriend.'

Everyone at the table is silent.

'Oh dear,' says Susie as she stirs a bit faster. 'I've shocked you, haven't I?'

'A bit,' says Roisin.

Susie sighs. 'Don't feel sorry for me, please,' she says. 'He pays for everything. I have a good life and, anyway, I don't really care if my husband's having an affair – at least he's still having sex with me.'

She then looks up. 'Ah, Anti and Alli,' she says, noticing her children, both clad in rolled-down wetsuits, coming up the steps into the café. 'Perfect timing.'

Later on, when we've all left the beach and made our way to the car park, Roisin says, 'I think Susie's very unhappy. I feel sorry for her. I mean, you're here on your own, but your husband is coming down at the weekend. I'm here on my own because I chucked my husband out. But Susie's here alone because her husband chooses to be with another woman. That's not great, is it?'

We both look towards Susie. She's sitting sideways and facing out of the driver's seat of her BMW 4x4, smoking a cigarette. Her long, slim brown legs are dangling down the side. Her two daughters are sitting in the back seat. Meanwhile, Jolka is loading the beach bags into the boot of the car.

'I don't feel sorry for her,' I say, suddenly feeling irritated as I lunge to stop the pushchair from rolling down the hill as I try to collapse it. 'Why doesn't she do anything for herself?'

'Maybe because she's making her husband pay for being unfaithful,' says Roisin. 'Maybe that's the only way she can get back at him.'

'I don't know,' I say, 'and in many ways I don't care. I've got a fête to organize and . . .' Then I remember what Roisin had said about the tickets. I was so stunned by Susie's revelation that, up until now, I'd totally forgotten the whole French puppet thing.

'Roisin,' I say, 'what on earth are you playing at?'

'What do you mean?' she says innocently, fixing her sun hat on her head.

'About the puppet show. I don't even know if it's coming here. And what's all that stuff about it being sold out and tickets going for a fortune on eBay?'

'It's all blarney,' says Roisin happily, 'but, look, I've made you sixty pounds already and that was in five minutes flat.'

'But what if it isn't coming?'

'Now that ain't my fault, Mrs Smythe,' says Roisin. 'That's between you and y'man. C'mon, Samantha. You'll just have to be persuasive.' She raises an eyebrow at me.

'God, Roisin,' I say, half frustrated and half amused. 'You really are . . . you really are . . .'

'Irish,' says Roisin. 'That's right. I really am Irish,' and she laughs as she walks off.

I get in the car to go, shaking my head in disbelief, but then, as I start the engine, I hear a horn peeping next to me. It's Susie. Her window is down. I stall the car and wind my window down as well.

'Is anything up?' I ask her.

'Actually, it is,' she says. 'I don't know if I should . . .' She looks behind her at her daughters. One of them, I don't know which one, nods her head. 'OK, here goes,' she says. 'Look, Anti told me just a minute ago that she saw your eldest son earlier on today. What's his name again?'

'Edward.'

'Yes, Edward, and apparently he was being very, well, very –' she turns her head back towards her daughter – 'he was being very strange.'

'What do you mean, strange?'

'Apparently he was with a girl and they were behaving weirdly.'

'What do you mean, weirdly?' I ask.

'I don't know,' Susie says sharply. 'Just in an odd fashion. That's all Anti would say and I thought I ought to let you know because, well, because you're his mother.'

'Right,' I say. 'Thanks.' I go to wind up my window, but Susie puts her hand on my door to stop me.

'Actually, Samantha,' she says, 'where is Edward?'

'He's with his friend Isabel at her grandfather's house.'

'Yes, but do you actually know that?'

'Yes,' I say.

'OK,' she says, 'just asking. I mean, I wouldn't even let Anti and Alli go to the loo by themselves.'

'He's twelve years old, Susie, and he's not by himself. He's at my friend's house.'

'Yes, but you don't know what he's been up to, do you?' she says, looking a bit triumphant. 'That's why you should have staff, dear.' Then she winds up her window and drives off.

A few hundred yards up the road, I come across Roisin. She's walking along, swinging hands with Lorcan. I pull over in front of her and stop the car. She comes to the window.

'What's up?' she says.

'I thought you might want a lift.'

'No, we're fine,' she says. 'I could do with the exercise after my two ice creams plus the bleeding tiffin.' Then she looks at my face. 'Then again,' she says, 'it's been a long day so, yes, thanks for the lift. C'mon, Lorcan. Let's get in the car.'

She puts Lorcan in the boot with Bennie, who has found a packet of crisps to share with him, and then she gets in the front.

'What's up?' she says as I drive towards Lower Strand.

I tell her about what Susie has just told me.

'What does "behave weirdly" actually mean?' asks Roisin when I've finished. 'I mean, Jesus, most kids behave weirdly, it just depends what you count as weird. I mean, I think that wearing a wetsuit halfway down your body is weird, but what would I know . . .'

'I know,' I say, 'you're right. I can't put my finger on it though, but there *is* something odd about Isabel.'

'What kind of odd?'

'She wears a G-string.'

'Yes, but she is thirteen. Lord, I was doing much worse things than that at her age.'

'Were you?' I say, intrigued.

'Oh, I smoked and drank and – Edward's a good kid, isn't he? That's what you were telling me on the beach really, weren't you?'

'Yes,' I say.

'Well, you have to trust him then,' she says. 'C'mon, Samantha. He's not a little boy any more. He's nearly thirteen and this is a small, safe place. If you're ever going to give him some freedom, this is the place to start. I mean, what harm can he and his friend be getting up to anyway?'

'I'm not used to giving him freedom,' I say.

'Well, get used to it,' says Roisin. 'You've done him proud. He's not an eejit, is he?'

'No.'

'So, maybe he'll drink an alcopop here and there. He's definitely going to drink his fair share of alcopops and maybe he'll smoke a cigarette and do all that stuff in his life anyway. At the end of the day, he has your values held in his heart so . . . do y'know what I'm trying to tell you?'

'Yes, but I worry. I've barely been able to concentrate on him for ages because of the other children . . . but, yes, you're probably right. I'll try to stop worrying so much.'

When we get to Lower Strand, Roisin asks me to drop her outside the village shop.

'Here's grand,' she says. 'I need to get some bacon and eggs for dinner.'

'I love bacon and eggs,' says Bennie from the back. 'I'm starving.'

'Ma,' says Lorcan, 'can Bennie come for tea?'

'No, Lorcan,' I say. 'Your poor mum's had Bennie all day.'

'He's no trouble,' says Roisin, 'and he's more than welcome to come for tea.'

'OK, thanks, Roisin,' I say. 'I'll return the favour another day.'

I leave her and Lorcan and Bennie at the shop. Bennie waves to me as I drive off.

12. Night Trapping

When we get to the house, I get Jamie and Baby Sparkle from the car and start running Jamie a bath. Once it's ready, I go to get Jamie and carry him through to the bathroom.

'Right, Jamie,' I say to him, 'it's time to give you a bath.'

'My no sike baths,' he says, trying to scrunch his feet up to avoid getting in.

'It's "I don't like baths", Jamie, remember? That's what Noel has taught you and you are covered in sand. If you don't have a bath you'll get sand all in your bed.'

'I like sand in my bed.'

'No, you don't. No one likes sand in their beds.'

'I do,' he says truculently. 'I'm going to put sand in my bed and in Sparkle's cot.'

'Jamie,' I say, 'you've been so good and kind recently. I don't want to see you being naughty again.'

'I AM NOT NAUGHTY!' he shouts. He grabs the side of the bath and tries to get out.

'You're not getting out,' I say firmly, trying to remember what the child psychologist had said: 'Reward good behaviour and ignore the bad.' She had made me repeat it like a mantra. So I ignore the fact that Jamie is in the process of clambering out of the slippery sides and instead I start soaping his body down.

'Get off!' he says. 'Go away! I want my daddy!'

'Tough luck,' I say. 'You've got me and I'm not going

away. I'm going to wash you and then you can get out of the bath.'

'I want to get out now!' he yells. 'I WANT MY DADDY!'

I carry on soaping away.

'I want to get out NOW, YOU STUPID!' he yells again.

I reach over and grab the shampoo bottle from the shelf. Jamie looks at me in horror. 'Nooo!' he says. 'You are not to wash my hair.'

'Well, Jamie,' I say, trying to keep my voice steady and calm like the psychologist told me to. 'I'm going to wash your hair because you've been itching it all day and it has sand in it.'

'Nooo!' says Jamie again as I approach him with the shampoo. 'YOU DO NOT WASH MY HAIR!'

But I'm not to be deterred. I find a plastic bucket that has been handily abandoned on the floor and I fill it with bath water and – whoosh – I pour it over Jamie's head.

'Arrgghh!' screams Jamie loudly. 'You get off! You get off!'

But I'm into the rhythm now. I'm empowered. This little child is not going to get the better of me. I grab the bucket again.

'No water!' yells Jamie, flailing his arms around like an injured sea anemone.

'I've got to get the soap out,' I say, holding his arms down firmly.

'Aarrgghh!' yells Jamie once again. 'Daddy! Daddy! Get my daddy!' But just as I'm about to pour another bucket of water on his head, I hear a noise from the kitchen. It's a wailing, crying noise and it's obviously coming from Baby Sparkle.

'Waaa!' she howls.

'Baby Sparkle is crying, Mummy,' says Jamie, his head covered in soap suds.

'Right,' I say, letting him go. 'Do not get out of the bath, Jamie. When I get back I'll finish washing your hair.'

I run into the kitchen. Baby Sparkle is in the middle of the room, sitting on her bottom. As soon as she sees me she starts crying again, even more loudly than before. Her pretty face goes bright red and she reaches her arms up for me.

'Oh, my darling,' I say to her as I scoop her up. 'What happened?' Baby Sparkle cries even more and moulds her body into mine, pressing her face into my neck.

'Why's she crying?' asks Jamie, who is now standing in the kitchen doorway, dripping wet and still covered in soap suds.

'Jamie! I told you not to get out of the bath.'

Jamie smiles at me.

Then we hear a knock at the back door. 'Hello!' says a cheery voice. It's Noel.

'Noel,' I call out to him. 'Come in.'

'Are you all right?' he says as he comes into the kitchen.

'No. Is Edward with you?'

'Not right now. He and Isabel are watching a DVD.' Noel then turns and sees Jamie. The soap suds seem to have dripped off his head and are gradually working their way down his body.

'Ah, James,' says Noel. 'You're covered in soap. I could hear you crying about it halfway up the street.'

'Yes,' says Jamie, smiling sweetly at Noel.

'Well, why don't you get back in the bath and rinse off because I have something very interesting for us to do.'

'What?' asks Jamie, his eyes like saucers.

'Tonight, my dear boy, we are going to try and catch a *Tetheella fluctuosa*.'

'A what?' I say.

'A Satin Lutestring. It's a lovely little moth, brown with a small dark crescent in the centre of its forewing. They're quite common round here and they like light and also, very much, wine strings.'

'What a lovely name!' I say. 'A Satin Lutestring.'

'Oh, they are very lovely,' he says. Then he goes and kneels down in front of Jamie. 'Would you like to help me find my Satin Lutestring? I have to make a record of them in my book and then send it to the *Entomologist's Gazette*. They are very keen to know what variety of species we have here as so few people actually log down what they see. You could be my little helper, James. How does that sound?'

'Ooh,' says Jamie excitedly. 'That sounds lovely!' Then he turns round and tiptoes back to the bathroom and we hear a splash.

'I really think you're a magician,' I say to Noel. 'You have put a spell on Jamie and magicked good behaviour from him.'

'I'm here to please, Samantha,' he says. 'And being with James takes me back to when I was a child. I used to go moth hunting with my grandfather. He was an amazing man. He wasn't a rich man, but he made a small living working for the Daubeny-Fortescues who lived at the big house.'

'What did your grandfather do for them?' I ask, intrigued.

'Well, the lord of the house's wife was mad on butterflies. She'd catch them in her net and chloroform them and pin them very neatly in rows in glass cases. Then she'd write their names in tiny neat handwriting underneath them.'

'Yes, I've seen cases of butterflies in museums. I always feel sorry for them.'

'Oh, don't feel sorry for them! Some butterflies barely live the summer. Isn't it better to be immortalized in all your beauty? To be drugged to a sleepy death and then pinned forever in a case to be admired by generations of people? How wonderful! Butterflies look to me as if they were meant to be put on show, for they are such showy creatures, don't you think? Anyway, Lord Fortescue decided that he wanted his own comprehensive butterfly and moth collection to give as a gift to his wife. He asked around for someone to do this for him and that's how he met my grandfather, who was well known locally for his love of entomology. He would catch butterflies and then spend hours on end making illustrations of them in a book.'

'He must have been delighted when he was asked to do his hobby as a job.'

'He was. Lord Fortescue gave him the gatehouse to live in and some money on top, and he spent his days travelling around in order to chase down and collate information about every butterfly and moth in the country. He made a comprehensive illustrated catalogue of the butterfly and moth population. His books came to be known as the *Daubeny-Fortescue Catalogues of Lepidoptera*.'

'And did Lord Fortescue like these books?'

'Oh, yes. But as my grandfather grew older, he started having a problem with moths. Interestingly, my grandfather worshipped butterflies. He could tell you at great length about the mating habits of the Dingy Skipper or the Green Hairstreak, but if you asked him about the Tree-lichen Beauty he'd become very quiet.'

'Why?'

'My father said that, as he got older, he became a very depressed man and that his depression seemed to be directly linked to moths. You see, my grandfather lived through both World Wars. He hoped he'd spend his dying days collecting butterflies and drawing them, but he found that, after the Second World War, the butterfly population went into deep decline and he thought it was because the moths were eating them. He went quite loopy, but maybe that's because he drank so much. It's the affliction of the Rideouts, you see. My grandfather became convinced that moths and butterflies were locked into some deadly battle – a battle between good and evil, where the colourful, pretty, daylight-loving butterflies represented the good and the dark, dangerous night-time moths were the bad. He wouldn't listen to anyone. My father said he died a broken man.'

'God, this is such a tragic story!'

'Yes,' says Noel simply. 'He was broken on a wheel as they say – apt really, isn't it?'

'What happened to his collection?'

'Lord Fortescue died quite a time before my grandfather, so the collection was left to the next Lord Fortescue, who was also potty about butterflies. After he died, my father tried to get the books back but, by then, no one seemed to know where the books were.'

'You mean they've gone?'

'Yes, totally disappeared.'

'But that's terrible. They'd be worth a fortune, wouldn't they?'

'A catalogue of every butterfly and moth living in the British Isles from 1910 onwards? Definitely worth something.'

'But where were they last seen?'

'In Sarah's house. She's really Sarah Daubeny-Fortescue, but she changed her name back to her maiden name after Gerrard died because some uncle of hers stipulated she had to do so in order to inherit his money. Mind you, there's none of that money left. The house costs a fortune to run.'

'Hang on a minute, Noel,' I say. 'Are you seriously telling me that your grandfather's priceless butterfly and moth journals are somewhere in Sarah de Salis's house?'

'No, I'm not telling you that. I'm just saying that the last time anyone saw them, which was in the fifties or something, they were in that house, but no one has seen them since.'

'We must find them then. They are the answer to our problem. We find them, sell them and pay for the house to be restored.'

'Yes, Samantha, I had already thought of that obviously, but, believe me, Mrs de Salis and myself have been through every inch of that house and they are not there. Sarah is looking through everything she can lay her hands on to see if there's the slightest mention of the *Daubeny-Fortescue Catalogues of Lepidoptera*. So far we have found out nothing of interest.'

'There's a way out of all of this,' I say. 'We just have to find those catalogues.'

'That would be wonderful,' says Noel, 'but, right now, I'm taking your youngest son out into the garden to look for a Satin Lutestring, a task which I hope he will very much enjoy.'

And, right on cue, Jamie appears in the doorway, clean and washed and wearing a pink T-shirt with roses on it.

13. Food Plants

I wake up the next morning feeling cross. At first I'm not exactly sure why I'm cross, but then I remember that, last night, everyone came in very late and I had to put them all to bed and I was tired and it took an age. First of all, Roisin kindly dropped Bennie home after he had tea.

'Goodness, your son eats a lot,' she said. Bennie told me that Roisin had cooked burgers and sausages and chips and salad, and that he'd had two burgers and three sausages and, as he put it, 'not much salad'. I told Roisin that I would have to repay her kindness by definitely inviting her over to eat the following night. As she was about to leave I also told her, as briefly as I could, about the *Daubeny-Fortescue Catalogues of Lepidoptera*.

'They've gone missing, have they?' she said. 'Let me think about this one. Y'know, the firm I work for deals in lots of wills and you'd be amazed how often things of great importance go missing over time. They leave them to second cousins who then leave them to another second cousin and gradually the catalogues could have got lost that way. Or maybe a past Lord Fortescue hid the catalogues and then left a code in a will to hint where they were hidden. The Anglo-Irish aristocracy were really into that type of thing. Has anyone actually looked into the wills of the past?'

'I don't know,' I said. 'I'll ask Sarah when I next see her and you can talk to Noel about it over dinner.' I told her to come around 7.30 p.m. for 8 p.m.

I was about to telephone John and tell him about the dinner party when Noel popped his head round the door and said he wouldn't come in, but that he and Jamie had had a great time. They hadn't spotted a Satin Lutestring, but it had been most enjoyable anyway, and then he sprayed some Gold Spot into his mouth and walked off down the garden path so quickly that I had to run after him to ask him if he wanted to come to dinner the following night as well.

'Yes,' he called behind him, marching out on to the road without even looking at me.

'Seven thirty for eight,' I yelled after him. 'And send Edward home.'

I put Bennie and Jamie to bed, which involved me going up and down the stairs about twenty times. First they wanted a glass of water each, then a story, but only the story in a particular book which happened to be back down the stairs, then Bennie said he was hungry and, eventually, while I was downstairs making a fruit plate, Edward finally appeared. He walked in the door, told me he was feeling really tired and went up the stairs. After I'd delivered Bennie's fruit plate, I carried on up to Edward's room to find him fast asleep. His mouth was open and he was snoring gently. I pulled his covers over him. He didn't stir.

But now I'm awake and I'm cross. I remember that I still haven't rung John to ask him about the status of the puppet show and that, in a few hours' time, he and Dougie will be here and that they won't know about the dinner party, and I realize I'm not sure what to cook. It also occurs to me that Dougie may be able to help in the search for the butterfly catalogues because he's a solicitor and that means a) he has an ordered mind, although it never seems to be that obvious when it comes to Dougie, and b) he'll be able to look for them with Roisin because they would know what to look out for in terms of past paperwork when I most definitely do not.

I put on my robe and go downstairs to find all the children are up and in various states of undress, watching the television. Even Baby Sparkle is awake and sitting on the floor, pushing a toy train one way and then back the other.

'Hello, children' I say. Then I notice Edward isn't here. 'Where's Edward? Who got Sparkle up?'

'I did,' says Bennie, who's eating a bowl of cornflakes. 'I lifted her.' He raises his arm up to show his muscles. 'I'm strong, see?' he says. 'Because I eat a lot of food.'

Just then I hear Edward groaning in the kitchen. I go in to find him sitting at the kitchen table.

'What's the matter?' I ask him.

'I don't feel that well,' he says. 'I've got a stomach-ache and my head hurts.'

'What kind of a stomach-ache? A painful one or a sick one?'

'A sick one.'

'Did you eat anything yesterday? Have you had something that would make you feel ill?'

'No, not really,' he says. 'I had a sandwich at lunch time and I had some crisps at Isabel's granddad's house.'

'Well, there shouldn't be anything in those that would make you sick. Did you drink any water?'

'No, not really.'

Edward lays his head on the table. He's really looking very ill.

'Christ, Edward,' I say as I go to the sink to get him a large glass of cold water and try to resist the urge to ask him if he's ill because he's hung over. I try to remember what Roisin has said. I must give Edward space and time and the chance to find out about life for himself. Instead I say, 'I'm sorry I didn't see you all day yesterday, but surely you didn't need me to ask Noel to remind you to drink some water?'

'We were at the beach,' says Edward. 'There wasn't any water.'

'I know you were at the beach because Susie told me.'

'Who's Susie?'

'The mother of those pretty twin girls you met down on the beach.'

'The ones with the odd names?'

'Yes, them. She told me yesterday that the twins saw you and you were acting in a weird fashion.'

'Well, they should know. They're weird themselves.'

'What do you mean?'

'Oh, we saw them down the beach and they were pretending to speak in some twin language and that boy Aaron was there and they were all playing on his PSP and they wouldn't let us play.'

'And?'

Edward looks shifty.

'What happened?'

'Isabel got cross with them. She told them to, you know . . .'

'To eff off?'

'Yes.'

I sigh. 'That's not great, is it?'

'No, but they started it, Mum, honestly. They have everything. They were messing about in these wetsuits. They were undoing the zips and then doing them up again and showing us their boobs and Isabel called them, you know, whores.'

'Whores?' I say. 'Well, I suggest that from now on you and Isabel leave those girls alone and the next time you go off you make sure you have something to drink.'

'I will if you give me some money.'

'I will give you some money.'

'If I had a mobile phone it would be so much easier, Mum. Why can't I have one? Isabel has one.'

'Then I'll get her number off her and call you on that,' I say. 'And why you didn't have a meal at Noel's, I have no idea.'

'He wasn't there much. He left us some food, but . . .'

'You didn't cook it.'

Edward looks a bit shifty now. 'No, we didn't. Sorry. We thought Isabel's granddad would come back and cook it for us.'

'How on earth was he supposed to do that? He was out with Jamie. He very kindly offered to take him to look for moths and, I tell you, Edward, he's doing marvellous things for Jamie. Yesterday Jamie even ate some mashed potatoes and some bread, and when he was having a fit in the bath in the evening Noel calmed him down.'

'Really?' says Edward, looking amazed.

'Really,' I say.

I leave Edward sipping his water and go back into the sitting room as the telephone starts ringing.

'Edward,' I shout, 'can you pick that up? Baby Sparkle's crying and I can't get the phone.'

'No,' shouts Edward from the kitchen. I put Sparkle back down on the seat with Bennie. 'Hold her,' I say. 'And make sure she doesn't choke on anything.' Bennie nods his head.

I get to the kitchen and pick the phone up.

'Hello,' I say loudly as I hear Jamie beginning to have an argument with Bennie.

'I want to sit with Baby Sparkle,' he's saying. 'She's my Baby Sparkle.'

'Mum told me to look after her,' Bennie replies. 'And you'll hurt her.'

'I won't hurt her. She's MINE!' yells Jamie. There's a crash and some wailing.

'Edward!' I say, motioning wildly for Edward to get up from his slump on the kitchen table and go and help out in the sitting room.

'What?' he says, wiping his hand dramatically across his brow. 'What can I do?'

'Go and help,' I say.

'Hello,' says a voice down the phone. 'Samantha, are you there? It's me, John.'

'John!' I say as Edward finally gets out of his chair and heads off to the sitting room.

'Is everything OK, Samantha?'

'Is everything OK?' I say tetchily. 'No, it isn't. Bennie has just dropped the baby, or Jamie's attacked her or whatever, and no one else is here but me and Edward's sick and . . . oh God, we're having a dinner party tonight.'

'Great,' says John. 'I'm waiting for Dougie to arrive and then we're leaving. Now, what do you want me to bring?'

'Another me,' I say.

'Well, apart from that.'

'Some headache pills and wine. Lots of nice wine. I'll go and get some food this morning. When will you be here?'

'Early afternoon,' he says. 'Ring if you want anything else. I can't wait to see you. I've really missed you. Oh and

I've got some good news. The puppet show people have said yes. They're delighted!'

'Oh, good,' I say.

'But where can they stay?'

'You can try the Cutlass Estate, just don't tell Noel.'

'Oh, you mean the man with the wine string. Am I going to meet him?'

'He's coming for dinner,' I say. 'There's much to discuss. You should see the effect he's had on Jamie!'

Then John says that Dougie has arrived and that they will stop at the off-licence.

'I love you,' he adds.

I go into the sitting room to find utter chaos. Baby Sparkle is lying on her back on the floor. She has a bemused look on her face. Jamie is sitting next to her, shaking a dolly covered in milk in her face, so much so that droplets of milk are falling from the dolly's hair on to Baby Sparkle's face. She's cooing with delight. Bennie's bowl of cornflakes has tipped over and there's milk all over the carpet. Meanwhile Edward and Bennie are both crammed in the armchair, locked in a battle over the television remote control.

'It's mine!' yells Bennie. 'I was here first.'

'Don't be such a butt, Bennie,' says Edward. 'I'm the eldest and Mum told me to look after you.'

'I'm going to tell on you,' says Bennie, going red.

'Yeah? Who are you going to tell then?'

'Mum,' says Bennie. Then he sees I've come into the room. 'Mum, Edward's being mean to me!'

'Children,' I say authoritatively, 'I'm not getting involved in this. You've all got to get ready because we've got to go shopping. Daddy and Dougie are coming today and every-one's coming for dinner and there's no food and —'

'I'm not coming,' says Edward moodily, finally moving off the chair.

'I'm not coming either,' says Jamie.

'Are you getting food?' asks Bennie. 'I'll come.'

'You all have to come,' I say. 'There's no one here to look after you.'

'I'm not coming,' says Edward. 'I don't feel well.'

'Look,' I say, 'don't you get it? You all have to come.'

'I know,' says Edward suddenly, 'why don't you ask Shel-ley to come over and look after us?'

'Why on earth would Shelley want to come at this time in the morning?' I say. 'Anyway, I thought you didn't like her perfume.'

'Maybe she won't wear it,' says Edward hopefully. 'She might want to use the computer.'

I think for a bit. 'Actually, Edward,' I say, 'I will ring her. I need someone to make a flyer for the puppet show at the fête. Would you help her if she came over?'

'Yes,' says Edward enthusiastically.

'So will I,' says Bennie.

'I won't,' says Jamie, smiling at Baby Sparkle. 'I'll play with Baby Sparkle.'

I look at Jamie in surprise.

An hour later and I'm driving up the hill, past the Cutlass Estate towards Ilfracombe. I haven't decided what we'll have to eat for dinner yet, but I thought I should look for some fish. The children are at home with Shelley, who seemed very pleased when I rang.

'Look, Shelley,' I said, 'I know this sounds a bit mad but —'

'You want me to come and help with the kids?' she said. Then she said it was fine and that she'd be over in a minute. 'I need to earn some money before I go back to college,' she said.

When she arrived she told us she had some wonderful news to share with us. 'I've been signed by a manager!' she said excitedly.

'You've been signed by a manager?' I said, feeling quite astounded. 'How? Where? You've just been here in Lower Strand. When did you go and meet this manager?'

'I haven't met her,' she said happily. 'She went on to my web page and listened to my music and she told me she loved it! We've been blogging about it all night. So now I just need to burn some more of my songs on to this CD and then send it to her. You don't mind if I do that, do you?'

'Not at all,' I said. Then I remembered about the flyers. I told Shelley I'd written down everything I could about the event and that Edward was keen to help her, so if they designed a flyer to promote the fête and the puppet show, that would be great.

'Yes, I'll do that,' she said. 'Actually, this could be part of my coursework, couldn't it? It's promoting tourism in the area, isn't it?'

'Absolutely,' I said.

'I love the idea of a French puppet show. But I can't afford ten pounds.'

'Oh, you don't have to pay, Shelley,' I said. 'I'll buy you a ticket and that will help save Mrs de Salis's house.'

'Do you think I could play at the fête?' she asked.

'I don't know. You'd need a stage and an amp, wouldn't you?'

'Oh, yes, but they have that at the fête because someone usually makes a speech to thank everyone for coming. They read out the raffle ticket numbers over a microphone.'

'Well, I can ask,' I said.

'I could sing in French, you know, "Chanson D'Amour", that type of thing.'

'What's that?' asked Edward.

'Song of Love,' said Shelley. 'Are you bringing your girlfriend to the fête?' Shelley winked at him when she said this.

'She's not my girlfriend,' said Edward and then he mooched off back into the kitchen.

But now, as I'm driving, I realize I don't even know if there's a supermarket in Ilfracombe, let alone a fishmonger's. I have Baby Sparkle with me. I almost didn't bring her as it took me an age to prise Jamie off her.

'No, Mama,' he said when I told him I was taking Baby Sparkle with me. 'I wanna play with her.' He then lay right next to her and wound his legs in with hers and held her hands firmly in his. Baby Sparkle turned towards him.

'Ra-la-ra-la-ra,' she said, smiling at him.

'I love you, Baby Sparkle,' Jamie said, kissing her on her head.

'And she loves you,' I said to Jamie, almost in disbelief.

I said that if he couldn't bear being parted from his sister then he should come and look for a wet fish shop with me and he looked very doubtful about that.

'Wet fish smell,' he said. He decided he would, in fact, let go of Baby Sparkle's hands and disentangle himself from her legs and I put her in the car.

At this moment, Baby Sparkle is looking at me and

smiling. She's wiggling her toes around, which is something she always does when she's excited.

'What shall we cook for dinner?' I ask her.

She cocks her head and gazes back at me.

'Shellfish? Sea fish? Or maybe no fish at all?'

'Ra-la-ra-la-la,' she says.

Just then, we pass the fork in the road that leads towards Sarah de Salis's house.

'Do you know something, Baby Sparkle?' I say, as I take the fork down the valley rather than up and out to Ilfracombe. 'Let's go and pay a visit to Sarah. We can do her shopping for her. She's very old and it's the least we can do.'

We turn right past the rhododendrons into her beautiful horseshoe-shaped drive and park at the top next to the house. I unstrap Baby Sparkle, put her on my hip and knock on the door with the lion's head. Nothing happens. I wait for a bit and try again. Finally I hear someone walking towards the door.

'Yes?' says a small, tired voice.

'It's me, Sarah,' I say as the door opens very slowly. 'It's Samantha Smythe.'

'Oh, Samantha,' says Sarah de Salis. When the door is finally open I can see she's still wearing her peacock housecoat. She has cobwebs in her hair and she looks very frail and tired. 'I was up a ladder,' she says. 'I was trying to get the cobwebs from the ceiling in the back hall, but it's quite high up.'

'Sarah,' I say, walking into the house. 'You shouldn't be doing that. Why are you up a ladder? You're too old to be clearing the cobwebs.'

'I suppose I am,' she says, 'but there's no one else to do it.'

Then she sees Baby Sparkle. 'Oh, your beautiful baby is here,' she says. 'Why don't you bring her through to the Long Room, then I can make us some coffee and she can play in the high chair. I remember how much your baby liked playing with the abacus.'

'I'm not staying long, though,' I say. 'I'm going shopping. I was wondering . . .'

But Sarah has already disappeared into the back of the house, heading for the kitchen.

By the time she reappears, Baby Sparkle is in the high chair pushing the abacus rings round and I'm looking at an ancient book, more like an album, with a faded red velour cover, that's sitting on the table.

'What's this?' I ask Sarah as she pushes the hostess trolley towards me.

'It's the accounts of the house,' says Sarah. 'I found them in the family archives and I'm going through them all in turn.'

'Are you looking for evidence of the catalogues?'

Sarah sighs. 'I don't know really. I'm looking for a mention of the catalogues, I suppose but, honestly, I don't think I'll ever find them. If I didn't know better, I'd think they didn't even exist, but . . . Noel swears by them.' Sarah pours out the coffee from a pot. 'Now I have something to tell you, Samantha,' she says.

'What?' I say, intrigued.

'This coffee is instant.'

'I'm sorry?' I say.

'This coffee, it's instant coffee. I hope you don't mind. Gerrard told me I must never serve instant coffee. He said it was very common, but actually I quite like it and I put it in a pot so it looks the right thing.'

'I love instant coffee,' I say.

'Good,' she says, 'and here I have some of those biscuits I gave you the other day. Would you like one?'

'Oh, I'm fine right now,' I say. But then I see Baby Sparkle's face light up and she pushes her hands out and makes grabbing movements with her fists.

'I think your baby wants one,' says Sarah. I reluctantly give Sparkle a biscuit and she sits happily cramming as much of it as she can into her mouth.

Sarah sits down, puts some glasses on and opens the large book. 'The problem with trying to decipher all this is that my eyesight is going and, as you can see, it's all written in a flamboyant scrawl. Also, the ink is fading and they spelled words differently in those days. Fs are sometimes Ss, you see.'

'How many of these books have you looked through?'

'Quite a few,' she says. 'They're all stacked up in the library.'

'But, Sarah, this one dates from 1710. Why have you gone that far back?'

Sarah de Salis wrings her hands. 'I know,' she says. 'It's quite mad, isn't it?' She sips her coffee. 'I shall try to explain. Gerrard and I never had any children so there's no one to leave the Manor House to, as you know. So I wanted to find the *Catalogues of Lepidoptera* to show that, once I'm gone, we did actually exist and we did, sometimes, do good things. But as I've so far failed to find them and really hold out little hope, I've decided that while I still have my sight and my wits, I shall make a history of the Daubeny-Fortescue family and their time in Lower Strand. That's why I'm collating these old books. Then, even if that horrible Mr Cutlass buys this house, there will be something left.'

'That's amazing,' I say. 'How much have you done?'

'Not much,' she says. 'I've only just started really. That's why I've gone back to the beginning.'

'Well, I really admire you,' I say. 'I wish I was doing something worthwhile like that.'

Now Sarah de Salis laughs. It sounds like floorboards creaking.

'You're bringing up your children and you're helping me.'

'I don't think I'm being much of a help though, am I?' I say. Then I remember about the puppet show. 'Actually,' I say, 'I've got some news about the fête.'

I tell Sarah all about John and his job and the idea of previewing the show here.

'A puppet show?' says Sarah. 'Why not? I loved them as a child. Mind you, every year I have Mr Henderson and Mr Cutlass going on at me about Health and Safety. Last year Mr Cutlass paid to have the pond roped off, but I don't suppose he'll be so happy to do it if the money is going to save this house from his graspings.'

'I hadn't even thought of anything like that,' I say. 'But you're right, Sarah. We probably do need some Health and Safety certificate. Leave it with me. I'll call the council and find out.'

'It's a fearful bore for you, I'm afraid, Samantha,' she says.

'It's fine,' I say and then tell her I must go. We've finished our coffee and Baby Sparkle is looking sleepy. Her head keeps lolling down towards the abacus.

'I'm going to the shops at Ilfracombe and I wondered if you needed any food,' I say as I get up.

'Food?' says Sarah. 'No, I don't think so.'

'Are you sure?'

'Hadn't you noticed?' she says. 'I don't really eat much. I never know what to eat now I don't have a cook.'

I think for a bit, then I remember my mother telling me that my grandfather lived off Campbell's condensed soup. Mushroom was his favourite.

'What about some soup?' I say. 'I could get you some Campbell's condensed soup. It's very easy to cook. You just add water to it. Apparently the mushroom one is very tasty.'

'Mmm,' says Sarah. 'Maybe I could try that, but I don't want you to go to any bother.'

'It's no bother,' I say and I go to leave.

14. Determining the Sex

By the time I returned from Ilfracombe some hours ago, weighed down by endless bags full of endless food that we probably won't eat, no one was in except Shelley.

'Your husband's here,' she told me, 'and so's your friend, and the kids are showing them round the village. I'm still doing the flyers, is that OK?'

I told her that it was fine by me and I went to put Baby Sparkle down for a sleep. I then went into my bedroom and found John's bag on the bed. It was open and various shirts and T-shirts were sprawling out of it. On the floor lay a pair of jeans, some socks and shoes. Obviously John changed when he got down here. I started tidying up his things. I find I quite like doing this. I like smoothing his clothes and putting them in drawers and hanging up his shirts and trousers. I like seeing the ends of his stubble still evident on his razor and the smell of his wash bag. It smells of vetiver and shaving cream and deodorant. In a way it makes me feel as if I'm reclaiming him. I've always found it is in the minutiae of someone's life that you really know them. What lover could recognize the stubble on the side of a bathroom sink? The smell of the wash bag? The holes in the socks? It takes a real and sustained knowledge of someone to be part of that small everyday quality we all possess. This is what John and I have only, sometimes, it's hard to remember that. He always knows when to rub my shoulders, when I'm asleep or just pretending. He knows the perfume I wear, the mug I like to take my coffee in. This is the way in which we love each other.

When I had put his stuff away and lined his shoes up on the floor and budged my toiletries around in the bathroom to make way for his, I sat on the bed and looked at them. Their presence in the room made me feel as if we were united once more.

Half an hour later, John appeared in the garden. He had Bennie on his shoulders.

'You squeal like a piggy!' John was saying to him, tickling his bare feet.

'No, I'm not a piggy!' Bennie was saying, laughing almost too much to get his words out.

Jamie came behind them, holding Dougie's hand. He was wearing trousers. Behind them was Edward, who had Beady with him on a lead.

'Mum!' he said when he saw me come into the garden. He didn't look white any more, just a bit flushed. 'Dad's here!'

'Samantha, my darling!' yelled John. He walked towards me, swinging Bennie down from his shoulders and reaching out to grab me.

'Kiss me, my wife,' he said.

'No,' I said, pretending to be cross. 'Not until you show me wine.'

'I come with gifts,' he said, laughing.

Then Dougie came up and kissed me and suggested we all had tea on the lawn.

'I'll make it,' he said.

'Where's my baby girl?' asked John, lying down on the ground and stretching out. Bennie let out a whoop and lay on top of him. 'I have missed you, Daddy.'

'I've missed you too. Now where's Sparkle, where's my girl?'

'She's in bed,' I said. I then went and lay beside him.

'Are you cross with me?' he said.

'Not now you're here, but it's been quite hard without you.'

'I can't talk with Bennie crushing me,' said John. 'Get off, Bennie!'

As we lay there in the sunshine and John gently rested his hand up my skirt on my thigh, I told him everything that had been going on. We lay there for maybe an hour, just talking, all of us, and drinking tea while the noises of the afternoon went on around us. I told Dougie and John all about Noel and Mrs de Salis and Mr Cutlass and, in the background, we heard Bennie singing 'Cockles and mussels alive alive-o!' and Edward trying to play French cricket with Jamie. At some point I raised myself up on to my elbows to watch them. There was Jamie, his hair standing up on end, his slim body arching over as he tried to wield the plastic bat Edward had found in the shed.

'He looks like a boy,' I said to John. 'I haven't seen him look like that for an age. I can barely believe he's in trousers. How on earth did you get him to wear them?'

'He just put them on without me asking,' said John. 'It's amazing what moths have done for him.'

'What Noel has done for him,' I said. 'He seems to have engaged his brain. Then again, Noel's like that. He's old so he knows many things. He's very good company.'

'Ah,' says Dougie, 'you've got the hots for him, haven't you?' He winked at me.

'Dougie. Noel's in his late sixties. He may even be

seventy! You can't have "the hots", as you so engagingly put it, for a man who is in his eighth decade of life. It's not that. It's just that I appreciate what he's done for Jamie and the fact that he's been very friendly to me and involved me in what's going on in the village, and the fact that he's actually close by.'

'It's true that this is a lovely place to be,' said Dougie. 'I feel as if I belong here.'

'Do you?' I asked. 'I'd always assumed that you were quite committed to your life as a solicitor in London.'

'No, not really,' he said. He stretched back and closed his eyes. 'No, this is the life. Sun on your face, boys playing in the garden, the sound of the sea . . . If I was younger, I'd stay here and be a country solicitor. I'd find a nice country wife and –'

The plastic cricket ball hit Dougie across the nose.

'Aaarggh!' he yelled. 'You little monkeys!' Then he got up and chased Edward and Jamie round and round the garden and, while he was doing it, John leaned over me and his head shaded mine and he kissed me while no one was watching.

'I really mean it,' he said. 'I'm touched at the change in Jamie. I hadn't realized how worried I've been about him, but seeing him wearing a pair of trousers, well . . .'

Suddenly John looked more moved than I had ever seen him.

'John,' I said, stroking his face tenderly. 'It's fine. Everything's going to be fine.'

It is 7 p.m. now and Dougie is furiously beating eggs in a mixing bowl. 'We should have started making dinner hours ago,' he's saying, beating away.

I have appeared from the bath, where I've been for almost an hour.

'You've been in the bath for an age,' Dougie says, looking cross.

'What's wrong with that?' I say. 'I've had the kids here on my own for days. I've barely even had a shower and now John is here I thought I'd relax for a minute.'

'Or sixty of them,' says Dougie grumpily. 'There's cooking to be done, Samantha.' Dougie waves his hand at the kitchen table. It's still covered in groceries. 'I mean, it takes ten minutes just to find the ingredients, let alone cook anything, and I'm trying to do a cheese soufflé as there appears to be nothing else to start with.'

'Well, that should all have been put away hours ago,' I say. 'Shelley said she'd do it with the older children.'

'I haven't seen Shelley for ages,' says Dougie. 'All I've seen is Bennie who seems to have wandered off with a packet of blinis . . .'

'Blinis!' I yelp. 'They're the starter, with smoked salmon.'

Dougie gives me a look. 'You mean the smoked salmon that Bennie also took along with the crème fraîche that he thinks is cream.'

'Oh God,' I say. 'Where's John? Roisin and Noel will be here in half an hour and –'

'I'm here,' says John, coming into the kitchen licking his fingers. 'Fantastic smoked salmon, Samantha,' he says. 'Did you buy it round here?'

'John!' I say. 'That's the starter!'

'Oh,' he says. 'Well, I never think you need a starter, do you?'

'Yes,' says Dougie. 'That's why I'm doing the cheese soufflé.'

'This isn't a big deal, this dinner party, is it?' asks John.

'It is for me,' I say. 'These are my two new friends and Noel is a very important man. I haven't even told him about the puppet show yet and we've been making flyers without asking him.'

'I'm sure he'll be ecstatic,' says John, 'especially if you can get away with charging ten pounds a ticket.'

'But we can't,' I say. 'You can't charge local people ten pounds. They won't pay it.'

'No, they won't,' says Dougie. 'It's too much. Could you do a reduced rate for people who live here?'

'I don't know,' I say. 'We need to talk to Noel about it. I'm sure he'll have a solution.'

'But if the butterfly books turn up then it doesn't really matter, does it?' says John.

'No, but Sarah de Salis has been looking for them forever. She can't find them.'

'They can't have disappeared,' says Dougie.

'Why not?' I ask. 'Do you know what's gone missing in our house? We've lost remote controls and CDs and videos, let alone the amount of books that have vanished. Our house even swallowed a telephone once, so a book of butterflies would never be found and we've only got four bedrooms. Her house is massive compared to ours.'

'I had a Magimix once that disappeared,' says Dougie.

John and I both look at him incredulously.

'You're lying,' says John as Dougie raises his eyebrows.

Just then Shelley walks into the kitchen.

'I've finished the flyer,' she says. 'Sorry it took so long, but I was playing with Baby Sparkle.'

'Playing with Baby Sparkle?' I say. 'I thought John was supposed to be looking after her?' I shoot John a look.

'I was,' he says, holding his hands up in supplication. 'But Jamie wanted to draw a picture, and Bennie wanted me to help him put salmon on the blinis, and Sparkle was having such a lovely time with Shelley rolling on the floor . . .'

'Rolling on the floor?'

'Yes, she loves a roll around, your baby,' says Shelley. Then she spies Dougie chopping up some monkfish. 'I love fish,' she says. 'When I'm at college I get some fish and roll it in cornflakes and then cook it.'

'This is monkfish,' says Dougie grandly. 'It's very expensive so it's not the type of fish you roll in breakfast cereals.'

'Oh,' says Shelley. Then she brightens a bit. 'Do you want to see the flyer? I'm pretty pleased with it. I know how to use the application on the computer because we've been taught how to do Photoshop and all that stuff at college.' She looks at John. 'I'm sure it's not up to your standards. Samantha said you're very artistic . . .'

'Oh, no, not really,' says John.

'But I asked my friend Ryan to help and he's really talented, so I think it's pretty good.'

For a moment I'm confused. 'Your friend Ryan?' I say. 'But I thought you've been here on your own.'

'I have,' says Shelley happily. 'I talked to him on MySpace and he gave me some suggestions. Linda did too, but I don't rate Linda and neither does Ryan.'

'Ah,' says Dougie. 'These are online friends, are they?'

Shelley nods her head. 'I've got thousands,' she says.

'I've only got twenty,' says Dougie.

'Dougie!' I say, 'I didn't know you were part of this cyber network.'

Dougie turns round to whisk egg whites into his mixture.

'I'm young at heart, Samantha,' he says. 'You have to meet people somehow.'

By this I know Dougie means a potential partner because, ever since Dougie's wife and now ex-wife Maxine left him some years ago, the only person he has gone out with is my sister, Julia. They split up a couple of years ago when she moved to Los Angeles to study childcare. Dougie has been my best friend for such a long time I can barely remember when he wasn't in my life. All I wish for Dougie is that he meets someone and becomes happy because, despite his bonhomie, I always suspect that, in his very heart, he is lonely.

Suddenly there's a rap on the door.

'Christ!' I shriek. 'I'm still in a towel.' I run upstairs and lock myself in my room and start to get dressed. Soon I hear a gentle knock on my bedroom door. I open it up a crack to see who it is. It's Roisin. She's looking rather beautiful in a long red velvet dress.

'Am I over-dressed?' she whispers through the door.

'No, you look great,' I say.

'Now, here I am, and Lorcan is here, and I'm most impressed to find your friend Dougie in the kitchen making the dinner. I'm even more impressed that your husband, who's obviously charming and lovely and so great with his children, has served me a drink and I've deposited my son with your babysitter and I have to say –' at this Roisin lies down on the bed and stretches out – 'that this is the most luxurious and relaxing evening I've had in a long time even though I look like I'm going to a ball for old folks.'

'You do not,' I say, smiling at her. 'Your dress is lovely.'

'It's second-hand from a shop down the road from where

I live, but it's the best I can do,' she says. 'What are you going to wear?' She gets up and looks through my wardrobe. 'Hmm,' she says. 'Not much here, is there?'

'Well, I didn't think I'd be entertaining really. I've just brought beachwear and a couple of skirts.'

'What? No dresses then?'

'No, although Jamie would love me to wear a dress. He's mad on *Chitty Chitty Bang Bang* and he wants me to dress like Truly Scrumptious.'

'Why don't you then?'

'Because she wears white frilly dresses with sashes round the waist.'

'Yes, I get that,' says Roisin, 'but why don't you find something like that somewhere? It's grand to wear a dress sometimes. You should try it.'

'What on earth would I do that for?'

'Cos it's fun,' says Roisin. 'Ah, c'mon. Let's have a girly night one night. I'll curl your hair if you like and I'm really good at putting on make-up —'

'Roisin,' I say. 'Don't be mad.'

'Why not? You know, us mothers of boys, we forget to be girly sometimes. I miss that. I'm so bloody capable with my job and looking after Lorcan. I want to put on some scarlet lipstick! I want to dress up! Let's do it for the fête. Why not? Let's get Shelley in to do the kids and we'll go to, Lord, I don't know where, Barnstaple or somewhere, and find some pretty dresses. What do you say?'

'I'm not going without Baby Sparkle,' I say. 'She's a girl.'

'Absolutely,' says Roisin. 'Let's go and unleash our feminine side. I mean, when was the last time you did that?'

I've tried for many years to become more girly. When I was trying to get pregnant with Baby Sparkle, my mother told me I didn't have a hope in hell unless I learned how to be more feminine. I asked her what she meant by that and she said, 'You have to stop being so bossy.' But I've always been bossy. I don't mean to be really but, apparently, as a child, I made all my friends play exactly what I wanted to play and I wouldn't countenance it any other way so, consequently, I had few friends.

There was one girl I knew – let's call her Alison – who was even more manipulative than me. I was openly very manipulative. I was probably rather stupid about it. I'd say, 'If you don't want to play Cowboy and Indians, then I'll hate you all!' Alison, however, never wanted to play rough games like that. She always wanted to play Tea Parties or Mummies and Daddies, and her games involved doing domestic things in the communal Wendy House. Everyone wanted to play in the Wendy House at school. It had a cooker in it and pots, and pretend food like fruit and cakes and strange plastic slices of bread with plastic butter on. There were knives and plates and forks and cups and, of course, the prettiest pink flowered tea set I had ever seen. But because the Wendy House was so popular, there was a rota as to when you could play in it. You were only supposed to be in it once a day for about ten minutes at a time. This used to irritate me because, once I was in there, I never wanted to come out. I used to say, 'If you make me come out of this Wendy House then I'll hate you all!' The upshot of this was that the teacher used to have to come in and speak very sternly to me and sometimes it ended up with me having to stand outside the headmaster's office during break time. And yet, somehow, whenever I went to play in the Wendy House, there was Alison. She'd be sitting there in her school uniform looking very pretty, daintily pouring out tea and handing round the plastic bread. I used to marvel at how she managed to stay in there so long. One day, I watched her. There she was, with her hair tied up in regulation blue ribbon and her white lacy socks neatly folded down and her blue leather sandals with their pretty cut-out flowers that I coveted; there she was, serving out the tea, and along came the teacher. 'Time to come out, girls,' she said and out trooped all the other girls, but not Alison. She continued pouring the tea as if nothing had changed.

'Come on, Alison,' said the teacher. 'It's time for some other children to have a turn.'

Alison got up very slowly and came to the door. She had tears in her baby-blue eyes and she kept batting at them with her long dark eyelashes.

'Oh, Mrs Patterson,' she said, 'Of course I must come out. It's just that I've made some tea and I haven't finished drinking it and do you think it would hurt tremendously if I served some out to these fellow pupils of mine before I left?' She then looked piteously up at Mrs Patterson, as if a negative answer would break her heart entirely, and Mrs Patterson said, 'Oh dear, Alison. Well, I'm sure the pupils who are about to come in would love your tea, but promise me you'll only stay in for another five minutes, OK?'

Alison nodded her head fervently and Mrs Patterson wandered off and then obviously forgot about Alison's promise because when I came back half an hour later Alison was still serving tea.

I got invited to Alison's house once. I'm not sure why. Maybe her mother took pity on me. She would always give me an odd look when I came out of school. I think it was because Alison was so neat and I was so scruffy. On the afternoon I went to tea, Alison's mother had made pretty biscuits in the shape of animals and she'd iced them in different-coloured icing – pink, mauve, yellow. They looked so wonderful that I was delighted when Alison's mother said we could have two each. I chose a pink dog and a yellow squirrel, and Alison chose two pink cats.

'I only like cats,' she said as we went to her bedroom to play. I was so looking forward to eating my animal biscuits. I had even decided which order I was going to eat them in. I was going to eat the squirrel's tail first to see what a squirrel would look like without a tail and then I was going to de-nose the dog and . . . but when Alison opened her bedroom door, I dropped my plate. I had never seen anything like it. It was like a dream. Everything in it was pink or white. The walls were pink. The carpet was white and deep and fluffy. The walls had spangles and stars stuck all over them and the lampshade was made to resemble Cinderella's castle. The pièce de résistance was the bed. It was a four-poster and it was high off the ground. The canopy above it was made of heavy pink silk. The pillows had Snow White on them, as did the duvet cover and, on top of the duvet, lay a patch-work quilt.

'Oh, Alison,' I said. 'I've never seen such a bed.' This was true. I had never seen a four-poster before. Then I noticed she had a Holly Hobby rotating bedside lamp and that she had Flower Fairy pictures framed and mounted on her walls. On the back of her door hung a pink ballerina costume and in the corner of the room was a golden chest that, when Alison opened it up, contained bead sets and paints and pencils with fluffy tops. Alison then beckoned me to come to the other side of the room.

'Look,' she said, and there was a miniature theatre with lots of miniature people from story books. Next to that was a china tea set with matching plates and two chairs and a table.

'Shall we take tea?' Alison said.

Suffice it to say, I never went to Alison's again. My mother took one look at my face when she picked me up and decreed that it wasn't healthy for me to be around someone who had so much stuff.

'What on earth have you been up to?' she said when she saw the make-up Alison had put on my face and the Flower Fairy book I was clutching that Alison's mother very kindly let me have.

'Alison's made me look like a girl,' I said.

In the car my mother told me that I mustn't try to copy Alison.

'Why not?' I wailed. 'She's so pretty.'

'Yes, but she'll also end up being pretty stupid if she carries on the way she's going,' said my mother. 'She goes to Brownies.'

My mother always had a pathological hatred of Brownies and refused to let me be in them. I used to beg her.

'They go camping,' I'd say.

'They take hostess badges,' she'd say, 'and that's not right.'

And so I spent my childhood in jeans and jumpers and big boots and hats and scarves and mittens, and I've never really grown out of that.

Since then though, when I've tried to be a bit more girly, I've often thought of Alison. What was it about her that made her such a girl? I could put on stockings and high heels and a skirt and a low-cut top and pretty earrings and make-up, and have my hair curled, and I still wouldn't look very girly. I could find the most exquisite Truly Scrumptious dress, yet

I'd still walk in my clunking fashion. I'd still trip up too often and laugh too loud and say all the things girly women don't say. It doesn't bother me. I look good walking a dog or weeding the garden or messing about with the children.

I just don't look good in a dress.

As I'm finishing putting on my make-up, there's another knock at the door and then I hear male voices greeting each other. I go to put a hair pin in and miss, and end up stabbing my finger. I look down at it. The hair pin has nicked my cuticle and it's bleeding slightly. Christ! I should be downstairs by now. I hear Roisin's voice. She'd left my room a few minutes ago when we both heard Dougie shouting a range of expletives which seemed to imply he'd burned something.

'Samantha!' he yelled. 'Come downstairs. I can't cook on this useless range! I've never cooked on an electric hob. Never, ever, ever. Do you know how hard it is to get a soufflé to rise in a crap oven? Do you?'

I sent Roisin down in my place.

'Call him Chef,' I said to her. 'That'll flatter him.'

I'm hoping that the soufflé is fine as I wrap a piece of loo roll round my finger. Then I shake my head a couple of times. I haven't had time to wash my hair and I've still got sand in it. Some people think beach hair is a good look. All I can say is, it's not a good look on me. My ends are dry and my hair has gone curly in a horrible fuzzy way rather than a ringletty type of way. It hardly cascades down my back, more just sits there looking like the unkempt coat of a small and unpleasant animal. I fumble about in my wash bag for an elastic band, then scrunch my hair up and secure it with the band. Now I look like Olive Oyl from *Popeye*, so

I try to persuade some strands of my hair to become unbunched and fall artfully around my face. I can hear someone coming up the stairs now. Edward's face appears at the door.

'Mum,' he says. 'Everyone is downstairs waiting for you. Dad says can you hurry up. I think he may be getting cross.'

'Right, I'm coming,' I say. 'How do I look?' I smooth my white linen skirt down and hoick the straps of my T-shirt up a bit to cover my bra straps.

Edward scrutinizes me for a bit.

'You look like you,' he says.

'Oh,' I say, disappointed.

'I mean, you look nice. You always look nice. Anyway, Isabel's here with Noel and I was wondering if we could –'

'Could what?' I say a bit snappily. 'Your father is here, Edward, and you haven't seen him all holiday and, really, I should think that you and Isabel could stay here and socialize for once in your life, couldn't you? Honestly, I have no idea what you two get up to, but –'

'We were going to deliver the flyers,' says Edward. 'We thought it might help.'

'The flyers?' I say, rather chastised. 'Well, that would be great, but I haven't even told Noel about the puppet show and I have no idea what he'll say . . .'

'Dad's told him.'

'Dad's told him?'

'Yes, I heard him, and Shelley's shown him the flyers and Noel thinks it's all marvellous. That's what he said. He said, "That's marvellous!" So Isabel and I thought we'd go and deliver some for you.'

'Right,' I say. 'Well, I'll come down now and check everything out and, yes, I'm sure you can as that's very kind of you both.' I suddenly feel suffused with love for Edward. I go and pull him to me a bit awkwardly as Edward is not expecting it and instinctively pulls back.

'Steady on,' he says.

I hold him at arm's length and look into his eyes. 'I love you, Edward,' I say. 'I really want you to know that. Both Daddy and I love you and we both trust you. I have to let go of you. I know I do. But that doesn't stop me worrying about you. Do you understand that?'

'Yes,' says Edward. 'But we're just going round the village with flyers, Mum. Don't make a big deal about it.'

By the time I get downstairs, everyone is seated at the table. Noel gets up as I walk in. He's looking smart in a tweed three-piece suit and shiny shoes. His trilby is hanging up on the door.

'Samantha,' he says, 'you look magnificent.' He pats the seat next to him that has obviously been left vacant for me. I go towards Noel and kiss him on the cheek. His skin is thin and papery. He smells delicious though, like a pine forest, and as he turns his head towards me slightly, I can smell mint on his breath.

'Sit here,' he says. 'I have the honour of your company.'

Dougie snorts as he gets up to check the soufflé in the oven.

'She's spent hours up there,' he says.

'Dougie!' says Roisin. 'You must never tell a gentleman that about a lady.'

Noel looks at her, vaguely surprised. 'That's right, my dear,' he says.

I notice that John is not in the kitchen.

'Where's John?' I ask.

'Oh, he's doing some twiddling or something with Shelley's flyer,' says Dougie.

'Oh, the flyer,' I say. I look at Noel. For some reason I feel guilty.

'I should have asked you about this,' I say to him. 'I'm sorry. It all just seems to be happening so quickly.'

'Do not apologize, my dear,' says Noel, waving a hand at me. 'I'm in awe of you. That's why I wanted you involved. You have the passion and the creativity of youth.'

'She certainly does,' says John. He has come into the kitchen holding a piece of paper. He waves it at me. 'What do you think?' He passes the flyer to me. I look at it as John opens some wine.

'It's great,' I say. 'I like the fact that the background is in the colours of the French flag. I like the drawing of the puppet theatre. Who did that?'

'I think that was Magnus.'

'Magnus? Is he another one of Shelley's friends?'

John nods his head.

'I like the fact it's in French,' says Noel, swirling a smidgeon of red wine around the bottom of his glass and then gulping it down. 'So clever of you to think of that, Samantha. Lovely wine,' he says to John. 'What is it?'

'A Rioja.'

'Oh, interesting. A Rioja with a soufflé.'

'What would you have served?' asks John.

'Oh, I don't know,' says Noel. 'I'm no wine buff, really, I just like to have a few glasses of an evening. You can do that when you're old but . . . maybe I'd have put a white with it.'

Now it's Roisin's turn to snort. 'Just pass me the bottle,' she says. 'I'm desperate for a glass and I don't care what colour it is.'

'I can open a white,' John says to Noel, looking a little worried. 'I have a Sauvignon Blanc here or a Zinfandel.'

'No, no, do not concern yourself. Really I'd prefer a Californian Chardonnay, but as you don't have any I'm sure my palate can adjust to a red. Now, Samantha,' he says, turning to me, 'all we have to do is persuade Mr Henderson to donate us the profits of the fête and half our job is done.'

'Yes,' I say, 'and I don't know how to do that.'

'We shall find a way,' he says. 'I say a resounding yes to the puppet theatre and I think you can get the children to deposit those flyers through people's doors. Then I think we should separate the puppet show. We could rope it off on the croquet lawn and charge ten pounds for that. Locals who don't want to see it or pay ten pounds will not be allowed on to the croquet lawn, you see? The rest of the fête can be held in the front garden and that way we solve all the problems.'

'That's a brilliant idea!' I say.

'Yes, it is, isn't it?' says Noel, drinking a glass of wine.

'There's another idea.'

'Yes?' asks Noel, looking interested.

'Roisin thinks that there may be a clue to the where-abouts of the catalogues in a past will, maybe a hidden code or something.'

'And what makes her think that?' says Noel, suddenly rather stiff. 'The firm of Rideout and Rideout looked after all the wills of the Lords Fortescue and, I can assure you, I have lived here all my life and made many wills and I've never come across a secret code or anything like that.'

'It's just that Roisin's a legal secretary and I asked her for ideas . . .' I say.

'A legal secretary?' says Noel to Roisin, raising an eyebrow.

'Have you looked at many wills? Because my legal secretary really just made the coffee and kept me abreast of the chitter-chatter in the office.'

'Actually, I've typed out hundreds of wills,' says Roisin shortly.

'Typed out, eh?' says Noel. 'Yes, women are very good at typing I find.'

'Noel,' I say reproachfully as I see Dougie now staring at Noel.

'Damn this oven!' says Dougie, suddenly slamming the soufflé down into the middle of the table. 'It rose and now it's flopped.'

'I'm sure it will taste the same,' I say.

Dougie sighs as he serves it out. 'Now, remind me, why are you so keen to save your friend's house from being built on?'

'You haven't seen the Cutlass Estate, obviously,' says Noel. 'A fine and historic gatehouse was destroyed to make way for those dreadful holiday homes. I mean, what kind of person does that? And what kind of person would choose to stay there?'

'Me,' says Roisin, her voice ringing out slightly over-loudly.

We all turn our heads to look at her.

'I'm staying there with Lorcan, actually,' she says defiantly. 'And I'll let it be known we're very happy there, thank you very much.'

'Good for you!' says Dougie as he gets up to clear the plates.

'My dear girl,' says Noel, looking at Roisin and pouring himself and her some more wine. 'Of course you're happy there. I hear the bungalows are well-insulated. But your happiness is not the point, I'm afraid. Surely you can see what an eyesore they are? They are inappropriate for this landscape. You can see that, can't you?'

Roisin looks right at him. 'Have you been to the north-west of Ireland?' she asks.

Noel doesn't reply.

'Because, if you had, you'd realize that precisely the same has gone on there. We've built bungalows everywhere and now places like the Donegal coast are full of German tourists and do you know what I say to them?'

'*Achtung* baby?' says Dougie.

'No,' she says. 'I say good on them, because you know what? That's what progress is.'

'I fear you are wrong,' says Noel. 'Not all progress is good.'

'This area is just like Ireland,' continues Roisin, talking over him. 'It's beautiful, yes, but without tourism it's going nowhere. Everyone here is desperate for tourists. Look at that beach café. It's six pounds for a sandwich and who's buying those over-priced sandwiches? I am. I'm eating that ciabatta drizzled in whatever and so's my son and if we choose to offset that cost by staying in a relatively cheap bungalow then so be it.'

'More wine?' says John, getting up and going towards the fridge. 'I've still got the Zinfandel.'

'I can't agree with you, my dear,' Noel says to Roisin. 'There are plenty of cottages you could stay in –'

'Yes, overpriced ones,' says Roisin.

'– and surely you can't enjoy the aesthetics of where you are if you stay in something so unappealing.'

'Jesus, Noel,' says Roisin. 'You're just a snob. You want everything to stay the same, but life moves on. I've learned that. Why can't you?'

'Right,' says Dougie smoothly, getting up from the table. 'Sorry to break up this fascinating discussion, but who wants monkfish rolled in cornflakes à la Shelley?'

'I'll just check on the children,' says John, heading for the door.

'I'm sure they're fine, John,' I say warningly, but luckily, as John reaches the door, Shelley comes into the kitchen followed by Bennie and Lorcan.

'Do you like those flyers then?' she says. 'Cos if you do, we were going to deliver some, weren't we, boys?'

Bennie and Lorcan nod their heads furiously.

'It's still light,' says Bennie, looking imploringly at me. 'Can we?'

'Yes, of course you can,' I say, 'but I thought Edward and Isabel were going to do it.'

'They are,' says Shelley. 'They've got a whole load and they're waiting outside for you to tell them it's OK to start taking them round the village.'

I look out of the window. I see Isabel and Edward waiting by the gate. Edward notices me and points enthusiastically at a bright pink plastic bag that Isabel is carrying. I give him the thumbs up. He returns the gesture.

'Edward says they've got a hundred and one flyers in that bag,' says Shelley. 'He counted them.'

'Typical Edward,' I say. 'But where's Baby Sparkle and Jamie?'

'I put Baby Sparkle to bed,' says Shelley. 'She was really tired and I didn't want to bother you, and your husband said that it was fine for me to bath her and pop her down.'

I look at John. He nods his head.

'Jamie's in the sitting room looking at a book,' continues Shelley. 'I think it's *Cinderella*. He says he doesn't want to come.'

'That's a surprise,' says John.

'Right, we'll be off then,' says Shelley.

'Well done, Shelley,' says Noel.

'Don't forget to leaflet the Cutlass Estate, Lorcan,' says Roisin pointedly. 'I'm sure everyone there will pay ten pounds to support the village.'

Noel pours himself another glass of wine.

An hour later we're all sitting at the table laughing. Whatever tension there was earlier seems to have gone and most of this is down to Jamie. He has come into the kitchen and deposited himself on Noel's lap.

'I want you to take me to the pub,' he says, staring into Noel's eyes.

Noel laughs. 'The pub, James?' he says.

'Yes, the pub,' he says. 'We can go and look for moths and then we can go to the pub. I can get a juice.' Jamie then gets off Noel's lap and starts tugging him towards the door.

'Oh, Samantha,' says Noel. 'I hope you don't mind but last night, after we went looking for moths, we popped into the Poltimore Arms. James said he was thirsty. I didn't get him one of those horrible fizzy drinks. Just a juice.'

'That's fine,' I say.

'He also ate some nuts, didn't you, James?'

'I like nuts,' says Jamie.

'Christ, at least he's eating,' says John. 'Out of interest, what moths did you find last night? Samantha says Jamie has really taken to it but, without wishing to be rude, does he have any idea of which moth is which?'

'Is that important?' asks Noel mildly. 'I always think anything that captures a child's mind is worthwhile pursuing, surely? But, actually, James does know some of the names of the moths. What did we look for last night, young man?'

Jamie looks hard at him.

'I don't remember.'

'Yes, you do,' says Noel. 'Remember, it has a lovely name, like a material beautiful clothes are made of. Can you tell your father what it was called?'

'I know!' says Jamie suddenly. 'A satin winestring!'

Noel laughs. 'Nearly,' he says. Then he turns to John. 'We were actually looking for a Satin Lutestring.'

'Why one of those?'

'Oh, because they're rather unique. You can find Common Lutestrings all over the place, but Satin ones are precious, just like your son.'

'Do you liken everyone to moths?' asks Roisin.

'In my mind I do,' says Noel. 'For example, Shelley is a Common Lutestring.'

'Oh, stop it, Noel,' I say.

'And you, Roisin, are a *Parasemia plantaginis*.'

'What's that?'

'A Wood Tiger. They're black and yellow and they like coming out in the late afternoon and evening. You don't really find them round here, but they're common in downland and scrubby places, particularly in Ireland.'

'Touché,' says Dougie. 'What am I then?'

'You're a difficult one. I think you're some type of Hawk-Moth. Yes, you're an *Acherontia atropos*, a Death's-Head Hawk-Moth.'

'That sounds scary,' says Dougie.

'They're wonderful creatures though,' says Noel. 'They have an unmistakable skull-like marking on their thorax and when they're disturbed they make an audible squeaking sound. They feed on potatoes and honey and are regarded as the omen of death.'

'Christ,' says John, 'that's a bit serious, isn't it?'

'I like the potatoes and honey idea though,' says Dougie. 'Now, what's Samantha?'

'No,' I say. 'I don't want to know. I'm not sure I'll like it.'

'Samantha,' says Noel, looking at me, his eyes almost closed. 'I've thought long and hard about you, Samantha, and I've decided you're an *Autographa pulchrina*, a Beautiful Golden.'

'Oh, there's a surprise,' says Dougie.

'You have a golden Y-mark and you feed on flowers in the half-light.'

'How lovely,' I say.

'Yes,' says Noel, still with his eyes cast down. 'You really live up to your name.'

There's another silence.

'Right,' says John this time. 'I'm going to put Jamie to bed. Come on.'

Jamie gives Noel a kiss.

'Goodnight, little Satin Lutestring,' says Noel.

'Night night,' says Jamie.

I turn to watch Roisin as Dougie and Noel start talking. She doesn't look very happy. She's playing with her wine glass, swirling some of the deep ruby liquid round and round one way and then back the other, so that it creates a small tidal wave of wine. I reach out and touch her hand.

'Are you all right?' I ask her.

'Actually, I think I've drunk too much,' she says. 'I'll have to go home soon, but I was wondering where Lorcan was.'

'I'm sure he'll be back in a minute,' I say. 'The light's going. Shelley won't be out in the dark.'

'I'm not sure if Wood Tigers can find their way in the dark,' she says, sounding upset.

'I'm sure they can,' I say. 'It's not real, Roisin. Noel's just having some fun.'

'At my expense,' she says.

'Well, at least you're not common, like Shelley,' I say. 'Look. He's old, Roisin, and he's the kind of person who likes everything to be in its place.'

'Every*one* to be in their place, more like. He reminds me of my ex-husband, you know. He'd also get aggressive for no real reason and it was always after a few drinks.'

'Roisin,' I say. 'Noel's not being aggressive. He's just being cranky. All old people get cranky.'

'Yes, but then they use the excuse of being old to behave rudely towards someone. You tolerate him like you would a child, but I was only trying to help, y'know. And he's obviously drunk.'

'Oh no, I think he's just tipsy, isn't he?'

'Not with the amount of wine he's knocked back he's not! Now I feel like finding those bloody butterfly catalogues just to show him that women who are merely legal secretaries do have brains.'

Just then we hear footsteps coming up the garden path.

'Lorcan!' says Roisin, obviously relieved. She jumps up and sends her chair flying across the kitchen.

'That desperate to get away, are you?' Dougie asks her, breaking off the conversation with Noel. He walks over to the cupboard and brings out a bottle of brandy. 'I was just going to suggest a nightcap.'

'No,' says Roisin. 'I don't want any more to drink and I'm a bit tired. Actually, I'm a bit gone. Sorry about that but, you know.'

'But we're amongst friends,' says Dougie. 'We're on holiday. We're having fun, aren't we?'

'Yes,' says Roisin, 'and thanks for the food and all that. It was delicious, Dougie.'

'Thank you for eating it,' says Dougie. 'Now, how will you get home?'

'We'll walk,' she says.

'Then I'll walk with you.'

'No, you don't have to.'

'Yes, I do,' says Dougie. 'I don't want you wandering off a cliff or something.'

'I'm not that bad,' she says.

'Anyway,' says Dougie, 'I want to see these famous Cutlass houses or whatever they're called. Noel's got me intrigued and, remember, no one's going to cross my path. I have the sign of the skull on my thorax.'

Roisin starts laughing.

'OK, then, you can walk us home,' she says. She turns to me. 'That was grand,' she says. 'I enjoyed it.' She nods her head towards Noel. He inclines his head back at her. 'Say goodbye to your lovely husband,' she says to me, and then she and Dougie and Lorcan walk back down the garden path.

Once Shelley has left and Bennie has gone upstairs to find his father, Noel and I retire into the sitting room. He told me that when he used to be here with Janet they'd usually go and sit by the fire.

'Is that comfortable armchair with the footstool still in situ?' he asks me and I tell him it is, so in we go. I absent-mindedly take the bottle of brandy with me.

'Good girl, Samantha,' Noel says when he sees it. 'I like

to have a nip before I go to bed. It stops my joints from aching. Would you mind?' I pour him out a glass.

'You are a wonder, Samantha,' says Noel. 'You take care of everyone, don't you? I was watching you that first day you came here. You were looking with some dismay at Janet's garden and trying to sort out all your children and I knew then and there that you're someone who cares. It's so lovely to be with someone who cares. Not many people can be bothered with the old and infirm, but you will look after me, won't you?'

'Of course I will,' I say. 'I think I'm programmed to look after people, young and old.'

Noel sinks back into the chair and tells me he's feeling a bit cold and his back hurts. I plump up a cushion from the sofa and position it behind his back and then go to find him a travel blanket.

'Here,' I say as I wrap the blanket over his legs. 'Is that better?' Noel smiles weakly at me and says that maybe it would be nice to have a fire. I point out it is midsummer, but Noel closes his eyes and says he's really feeling quite chilly, and suddenly he looks rather tired so I tell him I'll go and get some coal from the storehouse outside and stoke a fire for him.

I go into the garden. The sky is clear and everything is still. I stop and look around me. I can see everything with an odd clarity. I hear an owl, the sea, something rustling in the leaves. I wish Noel hadn't mentioned the garden because it reminds me that I haven't even started it. I resolve that, in the morning, I will persuade the children to weed with me. I'm sure Edward can help. Then I remember that Edward and Isabel are still out. I get the coal, go back inside and find that John is sitting with Noel. They're both sipping at glasses of brandy and seemingly chatting away quite contentedly. I mention my concern about Edward and Isabel.

'They'll be fine,' says Noel as John stoops to make the fire. 'They're probably at my house watching television or something. It's only ten thirty, Samantha. It's just that you think it's later than it is.'

'But ten thirty is late, isn't it, John?'

'I'm not sure,' says John. 'Edward's old enough to take care of himself now and if he's with Isabel in this small village then I don't see what could happen to them really.'

'Exactly,' says Noel. 'Samantha, my dear, they are probably off sharing secrets of one type or another.'

At 11 p.m. we finally hear Edward and Isabel come home. 'Thank God for that,' I say. I realize I must have been dozing, for when I hear their footsteps I find that John and Noel are talking about wine. We listen as Edward and Isabel shuffle into the kitchen. I'm about to get up and read Edward the riot act when something makes a loud BANG! as it drops on the floor.

'Shhh,' I hear Edward say as Isabel dissolves into giggles.

'Isabel, my darling,' calls out Noel in a warning tone. 'Is that you?'

'Edward,' I say more loudly, 'come in here right now. It's very late and I've been worrying about you so . . .'

'Ooh, Granddad,' calls out Isabel, stifling more giggles. 'I thought you'd be in bed by now.'

'Obviously not,' says Noel.

'Edward, come into the sitting room,' John says sharply. The door handle turns and Edward pokes his head round the door.

'Hi,' he says, looking flushed.

'Come in the room,' says John. 'We have some things we need to discuss with you.'

'I'm not coming in,' he says as Isabel dissolves into even more giggles behind him. 'You can't make me. I'm going upstairs to bed.'

'So am I,' Isabel calls out from behind him, then we hear the pair of them rampage up the stairs.

'Edward,' says John, suddenly angry. 'You bloody idiot. You're going to wake up —'

'Waaa,' cries out Baby Sparkle.

'Too late,' I say. 'John, do you think Edward's OK?'

'Jesus Christ!' says John, heading for the stairs. 'I don't bloody care! He's a rude bloody boy. I'll settle the baby. Samantha, you get Isabel down here so Noel can go home. Tell Edward I'll deal with him later.'

He slams the door as he exits to go up the stairs. Noel raises his eyebrows at me.

'Oh dear,' he says. 'Your husband has quite a temper.'

'I think he's right to be cross,' I say. 'It's so late and they woke the baby up.'

I then tell Noel that, actually, Isabel can stay the night if she wants to as Edward has a truckle bed in his room.

'I think Jamie's in with Bennie,' I say. 'It's fine. I'll sort them out. They do seem a bit worse for wear and it's very late really. Noel, do you think something's going on?'

Noel looks at me for a bit.

'I'm not sure, Samantha,' he says. 'I mean, yes, something is going on. Something is very obviously going on. They're enjoying each other's company, but are they falling in love? Are they discovering the joys of the world together? Who can say . . .'

'Noel!' I say, shocked. 'I hope you're not implying . . . that's not what I meant.'

'Didn't you mean that? Oh, young love, first love, Samantha. Can't you remember it? The tingle of that person's hand in yours? The way you felt deliciously warm every time they looked at you? It's nothing to do with carnal knowledge, my dear. It's to do with recognizing a certain something, something so special, in that other person, and that can happen at any age, can't it? You know that, my Beautiful Golden, don't you?'

'Noel,' I say a bit crossly because he doesn't seem to be concentrating on my original question. 'Do you think they're drunk? That's what I'm talking about.'

But before I can say any more, Noel says, 'Send Isabel home in the morning. Now, don't see me out. I'm fine as I am,' and he heads towards the door. 'I'll leave you my brandy,' he says. It's only after he's set off down the road that I realize there's none left.

Everything upstairs is quiet now. I look at the dining table and all I can see is a mess. I decide I'll clear it up in the morning. I get two glasses of water and go up the two flights of stairs to Edward's room. I'm determined to find out what's going on, but Edward has collapsed on his bed, fast asleep, still in his clothes. Isabel has fared better. She's wearing her T-shirt and some knickers – not a G-string, thank God – and has at least managed to pull the bedclothes down on the bed. I tuck her in and place one glass of water on the floor for her and another one next to Edward's bed in case he wants a drink in the night. I go downstairs, intending to talk to John about Edward, but when I get into the bedroom I find John is also fast asleep. He's in bed and tucked into his arms is Baby Sparkle. She's lying flat on her back with her tiny arms laid out beside her. She's breathing deeply. They are bathed in the moonlight that's flowing in through the veranda windows, so much so that they are almost glowing. I stand and watch them. Then I slip off my clothes and carefully climb into bed next to them, falling asleep to the sound of them breathing in unison.

15. Life Cycle

When I get up in the morning, I find Dougie asleep on the sofa in the sitting room. I look at him and remember how long I've known him. He has been such a part of my life. Before I met John, I knew Dougie. I met him after my first John and I broke up. He was married then, but his wife left him soon after and so we helped each other through divorce and pain and recriminations. Then I met John the Second, and Dougie . . . well, he's single, but my dearest wish is for him to meet someone and be happy.

He's snoring gently and, in between snores, he looks as if he's smiling slightly. I have no idea what the time is but, for some reason, I'm the only one up. It must be earlier than I thought. I look outside. The sun is low in the sky yet the bees are already humming outside. They keep head-butting the window in a rather dozy fashion. I step outside on to the lawn and feel the dew between my toes. It's cold and heavy. I walk through the garden and look at the flow-ers and then I feel guilty. The sweet peas have totally overrun their trellis and have spread along the back bed and become entwined round the bottoms of the delphiniums. The Sweet Williams are as tall as sunflowers, but their leaves at the bottom of their stalks are dry and curling up. The flower beds are a riot of hollyhocks, lavender, summer lilies and marigolds. There's a wonderful scent coming from somewhere. I sniff the air and follow the heavy scent over to a bush desperately in need of pruning. I bend down to sniff the little white flowers on it. They smell like oranges. Then I look at the honeysuckle growing up in the shade of the house and the climbing wisteria. I open the shed at the bottom of the garden and find a trowel. I kneel down at the nearest bed and start digging up weeds in a desultory fashion. I hear a noise behind me so I turn round to find Isabel standing at the doorway of the house. She's still wearing her knickers and a T-shirt and she's yawning. She stretches her arms above her head, screws up her eyes and opens her mouth in a wide O-shape and, as she does this, her T-shirt rises up above her knickers to show her tanned stomach. Without all her make-up on and with her hair hanging down, I realize she's really quite pretty.

'Isabel!' I call out to her. She opens her eyes and looks blearily down the garden and then, when she sees me, she steps out on to the lawn.

'Och,' she says as her feet hit the wet, cold ground. 'Jeee-sus.' She tiptoes down to me, almost rising on to the tops of her toes with every step and then letting out a little gasp of air every time the soles of her feet touch down on the grass.

'Come and stand here,' I say. 'The sun's dried it out a bit where I am.'

She reaches me and stops and yawns again.

'What are you doing?' she asks me.

'Weeding,' I say. 'Don't ask me why.'

'I dinna like weeding,' she says.

We both stand there and watch as a red and black butterfly floats over and settles on the buddleia bush.

'Do you know what butterfly that is?' I ask Isabel, trying to make conversation.

'No,' she says.

'Is it a Red Admiral?'

Isabel yawns again.

'Are you very tired?'

'Yes,' she says. Then she says, 'It's Granddad who likes butterflies and moths and that sort of thing, not me.'

She turns round and starts walking back to the house. I turn to watch her and find that John is standing on the balcony outside our bedroom window. He's wearing nothing but a pair of jeans and he has Baby Sparkle in his arms. His hair is sticking up but he looks good – tanned, relaxed. He waves at me when he sees me.

'Come and see us,' he says. 'We want you.'

I go back through the garden and up the stairs. I hear Bennie and Jamie in their bedroom. I can hear Jamie saying, 'Let's get my dolly some breakfast,' and Bennie is saying, 'No, let's get me some breakfast.'

I go into our bedroom. John is still standing on the balcony so I go up behind him.

'I want to talk about Edward,' I say.

John turns and kisses me.

'No,' he says, now kissing the top of the baby's head. 'No talking. Not now. Tell me everything later. All I want to know is, is anyone up?'

'Bennie and Jamie are.'

'They'll do,' says John.

'What do you mean?' I say.

'Wait here,' he says, then he walks out the door.

Five minutes later he comes back with no baby.

'Where's Sparkle?'

'She's in with the boys.'

'In with the boys? Why?'

John reaches out for me and pulls me towards him. 'Why do you think?' he says, nuzzling my neck.

'Oh my God,' I say. 'You'll do anything . . .'

'The time is right,' says John.

'Is it?' I say, running my hands through his hair for, somehow, the time does seem right with the morning heat still on my skin and him smelling of fresh sweat.

'Mmm,' he says, not really concentrating.

'I mean, can we leave Sparkle with the boys?'

'Mmm,' says John again, undoing my skirt. As he does so, I can taste the salt on his skin. We move towards the bed.

'I don't mean Bennie. I mean Jamie.'

'Jamie's fine,' he says.

'What if he hurts her?'

'Please be quiet,' says John, pulling my knickers down.

'I'm still worrying about Sparkle,' I say.

'Stop worrying. I'll be quick,' he says.

Afterwards, we get Baby Sparkle from Jamie and Bennie's room where we find her lying on the bed being cuddled by them both.

'I love Baby Sparkle,' says Jamie.

'Do you?' I say, sitting down next to him and giving him a big kiss.

'I love Baby Sparkle too,' says Bennie.

'Ra-la-ra-la-ra,' says Baby Sparkle.

'We all love Baby Sparkle,' says John. 'Now let's go downstairs and decide what to do today.'

When we get into the kitchen we find Dougie is clearing up. He's whistling as he carries plates from the table to the sink.

'Good morning, Dougie,' John says.

'Good morning,' says Dougie, 'and what a lovely morning it is.'

I go to the sink. 'I'll wash up,' I say. Then I realize that Edward isn't up so I ask John to go and see if he's still in his bed.

'Maybe you could talk to him now, could you? But don't be rough. Just ask him what he's been up to.'

'I'll try,' says John, 'but I can't guarantee he'll tell me anything. I'm still pretty cross with him.'

'Well, don't be. Being cross will not help anything.'

'Oh, all right,' sighs John as he heads to the stairs.

Dougie is still whistling.

'You're in a good mood,' I say to him. 'What time did you come home?'

'Oh, about midnight,' he says. 'Actually, I wanted to have a bit of brandy and sit outside on the veranda, but it had all gone.'

'I think John drank it.'

Dougie snorts.

'Why are you snorting?'

'Well,' he says, 'he doesn't smell like he drank it. You know how alcohol leaves that slight smell on someone? Maybe Noel drank it.'

'Oh, no,' I say. 'Noel smells all grown-up, of aftershave and clean, fresh breath and mouthwash.'

'Have you lost your mind? Every alcoholic smells like that . . .'

'What?' I ask. 'What do you mean?'

'He's a drinker! Haven't you noticed?'

'He's an old man, Dougie,' I say. 'I should think that, having got to nearly seventy, he can do what he likes. What's wrong with having a few nips of brandy because your joints hurt?'

'Oh, I think it's a bit more than that, Samantha,' says

Dougie. 'I thought he'd had a couple before he'd even got to the dinner party and that's why he was so tetchy with Roisin.'

'What if he had? Maybe he gets lonely sometimes. He hasn't had a great life, you know. Sarah de Salis told me his wife left him and he barely got to see his own —'

'That's no excuse for being drunk and rude,' says Dougie.

'You're being very judgemental. We were all drinking, Dougie. It was a dinner party. We were all in a drinking mood. Noel drank no more and no less than any of us. It wasn't him who had to be escorted home.'

'Yes, but that's because Roisin's not used to alcohol, you see? Anyway, have you been to see her place on the Cutlass Estate? It's very nice. I have no idea what that old bore's got against it.'

'Old bore? Who? Noel? Jesus, Dougie, you've only just met him and —'

Just then a shadow passes across the door and a letter drops through the letter box.

'What's this?' says Dougie, bending down to retrieve it. 'Oh, look, it has your name on the front of it. Let's open it.'

'It's for me, Dougie,' I say as he opens the envelope and holds the letter high in the air.

'Oh, is it a love letter?' he says, waving it just out of my reach. 'Does it say "Dear Beautiful Golden . . ."?'

'Give it to me,' I say, getting cross.

'Oh, stop fussing,' he says. 'It's not from Noel. It's some boring letter to do with the house. Look. It says "Dear Mrs Smythe, I wish to introduce myself. My name is Gordon Cutlass and I am the proprietor of Cutlass Candles and —"'

'It's one of those letters!' I say.

'What letters?' asks Dougie.

'Read on. Does he offer to buy the house?'

Dougie sits down at the kitchen table and smooths the paper out. 'Blah blah blah . . . oh, here it is. Yes, it says "if you ever wish to sell your beautiful cottage then I would be more than happy to meet with you and discuss terms that are favourable to yourself . . ."'

'My God!' I say. 'That man has no shame!'

'Who has no shame?' asks John, reappearing in the kitchen.

'Mr Cutlass Candles! He's just written asking if he can buy the house.'

'Under favourable conditions,' says Dougie.

'Under no conditions,' I say. 'It isn't even mine to sell.'

'Well, how could he possibly know that?' asks Dougie.

'Why are you trying to defend him?' I say hotly.

'I'm not,' he says. 'It's just that lawyers such as myself see all sides. There is nothing wrong with Mr Cutlass wanting to buy this house. Roisin told me he paid for the church bell to be repaired and that he bought the interactive whiteboards for the schoo—'

'With money made by forcing child labourers in China to put wicks into his candles!'

'Can this be substantiated?' asks Dougie, raising his eyebrows at John.

'John . . .' I say pleadingly.

'I'm not getting involved,' says John. 'I have only come downstairs to report on the matter of Edward, which is what you asked me to do, Samantha, so . . . Edward says that he and Isabel delivered their flyers all over the village and that it took ages because there were a hundred and one of them and that by the time they got home they were very tired and that's why they went to bed. He says he's been having a great time with Isabel who, by the way, has already gone home so that Noel doesn't get worried about her.'

'Oh,' I say.

'You're worrying too much about everything,' says John as he goes towards the telephone, which has started to ring. He picks up the telephone. 'Yes,' he says. 'Yes. She's here. I'll just get her. It's for you,' he says to me, beckoning me to come through from the kitchen. 'It's Sarah de Salis for you.'

I pick up the phone. 'Sarah,' I say.

'Samantha,' she says. 'I was wondering, if it's not too much bother, if you could come round this morning?'

'Yes,' I say. 'I'm sure I can. Is there a problem?'

'No,' she says, a bit too quickly. 'I've just found something out that I need to discuss with you, Samantha.'

'Is it about the butterfly catalogues?'

'No,' she says. 'It's about something else. I can't talk about it on the phone. I just need to see you.'

'OK,' I say. 'We'll leave in a minute.'

I put the phone down and go back into the kitchen. John is making coffee and toast.

'What was that about?' he says.

'It's very odd,' I say, sitting down. 'Sarah's just asked me to go round. I think she sounded a bit upset. I think I'd better go now really.'

'Why don't we all go?' says Dougie. 'I'm desperate to see the house and John probably needs to see the place where the puppet show should go.'

'I don't know,' I say. 'I think it might be too much for her.'

'What? Even if we just looked at the garden? Or stayed in the driveway or something?'

At that point Edward mooches into the kitchen. 'I'm bored,' he says, picking up a piece of toast, 'and Bennie and Jamie have tied Baby Sparkle up with a piece of string.'

'What!' I say, rushing out towards the sitting room.

'Only joking,' he says.

'Right, that does it,' says John. 'We're all going for a walk.'

'A walk!' says Edward, incensed. 'I'm not going for a bloody walk.'

John gets up and walks towards Edward. He pulls himself up as tall as can be and he puffs his chest out and then he says to Edward, in a low voice, 'I said we're all going for a walk, so that is what we're doing.'

Edward looks at him nervously. 'All right,' he says. 'I'll go and get dressed.'

'Good,' says John and he sits back down again.

After Edward leaves the room I ask John what all that puffing up was about.

'You looked like a chaffinch,' I say. 'Why did you do that? Why did you go towards Edward and do that standing thing?'

'I'm showing him who's boss,' says John. 'One day that boy is going to be bigger than me but, until he is, I'm using my physical strength to show him that I'm in charge.'

'Gosh, that's a bit basic, isn't it?'

'Yes,' says Dougie merrily, 'of course it is. We're men!'

While the others get ready, and Jamie, surprisingly, puts on a pair of jeans, I call the local council. The lady who answers the telephone tells me that she doesn't think she can help me as she's not sure if I need a Health and Safety licence to put on a puppet show.

'I can't really help you, my dear,' she says in a strong, slow

Devonian accent. 'Puppet shows don't come under my jurisdiction.'

'It's not just a puppet show,' I say. 'There's a fête that happens every year. It's at the Manor House. Maybe you've heard of it?'

'The Maanoor House,' she drawls. 'I don't know nothing about that.'

'I think maybe they do get a licence every year for it, but I'm not sure. They serve food there though.'

'And what name would that licence come under, my dear?' she says.

'Oh, maybe Noel Rideout. It's spelled Rideout, but pronounced –'

'I know how it's pronounced,' she says. 'His firm is in Barnstaple. But no, Mr Rideout has never applied for a licence here as far as I know. Would it be under any other name maybe?'

'Sarah de Salis?' I say. 'Or maybe Sarah Daubeny-Fortescue.'

'Nooo,' she says. 'I'd remember those names.'

'Well, all I know,' I say a bit desperately, 'is that Mr Cutlass usually pays for the pond to be fenced off.'

'Ah,' she says. 'Mr Cutlass did you say? Mr Gordon Cutlass?'

'Yes, that's him.'

'Ee's just bought my dad's place near Lower Strand,' she says. 'Paid a fortune for it. Oh, we love Mr Cutlass we do. You just get him to give me a tinkle on the phone and I'll get you whatever it is you need. If it's a certificate you want, then it's a certificate you'll get. You just ask 'im to call me. He knows who I am.'

'I can't do that,' I say. 'I'm organizing the fête so I think I have to apply for it.'

'Well, I'm sure Mr Cutlass wouldn't mind helping out. He's very kind in that way.'

'No,' I say sharply. 'It has to be me.'

'Well then, my love,' she says, a bit coldly. 'Then yous is going to have to come here to the offices and get the forms, I'm afraid. No other way round it.'

'Right,' I sigh, 'and where are your offices?'

'Barnstaple,' she says and rings off.

We end up driving to Sarah de Salis's house because I decided it might be good to show Dougie and John the beach. As we were getting ready to leave the house, the telephone rang again and this time it was Jean-Paul, the lead French puppeteer, who told John that the chateau he had carefully made from reclaimed wood that was an integral part of his *Pulcinella* set design had caught fire when one of the glove puppet operators lit a cigarette and then inadvertently dropped it on top of it.

'Oh God,' groaned John.

'Maybe it's hard to smoke at the same time as having a glove puppet on your hand,' said Dougie.

The upshot is that John has to go back to London today.

'I am so sorry, Samantha,' he said, kissing the top of my head. 'I won't leave till late afternoon and I'll be back next weekend.'

'Oh, that's OK,' I said, feeling that it actually wasn't OK at all.

'It took me an age to make that chateau,' he said as he heard me sigh.

'I know,' I said. 'It's just that it's so nice having you here. I think the boys have really appreciated spending some time with you and . . .'

'Is that all right with you, Dougie?' John asked him, talking over me.

'Me?' said Dougie. 'What on earth have I got to do with it?'

'Well, I'm taking you back to London, aren't I?'

'Are you?' says Dougie.

'Well, yes, or else how else are you going to get back?'

'I don't particularly want to go back. If it's all right with Samantha, I thought I might stay a bit longer. Roisin and I were having a chat last night and she seems determined to find those catalogues. You know how I like a challenge, Samantha, so I said I'd stay and help her look. Is that OK?'

I nodded my head. 'That would be lovely,' I said.

When we get to Sarah de Salis's house, Dougie driving my car and John taking his, we find that Noel is already there. He's standing on the doorstep about to knock on the door. He looks slightly confused when he sees two cars pull up on the drive, but relaxes somewhat when I get out of the first car.

'Oh, it's you,' he says. 'You've brought your brood.'

I explain about everyone wanting to see at least the garden and maybe even the house. 'I think John needs to know where to put the puppet show and he has to go back to London today,' I say. I then ask him why he's here as well. 'Did Sarah ring you?'

'Yes,' he says shortly. 'I was in bed. Isabel took the call.'

Isabel appears from round the back of the house.

'I can't see her,' she says.

'What's the problem?' I ask her.

'There seems to be no answer at the door,' says Noel. 'I've tried knocking three times now.'

'Oh God,' I say. 'I hope she hasn't fallen off her ladder. I was round here the other day and she'd been cleaning cobwebs in the back hall.'

Edward emerges from the car when he sees Isabel. 'Hi,' he says to her, nonchalantly kicking a pebble off into the flower beds.

'Hi,' she says. They stand in silence. Then Isabel says, 'I'm sorry for leaving without saying goodbye this morning.'

'S'all right,' says Edward.

'Come on, Isabel,' says Noel sharply. 'Go back round the east wing and see if you can see Sarah. Take Edward with you.'

A minute later, Edward and Isabel appear again. They're running towards us.

'Quick, Granddad,' Isabel says breathlessly. 'You have to come.'

'What's happened?' I say as Noel and I start to walk round the back.

'There's an old lady sitting at the kitchen table,' Edward says. 'Isabel picked me up so I could look through the downstairs bathroom window and I saw her slumped over the table. I think she might be . . . she might be . . .'

'Dead!' says Isabel.

Noel and I now break into a run. I get to the back door first. I turn the handle. It won't move. I rap on the door, hard, then harder. Nothing happens. 'Sarah!' I cry out.

Noel appears at my side. He tries the door handle. It won't budge for him either.

'Right,' he says. 'It's locked. Now, did Edward say he saw her through the bathroom window?'

'Yes.'

'We need to find a ladder.'

Noel and I both turn to go towards the old coach house that Sarah showed me just the other day but, as we do, the handle of the back door begins to turn.

'A ghost!' screams Isabel, laughing.

'Aarggh,' says Edward, looking bug-eyed. He starts running back round the side of the house.

The door opens and there is Sarah de Salis. Her eyes are red, her hair is straggling over her face.

'Samantha?' she says, looking this way and that like a blind woman. 'Is that you?'

I go forward. I take her hand.

'Yes, it's me,' I say. 'Noel is here too. You called me. You asked me to come.'

'I know,' she says, finally focusing on me. 'I did ask you to come and here you are and I'm so glad. Something awful has happened, Samantha. I've discovered something so awful . . .'

'Not here,' says Noel quietly. 'We need to go inside, Sarah. I shall make some tea.'

We go into the kitchen. It's cold and it smells. Edward reappears at the back door.

'Go,' I tell him. 'Go and help Daddy. I'll be out in a minute.'

'She's not a ghost then?' says Edward, staring at Sarah.

'No, now you need to tell Daddy and Dougie not to come in for a while. Go now.'

'Is your husband here?' asks Sarah. 'He must come in. He must have tea.'

'It's not necessary,' says Noel, putting the kettle on. 'He's only here to find where to put the puppet show.'

'The puppet show?' says Sarah. 'I don't want it here.' She looks wild-eyed again.

'I thought you did?' I say, sitting down at the kitchen table next to her. 'It's to help save the house.'

'Save the house?' she says. 'Save this house?' Then her voice goes very low and she half talks, half whispers. 'This is a bad house. It's a very bad house.'

'What do you mean?' I say. I can see Sarah is close to tears. 'It's not a bad house. It's a beautiful house.'

'Yes, maybe, but it's been built on bad things.'

'Now, Sarah,' says Noel, calmly pouring out some tea and sitting down at the table. 'Why don't you tell us what the problem is?'

Sarah sits and holds a cup of tea. Her hands are shaking so much I keep thinking the cup will slip from her grasp, but she manages to steady herself enough to take a sip.

'I was looking through the records,' she says. 'You knew I was doing that, didn't you, Samantha?'

'Yes,' I say.

'I wanted to leave something behind, you see? Do you see?'

'Yes,' says Noel slowly as if talking to someone who has lost their wits. 'We do see.'

'Well, I don't want to now,' she says suddenly. 'I don't want to at all.'

'Why not?' asks Noel. 'What has changed your mind?'

'I found something out,' she whispers. 'Something horrible.'

'What?' I say. 'What is it?'

Sarah de Salis looks straight at me. 'What I've found out is so horrible that, at first, I could barely believe it. But now I've checked and double-checked and I've talked to an expert archivist in Barnstaple and she has confirmed what I think and so it can only be true.'

'What?' says Noel. 'What on earth is it?'

'Gerrard's forefather, the one who built this house, was a merchant, you see. Did you know that?'

'No,' says Noel.

'He bought his title. He didn't earn it. He bought it.'

'Is that it?' says Noel. 'There's no shame in that! Loads of people buy their titles. I think even Rupert Howse, the man who bought Rideout and Rideout off me, is a Right Honourable or something.'

'I'm just explaining what type of man the first Lord Fortescue was,' says Sarah. 'He was the type of man who bought the trappings. He didn't earn his title.'

'But he earned the money to buy the house, didn't he?' I say.

'Oh, yes,' says Mrs de Salis. 'He earned it.'

'So what's the problem then?' asks Noel.

'The problem is, he was a slave merchant,' says Mrs de Salis.

'He was a what?' says Noel, looking aghast.

'He bought and sold slaves. I know that because in those dusty books in the library are all his accounts and someone – him maybe? his wife? I don't know who – logged it all down. The slaves came from Nigeria and he bought them in the West Indies and he had them shipped over here to Bristol and then he sold them. That's how he made his money. And then, when the Old House burned down, he took the opportunity to build this house, just the way he wanted, on the backs of those poor African people who were taken from their families and sold into slavery.'

There is a long silence. Then Noel says, 'Are you sure?'

'Yes,' says Sarah. 'I have no doubt at all.'

'What do you want to do then?' I ask her.

'We must cancel the fête,' she says. 'I no longer want to save this house and I can't have that type of celebration in a place that is tainted like this house is.'

'But it's not the house's fault,' I say. 'And isn't there an argument for retaining this house, for not selling to Mr Cutlass Candles? If you sell it to him, which you will have to do if we cancel the fête, then the immoral people in this world who make money out of slavery have won and we've lost. Isn't that so?'

Sarah de Salis doesn't say anything for a moment. Then she says, 'Noel says houses always retain a bit of the people who lived in them. This house belonged to a slave driver. Let it go back to another.'

'But you and Gerrard lived here,' I say. 'You still live here. Why wouldn't the house retain your character?'

'I have no one left,' says Sarah, now looking worn out. 'Why should I save it? I've spent my life trying to save people. I tried to save Gerrard, but he died. I have nothing to look forward to. For me there is only death waiting round the corner. Nothing else. This is my final word on it.'

Noel says that we should go. I turn to look at the house as we walk out to the driveway.

'I can't bear it, Noel,' I tell him. I feel tears in my eyes. 'We've failed, haven't we?'

Noel doesn't say anything.

16. Common Status

On the way to the beach, Noel is very quiet. Somehow we have managed to squash him and Isabel into our car. Dougie has taken my car and, along with Bennie, has gone to find Roisin and Lorcan.

'I said I'd pick her up in the morning,' he told me. 'Do you mind?' I told him I didn't and that, in fact, I thought it was a good idea. We arranged to meet at the beach café and then Noel said he thought he would like to go to the beach to get some sea air.

'You want to go to the beach?' I said to him, looking at yet another heavy three-piece suit he was wearing and his shiny brogues.

'No, not the beach,' he said tiredly. 'The beach café. There is a café there, isn't there?'

'Yes,' I said. 'It's just above the beach.'

So now, as John drives us, I find myself filling him in about what has just happened.

'Slavery?' says John, giving a low whistle. 'That's not good.'

'No, it isn't,' says Noel. 'It isn't good.'

'Sarah doesn't want to go ahead with the fête,' I say. John notices I'm upset.

'Maybe she'll change her mind,' he says.

'I don't think so,' I say. 'She sounded pretty sure that she didn't want to keep the house any more.'

We all sit in silence. I can see Noel's face in the rear-view mirror. He looks pale, exhausted. I sigh. 'It's such a shame,' I say to no one in particular, 'because I really feel the fête is a chance to bring everyone together – the people who live here and those who are just on holiday. I thought it would be a good thing, a happy thing.'

'That's true,' says John. 'It's such a shame. I do hope she doesn't end up regretting her decision.'

'I fear she may,' says Noel, 'because I'm sure, deep down, she will want to leave it as it should be in all its wonderful ancestral glory, not being turned into small flats for newcomers.'

'If she sells the house,' says John, 'where will she end up?'

'Probably on the Cutlass Estate,' says Noel, grimacing. 'Mr Philanthropy will no doubt offer her one of his bungalows with its Formica kitchen and linoleum on the floor. He'd save face that way. I can just hear him telling the AGM that although he has put in for planning to convert the Manor House, he has given Sarah a new home. They'd probably fall for it, which is a shame, because I had a call from Mr Henderson last night to tell me he was so delighted by the idea of a puppet show that we could put the profits from the fête towards renovating the house after all.'

'You're joking,' I say. 'What did you do to make him say that?'

'I appealed to his feminine side or, in this case, Mrs Pat Pucklechurch.'

'How?'

'I went round to her stables and gawped at all her equines and then I asked her about hunting and she droned on for an age. Then I told her about the puppet show and, crashing snob that she is, when she heard it was a sell-out show in London she got very over-excited.'

'Really?'

'Yes. She stamped her hooves and whinnied.'

'You're brilliant, Noel,' I say. 'Just brilliant.'

'Ah, the body may be slow but the brain is willing,' he says.

'I mean, that's it! This is the sign Sarah needs to see and understand that her house is worth fighting for. This is all she has – this village, the people who live here and the people like us who visit. As you've always said, her house is of historical importance and I think she will come to see that despite the past history of it, it's something worth saving, that the Daubeny-Fortescue name can mean more than the ancestors who made money from slavery. It should be a celebration of her life. She shouldn't be allowed to die a sad woman holding on to a bitter secret.'

I tell Noel he must go to see her and change her mind.

'Tell her that the village wants to give her the money. Tell her the puppet show is on the way. Tell her that she has to do this now or God only knows where she will end up.'

Noel says he will go and see her as soon as he can.

'I shall try to be as persuasive as possible.'

'That may mean actually eating her food,' I say, 'even the biscuits.'

Noel sighs dramatically. 'If I must . . .' he says.

As soon as we pull up in the car park, Edward and Isabel clamber out of the boot and start running off down the path towards the sea.

'Don't run off,' I yell after them. 'Come back soon and get some lunch.'

'All right,' yells Edward, not looking round. The last I see of them they are running on to the sands, whooping with delight. John gets out of the car and unstraps Baby

Sparkle, who has been asleep for the entire journey. She gives a little yawn and stretches her arms upwards, then smiles at John. He holds her close and gives her a cuddle.

'I love you, my baby,' he says as she nestles her head on to his shoulder. I go to the boot to get her pushchair. John follows me. He's looking at me in a quizzical fashion.

'Are you sure you really want to go ahead with the fête?' he says.

'Yes. Why wouldn't I be?'

'I don't know how to say this without sounding mean but, you don't live here, Samantha. You're on holiday. In a few weeks you'll be home and Lower Strand will continue, fête or no fête.'

'I can't believe you just said that!' I say. 'I care about this village. I've known it for a long time, ever since Janet lived here. People in this village need to take care of one another and, although I'm an outsider, I feel like an insider. I don't want to just come here and use the beach and buy food in the shop. I want to make a difference. That's the only way this village and the people who live in it will survive. Look at Noel. Before I came along, who did he have to pour him a brandy and make him a fire when he's cold? No one. Who was going to look for the *Daubeny-Fortescue Catalogues of Lepidoptera*? No one. Now Roisin and Dougie are going to find them.'

'But how are you going to make all this happen?'

'Roisin and Dougie will find the catalogues and Sarah will then have something to feel seriously proud of and Noel will tell her that the village is willing to come together and help her. It's the only way to save the house from probable destruction.'

'But, Samantha, my dearest wife,' he says, holding out

his hand to take mine, 'you're doing what you always do. You're trying to save people. You can't do that time and time again.'

'Why can't I? It's my job to help people. That's what good people do. Anyway, I owe Noel. Surely you can acknowledge that Noel is the only person who has got through to Jamie in the last twelve months? That makes him and his concerns very special to me.'

'Yes,' says John. 'Noel certainly has made a difference. I can't disagree with that. I'm just wondering if all this is worth it.'

'How can you ask that, John? You haven't been here so you don't realize how this community works, what the needs of this place are.'

'Oh, sorry,' he says shortly. 'I thought you were doing this for Noel.'

Just then, Jamie appears at the back of the car. He has his dolly with him.

'Why don't you leave your dolly in the car?' I say to him. 'Or else she'll get sandy.'

'NO!' yells Jamie, looking angry. 'I SHALL NOT!' He then runs round the side of the car and cannons into Noel.

Noel staggers back and flails his arms out to balance himself.

'Jamie!' I say as I rush forward to grab hold of Noel's arm before he topples over. 'What on earth are you doing?'

'Oh dear, James,' says Noel, trying to regain some composure. 'You nearly had me base over apex there. Phew. I'm an old-timer, James. If I fall, I break.'

'If you fall, you break?' says Jamie, looking upset. He reaches out to Noel. 'I'm sorry,' he says, now looking as if he's about to cry. 'I'm really sorry.'

Noel bends down and holds Jamie in his arms.

'That's a nice thing to say, James,' he says. 'I can see that you're sorry, but you must stop shouting. How can we go and look for a Dark Dagger if you shout at your mother?'

'A dark dagger?' says Jamie. 'Will it hurt me?'

'Oh no, not that type of dagger,' says Noel. 'A moth one. It likes goat willow, you know, and it has a long dagger mark near its trailing corner.'

'Goat willow?'

'It's a plant,' says Noel. He straightens himself up and winks at me. 'Now, if you're a good boy, James, you may find one here on the beach.'

'Really?' says Jamie, his eyes as round as small gobstoppers.

'Absolutely,' says Noel. 'Now I'm sure your father will go and help you look.' He turns to John. 'You need to look on the scrubland near the rocks. Goat willow often grows there.'

'Oh,' says John, sounding a bit put out. 'I was going to get a —'

'Please, Daddy,' says Jamie, putting his hands in his father's. 'Please can we? I'm very good at finding flutterbyes.'

'Remember, James,' says Noel, 'they're not butterflies. They're moths.'

'But don't moths only come out at night?' asks John.

'Not all of them,' says Noel smoothly. 'If you look carefully, you'll find out, won't you?'

'All right,' says John, sighing. 'Come on, Jamie,' he says. 'Come on, Baby Sparkle.'

'Is Baby Sparkle coming?' asks Jamie. I see John brace himself for an onslaught of shouting.

'Yes,' says John.

'Good,' says Jamie. 'I love Baby Sparkle and I want her to see a Dagger Dark.'

Before Jamie walks off, Noel touches him lightly on the shoulder. 'Much as I do like your pink dress,' he says, 'I do think you look very spiffing in your blue jeans.'

Jamie blushes to the tips of his ears.

Noel tucks his arm in mine as John wanders off towards the bottom of the cliff with his two youngest children.

'Good,' he says. 'I've got you to myself, Samantha.'

'Noel,' I say, 'is there really a moth called a Dark Dagger?'

'Of course there is,' he says, 'but they don't really come out in the daytime. They do like lights, but only really of the electric variety at night. Oh, and they tend to be seen most in suburban gardens, but . . .'

'Well, why did you send John off then?' I say, trying to sound cross when, in fact, I secretly feel a bit flattered.

'Because I want to talk to you,' says Noel, arching his eyebrows.

We walk into the café but, as Noel and I are about to sit down, I hear a familiar voice say, *Bonjour, Samantha. C'est moi.*'

It's Susie. She's standing in front of us, clad in a white string bikini, high heels and a cowboy hat. Her electro-magnet pendant is swinging down low between her breasts, as is a necklace made of turquoise stones. She has on a matching bracelet and a pair of wraparound sunglasses. Next to her is Karin. She's carrying a tray with two coffees on it and two chocolate brownies.

'I just can't resist it, Samantha,' she says, giggling. She's wearing a black one-piece swimsuit. I notice that her right

shoulder is somewhat burnt. 'I fell asleep in the sun yesterday,' she says, blushing when she sees me looking at her
shoulder. 'Silly me.'

'Yes, silly you,' says Susie.

I remember that Noel is with me.

'Noel,' I say. 'This is Susie.' Noel politely stretches out
his hand to shake Susie's hand. For some reason this seems
to take Susie by surprise.

'Oh,' she says, putting her hand out to meet his. 'What
a gentleman. How lovely.'

'And this,' I say, pointing to Karin, 'is Karin.' Noel shakes
her hand too.

'And who, might I ask, Samantha,' says Noel, turning to
look at me, 'are Susie and Karin?'

'Well,' I say, feeling a bit embarrassed, 'they're my friends.'

'Your friends,' says Noel, carefully emphasizing the word
'friends'. 'Are they really? How interesting.'

HOW TO MAKE FRIENDS ON HOLIDAY

Making friends on holiday is one of the most difficult and
dangerous pastimes known to humankind. It's impossible to
know this until you're an adult for, when you're a little child,
you make friends with impunity. You have no concept of
whether or not you actually like the person you have suppos-
edly made friends with. All you know is that they are roughly
the same size as you and they seem a lot of fun. The rest –
what language they speak, what class they are, what they look
like, who their parents are – seems immaterial. I once made
very good friends with a small girl called Vicky. We played
every day on the beach in France and we hung out together
and lent each other our dollies. We had sleepovers in each
other's apartments and we laughed at the same things – doing

high-jumps on the holiday park trampoline, watching adults try to eat *fruits de mer* as most of it marched off their plates – and we cried at the same things. We were especially upset at the thought of being parted and we promised, hand on heart, to write to each other every day without fail once we got back home to the opposite ends of the country. The day came two weeks later when we had to part and I cried as Vicky got on the tour bus that took her away from me. As the bus rounded the corner of the road, when I would no longer see her and had no one to play with, my mother said, 'You played with Vicky so nicely, Samantha. Honestly, it was as if you'd never noticed that she had only one arm.'

'ONE ARM!!' I said in horror. 'What do you mean?'

For, in truth, I hadn't noticed. I hadn't been interested in Vicky's arm or her legs or anything very much. That's how real friends are. Mind you, that afternoon I met Elizabeth and we got on very well too. All of a sudden it was her I was laughing with about the crawling crustaceans and the bouncy trampoline, and this time I did look very carefully at how many arms she had just so I wasn't caught out again.

Interestingly enough, when Edward was three and we were on holiday in Greece, just the two of us, he made very good friends with a little Greek boy. This little boy spoke no English and Edward spoke no Greek, but still they had a wonderful time on the beach, making sandcastles and swimming together in the shallows. Eventually we had to leave and Edward hugged and kissed this little boy goodbye. About a year later when I was telling John the Second all about it and I was describing how well the boys had got on despite the language barrier, Edward said, 'What language barrier?' and I told him that the boy had spoken no English at all. Edward was very affronted.

'He did speak English,' he insisted, 'or else how did we play so well together?' Nothing would deter him, not even the truth.

But as an adult it's a totally different scenario. Everything, every gesture, every look, every sentence, is loaded with meaning.

The beach is, of course, the prime place to meet people. In many ways it's obvious. You are, quite literally, stripped bare and rather vulnerable. As an adult I have talked to far more people on the beach than I ever do in my normal life, except when I'm walking the dog. I meet hundreds of people walking the dog and we all know each other by our dogs' names, so if I see Spotty the Dalmatian galloping towards me and, behind him, his owner, I'll say, 'Hello, Spotty's owner!' and Spotty's owner will wave at me and say, 'Hello, Beady's owner!' Actually, he doesn't do that. He says, 'Hello, Beady's mum!' which rather freaks me out as I have obviously never given birth to a puppy. This concept makes John laugh. He always strokes Beady of an evening and says, 'Come to Daddy,' because he knows it winds me up. But dogs are a great way of meeting people and I like to think that's because Beady is so generally loveable and fantastic that everyone wants to pat her.

The same cannot be said for my children. Oh, no. I've seen people shrink in horror from them, but it is true that if you go to a family-orientated beach with your children you will meet people. They're usually other mothers and when you all notice each other and work out that their children, or some of their children, are the same age as your own children, then it's more than likely you will have a vested interest in making friends with each other. And, for the duration of the holiday, that person may truly feel like a friend. You'll sit and chat to them as your children get covered in sand. You'll somehow reveal all sorts of things about your life to them. For the joy of the beach friend is that you'll only know them for such a very short time. In the blink of an eye you'll become as close as siblings. Over a glass of wine or a cup of coffee or a smoothie, you'll find yourself telling them the most intimate details of your life. Marriage break-ups will be spoken of in great detail, husbands' affairs will be revealed, children's behaviour will be scrutinized. Sometimes, you might even come to believe that this person really means something in your life. You may be subconsciously looking for this the very second you step on to that warm sand, for spending the holiday with a new friend can be magical. You can guarantee you'll never see them again, so everything is up for grabs.

But, of course, the first and most important thing you must do is make sure that the potential beach friend is someone who you might actually get on with and, to do this, you must use the Codes. The Codes become very important very quickly because, after all, you may only have a week or two to make this person your very best friend. If you manage it, you will have someone to hang out with and your children will amuse each other, and your holiday will suddenly go from looking as if it's going to be a bit of a nightmare to total joy.

Here are the codes you are looking for:

1) What are they wearing? If you are clad in a designer bikini with designer sunglasses and towels from Harvey Nichols, then you have to accept that the overweight woman sitting opposite you wearing a cheap one-piece is not going to be like you. That doesn't mean you won't get on with her. You might have the best time together, but you may not share the same type of interests in the long term.

2) What are they reading? There you are, mired in your

Tolstoy, while they're very obviously reading the latest autobiography by a C-list celeb. Will your match work? Probably not.

Having said that, those indicators could be misleading. She may be wearing a one-piece from Primark, but Primark is very trendy. She may be overweight because she's a middle-class foodie like me who spends every waking hour gorging on Parma ham. She may be engrossed in celeb-land in a sort of post-ironic type way.

3) OK, so the next step is to look at the kids. If they have shaved heads, tattoos (real), wear body jewellery and have names like Chardonnay and Kyle then, once again, you might not be singing from the same song sheet.

Then again, the children could recently have had nits – hence the shaved heads (bit extreme, I know, but some mothers swear by it) – and maybe their parents are so retro-cool that names like Rex and Randy are supposed to be tongue-in-cheek.

4) What are they eating? Are they a grilled-ciabatta-with-roasted-Mediterranean type family or can you see them tucking into bucket-loads of fast food?

But, yet again (sigh), you're on holiday. Everybody eats fast food on holiday. It's almost an unspoken rule – You Must Eat Pizza.

So, really, it's pretty hard to tell what people are like on holiday. Everything is misleading – consequently, you can take a chance with anyone.

As Noel goes to get us some coffees, Dougie arrives with Roisin, Lorcan and Bennie. The boys tear down the cliff path, the wind blowing their hair back. Dougie runs after them. He stops when he gets to the café and sees me.

'We've got a kite,' he says. 'Do you want to come and fly it?'

'No,' I say, nodding my head towards Noel who's returning with a tray.

'Oh, right,' Dougie says. 'I just thought you'd like to come and have some fun with me and Roisin.'

I tell him that as much as I would like to have fun, Noel and I have some planning to do. 'We really need to sort out the fête,' I say.

'Who are you?' asks Susie, lighting a cigarette and finally noticing I'm talking to someone of the male variety. 'Are you Samantha's husband or a French puppet master?'

'*Mais, non,*' says Dougie, not really looking at her but, instead, watching Roisin come into the café.

'Well, who are you then?'

'He's Dougie,' says Roisin, arriving at the table. 'Samantha's friend.'

'Well, where's your husband then?' asks Susie. 'Is he here?'

'He's with Jamie on the beach,' I say. I squint and put my hands above my eyes to shade them. 'Yes, he's there.' I point to the other side of the beach.

'Oh, I think Aaron and the girls are over there,' says Karin.

'Where's Jolka?' I ask.

'Actually, she's ill,' says Susie. 'She ate a dodgy prawn last night, so she's in bed.'

'Jolka's allowed to be ill then, is she?' says Roisin. Karin looks at her nervously.

'Not usually,' says Susie, not missing a beat. 'Just this once.'

'Well,' says Dougie. 'I think it's kite time. What do you say, Roisin?'

'Grand,' she says. 'Let's do it.'

'Are you going past John?' I ask. 'It's just that Jamie needs some lunch, so if you could ask John to bring him up in a bit. Oh, and if you happen to see Edward . . .'

'But Edward and his friend, that girl, are with Aaron and Anti and Alli,' says Karin. 'I just saw them. They're still playing that PSP thing in the shade by the rocks.'

I get up and call down to Dougie and Roisin, who are setting off for the cliffs on the other side of the beach. 'Can you get all the kids to come?' I call. 'Apparently Edward and the others are over there.' I point at the place where there's a shady overhang. Dougie nods his head and waves as he walks off.

I look up from studying the lunch menu a few moments later to find Aaron, Antigone, Allegra, Isabel and Edward standing right in front of us. The twins look as beautiful as usual. They both have their hair tied back and are wearing pink mini sundresses. Isabel, in contrast, is wearing a big black T-shirt with a skull and crossbones on it, lots of black eyeliner and a pair of tight black jeans. She has no shoes on. Her toenails are painted with black varnish which is badly chipped.

Susie stares at her as if she's from another planet.

'Aren't you hot?' she says.

Isabel doesn't look at her. She just shakes her head.

'Of course she's hot,' says Antigone, sitting down next to her mother and letting out a deep sigh.

'Yes, she's hot,' says Allegra. 'Look, Mummy. I'm in this tiny dress and I'm baking.' She flops down on a seat on the other side of her mother. I notice she has cowrie shells wrapped round her wrist. Noel notices it too.

'Do you know that many centuries ago in Africa they used cowrie shells for currency?' he says to her.

'How do you know that?' Allegra asks him.

'Were you alive then?' sniggers Aaron.

'Aaron!' says Karin quickly.

Noel takes no notice. 'Did you know that?' he says.

Allegra shakes her head, looking bored.

'Don't they teach you anything at school then?' he says.

'They teach me stuff at school,' says Edward suddenly. 'They teach me to write good stories on the computer.'

'Oh, what do you know about computers?' Allegra says. 'You and your girlfriend can't even play Doomscape.'

'No, you can't,' sneers Aaron. 'You're like your girlfriend. You're a total spaz at it.'

'At least I've got a girlfriend,' says Edward, going red.

Allegra laughs. 'Yeah, but only gaylords have girlfriends, Edward. That's what I'm going to call you. Gaylord.'

Before I can say anything, before anyone can say anything, Isabel suddenly moves forward and grabs Allegra by her throat. At the same time she pinions her down on the seat with her knees.

'Don't call him a gaylord,' she says, spitting in Allegra's face and ignoring Susie, who has leaped to her feet and is trying to pull Isabel off her daughter. 'You're a fucking gaylord and you –' she turns to Aaron – 'are only good on your fucking PlayStation because that's all your stupid mother ever gets you to do, you stupid moron.' Then, in a millisecond, she lets go of Allegra and, forcing Susie away from her, she grabs Edward's hand and they rush, her pulling him, out of the café and up the hill towards the car park.

Allegra sits there, elaborately choking. 'Mum,' she wails. 'That dreadful girl nearly killed me.'

'Oh my God,' says Susie, bending down to look at Allegra's throat, which has gone scarlet. 'Oh my God.'

Once she has quickly checked to see that Allegra is all right, she turns on me. 'Who is that girl you're letting your son hang out with?' she shouts angrily. 'What's the matter with you? There's something wrong with her. She's feral.'

'Yes,' continues Karin, looking very upset. 'She called my son a moron! You're not a moron, are you, Aaron?'

Aaron croaks, 'No, I'm not,' and then he buries his face in his mother's lap like a baby.

'See?' says Karin. 'He's upset.'

'Hang on a minute,' I say, feeling incensed. 'Didn't either of you two hear what your children said to my son?'

'It was harmless,' says Karin tetchily. 'I can't believe what that girl did to Allegra. How can you compare their words with that violence?'

'Who on earth is that girl?' says Susie. 'She's obviously as common as muck.'

'Actually,' says Noel calmly, 'I think you'll find that girl is my granddaughter.'

Once John and Jamie get back to the café, I tell John what happened. Susie and Karin have already gone down to the beach, accompanied by their children. They all gave me a resentful look as they went.

'It was horrible,' I say to John as Jamie eats a sandwich.

John asks where Edward and Isabel are and I tell him that Noel has gone to find them.

'I had to wait here for you,' I say. We go back to the car park, where we find Isabel and Edward sitting in the boot of the car. Noel is standing, looking out to sea. He takes a deep breath in.

'Sea air,' he says. 'It sorts out everything.'

'Is Edward OK?' I ask him and he just nods.

'Don't make a scene,' he says. 'Sticks and stones, Samantha. Sticks and stones.'

But still, no one speaks on the journey home and when we get there John says he has to pack.

'It's been a long day,' he says. 'I'm tired, so I'll go now. If I don't go now, I'll fall asleep.' He says goodbye to Noel. They shake hands. Noel tells me that he's going home too.

'I must eat,' he says. 'I need to have tea.'

'But I didn't see a Dagger Dark,' says Jamie plaintively, 'and I need some tea because I'm hungry too.' He looks at Noel. 'I want to go and have tea at your house. I very much like eggs . . .'

'Actually, you can come for tea,' says Noel, sounding rather surprised with himself. 'I could do with some company really and I'm a dab hand at chips. Would you like some egg and chips, and then I'll take you to look for a Dark Dagger?'

'Oh, yes please!' says Jamie, hopping from foot to foot. 'I would like eggs and chips.'

'We want eggs and chips too,' say Edward and Isabel from the back of the car, suddenly perking up a bit. They're still in the boot.

'OK, OK,' laughs Noel. 'I'll make egg and chips all round.'

'Can we go?' says Edward when I finally open the boot. 'Please say yes. Isabel's got a really great DVD we can watch.'

'I don't know, Edward,' I say. 'It's been a hard day, hasn't it? I mean, that scene on the beach was hardly pleasant.'

'I know,' says Edward, 'and I'm sorry. But Isabel was right to defend me, wasn't she?'

'Sort of,' I say. 'She was a bit over the top though, so . . .'

'But I'll bring Jamie home with me when the DVD has finished. I promise.'

'Well, what time do you think that will be?' I ask Noel.

'I think around seven,' says Noel.

'That sounds good,' I say, relieved. 'I think after today's events we could all do with an early night.'

I watch Noel and Jamie wander up the road holding hands. They're flanked by Edward and Isabel. I'm about to go up and talk to John when Dougie draws up in my car. Roisin is sitting in the front. She smiles at me happily.

'Do you need your car tonight, Samantha?' Dougie asks me. I tell him I don't. Roisin gets out of the car, followed by Bennie and Lorcan, who tear off into the house.

'Samantha,' she says to me. 'I don't want to be a burden and I really would want you to tell me if this is too much, but . . .'

'But what?' I say.

'Would you mind having Lorcan for a couple of hours?'

'No, that's fine,' I say. 'What are you going to do?'

'Well, Dougie thought he'd take me for a meal maybe.'

'Dougie?' I say.

'Yes, me,' says Dougie. 'What's wrong with that? Someone at that beach café told me about a new restaurant in Ilfracombe and I thought Roisin and I could check it out.'

'Sounds perfect,' I say.

'We're going to finesse our game plan, aren't we, Roisin?' says Dougie.

'For sure,' she says. 'I'm going to show your friend Noel that legal secretaries have brains.'

'Well, why don't you invite him too? I'm sure he can help.'

Roisin looks at Dougie again, nervously this time.

'I'm only joking,' I say. 'Noel's actually going searching for a Dark Dagger with Jamie.'

Roisin shivers slightly. 'Why do moths have such horrible names?' she says.

'Not all of them do,' I say. Then I tell Roisin that, actually, it's easier if I have Lorcan for the night.

'At least then I can go to bed early and I won't have to wait up for you two to get home.'

'Are you sure?' says Roisin.

'Absolutely,' I say.

An hour later, John comes into the garden to say goodbye. I've been cutting back the borders of the flower beds with some hand-held secateurs, a very labour intensive job, while Bennie and Lorcan have been pulling up trails of ivy from the bushes and trees. Baby Sparkle is sitting next to me, digging up bits of earth with a table fork and then staring at the small clods in amazement. 'Ra-la-ra-la-ra,' she says.

'I've found some sticky,' I heard Lorcan say a while back, waving around long tendrils of that green plant that sticks to your clothes and hair and suchlike. 'I'm going to stick it on you.'

'No!' said Bennie. Then he found some behind the shed and turned back to Lorcan. 'Ha! Now I've found some.' They went tearing round the lawn, trying to stick more and more plant stuff on to each other. Eventually I had to reel them in and put them back on their deforestation project.

'You're explorers going through the jungle, clearing a path,' I told them and the next thing I knew they were swiping away nettles with Beady's chewed sticks that she had left on the lawn and chopping back ivy and generally doing a marvellous job. They both agreed, as they swished their way through the jungle that, the next day, they were going to help me plant out some explorer pots.

'What will they have in them?' asked Bennie. 'Food?'

'Sort of,' I said. 'I was going to plant out tomatoes and French beans and runner beans. I hope it's not too late in the season.'

'We'll help,' said Bennie.

'Explorers like to help,' said Lorcan and they went back to playing their game.

But now John is leaving. 'I love you, my sweet,' he says as I stand up to wish him goodbye. I smell of earth and weeds. 'You smell like a peat bog,' he says as he leans down to kiss me.

'Good,' I say, kissing him back. 'I'm so glad I meet with your approval.'

'I wish you'd slow down though,' he says, looking at the garden. 'This garden is a major job.'

'I know that,' I say, 'but I promised her – well, I promised myself – that I'd restore it to its former glory. I feel dreadful that it's got so run down. You know this all started out because I wanted to make Janet's house a happy place for her memory and for Edward.'

'Yes, but Edward isn't interested really,' says John. 'He's experiencing his first crush.'

'Oh God, don't talk to me about Edward. I'm still trying to sort out Jamie.'

'I think you'll find though,' says John, getting into the car, 'that you, my Samantha, are going to have to pick up the pieces of that one. It's not the names that hurt. It's having your heart broken into teeny tiny pieces.' He surveys the garden one last time. 'I'll help when I come down next weekend. I'll bring the mower and some garden tools from home.'

'Oh, you're lovely,' I say, bending down and kissing him again through the car window, 'even though you're leaving all this to me.'

'I shall help next weekend!' he calls out as he drives off up the little lane that leads out of Lower Strand and back to the world I realize I've almost forgotten about.

17. Malaise Traps

By eight o'clock no one is back and no one has rung me. I've started to become worried. I've rung Noel's number at least ten times, but no one has picked up the telephone. I can't leave the house as Lorcan and Bennie are here in bed. I've rung Dougie and Roisin just in case they've seen Noel and Jamie or Edward, but they're not answering their mobile phones either. In desperation I ring Shelley. She says she'll be with me as soon as she can.

Half an hour later, she appears holding what I assume is a homework folder.

'There's only Bennie and Lorcan here, Shelley,' I say to her as I grab some money and my mobile phone from my handbag and head for the door. 'Baby Sparkle's in bed and the boys are asleep.'

'Right,' she says. Then she must notice how flustered I look because she asks where Edward and Jamie are.

'I'm just going to get them,' I say quickly. 'That's why I need you here.'

'Well, will you be long?' she says.

'No,' I say. 'I'll grab them and then come home.'

'It's just that I need to do an essay on the future of tourism in Lower Strand. We were told to pick a subject close to us and I heard you all talking at dinner the other night so I thought maybe you could help me.'

'Yes, I can help you,' I say. 'I'm sure I can, but not right now. You could start the essay on the computer if you like and then I could look at it when I get back. Is that a good idea?'

'Oh, yes,' says Shelley, 'that's great. Well, you go off now and have a good time and I'll see you later.'

I run out of the door and head towards Noel's house. Why is he not answering his telephone? If he was at home he'd answer his telephone, wouldn't he? Old people always answer the telephone, so why isn't he? Edward and Jamie should have been home an hour and a half ago. Why hasn't anyone rung me to tell me where they are? I realize I'm feeling rather nervous. I tell myself I'm being ridiculous. Noel offered to take Jamie to look for moths and that's probably what they're doing. They've probably gone up somewhere near the Cutlass Estate. After all, moths like light and the lights are always on at the Cutlass Estate. Isn't that what Noel told me? Yes, that's it. Noel and Jamie are looking for a Dark Dagger, or whatever it is they've gone to find, up there at the estate and Noel's lost track of the time. What I must do is go there and find them and watch moths with them. But then I can't make a decision. Should I go and check Noel's house? Or should I head straight for the estate? Suddenly I realize I don't actually know where Noel lives. He said he lived in a former pub, but at no point has anyone been there apart from Edward. God, it could be anywhere. I peer down the street. I can't see any house that looks like an old pub. It's getting dark now and I have no torch. Soon I won't be able to see anything but the lights of the Cutlass Estate. I decide I'll try there first. If I can't find them I'll walk back to the Poltimore Arms and ask where Noel's house is. The lights are on in the pub and, as I pass by, I can hear raised voices.

I turn round to head out of the village and climb up the hill to the estate. I feel calmer now. I'm sure Jamie will be

here, crouching down behind some poor person's bungalow, staring at a patch of grass or something. The sign
saying Cutlass Estate is lit up. I reach the first bungalow.
It's only then that I remember there are about twenty or
more of these blasted things. It's going to take me an age
to go round every one of these in the increasing darkness.
Instead I stand in the road and whistle loudly. I have no
idea why I whistle. I think it's because I'm worried that if
Noel and Jamie have found one of these Dark Daggers
and I go around shouting their names, I'll scare it off and
ruin their evening. Noel has been good for Jamie. That's
what John said. He was impressed by Jamie sitting on Noel's
lap the night of the dinner party. So I don't want to ruin
their moth-searching time. I just want Jamie to come home.

Then I think of Edward. Goddamn Edward. If it wasn't
for him and that bloody Isabel, I wouldn't even be here. He
promised me. He promised to bring Jamie home. In fact, he
looked me straight in the eye when he said it and now where
on earth is he? Probably down that bloody rec again. But
what do he and Isabel do there? In fact, the more I think
about it, the angrier I get. Edward has been behaving in a
shady fashion. He's been getting in late and falling asleep
before I've even had a chance to speak to him. I actually have
no idea what he's been up to at all. This now starts to worry
me. Something is obviously going on with Edward. I know
that because I've never known Edward not stick to something he has promised when it involves one of his brothers.
If Edward said he was going to bring Jamie home, then that's
what he should have done. Now it's obvious to me that
Edward must have abandoned Jamie or else the two of them
would be at home. It's the first time this has happened in our
family. God, why would he leave Jamie in danger?

Then I stop myself. Why do I think that Jamie's in danger? I don't know. But I do. It's late, it's dark and I don't know where Jamie is, and realizing this makes me start running through the Cutlass Estate. I run, whistling madly as I go, and then I stop to listen. Nothing. I run again. I stop to listen. Nothing. I'm just running down a back row of bungalows when I hear a noise. It's voices. One low, one more high-pitched.

'Jamie!' I call out quietly but urgently. 'Jamie!' I run to where I think the voices are. There's no one there. The voices have gone. Just then I notice there's a light on in the bungalow I'm standing next to. Thank goodness. I'll knock on the door and . . . I hear the voices again. They're coming from the bungalow. Not Jamie and Noel then. I'm just about to walk up the short path to the door when I see two people in the window. They are kissing. The man is cupping the woman's face in his hands and he's kissing her deeply. I realize that the man is Dougie.

'Oh my God,' I say out loud as I see the woman, who's obviously Roisin, pull away from Dougie and smile up at him. 'Oh my God,' I say again to myself. 'You didn't go to Ilfracombe at all!' Dougie and Roisin? Of course. It's perfect.

Still no Jamie though. I'm almost tempted to knock on the door anyway and ask them if they've seen Jamie or Noel, but they're so engrossed in each other I don't want to spoil it. Instead I look back down the hill to the Poltimore Arms.

I'm out of breath when I burst through the door. Everyone at the bar turns to look at me. I recognize Mr Henderson and Mrs Pat Pucklechurch, the bridleway lady, and Dilys, Shelley's mother. Mr Smullen, the man who wanted the zebra crossing, is serving behind the bar. The lights in the

281

pub are bright and suddenly I feel rather ridiculous. Everything seems so normal. Wasn't I in here the other night having wine with Noel? Of course I was. I tell myself I'm not being silly. I just want to find my children, that's all.

I walk up to the bar.

'Can I help you?' says Daniel Smullen.

'Yes,' I say falteringly. 'I know this sounds a bit crazy, but I seem to have lost two of my children.'

'Oh,' he says.

'One's my eldest son Edward, who's twelve, so I'm not so worried about him, but I'm also looking for my youngest boy . . .'

'Has he got blond hair?' asks Mrs Pat Pucklechurch.

'Yes,' I say. 'And I was just wondering if –'

'Very cute?'

'Yes,' I say. 'That's him. He went out tonight with –'

'Noel Rideout,' says Mr Henderson.

'Yes,' I say, looking at him intently. 'Have you seen him? They went to look for moths and –'

'Don't think they found many o'them,' says Daniel Smullen.

'What?' I say. 'You have seen them? Where were they? It's just that I've been trying to telephone Noel for hours and no one's answering and I've looked for them at the Cutlass Estate and –'

'You won't find them up there,' says Daniel Smullen. I notice he won't look me in the eye. In fact, no one seems to be looking at me at all.

'I know,' I say. 'I've just come from there and all I want to know is where –'

'He's at home,' says Mr Henderson, studying his pint of beer.

'At home?' I say. 'Jamie's at Noel's house?'

'Yes,' says Mr Henderson.

'Right,' I say. 'Well, can anyone tell me where that is?'

No one speaks. Suddenly Shelley's mother gets up and comes over to me. She takes my hand in hers and looks at me softly.

'Noel Rideout lives down the lane at the back of this pub,' she says gently. 'It's the last house on the right. You'll find him there with your son. You're not to worry. Your son is fine.'

'Thank you,' I say to her, rather puzzled. Just as I'm about to leave, Mr Henderson turns to me and says, 'Mrs Smythe. How well do you know Mr Rideout?'

For some reason this question irritates me.

'Pretty well,' I say. 'Well enough to leave my youngest son with him.'

'And yet you went looking for him at the estate,' he says. 'Why?'

I see Mrs Pat Pucklechurch place a hand on Mr Henderson's shoulder.

'Now, Donald,' she says warningly.

'You should have looked in here first,' he says, turning back towards the bar. 'I would have thought you'd have known that.'

I leave the pub and run down the lane. It's not very long. It takes me two minutes maybe. The lights are on in the last house on the right. I breathe a sigh of relief. Thank God. Noel and Jamie are probably so engrossed in studying the moths they've found that Noel's forgotten the time. And Edward, well, Edward's in a lot of trouble, but I'll worry about him once I've got poor, tired Jamie home. I open the creaking gate and go up the path. The door to the cottage is slightly open. There's no knocker. There's no bell. I'm not sure what to do so I rap on the door with my knuckles. The wood is so old and damp that the sound is muffled, deadened. No one moves inside.

'Hello,' I call out as I push the door open. 'Noel? Jamie? It's me.'

I go into the house. The door leads straight into the sitting room and there, lying on a small old sofa that has stuffing coming out of the corners, is Jamie. He's all curled up with a pink cushion under his head. Someone, probably Noel, has wrapped a tartan blanket over him.

'Jamie,' I say softly. I don't want to wake him as he looks so peaceful. I go and kneel down next to him. His mouth is slightly open. I bend to kiss him and then I notice he's clutching something in his hand. It's a straw.

Just then I hear something clinking towards the back of the house.

'Noel?' I say. I walk through the sitting room door and through a small hallway towards another door. I hear more clinking. It's coming from behind the door.

'Noel?' I say again.

Suddenly the door opens and Noel is standing there, framed by the light.

'Samantha!' he says. 'Come in. Come into my humble abode! Oh, but you are in, aren't you? Clever old you. Now come into my kitchen and have a brandy with me.'

I walk into the kitchen. It's cold and bare and it smells slightly. On the Formica table is a bottle of brandy and a glass. Most of the brandy has gone.

'Have a drink,' says Noel, waving his arm towards the table.

'No, I don't think so,' I say. 'Actually, I think I'll just pick up Jamie and go.'

'Go?' says Noel, finding another glass from a cupboard above the sink. 'Go? But you've only just got here.'

'It's late. I need to get Jamie to bed.' I watch as Noel pours himself out a brandy.

'But he's asleep, isn't he? Now, don't be mean. You wouldn't leave an old man to have a brandy on his own, would you?'

Noel sits down on a rickety chair. I stay standing.

'You don't like my kitchen?' he says.

'It's not that,' I say. 'It's just that . . .'

'Well, sit then.' He pats the seat again. 'We're friends, aren't we?'

I nod my head. Noel pours me a brandy. My glass empties the bottle.

'Noel,' I say. 'It's late. You've been out looking for moths with Jamie for hours and I need to get him home.'

'How did you find my house?' he asks, closing his eyes a bit and drinking a huge gulp of brandy.

'I asked at the pub.'

'Oh, the pub,' he says. Then he whispers, 'And did they tell you they'd seen me?' His eyes turn to slits when he looks at me.

'Yes,' I say. 'They did.'

'Ha!' says Noel loudly, suddenly standing up and reaching for the cupboard again. 'They're bloody nosey so-and-sos. Now, more brandy I think.' He gets another full bottle down from the cupboard above him.

'So, did they tell you then?' he continues.

'Tell me what?'

Noel opens the bottle of brandy and sloshes some more into his glass. 'Drink up, Samantha,' he says, noticing I haven't had a sip.

'What didn't they tell me, Noel?' I say again.

Noel sighs. 'Oh, well,' he says. 'I suppose I might as well tell you or else some other bloody do-gooder will.' He drinks some more brandy. 'Here goes. I didn't take Jamie moth hunting, you see.'

'You didn't take him moth hunting?'

'No.'

'Not at all?'

'Not at all. I meant to. I had all my kit but, well, he said he didn't want to go and look for Dark Daggers. I told him we were going to look for Dark Daggers and he kept saying he didn't want to or something like that, and I think he was frightened, so we went to the pub instead.'

'You went to the pub?'

'Yes, we went to the pub. Your son likes going to the pub.'

'But, Noel, you left hours ago. Are you seriously telling me that you didn't go and look for even one moth?'

'Not a single one,' says Noel, helping himself to more brandy.

'Oh God, Noel,' I say, shocked. 'You're drunk. You took my four-year-old son to the pub and got drunk. That's why everyone there was being strange. They all saw you with him getting drunk, didn't they?'

'Touché, as your friend Hawk-moth man would say,' says Noel. 'Well observed, Samantha. Top marks. Yes, I am probably drunk.'

'I can't believe it.'

'Why not? Most people get drunk after they've downed a bottle or more of brandy.'

'How could you get drunk in front of my son? How could you be so irresponsible?'

286

'Oh, stop being so pious. We were ratted the other night at your house. Stop being so bloody holy about it.'

I get up. 'There's a difference between social drinking occasionally and getting drunk all the time and, as you obviously fall into the latter category, I'm not going to continue this conversation. I just want to take my son and go. We'll talk about this tomorrow.'

'Aren't you going to help me?' says Noel suddenly.

'Help you?' I say.

'I thought you would.'

'How can I help you? You've deceived me. God, I can't believe I didn't see it before.' I suddenly remember him being so cantankerous towards Roisin. And all that spraying of Gold Spot. How could I have missed all the warning signs? 'I mean, I knew you liked a drink. I thought it was because you were lonely. But I never expected you'd do this to me and Jamie.'

'Why? Because you thought you were special?' he says, almost sneering.

'Yes,' I say angrily. 'Because you treated us – me and my son – as if we were very special.'

'You are deceived in that. In fact, you wanted to be deceived. You were like a moth to a flame,' he says.

'Well, this flame has just gone out for me,' I say angrily, going towards the door.

'But Jamie's had a great time!' says Noel. 'And, anyway, what was all that you said about helping people down by the beach? I heard you talking to your errant husband. You should help me. I need you.'

'How can I help you when I don't know why you drink.'

'I drink because I like it. Oh, sorry, my dear Samantha. That's not the answer you want, is it? You want me to reveal

287

why I drink. Now that would make you really happy. It would make your night, wouldn't it?'

'I'm going, Noel,' I say. 'I can't deal with this. You asked me to stay, but I'm not putting up with this . . .'

'Please stay,' says Noel. He looks so piteously at me. 'I'm sorry, Samantha. Oh, I drink because I was devastated by my wife leaving me all those years ago. I drink because I have a broken heart.'

'Do you?' I say.

'I don't know. I can't remember. Oh, but you're judging me, aren't you? You're probably looking at me now and pitying me. You're probably thinking you can help me if you could just get me to o-p-e-n up.'

'No, I'm not.'

'Of course you are. Ever since you first met me you've been wanting me to open up to you, haven't you?'

'No!' I say. 'I just thought we were friends.'

'Friends? You've only just met me and yet here you are, in my house, thinking I drink because I'm sitting on some dreadful secret. You're one of those bleeding-heart liberals who thinks that if we all just talked about our emotions then we could live off a glass of elderflower juice a day. You really think you know me, don't you? You really think that we are part of each other's lives, that somehow, because you're going to help save that house, you belong in this village – but life, Samantha, my dear, just ain't that simple.'

I sit and look at him. I'm still in shock. I'm not sure if I feel angry or sad or both. I'm too confused to know.

'Noel,' I say. 'Why are you being so mean to me?'

'All alcoholics are mean,' he says. 'We are devious and we are mean. We spray Gold Spot in our mouths so no one can smell the alcohol, see? That's how devious we are.'

'You're just making excuses,' I say. 'You've spent hours with me and Jamie.'

'Only because I was bored.'

'What do you mean?' I say.

'Oh, sorry. Don't you know what bored means? Bored is sitting in that café listening to you and your mummy friends. There you all are, bringing up a generation of cry babies who can't lose at anything. Look at your so-called friends. They're all dreadful, awful yummy mummies. They say they love their children, but they send them away to school and what happens to them? They become cold and arrogant and bored and stupid and they have no sense of adventure. If you're going to send them away, send them to Eton or somewhere where they might actually learn something rather than these ghastly pseudo public schools that don't teach them anything other than a superiority complex.'

'What are you talking about? I'm not sending Edward away to school.'

'Not you. Them. I saw them. I saw them look at Isabel. They were looking down at her, snubbing her. Who are they to snub my granddaughter? At least Isabel's experiencing life.'

'What, drinking a Bacardi Breezer down the rec?' I say angrily. 'Dressing like death warmed up? Swearing?'

'Absolutely. Actually, I think if she and Edward looked in that rec a bit more closely, they'd find a Dark Dagger down there.'

'Is that where Edward and Isabel are, Noel?'

'I don't know,' he says. 'I don't care.'

'Well, I do and so should you. She's in your care, Noel, and from where I'm sitting right now you don't seem to have really grasped that.'

'Oh, so you think I don't care?' he says, sounding venom- •
ous. 'You think it's only you, do you? Only you who knows
how to care for children? I mean, look at you. What do you
know about anything? All that education and what have
you done? You do nothing but endlessly worry about your
children and talk about your children. You never leave them
alone. Do you know how tedious it is for everyone else?
How dull you sound? Do you know how boring it is for
your bloody children? You've wasted your life. You don't
even know about moths.'

'So what?' I shout at him, finally losing my temper. 'I
don't care about your bloody moths!'

Noel suddenly lunges across the table and grabs my arm.
The bottle of brandy goes spinning towards the edge of
the table. Noel is focusing on me with such intent, he
doesn't even notice.

'Well, you should,' he says, spitting out his words one by
one. 'Why don't you? They would tell you about your life,
Samantha, a life you seem to know nothing about.'

'Let go of me,' I say, close to tears. 'I want to go. You're
frightening me.'

Noel grips my arm even tighter, leans forward and talks
to me in a low, threatening voice.

'Do you know what your husband is? He's a *Pasiphila
debiliata*.'

'I don't care,' I say, desperately trying to pull my arm away
from him.

'He's a bloody Bilberry Pug, that's what he is. You know,
drawn to the light, pupates underground. He's a shady
bloody man who only comes out when he sees you. Christ!
It's not my fault your beloved Jamie is starved of attention.'

'What are you talking about?'

'Oh, don't tell me you haven't thought about it, Samantha, late at night when you've had your fill of wine? You've lain there and wondered if, deep down inside, your son's an angry little boy because his father is never around. Christ! He's off doing some bloody puppet show when he should be concentrating on what's going on in his family.'

'How dare you, Noel. How bloody dare you!'

'You think you know so much about your children, but you can't see what's in front of your own eyes! At least I've got an excuse. I'm too drunk to see what's in front of mine, but I'll tell you one thing, you could learn a lot from moths. Your stupid friend Susie's a *Colobochyla salicalis*. A Lesser Belle, Samantha, a Lesser Belle. You should study moths, really you should. Did you know there's one called the Flounced Chestnut? The Flounced Chestnut, that's your blubbery friend Karin. And then there's the Maiden's Blush. Is that you, Samantha, is it?'

'No, it's not,' I say, fighting back tears. 'You told me I was a Beautiful Golden.'

'Such a common moth,' he says nastily. 'Oh, didn't I tell you that? No? Well, maybe you're a True-Lover's Knot, Samantha. A *Lycophotia porphyrea*. It likes acid heathland, you see, acid heathland like me.' Suddenly Noel releases my arm. 'Now go,' he says tiredly, reaching out to grasp the brandy bottle before it finally topples off the side. 'I've had enough of you. This pool is empty, Samantha. Utterly and totally empty, and you don't belong here.'

I get up and, without looking back at him, go into the sitting room as steadily as I can manage. I bend down and pick Jamie up, hugging him to my chest, and then I leave, pushing my way back out of the front door. I stop at the gate. I almost expect Noel to come after me, but he doesn't.

I walk quickly back down the road towards the Poltimore Arms. I don't look behind me. I hear nothing until I pass the pub. Shelley's mother, Dilys, is leaving. She stops when she sees me.

'Oh,' she says, noticing the tears streaming down my face. I try to push past her, but she's standing right in front of me.

'Oh, oh,' she says. Suddenly the look on her face, the look of shock, of regret, of sadness, makes me feel intensely angry.

'Why didn't you stop him?' I shout at her, rubbing the tears from my face with my free hand. 'You could have stopped him! Why didn't you?'

'Oh, no,' she says. 'Oh, no.'

'You could have,' I say. I can hear how desperate I sound, but I can't stop. 'My son is four. He's only four years old. You sat there. You sat there in that pub and –'

'No, I didn't,' she says desperately. 'He was leaving as I was coming in. I would never . . . Please, you don't understand.'

I'm sobbing now. Dilys reaches out for me, but I back away.

'You should have stopped him years ago,' I shout at her. 'Why didn't you? Why didn't you?'

Then Dilys looks at me sadly. 'Oh, my dear,' she says. 'Don't you understand? No one could ever have stopped him.'

She comes towards me. I turn and run down the hill towards my house. But Jamie is so heavy. When I get to the village hall I sink down on to the bench outside it. It's so dark now. Barely any stars are out. The moon is clouded. I hold Jamie close on my lap and bow my head and cry. My tears fall on to his face and he stirs. I find some tissue paper in my skirt pocket. It's tiny and balled up. I unfurl it. It has a small spot of blood on it. It's the paper I used the night before at the dinner party, the night I pricked my finger with a hair pin, the night I was the Beautiful Golden. It seems like such a long time ago. I start to feel very tired. I'm about to gather my strength to pick up Jamie when I see something fluttering just to the right of the bench. I look down. There's a bag stuffed under the bench, pushed back to be hidden by the undergrowth. I look again. The moon comes out. I recognize this bag. It looks like the bright pink carrier bag Isabel and Edward went off with last night.

I bend down, carefully avoiding squashing Jamie. I pull the bag up from under the bench and, as I do, the side of it snags on a bramble and rips open, gashed along the side, and I sit and watch as one hundred and one red, white and blue flyers go fluttering off down the streets of Lower Strand.

18. Natural Habitat

I wake up the next morning feeling as though I have a hangover even though I know I don't. For a minute, I can't remember where I am. I think I'm at home, my real home where John and I live amongst the hills and the deer and the damp misty early mornings. I reach my hand out to touch John. Is it true what Noel said? I can hardly bear to think about it. Is Jamie really trying to get his father's attention? I feel the cool crisp linen beneath my fingertips. How many times have I reached out to touch John? He has always been there for me, for all of us surely? All the times I've cried, all the times I've laughed, he has been there. I remember how he turns to me in the morning, when his face looks hazy because the sunlight coming through the curtains has shone directly into my eyes, leaving me unable to see him in definition. I want him here now. I want to open my eyes and see him with the sun on his face and his bleached outline. I want to squint my eyes up so I can see his smile. I want to ask him what's going on. Maybe if I open my eyes, he will be here. I try, but everything seems blurred. I can see the white material of the duvet cover and some curtains. These are not my curtains. I'm not at home. There is no John.

I'm at Janet's house. I'm in bed in the main bedroom. I can smell the garden – roses, honeysuckle, buddleia, sweet peas, the wonderful mock orange – yet my head feels dull and thudding and my heart hurts and I've woken up with a terrible sense of dread like I did the morning I knew John the First was leaving. Everything had faded by then – our love, our friendship, our ability to take care of each other and hold each other. The garden hadn't faded though. It was the beginning of summer and everything was blooming. I remember John the First, the night before he walked away from us, wandering around stroking the heads of lavender and then inhaling deeply, as if trying to get the spores to go into his throat and down into his body and lodge there somewhere, somehow. Maybe it was that he wanted to remember something of us, the garden and the lavender and the mint that took over the vegetable beds because we never got round to planting anything else. How do you retain the essence of something you've lost? But I have retained the essence of the hurt, of the pain. It has been etched in my heart for all these years. My John the Second poured salve on it and healed it, and yet here I am, numb, shocked. Everything I've believed in has abandoned me. Love, friendship, my relationship with Edward – all seems meaningless and lost. How has this happened? Was I really that distracted not to notice what has been going on? This was meant to be my summer of achieving something. This was meant to be my family's turn in the sun and now look. I've gained nothing from being here.

Suddenly I have a desperate need for John to be with me. I want him to be lying here next to me, to tell me that Noel is wrong, that Edward will come back to me, that Jamie will be fine and that I haven't turned into the woman I never wanted to be. I want him to tell me that I'm not dull and needy, with children who lie to me, and as I think about this a terrible pain rips through me. Noel, the man I admired, the man who I thought admired me, thinks I'm boring. Everything he did with Jamie was fake. I thought he cared for Jamie. I thought he was reliving his lost youth through his relationship with my lovely but disturbed youngest son. I think of them in the pub, Noel and Jamie, surrounded by all those people as Noel got drunk and my poor little Jamie sat there with his juice and his straw, and everyone knew what was happening and no one moved a muscle to prevent it and the thought of this, the thought of how I wasn't there to wrap Jamie up and take him home, makes me feel so angry and so sad that I find myself shouting out loud: 'This is not how it was meant to be!' At the sound of my voice, Baby Sparkle starts to cry from her room next door.

I get up and go to her. As I lift her out of the cot, I find that I'm crying. I hadn't known I was. I can remember everything now and I'm not sure what's causing me the most pain. Is it the fact that Noel turned on me? Oh my God. I cannot bear to think of the words he said to me. I remember coming home. I had Jamie in my arms and that pink bag and some sodden flyers stuffed into my pocket. Why? Evidence, I think. So I came home with those curled-up flyers and Jamie's sweet, sleeping breath on my neck and I set my mind against Noel. I kept hearing him in my head telling me how boring I was, how sick he was of me, but I didn't let go of Jamie. I made myself a test. If I got Jamie home without stopping, then the pain would go away, and by the time I got to the door I was exhausted. Shelley was there, looking concerned. She asked me why Jamie was in so late, but I didn't say anything, and then the telephone rang and I thought it was Noel. I thought he had come to his senses and was ringing to apologize, but Shelley got to the telephone before me and I heard her have a murmured conversation with someone. Then she put the receiver down and came back into the kitchen.

'That was my mum,' she said as I stood there looking at her, still holding Jamie.

'Your mum?' I said, as if stupefied.

'Yes,' said Shelley awkwardly. 'She wanted to know if you got home OK.'

'Got home OK?' I asked.

'Yes,' said Shelley even more awkwardly. 'I told her you did.'

'Oh,' I said.

Then I went to take Jamie upstairs and Shelley came behind me and she didn't say anything, but she looked very worried.

'Is Jamie OK?' she asked.

'Why do you keep saying "OK", Shelley?' I said, snapping at her, suddenly angry at what I knew her mother had told her.

'Sorry,' she said. 'I just wondered if —'

'He's fine,' I said.

Then Shelley told me that Edward had come in half an hour ago and that he'd gone to bed.

'He was acting very strangely,' she said. 'He barely spoke to me and he bumped into the wall as he went upstairs.'

I found myself slumping against Jamie's door when she told me.

'Do you think you should go and see him?' she said, almost in a whisper.

'I will,' I said. 'I will when I'm alone.'

Shelley stood, moving nervously from foot to foot, watching me as I closed my eyes and rested my head on the wall.

'Not everyone's bad in this village,' she said a little desperately. 'My mother wanted you to know that.'

'Thanks,' I said, but I kept my eyes closed and, eventually, I heard her go down the stairs and out of the back door. I opened my eyes slightly and watched her walk up the road, bathed in moonlight.

Then I went to Edward. He was pale and sleeping deeply.

'Sticks and stones,' I whispered to him and then I didn't know if I wanted to slap him across his face or stroke his hair. I just stood and looked at him and there he was with his freckles and his long brown hair and that scar on the bridge of his nose where he once fell off his chair and smashed it against the table top. I could still see the baby that I gave birth to in that face of his. How long and how hard I have loved him. I went downstairs for a glass of brandy and then I remembered the brandy was gone.

'Damn you, Noel,' I said.

But now it's the morning and for some reason I feel I must go into the garden. I can hear those bees again, buzzing as loudly as the thoughts in my head. It's warm and sunny once more and the blue sky and the breeze and the heady scent of the roses make me feel as if this is my punishment. Look at the beauty of the day! How can I feel so terrible on a day like this? My mother always told me that gardening was therapeutic. 'If you're ever depressed,' she said after John the First left, 'go and plant your garden.' So today is that day, the plant-the-garden day. Today I cannot concentrate on anything else. I find a rug and put Baby Sparkle down on it. She sits and gazes out towards the sea. Bennie then appears, yawning. 'Can I have some breakfast?' he says. 'I'm hungry.'

'We're having a picnic breakfast,' I say to him, trying to

298

keep my voice light and cheerful. 'Help yourself to some croissants and fruit.'

'Croissants!' says Bennie and he scampers back indoors.

Five minutes later he reappears with Jamie in tow. Jamie has on a pair of shorts. They're too big for him.

'Jamie, you've got shorts on today,' I say.

'Yes,' he says defiantly, putting his hands in both pockets.

'But they're my shorts,' says Bennie, taking a croissant. 'Jamie's put my shorts on and he won't take them off and Lorcan's in my bedroom looking at a book. I've given him an apple because he said he didn't want a croissant.'

'Well done, Bennie, that's very kind of you. Will you come and sit here with Baby Sparkle and me?' I say, patting the rug next to me. Bennie comes over and waves a croissant at Sparkle.

'Ra-la-ra-la-ra-la,' she says, pumping her arms up and down with excitement.

'Do you want one, lovely baby?' says Bennie, breaking a bit off his croissant and giving it to her. Baby Sparkle clenches the croissant in her hand and starts munching it in a thoughtful fashion.

'She likes it, doesn't she?' Bennie says contentedly.

'Yes, she does,' I say. Then I look down to speak to Jamie, who's now snuggled up in my lap. 'Jamie,' I say, 'do you remember much about last night?'

'Yes,' he says. 'I had a juice in the pub.'

'Yes,' I say carefully. 'You went to the pub with Noel.'

'That's not fair!' says Bennie heatedly. 'Why didn't I get to go to the pub?'

'Bennie,' I say warningly, 'you were here playing with Lorcan and, anyway, Jamie was supposed to be looking for moths, weren't you, Jamie?'

'Yes,' says Jamie, 'but we didn't see moths. I had a blue straw.'

'You went to the pub and then where did you go?'

Jamie looks as if he's thinking very hard.

'Don't know,' he says.

'I found you asleep at Noel's house and I carried you home,' I say. 'Do you remember that?'

'No,' says Jamie, looking very unconcerned. 'Can I have jam on my bready-thing?'

'Yes,' I say, relieved. Obviously Jamie doesn't really remember anything.

'Now that's really not fair!' says Bennie. 'I want another croissant and this time I want jam on it.'

'All right,' I say, laughing. 'I'll go and get some jam and plates. Just stay out here and watch Sparkle for me, please.'

Jamie gets up from my lap and goes to pick a daisy.

'For Sparkle,' he says. 'Pretty flower. Pretty baby.'

When I get to the kitchen I find Edward is there. He's helping himself to some cereals. He looks up as I walk in. To give him his due, at least he has the grace to look guilty.

'Hi, Mum,' he says, not looking at me.

'Edward,' I say and then I stop. I actually don't know where to start, so I just say, 'I think you have some explaining to do.' I motion towards a chair at the table and he sits down. I sit down opposite him where I can see the boys playing with Baby Sparkle from my view out of the back door.

'Yeah, right, well, I'm really sorry about Jamie,' he says before I can say anything, 'but you must've come and got him really early, cos Isabel and me weren't down the rec that long but by the time we got back to Noel's I saw you were there. You were in the sitting room, bending over Jamie, so I thought

300

you'd be taking him home, see? It's not my fault you came and picked him up. It was only just gone eight and –'

'Do you think I'm stupid, Edward?' I ask calmly as I know me being calm will unnerve him far more than my screaming and shouting, as he always expects me to do that.

Edward stops, surprised, even hopeful maybe. 'No,' he says.

'Do you think I'm illiterate?'

'Erm, no.'

'Do you think I can't read the hands on a watch?'

Edward pauses. He knows where this conversation is going. 'No,' he says finally, somewhat deflated.

'So are you going to keep on pretending that you and Isabel came back to Noel's by eight? Or are you going to tell me the truth?'

Edward swallows nervously. 'Maybe it was nine,' he says.

I get up and walk towards the door.

'Where are you going?' he says.

'I have no interest in talking to you, Edward,' I say. 'If you can't be bothered to tell me the truth, then I can't be bothered to listen to you.'

'I am telling you the truth.'

I suddenly feel incredibly angry. I turn to Edward and spit out every word. 'Are you such a stupid boy that you can't understand that when I came and got Jamie I actually looked at the clock and, when I did, it wasn't bloody nine o'clock. Can't you understand that? Because if you can't, then there's no point in me talking to you. It means that you don't care. You don't care what might have happened to Jamie and you don't care what time I came to get him and you don't care that you promised me, yes promised me, to have him home by seven because you

301

don't give a jot about anyone but yourself. Don't you understand that?'

'It wasn't just me!' Edward says hotly. 'It's Isabel's fault as well.'

That does it. I finally let rip.

'JAMIE IS NOT ISABEL'S BROTHER!' I yell at him. 'Jesus Christ! You are Jamie's brother. He was your responsibility.'

'But you told me at the beginning of the holiday that you didn't need me to take care of Jamie. You said it wasn't my responsibility just because Dad couldn't be bothered to come on holiday with us.'

'Edward!' I say. 'That's not the point. Dad is working. It's not the case that he can't be bothered and, last night, I didn't ask you to bring Jamie home – you offered! You wanted to go and play with Isabel and that was the deal and, while we are on that subject, what do you and Isabel actually do down the rec?'

'Nothing,' says Edward, looking shifty.

'Nothing?'

'Just stuff.'

'What kind of stuff?'

'Jeez, Mum,' says Edward, poking his spoon into his breakfast, 'we just hang out. Anyway, we've barely been down there.' Then he looks appealingly at me. 'We spent the other night delivering those flyers for you, remember, Mum?'

'Oh, the flyers?' I say. 'Oh, yes, you spent a long time doing that, didn't you?'

Edward doesn't miss the sarcasm. 'Why are you being like that?' he says. He opens his eyes wide and tries, almost convincingly, to look genuinely puzzled.

'Are you going to tell me the truth?' I say to him again.

'I am telling the truth,' he says, waggling his eyebrows up and down in an attempt to look innocent.

'So you're telling me that you and Isabel delivered all those flyers we gave you?'

'Yes,' he says. 'After all, how would people in the village have known about the puppet show if we hadn't?'

'Bennie and Shelley and Lorcan went out to deliver some, remember?'

'Oh,' says Edward, looking nervous again.

I get up and go towards the sitting room.

'What are you doing?' he asks quickly.

'Just wait here,' I say. 'I'm getting something.' I find the long cardigan I was wearing last night lying on the back of the sofa. I delve into the deep pockets and pull out the sodden flyers. The pink bag is hanging off the mantelpiece, draped near the fire. Shelley must have put it there to dry out. I unhook it and walk back into the kitchen. Edward looks up. He sees the bag. He goes red and then moves his mouth up and down like a goldfish.

'What's that?' he says eventually.

'A bag,' I say. 'It's the bag you and Isabel used to deliver the flyers.'

'No, it isn't,' he says quickly. 'How do you know it is anyway?'

I don't say anything. I just raise my eyebrow.

'Where did you find it?' he asks.

'Where you left it.'

'Oh,' he says. I can see his eyes twitching. He always does this when he has to think hard. 'I remember! We delivered all the flyers and then we couldn't be bothered to take the bag home. Oh, Mum, I'm really sorry. It's bad to litter, isn't it? I remember you always tell me that. You say, "Don't leave bags lying around because small animals might crawl in there and suffocate and die and that's cruel." That's what you say, isn't it, Mum?' Edward looks at me appealingly until I bring out the crumpled, damp flyers.

'Oh,' he says.

'Yes. Oh,' I say. Then I sit down opposite him and I ask him to look at me.

'Edward,' I say very calmly. 'I just want to tell you something. We're all part of a family, you see, and me and Daddy have worked very hard to make you all happy. Daddy may not be here all the time, but we do try every day to think of you and help you and make sure you understand what life is about –'

'I know,' says Edward rapidly, 'and I really do appreciate it and–'

'– and this,' I say, pointing at the bag and the flyers, 'could not hurt me more.'

Edward starts trying to speak again, but I raise my voice.

'You're not in this family right now, Edward,' I say. 'You have chosen to step outside it, so I hope you're happy with your choice because there's nothing I can do for you now.'

'No!' he says, panicked. 'No! You don't understand, Mum. It was Isabel. She told me to dump them. She said you'd never find out. She said a puppet show was a stupid idea and no one would come anyway and –'

'No, Edward,' I say firmly, putting my hand up to stop him from continuing. 'You made your decision. Now you must live with it.'

Then I walk back out of the kitchen and into the sunshine with tears in my eyes.

Two hours later, Dougie and Roisin appear to take Lorcan to the beach. They look so happy it's almost impossible to be around them. They sit down and eat croissants with the children, commenting on how amazing it is that Jamie is both eating and wearing shorts.

'Shorts!' says Dougie. 'Hallelujah!' Jamie smiles secretly to himself.

As they chat away, asking Lorcan how his evening was and twirling Baby Sparkle up into the air, which makes her go red and giggle, I start weeding the large flower pots that line the garden path. I have some twine and some secateurs with me and in the greenhouse at the bottom of the garden I've found some summer lily bulbs which I'm intending to plant out in the pots. I dig a bit and then I snip at the roses and tie them back to the trellis that loops over the path. I also try to thin out the mint that has obviously been running riot for years. Noel told me the other day, when he was looking at the moth book with Jamie, that there were at least six types of mint in this garden. He said there was black mint and Italian mint and . . . I can't remember the rest. Thinking of Noel makes my eyes smart. I wipe them on my dirty gardening glove which is not a good idea as soil gets into them and makes them water ever harder.

'Are you all right?' Dougie asks me, coming up behind me.

'Yes,' I say brightly, maybe a bit too brightly.

'No problems last night then?' he says, looking concerned.

'Absolutely none. I've just got soil in my eye, that's all.'

Then he sees Edward mooching around the garden. 'What's up with him?'

'We had a row. Nothing major.'

Roisin comes over and asks if I want to go to the beach with them and I tell her I don't because I'm determined to keep clearing Janet's garden.

'I want to finish the weeding today and plant out some summer lilies and the salad vegetables,' I say. 'I've sort of promised Janet in my head, if that makes any sense.' Roisin says it makes perfect sense.

'It's a very good day for gardening,' she says, 'and a promise is a promise.' Then she says that if I can't come to the beach, why don't she and Dougie take Bennie and Jamie with them.

'They're jumping up and down with joy at the thought of making sandcastles!' she says and the next thing I know the five of them have set off down the road.

This leaves Edward and me and Baby Sparkle but, by now, Sparkle is starting to yawn and rub her eyes. I take her up to her room.

'Time for a morning nap I think, Sparkle,' I say to her, kissing her head as she tucks her body into mine. 'You were up so early, my darling, and it's getting hot now.' I strip her down to her nappy and she pops her thumb into her mouth. 'Sleep peacefully,' I say as I gently ease her down into her travel cot. I shut the door quietly and go back downstairs into the garden.

Edward is sitting on the rug. He gets up when I walk past him and follows me down the garden towards where the sweet peas are over-running.

'What are you doing?' he asks me as I move towards the back flower bed.

'I'm clearing the garden,' I say as I start thinning the sweet peas back and tying them to the bamboo pole I've found for them. I don't look at Edward. 'This garden used to be beautiful when your Granny Janet lived here. She was very proud of it and I know she would want me to keep it the way she liked it. I feel I owe her that because she left you this wonderful house. It's a loyalty thing, Edward – not that I'd expect you to understand that.'

For a couple of seconds there is silence. Then I hear Edward take a huge gulp and when I turn to look at him I find that he's crying.

'Oh, Edward,' I say. 'Don't cry.' I'm about to reach out to him when, suddenly, he flings himself over the flower bed and lunges at me with his arms outstretched.

'I am sorry, Mum,' he says, tears pouring down his cheeks. 'Please stop being so horrible to me. Please, please . . .'

I open my arms and pull him towards me. He's so tall it's all a bit awkward, but still I hug him and give him a kiss on the top of his head.

'Edward –' I say.

'No,' he says. 'Please listen to me, Mum. I'm so sorry. Really I am. I've been a horrible boy and I'm really sorry I didn't bring Jamie home because I do love Jamie, even though he can very bad-tempered and he shouts at me sometimes, but I know I promised and –'

'It's OK,' I say, now feeling a bit overcome.

'And I do understand what family means, Mum, and I love my family and please don't tell me I'm not part of it any more. I'll do anything,' he says. 'Just ask me. Go on. Ask me.'

'OK,' I say and then I hold him at arm's length. 'I want you to tell me, without lying, what you and Isabel have been up to.'

Edward starts squirming a bit. 'Do I have to?' he says.

'Yes,' I say firmly.

'You won't like it,' he says.

'I know.'

'I didn't mean to,' he says.

'I know that too.'

'We've been spray painting on the cricket pavilion wall.'

'Yes, I thought so. What did you write?'

Edward stares at his feet and shuffles around.

'Edward,' I say warningly.

'We wrote "Mr Henderson's a wanker".'

I suppress a smile. 'Well, that's not very good, is it?'

Edward shakes his head.

'And what else have you done?' I say, trying to keep some severity in my voice.

'Nothing,' he says, but he won't meet my eye.

'Edward, you promised to tell me the truth.'

'Oh,' he says. 'It wasn't me, Mum, but, well, we've been drinking.'

I sigh.

'I didn't mean to. I mean, at first I didn't know what it was, but Isabel says she drinks these alcopops at home all the time and that everybody she knows drinks them and that sometimes they drink this stuff called scrumpy and she told me her granddad had some in his cellar and –'

'You've been drinking alcopops and scrumpy?'

'Yes,' he says miserably.

'Did you like drinking them?'

'Not really,' he says, hanging his head. 'They made me feel good at first, but then I felt sick.'

'Were you sick?'

He nods his head. I let go of him.

'Edward,' I say, 'I think you've learned your lesson then and I appreciate the fact you've been truthful, but you'll have to go and tell Mr Henderson that you've been vandalizing the cricket pavilion and that you've come to offer to clean it up.'

'Do I have to?' says Edward.

'Yes. And I don't want you to see Isabel for the rest of this holiday.'

'Really?' says Edward and, I have to say, he looks relieved.

After this, we spend the rest of the day gardening together and somehow my mood lifts. I show Edward how to tie up the sweet peas and then I watch him as he happily snips and ties while I go back to planting the lilies in the pots. Then he starts digging around a bed at the very bottom of the garden and soon he's leaping over the flowers up the path towards me.

'I've found some strawberries!' he says. 'There's billions of them down there.' I tell him he can eat some and pick the rest and then find some netting in the potting shed and net up the rest of the plants. I also show him how to gently dig up the ones that are over-crowded and move them to a spare patch of freshly dug earth.

'This is great!' he says. 'I never knew gardening could be so much fun.'

I tell him that gardening is a lot of fun when you do it with someone and you find things that you can grow and eat.

I spend the next couple of hours watching Edward trying to wheel a barrow around and pulling up nettles and ground elder from the beds. When Baby Sparkle wakes up we move the rug next to the flower bed we're working on and Edward gets her a washing-up bowl full of water and some plastic cups. 'These are boats, Baby Sparkle,' he says to her and he pushes them around the bowl so she can see how to play with them.

'Ra-la-ra-la-ra,' she says, bestowing on Edward an intense look of love.

'Oh,' he says, throwing himself down next to her and

kissing her on her rounded tummy that's poking out over the top of her nappy. 'I do love you so much, Sparkle. I love all my family.' Then he lies down and closes his eyes until Sparkle soaks him by pouring a cup of water on his head.

'Sparkle!' he says as she giggles away noisily. He shows her how to push the plastic cups under the water so that they bob up.

'Submarines,' he says and she tries to copy him and virtually tips up into the washing bowl. Then he gets up and goes to pick her some strawberries. 'Baby Sparkle likes these, doesn't she?' he asks me.

I tell him that she most certainly does so he bites the green leaves off for her and gives her the remaining fruit.

'Can we plant more food?' he asks me.

I tell him we can. 'We can try and grow beans and courgettes and things,' I say. 'We'll go to the garden centre once we've got this all under control and you can choose what you think Janet would like in her garden.'

Edward leaps up in delight, which seems to worry Baby Sparkle as she starts to cry.

'Oh, sorry, Sparkle!' says Edward and then he scoops her up in his arms and deposits her in the wheelbarrow. 'This'll show you!' he says as he wobbles off with the barrow, pushing Sparkle up and down the garden. She coos crazily with delight.

'We go up . . .' he shouts, wobbling the wheelbarrow around as she holds on to the sides and almost splits open like a ripe fruit she's laughing so much. 'And we go down . . .'

Eventually Edward slumps down next to me. I'm trying to slash the nettles back that are crowding a lobelia I've just discovered.

'There's something else I want to tell you,' Edward says as Sparkle crawls up the garden.

'What's that?' I say, holding some string in my teeth.

'I heard that conversation you had with Dad, the one when you were cross with him for not coming on holiday.'

'I know you did,' I say, 'and I'm sorry. You shouldn't have heard that.'

'But I think we're all angry with Dad,' he says. 'We wanted him to be here.'

'But, Edward,' I say. 'Your father is —'

'I know,' he says. 'He's working. That's what you always say. I'm just telling you how I feel. It's hard sometimes, being a teenager and all that.'

'Yes,' I say, once again trying not to smile.

'And I do keep feeling sad about my granny who lived here and died.'

'Yes, I know. But that's why we're doing her garden, to honour her.'

'Yes, we are, aren't we?' says Edward, suddenly looking happy again.

I stop and I crouch down next to him and reach out to gently ruffle the top of his head.

'Thank you so much for telling me how you feel,' I say. 'I shall definitely bear it in mind from now on.'

Later on, after everyone had come home and Dougie had gone back with Roisin and Lorcan to their bungalow on the Cutlass Estate and I had kissed all my children goodnight and told Edward that I did still love him and that, yes, he was now officially back in our family and, yes, I was delighted at his discovery of the strawberries, the sadness crept in and I went into the kitchen and found a bottle of wine left over

from the dinner party and I opened it. I suddenly felt defi-
ant. I'll drink the whole bottle, I thought. I'll drink a whole
bottle of red wine all by myself and then I'll stagger over
to Noel's house and tell him how much I've drunk and how
could he call me boring then? I had asked Edward earlier,
after he had finally released Baby Sparkle from the wheelbarrow extravaganza, if I was boring.

'Am I boring?' I said, pushing my hair behind my ears
with the grubby gardening glove.

'Boring?' he said, looking slightly amused. He smiled and
pulled up a perfectly healthy hollyhock and said, 'No, Mum.
You're not boring. You're dirty and a bit bossy, but you do
make me laugh a lot even though you're a bit too strict.'

I leant towards him and tickled him with some of the
sticky plants Bennie and Lorcan had found the night before.

Later on though, when I was preparing dinner, all the
children came in and stood in an embarrassed fashion in
the corner of the room, except Baby Sparkle who sat at
their feet. I stopped making their cauliflower cheese and
asked them what they were doing. There was a lot of shuf-
fling of feet and poking in the ribs by Edward. Eventually
Edward said, 'One, two, three,' and they all went into a
child-version of 'You're Beautiful'. It was rather out of
tune and Baby Sparkle did nothing but shout her way
through it, but it was so touching I thought I was going to
cry or laugh or both. Afterwards they all came and hugged
me, with Edward lifting up Baby Sparkle so she too could
give me a cuddle, and I told them how wonderful they all
were and Edward put Baby Sparkle down and then threw
his arms round my neck and kissed me and said, 'Now do
you feel better?' and I told him I did.

Still the sadness came later on when they'd gone to bed

and with the turning out of every light came each thought I had held in check during the day. I thought about Noel and the short but significant time we had spent together and I couldn't understand it. So I opened that bottle of red wine, but as I poured a second glass I thought of Baby Sparkle and her lovely face and how she throws her arms around me and cuddles me. And I thought of Jamie in his girl knickers and then of Bennie, solid, kind, decent Bennie who's always eating food. Finally I thought of Edward, my biggest challenge, my greatest success, and I put the wine down. I picked up the telephone and I called the one person who could make it all right again, but who also needed to know Edward's point of view.

I called John.

19. Drawn to Light

The morning of the fête dawns bright and clear. I can see pink skies through the open windows. A gentle breeze is making the curtains twitch. A butterfly hovers at the doors to the balcony. It flutters there hesitantly and then turns and flies off. I watch it loop away up into the sky. Yesterday I put some cut freesias on the dressing table. I've always loved the smell of them and now the room is full of their scent. I sigh, feeling contented yet apprehensive. Today is the day all these weeks have been leading up to. But, more than that, today is the day I will see Noel Rideout again. I can't tell anyone how nervous I am at the thought of this, even though John is lying here beside me as he has been often during this holiday. After the telephone call all that time ago, after I told him what Noel had said to me and how hurt I felt and then what Edward had told me about John being absent, he drove down the very next morning. He picked me up and held me and told me he loved me and that everyone loved me and that Noel was someone who was wrong. Just that. Simply wrong, he said, and he said it so emphatically that no dissension was possible. He asked me if I'd told Dougie and I said I wanted no one to know. I told him it was because I didn't want to put a shadow over Dougie and Roisin's happiness, but really, deep down, I felt embarrassed at what had happened. I told John I wanted to push it aside, to never think or talk of it again. I told him I wanted to pretend that I'd never met Noel and that Noel had never been so much a part of our family.

'He lied to me,' I said. 'He said he wanted to help Jamie, but he didn't really.' I told John I couldn't get over that and John agreed with me, for he, too, was hurt at the thought of Noel's duplicity towards Jamie.

'You'll never have to see him again,' John said to me.

Then we sat for a long time and I told John what Noel had said about him. John sank his head into his hands.

'It's not true,' I said hurriedly, stroking his hair.

'Yes, it is,' said John, finally looking at me. 'Noel may be a drunk, but he's turned Jamie around and how has he done it?'

'I don't know,' I said.

'By being there for him.' Then John told me how sorry he was for leaving me alone with the children.

'I don't know what I was thinking,' he said. 'How could I not have seen what was happening with Edward? How cross and sad Jamie is?'

'They're fine, John,' I said. 'I'm here and I've been trying so hard . . .'

Then John softened and held me in his arms.

'Oh, it's no criticism of you,' he said. 'Lord alone knows what we would do without you. No, it's time I took responsibility for my family.'

Then he called all the children in from the garden and asked them to sit round the kitchen table.

'I have something I want to say to you all,' he said. He then told them he loved them and cared deeply for them and that he would, from now on, be here as much as he possibly could. He also told Edward that he knew what he had been up to and, although he didn't approve of his behaviour, he knew I had dealt with it.

'I'm not going to punish you,' he said. 'I know you've had punishment enough from your mother. But I do want you to know something, Edward. I may not be your real father, but here in my heart –' at this point John beat his fist hard against his chest – 'I really am.' Edward looked overcome with emotion and came and hugged John so tightly I thought John might expire.

'Thanks, Dad,' he said, 'and I'm sorry for behaving like a prat.'

'But now I'm here for all of you,' continued John, once Edward had let him go, 'and I want to apologize to all of you for not noticing that you needed me.' Then everyone hugged him and I saw he had tears in his eyes.

'You were right,' he said to me after they had all gone back out to clear up the lawn cuttings from the mower. 'I should have taken more notice of Jamie. I feel like a fool. I've let you down.'

I kissed him then.

'You're here,' I said. 'That's all we need.'

As if by magic, I somehow didn't see Noel anywhere or even hear of him from anyone. Shelley came in and out of our lives to babysit and never once mentioned him. She seemed far too busy composing a song in French for the fête. 'I'm going to do a love song,' she said. 'Not "Chanson D'Amour". Something of my own.' Jamie discovered the delights of playing a rather skewed form of cricket with his brothers, Lorcan and Dougie in the back garden, all thoughts of moths and Dark Daggers seemingly gone from his mind. Only Sarah de Salis talked of Noel to me. She called me two days after my confrontation with him and didn't mention him on the telephone. Instead she asked me to come for lunch.

'I don't want to risk sounding repetitive,' she said, 'but I do have something to tell you.' So I left Dougie and Roisin with the children and went over with no one but Baby Sparkle as not even Jamie wanted to risk eating the ancient biscuits again.

It was while she was serving out some over-boiled potatoes that Sarah told me she wanted to ask me something very serious.

'Do you hate me for what I've done?' she said.

I was so startled I almost fell off my chair in shock.

'Hate you, Sarah?' I said, taking her hand. 'Of course not! How could I? Why would I?'

Sarah patted my hand absent-mindedly.

'Because I never told you about Noel,' she said.

'What about Noel?' I asked, almost overcome.

'You'll never see Noel again. You do know that, don't you?' she said.

'Why?' I said, almost in tears. In some way, perhaps, I'd still assumed I would bump into him one day and maybe, in a small place in my heart and mind, I'd imagined us looking for moths together in Janet's garden once more on a warm, balmy summer's night.

'Don't be upset. It's for the best, you know. Noel has always been an alcoholic, Samantha. I think he was that way even when Gerrard and I first knew him.'

'How do you know?'

'Oh,' she said faintly, 'because Gerrard was the same. He drank when the war was over. I forgave him because he had seen so many dreadful things. His friends had been killed around him. He'd been injured and he had shell shock. The man I first married had all but gone and so I let him drink. I bought him his brandy and whisky and

I thought it would ease his mental and physical pain, but what I actually did, I suppose, is watch him as he killed himself.'

'Oh my God, Sarah. That's terrible.'

'Is it? He wasn't the only one. I think all the men I knew in the area were like that.'

'But Noel wasn't in the war. He was too young.'

'No, you're right. He wasn't in the war and yet even as a young man with everything to look forward to, he drank, and I did nothing to stop it. Maybe I didn't even realize it until you came along. You affected him. He was taken with you really, I think. I liked to see him with Jamie. I always thought he was trying to reclaim the lost years he never had with his daughter, the poor young girl he so cruelly ignored because of her mother's misdemeanours.'

'If he was trying to reclaim that relationship, why didn't he look after Jamie better? That night when I found him huddled up on the sofa . . .'

'Never think of it again, Samantha,' she said. 'I think Noel was too far gone to know how badly he'd behaved. He can't help himself, you see. He won't mourn me when I'm dead. He probably wouldn't let himself.'

Then she shook herself a bit and carried on.

'Now, speaking of my death –'

'Oh, Sarah, please don't,' I said.

'Don't be sentimental,' she said. 'I have something that you need to hear because it's very important. I've decided not to sell the house. I thought about what you said to me that day and I've decided that you're right. Just because this house is built on the profits of slavery, it doesn't mean it should be damned to go back into the hands of someone who has made his fortune in the same way.'

'Absolutely,' I said enthusiastically.

'In fact,' she said, ladling some sort of meat stew on to my plate, 'I've made an even more momentous decision. I've been to see my lawyer. I've been thinking there should be a legacy that this family leaves to the village. The Daubeny-Fortescue family and the village are deeply entwined in each other's history so I've decided that the house itself must serve as a memorial. I shall leave it in trust and it shall be called the Daubeny-Fortescue Foundation. It will fund holidays here for underprivileged children from London. They shall be welcome here all year round and enjoy the house and the gardens and the sea. I have it all worked out. The Foundation shall be linked to a London charity who shall decide which children will come. They will provide the teachers and social workers to stay here and help the children adjust to country life. When I die, an administrator will be announced and the trust will be put in place.'

'That's amazing,' I said. 'That's a wonderful thing to do. But, without wishing to pry, how on earth is the trust to be funded?'

'Ah. I've thought about that and I've come up with a wonderful solution. I'm going to sell everything!'

'What do you mean, everything?'

'The car, Samantha. You said it must be worth a fortune and that may well be the case, so I'm going to sell it and the pram and the doll's house. I've asked Rupert Howse to get some antique experts to come and value it all. I'm sure even those small children's shoes in the cloakroom are worth something.'

'But I thought you didn't want to sell anything that Gerrard loved?'

'Gerrard is dead,' she said simply. 'He has been dead a

long time and soon I will be dead too, so what do these things matter to us? No. What matters is that children can come to this beautiful place and dance on these floors and run in these grounds and have the freedom here that I saw in Jamie the first day you came for lunch.'

I told Sarah I thought her gesture was magnificent.

'I can just imagine the children here,' I said. 'They will enjoy it so much.'

'Yes,' she said. 'I never had children to enjoy this house and it's a house that should be enjoyed. In fact, I'm even thinking of stipulating that one of the jobs the children can do when they are here is to work on the gardens. I think children like gardening, don't they? They could help restore the Italian sunken garden. It's a good way of learning about the cycle of life, isn't it? You know, life and death and pollination and fertilization and all that sort of thing.'

'Yes,' I said and then I told her that Edward and I had been working hard on Janet's garden.

'We've really made a commitment to it,' I said. 'It's changed Edward's attitude, I think. A project has been good for him and gardening is a life-affirming thing to do, even for a child.'

'He's not a child though, is he, really?' said Sarah.

I thought of all the times recently that Edward had needed me.

'He may not show it,' I said, 'but I think he actually still is a child. He still needs guidance and reassurance. He still needs a hot meal on his plate.'

'Yes,' said Sarah sadly. 'I've never known that. But then again,' she was brisk now, 'I mustn't dwell on that because we have a fête to be getting on with!'

*

The organization of the fête has taken up all my time. It has kept me busy. It has kept my mind occupied. I've spent half my time arguing with the Health and Safety people in Barnstaple and the other half trying to work out the logistics of the puppet show.

'We need electricity!' John said three weeks before the event. Then he said that instead of the three puppeteers scheduled to come down, the whole troupe had decided to come and that numbered ten, so I said I'd talk to Mr Cutlass Candles about hiring some bungalows.

'Ah, Mrs Smythe,' he said when I told him that I wanted to ask him a favour. 'Have you decided to sell me your wonderful house?'

'No,' I said, but I told him that I wanted to rent five of his bungalows for a weekend.

'They're all full,' he said airily. 'Anyway, I only ever rent them for a week.'

'Oh,' I said, disappointed.

But a few days later he called me back.

'I might have some space, depending on the price,' he said.

In the end we negotiated something for a long weekend on five bungalows which, apparently, had only become available minutes earlier due to the entire Long Marston WI cancelling their trip to Lower Strand, owing to the fact that their social secretary had inadvertently double-booked them to go to Dublin to see *Lord of the Dance* over the same weekend.

'Who are the bungalows for?' asked Gordon Cutlass.

'Friends,' I said.

'Friends coming to the fête?' he said, sounding a bit put out.

'Yes.'

'Well, business is business,' he said briskly.

I rang John and told him the accommodation was all sorted and he said that was fantastic, but weren't the bungalows self-catering and, if so, how could his puppeteers get any food if they were busy rehearsing and setting up the show? I ended up saying that I'd get some food in for them. He then told me that he'd noticed they were quite picky about what they ate. 'I don't think barbecue beans would cut it, Samantha,' he said. 'Can you do something special?'

After we finished talking, I went to the beach, somewhat reeling from the weight of all the responsibilities. I took the children with me. By now they'd bought boogie boards with their pocket money and they marched off down the hill past the café, each clutching a board, even little Jamie, who'd bought a small version with a picture of a mermaid on it.

Susie was at the café as they walked past.

'Isn't that a mermaid?' she said when she saw Jamie struggling down to the sea.

'Yes,' I said. 'He likes mermaids. He doesn't like sharks and things like that on a board because they scare him.'

'I don't blame him,' said Susie. Then she noticed Edward manhandling his shark-covered board down towards the water and she rolled her eyes and asked where the 'rude' girl was. 'Honestly, Samantha,' she said, 'I don't know why you let him hang out with that girl. She was so rude. Poor Allegra. Her throat hurt for days afterwards.'

Despite myself, I smiled. 'I'd forgotten that,' I said. 'Yes, I guess Isabel certainly had spirit.'

'What do you mean, *had*?'

I took a deep breath and explained that Edward was no longer hanging out with Isabel. 'They've had a parting of the ways,' I said. To change the subject, I ended up telling her about the French puppeteers coming to stay on the Cutlass Estate and instead of turning her nose up at the idea she said she thought it all sounded great fun.

'I rather like those bungalows,' she said. 'I drove up to see Roisin the other day and she was outside doing a barbecue with your friend Dougie. They're obviously totally smitten. I was just trying to tell you that I thought the Cutlass Estate was rather charming and handily low maintenance. I'd even stay there.'

'Would you?' I asked her.

'No, not really,' she said, laughing. 'It's not my style, but I should think ten French puppeteers will be very happy cooking Toulouse sausages there.'

I told her that John had said I needed to get some food in for them and that they were apparently quite demanding about their food, being French and all that. Karin, who had just struggled up to the beach and was munching on a Devon scone filled with jam and clotted cream, then announced that, actually, she was a Cordon Bleu chef.

'I mean, I'm not brilliant,' she said, blushing, 'but when I was first married, Henry sent me on a course because he said he didn't want to eat horrible food all the time and he thought the best attribute a wife could have was to cook properly.'

Susie raised an eyebrow.

'He likes his food,' said Karin defensively, 'and I like Aaron to eat well because you know how he gets . . .'

'How does he get?' I asked.

'He gets very cross and angry if he doesn't eat,' Karin said. 'He doesn't like vegetables so I have to hide them in other things.'

'Like what things?'

'Well, I might do meatballs Swedish style, but in the meat I'll put mushrooms and courgettes chopped up into tiny bits so that he doesn't notice they're in there. On this course, I learned how to chop things up into teeny-weeny pieces.'

'Well, I wish you'd chop Aaron into teeny-weeny pieces,' said Susie. 'You should stop mothering him so much. He's nearly a bloody teenager. Why don't you give him some freedom and hopefully he'll hang himself with it.'

'Susie!' said Karin.

'It's only an expression,' said Susie. 'You know – give him enough rope and –'

'What could you cook that's simple but tasty?' I asked Karin, interrupting.

'I could do a Vichyssoise,' she said, 'and then maybe a boeuf bourguignon.'

'Could you?' I said, rather amazed.

'Oh, yes,' she said. 'It's very simple really. You just –'

'Oh God, spare us the recipe,' said Susie. Then she softened a bit. 'Would you like Jolka to come and help you, Karin? She's a pretty good cook. She could be your sous chef. I can drop her off up there at the Cutlass Estate if it's a help.'

'It would be a help,' said Karin, a bit tetchily. 'I mean, if you don't mind.'

'I don't mind at all,' said Susie. 'I like being bountiful. It might even be fun.'

I spent a hot day in Barnstaple with Roisin when we went there to pick up the forms to obtain the Health and Safety certificate. Roisin had looked very relieved when I said I had to go there to sort everything out. She asked if she could come too.

'I've been through all those wills,' she said, 'and I've found nothing.'

'I don't think Sarah expected you to find anything,' I said.

'I know, but I'm worried that me and Dougie are letting everyone down. The money from the sale of the car isn't going to last forever and for that house to survive we need to find the catalogues.'

She said that, in a last ditch attempt, she had sent Dougie to Sarah's house to look for more clues.

'They could be anywhere and, now everything is being sold, I'm worried we've missed something vital.'

Barnstaple would be a relief, she claimed. 'And we can buy our dresses,' she said, perking up.

So Roisin and I went off first thing in the morning, leaving the children with John, and drove the hour to Barnstaple. We went to the local council office where they gave us the forms. The lady on the telephone was in reception. I knew it was her because she had the same voice.

'I've come to pick up some Health and Safety forms,' I said.

'For the Lower Straaand fête?' she said.

'The very same,' I said.

'Mr Cutlass not signing them?' she asked nosily.

'No,' I said. 'He doesn't need to sign them because I am.'

'Oh,' she said. 'I thought there was a pond involved. I thought there was *food*.'

'There is,' I said, 'and I'm going to rope the pond off and just apply for a food permit and that's all.'

'Food permits can take weeks,' she said, handing me the

forms before walking off into the myriad of offices behind her.

'Good Lord,' said Roisin. 'What a cow.'

'Oh, Mr Cutlass just bought her father's old farmhouse for way over the odds,' I said. 'So she loves him.'

'She may well do, but what's all that stuff about you being able to fence off the pond yourself? I didn't know you were going to do that.'

'Well, neither did I, but it has just occurred to me that Mrs Pat Pucklechurch of the Upper Strand Centre of Equitation is very keen on puppet shows. I bet she has fencing. All people with horses have fencing. I wonder if I went to see her and buttered her up a bit if she'd let me borrow it, then Dougie and John can fence the pond off.'

'Do you think Dougie and John are any good at fencing?' Roisin said doubtfully.

'No, not really,' I said, 'but how hard can fencing be?'

Then we went into the centre of town and found a dress shop full of frothy little summer outfits and tried on just about everything.

'Lovely dresses in here,' said Roisin, trying on a pink frilly number with a tutu for a skirt. 'I feel like a princess!'

'You look like the Sugar Plum Fairy,' I said.

The female assistant, who was young and very helpful, found a purple bias-cut dress for me to try. It was simple, calf-length, understated.

'Wow,' said Roisin when I tried it on. 'You actually have a figure.'

'A large figure,' I said.

'But this dress skims all that,' said the shop assistant. She was right though, the dress was very flattering.

'But it's not very Truly Scrumptious, is it?' said Roisin.

I was about to explain to the shop assistant what Roisin meant by that, but it turned out that *Chitty Chitty Bang Bang* was one of the shop assistant's favourite films when she was a child and that she too loved a Truly Scrumptious outfit and so she told me not to fear because she knew exactly what to do. She disappeared out to the rear of the shop and then came back with a beautifully large and floppy straw hat and some ribbon.

'Tie this ribbon round the hat and put some flowers in it,' she suggested, 'and then find some pretty shoes and I'm sure your son will see how lovely you look.'

I tried on the hat and it did look quite impressive with its wide brim and hippy-ish air, so I ended up buying my outfit and Roisin bought hers.

'This will give Dougie a turn,' she said as we looked in a shoe shop window at some delicate suede shoes with small heels and embroidered straps, and by the time we left Barnstaple we were crowing with delight. On the way home, though, Roisin became more serious. I noticed her looking out of the car window, away from me. I thought she might be crying.

'Roisin,' I said, 'what's the matter?'

'Nothing,' she said, still not facing me.

'Are you crying?'

'No,' she said, sniffing.

'You are crying! But why? I thought we'd had such a nice day?'

'I'm not really crying,' she said, turning towards me and looking rather desperate. 'I've only had one tear.'

'What's the matter?'

'I'm so happy, Samantha,' she said. 'I haven't been this happy for such a long time. I've met you and I've met Dougie and, well, I really like him. He's such fun and he's so wonderful to Lorcan and it's been great this summer, but after the fête it's over, really, isn't it? I've failed to find the catalogues. The Foundation may have to close after a few years, mightn't it?'

'I don't know,' I said, sighing. 'Where there's a will, there's a way. We might come up with another solution.'

'What solution? There is no other solution. Believe me. No. We'll have the fête and then we'll all go home and that will be that and I just can't believe it.' At that, Roisin started crying again.

I reached over with one hand to take Roisin's.

'I know what you mean,' I said. 'It's felt as though time has stood still and we'll all remain here forever.'

'But we won't, will we?' she said.

'No,' I said, 'we won't but, you know, we'll keep in touch, Roisin, I know we will. I'll come and visit you and you can come and visit me and we can all come back to Lower Strand on holiday every year.'

'But it won't happen,' Roisin said sadly. 'Everything will change and the children will grow up. Edward won't want to come back next year. He's outgrowing the beach already, really.'

'But Edward loves it here. He loves his house. It's very important to him.'

'But you're not going to stay here long term and neither is Dougie. He'll have to go back to London and his job and . . . I've given up my job,' she says.

'What?' I say. 'Why? For Dougie?'

'No, not for Dougie,' she said. 'Haven't you noticed? I've been away for weeks. I just realized that I didn't want to carry on as before so I called my boss and told him to stuff his job, but now I don't know what to do . . .'

'Why don't you go to London then?' I asked her quietly as, in truth, the thought had only just occurred to me. 'You could live with Dougie.'

'I don't know if me and Dougie would work in London,' she said. 'There's Lorcan to think about and, anyway, I have no idea how serious this all is. I barely know Dougie so . . .'

Then she changed the conversation.

But today is the day of the fête and now we're all here in the back garden of the Manor House. All our hard work has come together at last. I finally got the Health and Safety certificate and now even the pond has been fenced off. Not by John and Dougie, actually, but by Jean-Paul and Michel, the French puppeteers who kindly went and collected Mrs Pat Pucklechurch's temporary horse fencing and then strung it up around the pond yesterday. Susie and I sat there and watched them do it, and Susie spent the afternoon gazing at Jean-Paul with his fine muscles and dark skin. Later on, as the evening turned into night, instead of just dropping Jolka off to help with the cooking, Susie actually stayed and, the next thing I knew, Allegra, Aaron and Antigone were having the best time hunting for firewood by torchlight with Michel, who only looked about nineteen, while Susie talked at length in French to Jean-Paul. Aaron had started the evening complaining endlessly to his mother about the fact that she wouldn't let him play on his PSP.

'Why can't I play on it?' he said as Karin furiously stirred a pot of soup while Jolka served up bowlfuls of it.

'Because I said so,' said Karin.

'But I want to,' whinged Aaron.

'Well, you can't,' said Karin. 'We can't have everything we want.'

'If you don't let me have my PSP, I'm going to tell Dad.'

At that, Karin stopped stirring the soup and turned to face her son.

'Look, Aaron,' she said. 'I don't care if you tell your father because I will tell him how tiresome you've been this holiday. The truth is, things are going to change around here. You want your PSP, but you're not going to have it. I want to eat three bowlfuls of this delicious cream-laden soup, but I'm not going to have that either. This is how life is going to be from now on, so if you don't like it, lump it.'

'What am I going to do then?' asked Aaron, horrified.

'Go and play,' said Karin. 'I am not here for your amuse-ment.' And then she went back to her cooking. The next time she looked up, Aaron was off finding firewood and I saw a look of genuine relief flush across her face.

Then I noticed Susie sitting curled up in front of the fire, her long limbs tucked around her like a deer that had fallen down and her sheen of hair hanging down to one side of her face like a silken screen. She had on plain jeans and a large poncho. At one point Jean-Paul took her hand underneath her poncho and I raised an eyebrow at Karin who was by then in the process of cooking the most deli-cious boeuf bourguignon ever. She smiled back at me conspiratorially and carried on stirring.

I can see Susie right now, here in this beautiful garden. She somehow blends in with the perfection of this day. She's wandering around with Antigone holding one hand and Allegra holding the other. The girls are wearing glisten-ing gold sundresses and flip-flops, and Susie has on a red polka-dot sundress and her feet are bare. Her hair is straggling down her sun-kissed back. She's wearing no make-up. One of the girls is trying to pull her towards the large marquee that houses the cake stall and the makeshift bar. The other one is pleading for her to come and play the hook-the-duck game.

'Mummy,' calls whichever girl it is. 'Come and hook a duck.' Susie is laughing and, as the local brass band begins to blast away on their tubas and horns and cornets, Susie shakes off her children and puts her hands up to her ears in mock horror.

'Wow!' says John as he appears from the puppet tent and sees her. 'Your friend Susie's having a good time. I hear she enjoyed herself last night.'

'Did she?' I say. 'Go on. Do tell.'

'All I know is that she's splashing money around like there's no tomorrow. The lady on the gate –'

'That's Dilys, Shelley's mum.'

'Yes, her. She said that your friend Susie is paying over the odds for everything. Apparently she insisted on giving her ten pounds to enter even though it's only a pound, and that man over there doing the coconut shy –'

'Mr Smullen.'

'Yes, him. He said she gave him a fiver for three balls when it's only supposed to be fifty pence!'

'That's great, isn't it?'

'Mad,' says John. 'But that's what happens when you hang around with these French guys. You go barmy.'

'You haven't gone barmy though, have you?' I ask him.

'Only for you,' he says, kissing me. 'Now, have I told you how wonderful you look?'

'Yes,' I say. In fact, everyone has told me how wonderful I look. I had put my purple dress and my hat and shoes on at home and Edward had come into my bedroom whistling. When he saw me, he said, 'You look lovely, Mum.' I sent him out to get some flowers for my hat and, while he was gone, Jamie appeared.

He came into the room and stopped dead when he saw me.

'Mama,' he said in an admiring tone. 'You look like Truly Sumptious!'

'Do I?' I said, feeling rather tearful.

'Yes,' he said. Then he came over to me, climbed on to my lap and kissed me. 'I like it when you wear a dress. I like girls who wear dresses.'

'Does Sophie like to wear dresses?' I asked him.

He looked at me very solemnly. 'Sophie has gone,' he said.

'Gone where?' I asked.

'Gone away,' he said. Then he looked a bit sad.

'She can always come back, you know, Jamie,' I said. 'There will never be a problem with that.'

Then Edward came back with lilac and poppies, sweet peas and some morning glory.

'Will this do?' he said, and when Jamie saw the flowers he got very excited so Edward took him back into the garden to find some daisies and they both spent about half an hour trying to weave the flowers into my hat-band. By the time they were finished, I looked like a carnival queen.

'Oh, mama,' said Jamie as he felt the silk of the dress. 'You do look very pretty.'

'Mummy finally looks like Truly Scrumptious, doesn't she, Jamie?' said John when we all appeared downstairs.

'No, she doesn't,' said Bennie. 'She looks like a Flower Fairy.'

'I love Flower Fairies,' said Jamie, smiling, and then he went to his room and put on a blue shirt of Bennie's and some boy's swimming trunks. When he came downstairs I found he also had with him one of Baby Sparkle's prettiest dresses, a white cotton smock with peonies printed all over it.

'Look, mama,' he said, holding the dress out to me.

'That's too small for you, Jamie,' I said.

'S'not for me,' he said. 'It's for my lovely sister,' and he turned and kissed Sparkle on the head.

So, here we all are in this garden together and now the fête has been going for an hour and a half and everyone seems happy. People I have never seen before are sitting on the lawn eating ice-cream cornets and drinking pints of local cider. A handful of what I assume are holidaymakers are spending a fortune on the tombola. 'What have you won?' I hear one ask another in a cut-glass accent. 'A set of lily-of-the-valley candles!' says the other. 'It's got a picture of this village on the front. How sweet!' A man wanders past them. He sells them some pots of home-made honey he's carrying in a large basket. It turns out that he lives on the Cutlass Estate and that the honey is made by his own bees.

'Where are your hives?' Roisin asks him.

'In my back garden,' he tells us. 'Mr Cutlass says he doesn't mind me doing it. Says he likes bees.'

Edward and Aaron have finally decided they might like each other and now that Karin has confiscated Aaron's PlayStation they're spending all their pocket money trying to knock down bowling pins.

'Look! Five down,' yells Edward as Aaron takes his turn.

'Bet you can't beat that,' says Aaron, thumping Edward on the back.

'Of course I can,' says Edward, and he runs and the ball goes thumping down the grass and crashes into the skittles. 'Five!' he and Aaron yell at the same time.

Bennie and Lorcan are sitting on the grass eating ice creams with Karin.

'I like the pink flavour,' I can hear Bennie telling Karin as if he has known her all his life, 'and I also like the green, but Lorcan likes the brown ones. What ones do you like, Karin? Would you like Mummy to buy you one?'

'I like all of them,' says Karin, smiling, 'but I'm not having one today. Thanks for asking though.'

Dougie and Roisin have bought a skipping rope from the bric-a-brac stall and are trying to teach Jamie to skip, which is proving a bit tricky as the rope keeps getting stuck on the tutu of Roisin's Sugar Plum Fairy dress.

'You take your dress off,' Jamie is saying to Roisin, giggling away.

'Yes, you take your dress off,' says Dougie as Roisin attempts to jump over the rope.

Roisin gives Dougie a fake grimace.

Out of the corner of my eye, I see Mr Henderson and Mrs Pat Pucklechurch sitting at a table on the croquet lawn having tea with Mrs de Salis. They have cakes and biscuits and a rather sad-looking basil plant they've bought from the plant stall. I can see Sarah laughing with them. She keeps on picking up a ginger snap, but I notice she doesn't actually eat any of it. It makes me worry about her and about why we're all here. I've told her my concerns about the continued funding of the Foundation, especially since Dougie found nothing except more out-of-date biscuits in his search of the house, but Sarah said that the car would probably sell for thousands. Still, none of us will know until the sale happens. Until then, we're reliant on this fête.

My attention turns to Jean-Paul and Michel who, now that the puppet show is over, seem to be entertaining Jolka, Susie and the girls with the hand puppets. Jean-Paul keeps tickling Susie flirtatiously with the Pulcinella and she's squirming and laughing at the same time. The puppet show has been a massive success. Even the locals paid the ten pounds to see it and we all marvelled at the skill of the puppeteers and John's wonderful set, complete with spinning disco balls, a wand with sparks that came out of it and exploding sausages. Somehow it appealed to everyone, old and young.

'Your chateau is marvellous,' I whispered to John once the curtain went up. He grinned happily at me. I saw Mrs Pucklechurch doubled-up laughing at the banging bangers and, at the same time, Baby Sparkle came out with such a low, dirty giggle that she had people laughing even more than the puppet show. John was glowing with pride when it finished. 'That's my show,' he said and then he grabbed Baby Sparkle and threw her into the air. She squealed with delight. 'And that's my girl!' he said, catching her in his arms and kissing her all over her tummy.

But now the sun is getting lower in the sky and, as Shelley takes to the stage to sing her French love song – 'This is my version of a *chanson d'amour*,' she says – I look around for Noel. In fact, I've looked for him all afternoon. I've gone backwards and forwards to the Portaloo because I've been so nervous. I want to look confident when I see him. I want him to acknowledge that not only have I played a major part in organizing the fête, but that I've also managed to do it in style. I've repositioned my hat on my head maybe twenty times or more. I've reapplied lipstick and ruffled my hair. I've sprayed perfume from the small bottle in my bag. I've powdered my nose and straightened my dress and buffed my shoes and all to no avail for Noel is not here.

Quite a few people have gathered around the stage now and they're swaying to Shelley's wobbly but sweet voice. '*Je t'aime,*' she sings, bravely strumming away at her guitar. '*I love you . . .*'

'I lerve you!' Michel yells out from next to the puppet tent. Everyone starts laughing. Shelley smiles. '*Mon ami, je t'aime. Finis!*' she sings with some relish and then she stands up to take a bow and we all clap. Just before she puts the microphone down she yells, 'And I love you all!' We clap even more loudly, especially Dilys, who looks terribly proud. Shelley looks as if she's about to say something else, but Mr Henderson appears from the back of the stage, carrying a couple of chairs. He carefully puts them down and takes the microphone from Shelley. Dougie follows him with two more chairs and he lines them up at the front of the stage. As Mr Henderson clears his throat, Dougie disappears offstage again, only to return with a lightweight podium. He winks at me as he positions it right at the front.

'Can you hear me?' says Mr Henderson into the microphone. 'Can you?'

'Yes,' shouts Mrs Pat Pucklechurch, who has now come to stand next to the stage.

'Right,' says Mr Henderson loudly. 'Can all of you who are playing games just stop for a minute? I know you're having fun, but this is important so put down those pints of cider and desist from licking ice creams, as it were.' He pauses for a bit as people start turning round to look at him. 'Have we all stopped?' he says. He looks around the garden to check. 'Now, I want you all to come close to the stage because there are a few important things you all need to know.' He clears his throat again as people start gathering round. 'I just want to say thank you to Sarah de Salis for letting us have this fête in her garden. I must say, it's been a wonderful afternoon and I think we might well have raised a lot of money to save this wonderful house so . . . thank you, Sarah.' Everyone starts clapping as Sarah de Salis appears on stage. She looks suddenly even frailer than usual. She's smiling, but at the same time seems close to tears.

'In order to say thank you properly and to explain why we're all here,' continues Mr Henderson, 'I call on someone far more eloquent and knowledgeable about this area than myself. Residents of Lower Strand, holidaymakers, French puppet people and anyone else I've forgotten, I give you Noel Rideout!' And for some reason everyone starts whooping as the unmistakably elegant figure of Noel Rideout comes on to the stage.

My heart is beating so much I can barely breathe. I watch him move towards the microphone with such an intensity that my eyes hurt. I'm not aware of anything else but Noel. Up until this very second, I had no idea how I would feel on seeing him again, but now I know, deep down in my heart, that I forgive him. He is Noel Rideout, an old man and sometimes a kind and wise man, and that much I remember so very clearly. As he gets to the front of the stage, I find I can't see him properly. The sun is in my eyes. I squint up and see, for a moment, I'm sure of it, that Noel is looking right at me. I can't fathom his look. But now Noel has stopped looking at me and is, instead, looking down at the people gathered on the lawn in front of him.

Everyone is quiet but, for a little too long, Noel doesn't say anything. He just stares out above their faces while we all look up at him expectantly. At that moment, I see Edward. He's skulking at the back of the croquet lawn. He looks as if he's about to disappear into the rhododendrons. Aaron isn't with him. I can see Bennie whispering into Lorcan's ear and Roisin suddenly looks down and taps him lightly on his shoulder. I can see Baby Sparkle asleep in her pushchair, her hair catching the sunlight. John is standing next to her, his hand gently resting on one of the pushchair handles. I look for Jamie. Ah, there he is. He's in Dougie's arms. He waves at me and smiles. I smile back at him. They're all before me, my friends, my family . . . and then I look again at Noel, who now seems as if he's in a trance, like a sleepwalker. His eyes are open, he looks as if he's awake, but really he might as well be asleep because still no words come out of his mouth. Suddenly I feel that I must help him. I realize that something is wrong and so I must get up, in this instance, and help Noel Rideout. I don't care what he has done, what he has said, I just know that he needs me and that if I don't help him I'll never forgive myself. But before I can jump to my feet and move to his side, Noel starts talking.

'I suppose I'm supposed to thank you all for coming,' he says, swaying slightly. 'And I suppose I do. I mean, it's great you all came. We probably haven't made a bean more than we usually do and this beautiful house will no doubt be bought eventually by the awful Mr Cutlass Candles, who I don't even think is here. But that's not a surprise, is it? Nothing is real . . . but you came, we tried, didn't we? *Zut alors!* We even have French puppets here. That's a real effort, isn't it? So, yes, we have tried, *n'est-ce pas?* That's what we'll tell ourselves, you know, on our death beds. We'll say, "Oh, but I tried." That's what we'll say. This lady here –' and at that Noel waves his hand in my general direction – 'would say that. She's Samantha Smythe, you know, my Beautiful Golden, and she has tried to save this house. She is the person who told Sarah de Salis that the fate of the house could be changed. I am here to announce that, if we *can* save the house, Sarah de Salis will be leaving it to a charity that runs residential holidays in the countryside for under-privileged children. It's a worthy cause. It's the right thing to do and Sarah de Salis is so keen for this to happen. We have to right our wrongs, do we not?' At this point Noel turns and looks at me. 'Samantha thought French puppet-eers would help. She tried to save everything. I think she's even tried to save me, but I'm too far gone, you know. Anyway, this is what I want to say to you, Samantha Smythe, and, in fact, to everyone here. Do you know, by the time you die you may well look back on life and realize there have been great moments in it, but, before that happens, you've got to put up with a whole pile of shit.'

And then Noel Rideout falls very quietly backwards off the podium.

Epilogue

Strange how you can have feelings of love for someone who isn't there. I never told John that, in my own way, I felt so strongly for Noel and yet, of course, he knew all along anyway. I only found out the day after we went to visit Noel in the hospital in Barnstaple. We had gone to tell him that, despite his misgivings, the fête had raised a staggering £20,000. Half of that money had been donated by Susie's husband – 'Guilt money,' she had said to me before she drove off out of Lower Strand and back to her life in London, blowing Jean-Paul the biggest of kisses as she left – 'but who cares!' – and the rest had been raised by puppet show tickets and the fête in general. I wanted to tell Noel how the fête had rekindled some sort of village spirit, how Mrs Pat Pucklechurch had come up to me at the end of it, beaming about how much money we had raised.

'We can fix the house!' she said and then Mr Henderson told me he'd be more than happy to find some builders to begin work as soon as possible. Even Mr Cutlass announced at the next meeting of the Parish Council, hurriedly held the following day, that he would be donating his gardeners to work on the Manor House gardens and help bring the Italian garden back to life.

'You have to hand it to him,' said Dougie when he heard, 'that man knows how to turn every situation to his advantage.'

'What do you mean?' I said.

'He has the common touch. He knows which way the

340

wind blows. That's probably why he's so successful. I mean, there's no point in him buying the Manor House right now. The whole village has been swept up with the success of the fête and the charitable outcome that will happen because of it. Now is the time to appear to be supportive. We're all so busy congratulating ourselves that no one wants to be seen as a stingy curmudgeon.'

I had intended to tell Noel all of this, but when we got to the hospital he had obviously just come out of an operation. We saw him through the plexiglass window of the waiting room as he was being wheeled on to the ward. He had a bandage round his head and his right leg, stuck out at an angle, was also bandaged. Isabel was trotting along next to the gurney and, as they turned to put Noel back in his bed, she saw us and waved and then came over.

'Hello,' she said in her lilting voice. 'Have you come to see Granddad?'

We all said we had.

'Doesn't he look very sorry for himself with his leg all bandaged up?' she said. 'He's broke his ankle, you know. That's the problem with old people. The doctor said they don't bounce.'

I told Isabel that I wanted to see Noel, but she just shook her head solemnly and told me that the doctor had said her granddad shouldn't have visitors until he had rested for a while.

'I'm not sure he wants to see you anyway,' she said to me, giving me a sly look. Then she said she was going outside for a cigarette.

'You coming, hen?' she said to Edward and Edward shifted from foot to foot and looked nervously at me. I kept my expression as blank as possible.

'Nah,' he said eventually and then, after Isabel had left the waiting room, he came and sat next to me.

'Do you think Noel's going to be OK?' he asked.

'Yes,' I said.

'But how do you know? We hadn't seen him for ages before he hurt himself.'

'That's because he was being childish,' said John.

'In what way?' I said.

'Oh, in that "I won't apologize to her until she comes to see me" type way. Not that you had any reason to go and see him after he behaved so badly. Really, it's all attention-seeking behaviour, so babyish.'

'By the way,' said Edward, 'where are the baby and Bennie and Jamie?'

'Bennie and Jamie are with Roisin and Sparkle's with Shelley.'

'Sparkle's probably got her own web page now,' said John. 'I mean, honestly, what's wrong with this generation? Why do they want to exist solely as an image on a computer? Why don't they go out and actually meet people rather than talking to them over the Internet when, really, they're nothing but strangers to each other?'

'Well, I met Isabel in real life,' said Edward gloomily, 'and look what happened to me.'

'Isabel's disturbed,' said John. 'She's not normal.'

'Isn't she?' I said. 'She doesn't do anything that abnormal. She stuck up for Edward, remember?'

'In a manner of speaking,' said John. 'Anyway, she drinks and smokes and she's only thirteen.'

'Well, maybe that's normal now,' I said. 'I have a feeling she'll be OK, you know. She's a toughie, but she's got a good heart underneath all that odd make-up and hair.'

John sighed. 'You're just defending her because you think that I'm somehow attacking Noel by attacking her, but I'm not.'

'You don't like him though, do you?'

John sighed again.

'But I still miss him,' I said, 'and that makes you jealous and I can't stand it.' Despite myself, I started to cry. Edward looked nervously at me.

'Shall I go and get you some water?' he asked, trying to be helpful but obviously extremely embarrassed.

'Yes, please,' I said.

After he'd left the room, John did something unexpected. He kneeled down in front of me and took my hands in his.

'I know you're upset because you can't see Noel and that's making you sad but, in answer to your question – no, I don't like Noel Rideout, but it's not because I'm jealous of him. It's because he hurt you and he made you sad and it hurt me that you thought he was worth being sad about.'

'But he made me feel so good about myself,' I said, still crying. 'I don't know why I haven't said this before, but I didn't know how to. I was so angry with him about Jamie, but then I got angry with you too.'

'I know that,' John said. 'I've apologized. We've moved on, haven't we?'

'Yes,' I said. 'But it doesn't mean I haven't missed Noel somehow even though I don't really know why.'

'I know,' said John. 'He's probably missed you.'

'He made me feel worthwhile, you see. He made me feel that what I said might actually be important or interesting and I haven't felt that for such a long, long time.'

'Yes, but it wasn't him that did it, it was what you put on him that worked for you. It was you who decided he was such a great intellectual and so witty and dry and all that. You wanted him to make you feel those things.'

'But he chose to spend time with me. Don't you see that? When he had any spare moment he came round. It affected me so deeply that he spent time with me and Jamie.'

'He only came round because he had nothing to do and, as for Jamie, he's only four years old. Do you honestly think Noel was interested in Jamie or did it just give him something to do? He probably loved this idea of being a mentor to a young boy, the fact that he was, in part, reliving his childhood, but he didn't really care about Jamie.'

'Why are you being so harsh?'

'Because it's us who love you. You saw Noel as being some sort of saviour for you. The rest of us just saw him as a manipulative drunk. Ask Dougie or Roisin. They'll tell you the same thing.'

'So you're saying I just saw what I wanted to see? God, do you think I'm that desperate? Then it's true what Noel said to me. I'm nothing but a martyred mother with nothing interesting to offer the world at all. I've wasted everything I was given. I –'

'No,' said John. 'I won't have it. You're not wasted. You're so very loved by me, by your friends, your family and, above all, your children. You're our everything, Samantha, and we all love you and respect you and we all think you're the best thing that ever happened to us and I won't let those feelings you think you have for that pretence of a man take over the rest of our lives.'

And then I sat there for a while and watched Edward in the room next door pulling out paper cups shaped like triangles and putting water in them and gulping it down and pulling another one out and then staring at it as if it was the most wondrous thing he'd ever seen and, eventually, he saw me watching him and he smiled at me and I turned to John and took his hand in mine and we walked out of the door.

A few months later, we all went down to visit Sarah de Salis. We met Roisin and Dougie at her house for, by this time, they were living with her and taking care of her.

'I've done lunch,' Roisin said when we got there.

'I don't want lunch,' said Jamie.

'I've done you all a packed lunch,' said Roisin. 'No more ancient biscuits. They've been banished! You can have your lunch in the garden. I've put tables and chairs out for you. Now off you go, the grown-ups want to talk.' Roisin then told me that Sarah was now, in fact, quite frail and maybe it was better if the children stayed outside rather than rampaging round the house.

'Sarah won't mind,' she said, 'but I think she'd like to actually have a conversation rather than be drowned out by the kids.'

So off the children went, Lorcan running in the lead, Jamie bringing up the rear, and the last thing I heard was Jamie yelling, 'Where's the car? The Chitty Bang Bang car?'

Dougie went to get Sarah and she came into the dining room looking very fragile. She sat in a chair, a rug tucked round her legs, her eyes watery, and she pecked at a bit of bread and tried to eat some soup, but it kept dribbling down her chin. It reminded me, almost painfully, of the first time I'd met her when I'd sat round this table feeding Baby Sparkle the horrible consommé. It seemed like such a long time ago, I could barely believe those days in the summer had actually existed and now Sarah looked so much older.

She wasn't wearing the peacock housecoat any more and somehow that seemed significant.

'Here,' said Roisin gently as Sarah tried to feed herself again with the spoon. Roisin put a linen napkin under Sarah's chin and spooned small thimblefuls of soup into Sarah's mouth.

Eventually Sarah spoke and her voice sounded like someone's dying breath croaking out.

'The sale is in two days' time,' she said weakly, trying to focus on me and John.

'It's all fine, Sarah,' said Dougie reassuringly. 'Everything's ready and waiting in the garage and the auctioneer will be here early in the morning . . .'

'I have to say goodbye.'

'Yes, I know. I'll take you out there to see everything.'

Sarah continued, her eyes watering more than before as she turned to look at me. 'I have to say goodbye to Gerrard's and Philomena's things. You understand, don't you, Samantha?'

I took her hand.

'I do understand,' I said gently. 'I know you're feeling sad, but it's what you wanted, remember?'

Sarah nodded.

'Think of the children out there now,' I said. 'Can you hear them laughing outside this window? Can you hear their running feet on the earth? They're loving being here. You have left a legacy for so many children who will love it as much as them . . .' As I said it, I could hear the children whooping.

'Listen to them now!' I said, but as I was about to continue the whooping became louder until Bennie, Lorcan and Edward suddenly burst through the door.

'We found something! We found something!' yelled Bennie.

'What?' said John. 'What have you found?'

'Come with us,' said Lorcan, gulping for air. 'Jamie has it. It's . . . I don't know what it is. Come and see it.'

We all got up, even Sarah, who could barely walk, and made our way out towards the garage, Dougie supporting Sarah all the way. We wanted to run, that much was obvious, but we had to walk because of Sarah's frailty.

'What is it, Edward?' I hissed at him as we made our way down the corridors.

'You'll see,' said Edward conspiratorially.

By the time we got outside, the younger children were dancing around in front of the garage.

'Come in, come in!' they yelled.

We went into the darkness and stood, letting our eyes adjust, until Dougie turned a light on.

'Electricity,' he said, 'a great invention.'

There, in front of us, was the car, now gleaming green and magnificent, and by the car was Jamie.

'I've found something special, Mama,' he said. 'You'll like it.'

'What is it?' I said, intrigued, as Edward went to get into the front seat of the car.

'Be careful,' said Dougie. 'This beauty is being sold by the end of the week and I've spent months polishing it. It's going to raise a fortune, I hope, because that's what we need, so don't smudge it, Edward, whatever you do.'

'Did you polish the boot?' asked Edward, looking slightly smug.

'Yes,' said Dougie. 'I've polished everywhere.'

'Did you polish inside the boot?'

'Inside the boot?' said Dougie. 'I didn't know you could get inside the boot.'

'But you can, you can!' said Bennie excitedly. 'Jamie found a lever.'

'This lever,' said Edward, and he leaned forward and delved under the driver's seat. Suddenly the small boot door on the back of the car pinged open a little bit.

'Well,' said Dougie, 'that's great the boot opens, but –'

'Wait,' said Edward, holding his hand up in a commanding fashion. 'Now, Jamie, if you would do the honours.'

Jamie turned and buried his arms and head in the boot.

'What are you looking for?' asked John.

But, just then, Jamie re-emerged holding something that we couldn't quite make out.

'Give it to Mrs de Salis,' said Edward and as Jamie walked towards Sarah, his arms cradling something, we all knew what it was he'd found.

'The catalogues!' said Roisin. 'You've found the catalogues, haven't you? Is it? Have you? Were they in the boot? Were they?'

But no one answered because all we could do was look at Sarah, who had tears streaming down her face as Jamie presented her with a huge black and rather dusty book.

'There's at least another three of them in there,' said Edward helpfully, as Sarah just stared at the book, the weight of the volume bowing her arms.

'It's so heavy,' she said as Dougie went to hold it for her. He blew on the cover.

'Oh my God,' he said, reading the gold lettering on the front. 'You've found them! You've just gone and found the *Catalogues of Lepidoptera*. You are very clever children! Oh, well done, Jamie, well done, Edward.'

'And us,' trilled Bennie and Lorcan.

'And all of you,' said Roisin.

Dougie opened the book he was holding and showed it to Sarah.

'What a thing of beauty,' she gasped. 'Oh, how wonderful. How utterly wonderful.'

Sarah died in her sleep six months later and, once again, I thought I would finally see Noel, but he didn't attend Sarah's funeral and he didn't come to the reading of her will. He was fully expected to turn up at the office in Barnstaple that bore his name. We all went – me and John, Dougie and Roisin – but although we waited for him at the lawyer Rupert Howse's insistence, Noel didn't show up.

Roisin and Dougie told me that Sarah had died peacefully. They had been with her until the last, reading the entries in the catalogues out to her and nursing her as her health failed. Dougie told me that the reason the catalogues remained intact was probably because there was not much air in the small boot and so no damp had got in to rot them.

'They are amazing,' he said. He explained that he and Roisin had spent the last half a year collating the information in the catalogues before they were sold.

'It's what Sarah wanted us to do. The Foundation will be funded by the sale of the goods for the first couple of years and then the money from the sale of the catalogues should keep it going for many years to come.'

Roisin read from the catalogues to Sarah every night. She told me that Sarah loved to hear about flight paths and wine strings and the like. When Roisin tired of reading, Dougie would take over and he described how he once read the entire section on Satin Lutestrings three times over as Sarah was so enchanted by the thought of these delicate little moths fluttering by her on a nightly basis. Apparently she was very taken with moths. She liked the idea of all those living creatures carrying on unseen but contented in the very dark of the night.

In many ways, it was no surprise to anyone that she ended up naming Dougie as the person she wanted in charge of the Daubeny-Fortescue Foundation. In her will she had written of how impressed she was with Dougie and Roisin and their willingness to stay on in Lower Strand to look after her even when the summer of the fête was over. She wrote in the will about how she wanted them to have a future in Lower Strand and so she had come to believe that Dougie was the man to see her vision through. She also named Roisin and myself as trustees to oversee whatever the Foundation was up to. Dougie was delighted, but concerned.

'We didn't stay on purely out of charity,' he said after the will had been read. 'We wanted to be together, Roisin and me, so when Sarah offered us a chance to live with her at the Manor House in return for helping out with the cooking and gardening and general maintenance of the place, we leaped at the chance. Sarah must have thought we stayed just for her.'

'No, she didn't think that,' I said to him, giving him a hug. 'Sarah de Salis was no fool. I think she knew everything that was going on pretty much all the time. No, she would have appreciated the fact you and Roisin looked after her, and she was a romantic. Her love affair was ruined by something that was out of her control. Maybe she saw that you and Roisin should be together and she just worked out a way that benefited all of those involved.'

'But why didn't she name Roisin as the administrator of the Foundation? She's just as capable of running it as I am.'

'Because she was of a different generation,' I said. 'She knew you'd run it together anyway so stop worrying.'

It also turned out that Sarah had stipulated that part of the proceeds from the sale of the catalogues should be used to pay Dougie a salary, thus enabling him to remain in Lower Strand.

A month later the catalogues went to auction and were, surprisingly, bought by Gordon Cutlass for vast amounts of money. Then, even more surprisingly, he donated the catalogues back to the Manor House where he decreed they should remain, housed in specially created, humidified cabinets, so that the work of Noel's grandfather and the patronage of the Daubeny-Fortescues would never die and rot in the way all those poor moths and butterflies of the past did.

It seemed such an extraordinary action that I wrote to Mr Cutlass to ask him why he had done this.

'Much as the Foundation appreciates your donation of the catalogues,' I wrote, 'I must ask why you have done this? Why, having bought them, have you not kept the catalogues for yourself?'

His answer came by return of post.

Whatever you may think of me, Mrs Smythe, I am not as avaricious as you believe. I, too, can appreciate a work of beauty. I, too, have some sense of the value of the past. I bought these catalogues as they belong here, to remain in the home of a family that was once important in Lower Strand. I hope, in this way, the name of Cutlass will also be important in Lower Strand when I am dead and gone. My legacy – the Cutlass Estate and Cutlass Court – may look modern in your eyes now, but in hundreds of years' time I hope I will be as revered in the area as the Daubeny-Fortescues are now. Yours, Gordon Cutlass.

I showed the letter to John and it made him snort.

'My God, that man's self-obsessed!' he said.

'Yes,' I said thoughtfully, 'but he's done a good deed in buying those catalogues even if it was for the wrong reasons. The money will keep Sarah's vision alive. Without that sale, the Daubeny-Fortescue Foundation couldn't exist.'

And, as it turns out, Dougie is making a wonderful administrator of the trust. He has made links with various charities in London and every time we go to visit Dougie and Roisin who, on Sarah's legacy, are renting Janet's house from us as that seemed to be a perfect solution all round, we go and watch the children having fun in Sarah's house and garden. Even Janet's house looks amazing – Dougie told me that sometimes the children come to help him with the garden that Janet created so lovingly. 'These kids like to garden!' he said to me in amazement when I put my trustee hat on and asked him sharply if he thought it was appropriate for him to use the children from the Manor House to do his own dirty work. 'They offered!' he said to me. 'This year I reckon we can even get it into the National Garden Open Day.'

In reality, I don't have to do much as a trustee. Dougie sends me reports – as collated by Roisin – and I just check boxes and then sign on the bottom. To make ends meet, Roisin also found a part-time job as a legal secretary to Rupert Howse. When I asked her how she could work for him, she laughed and said, 'He's completely fine and he pays me properly and he doesn't ring me with ridiculous queries all the time. Without him, I couldn't stay here with Dougie and, anyway, he's a good lawyer. He doesn't get emotionally involved. He just takes on what's required of him and does the best he can. That's what lawyers are supposed to do.'

*

I never saw Noel again. Not once. I barely even heard about him. If Dougie and Roisin ever saw him, they didn't say. The only time I ever knew anything of him was when I was contacted by the caretaker of the graveyard in the church where Sarah de Salis was buried. He called to say that some flowers had accrued on Sarah's grave and that he didn't know what to do with them. 'I hope you don't mind me calling,' he said, 'but they're going rotten and slimy and they could present a hazard. I didn't want to throw away something that was a gift to the dead but I don't know who they're from.'

'Did they have a message on them?' I asked.

'Yes,' he said. 'It said, "I think Gerrard would have wanted to say sorry." But Gerrard was her husband, wasn't he, and he's dead a long time now, isn't he?'

'Yes,' I said. Then I told him he should dispose of the flowers as and when he saw fit.

'Health and Safety, I'm afraid,' he said.

'Yes,' I said. 'Health and Safety.'

And what of John and me? We're fine really – him with the stubble round the bathroom sink and me with my particular brand of perfume. For our love, this day-to-day love, just continues on as it always has. Here we find ourselves, back home, the same as we ever were and I know one thing: John and I have survived as we will always survive. We've done it before and we will do it again, for our love is not startling or breathtaking. Birds don't fall out of trees when we walk by. The fish don't leap out of the sea. Our love is quiet, sustaining, warm and, in many ways, more remarkable for it. It is an everyday love and, every day, I thank John for that.

As for the rest of us, Jamie is still wearing trousers and

T-shirts and sporting grubby knees and dirty fingernails. He does have his obsessive stages though. Right now he's into 'pirate wear', which means that everything has to have a skull and crossbones on it and John regularly makes him cardboard cutlasses to flash at people.

'I think I preferred him in dresses,' John said when I filled in the forms Candace-Miss-Harris sent me enquiring whether or not I wanted to take up the opportunity to have an annual follow-up session at her clinic.

'Child cured', I wrote on the top of the form under the bit where it said, 'Use this box to describe your child's symptoms'.

'Is he cured?' said John, as Jamie walked into the kitchen wearing nothing but an eye-patch.

'Yes, I think so,' I said, watching him as he went, 'but I don't think it matters really.'

Baby Sparkle, our gurgling girl, has everything before her and Bennie continues along his path upwards, for he has grown into a happy, bright child with many friends. He has an easy, uncomplicated life, as easy and as uncomplicated as Edward's was difficult and fraught. But I can't change this. I can as much make the moon turn into the sun as I can change the very nature of my children and the circumstances of their birth.

Yet increasingly I feel that Edward has left us and gone into the land of the teenager. Sometimes I find myself lying on the bed in his room and just existing in his space. I look at the posters on his wall and I smell that slightly acrid smell of him and I try to imagine being him. Sometimes, now Edward has got so big, I wear his clothes. I put on a sweat top or some sweat pants. I wore his trainers the other day even though they're too big for me and something about being dressed like him makes me feel young and youthful and athletic and all the things that I'm not. Edward actually doesn't seem to mind this. He'll come home and see me wandering around in his second-favourite top and he'll pretend he hasn't noticed. But I see him smile, secretly pleased. He still needs me, that I know, he just doesn't want anyone else to realize it. But there are the days, the weeks, when I barely see him and then I miss him so. I wait for him to come back, as I know and trust he will.

So what is the conclusion of these last few years we have all spent together? I think about all the people in my life like Janet and Sarah de Salis and even Edward's father, John the First, and I know that they are gone in one way or another. I'll never see them again and that makes me sad, for I loved them all and part of my life has been diminished by their absence, as if they have taken a small amount of me with them too. Then there are the ones that are lost to me, the ones that I couldn't save – Noel and Isabel – and they too have dented this life of mine. And then there are those who fill up empty hearts with love: Dougie and Roisin, who seem set to find happiness with each other. And there are, of course, my children, the children whose very essence I love, whose noise and chatter lifts my spirit and without whom I would be as empty and as dry as an old drum left to rot in an attic. For Noel was wrong: I have been right to give myself over to my children. How much joy have we all had together? Joy that, in many ways, I don't suppose Noel ever had the chance to find. He was, in the end, a Shaded Broad-bar perhaps, a *Scotopteryx chenopodiata*. In the guidebook to moths, the one I bought a few months after I came back from Devon when I found hundreds of them circling round our bedroom light one night after I'd left the windows open to the dark, it says the Shaded Broad-bar is in decline. I think Noel would rather like that analogy.

Finally, I see us here in our house in the country trying to find our path through life and now I know where mine has taken me, where it was always meant to take me. It is here, with John, in each other's arms, wrapped up against the chill of the night, the deer once again barking on the hill, the pheasants once again croaking in the wood. The children are asleep, our three boys, our beautiful girl, and I have been so fortunate to have them. While everything else changes, nothing does for us really. Together John and I are like the trunk of an old oak and our friends and family are the branches swaying and breaking and drifting off with the wind that surrounds us. But here we stand, firm and solid. It is where I will be, where I will always be.

I am, after all, Samantha Smythe.

Acknowledgements

I would, yet again, like to thank Cherry and Brian for letting me use their house to write in – and for Cherry's superior research skills – and for Noel Fielding for the use of his office. I couldn't have done this book without the inspiration of the marvellous North Devon countryside and the help and support of those who live there, especially E. J. Davies and Tom Butterworth. I am in debt to the *Field Guide to the Moths of Great Britain* by Paul Waring and Martin Townsend, without which I would have known nothing of lepidopterology. Much thanks also to my friend Rodolph's knowledge of period houses, including that of his mother, Jane, and for letting me use his rather unique surname. The other beautifully informative book which helped with all things of an architectural nature was *The Private Life of a Country House* by Lesley Lewis.

I could not have done this book without the staunch support and utter brilliance of my editors at Penguin, Louise Moore and Clare Ledingham, and the fine skills of Karen Whitlock, or without the sounding board that is Bridget Hancock. Thanks also to my friends, my family, my children, and to Michael, who is still, despite all these years and all these children, my love.

My final dedication goes to my agent, the magnificent Kate Jones – friend, mother, wife, bon vivante, celebrated wit, noted red-coat wearer and the kindest person you could ever hope to meet. She read two-thirds of this book and she loved it so much that I finished it imagining the wise and pithy comments she might have said in my ear were she able to. So this is to the memory of Kate because, for me, she is not gone. She is merely temporarily unavailable, and still so sorely missed.

He just wanted a decent book to read ...

Not too much to ask, is it? It was in 1935 when Allen Lane, Managing Director of Bodley Head Publishers, stood on a platform at Exeter railway station looking for something good to read on his journey back to London. His choice was limited to popular magazines and poor-quality paperbacks – the same choice faced every day by the vast majority of readers, few of whom could afford hardbacks. Lane's disappointment and subsequent anger at the range of books generally available led him to found a company – and change the world.

'We believed in the existence in this country of a vast reading public for intelligent books at a low price, and staked everything on it'
Sir Allen Lane, 1902–1970, founder of Penguin Books

The quality paperback had arrived – and not just in bookshops. Lane was adamant that his Penguins should appear in chain stores and tobacconists, and should cost no more than a packet of cigarettes.

Reading habits (and cigarette prices) have changed since 1935, but Penguin still believes in publishing the best books for everybody to enjoy. We still believe that good design costs no more than bad design, and we still believe that quality books published passionately and responsibly make the world a better place.

So wherever you see the little bird – whether it's on a piece of prize-winning literary fiction or a celebrity autobiography, political tour de force or historical masterpiece, a serial-killer thriller, reference book, world classic or a piece of pure escapism – you can bet that it represents the very best that the genre has to offer.

Whatever you like to read – trust Penguin.